THE
YOUNG
FRONTIERSMAN

The Flintlock Sagas
Book 1

The
Young
Frontiersman

WRITTEN BY

ALAN W. HARRIS

Inspired by the book <u>The Young Trailers</u> *by Joseph A. Altsheler*

~ ~ ~ † ~ ~ ~

Fruitful Tree Publishing
Lexington, South Carolina 29072

This book is published by:

Fruitful Tree Publishing

509 Aspen Glade Court

Lexington, South Carolina 29072

www.StoriesChangeHearts.com

Copyright © 2019 by Alan Harris

Printed in the United States of America

ISBN-13: 978-1-7341845-0-1
ebook ISBN: 978-1-7341845-1-8

1. Harris, Alan W. 2. Christian 3. Historical 4. Adventure 5. Family 6. Teen 7. Young Adult 8. Character Development 9. Faith Building 10. Nature Tales 11. Inspirational 12. Flintlock

This novel is a work of fiction. Names, characters, places and incidents are either the work of the author's imagination or are used fictitiously. Any resemblance to actual events, locales, organizations, or persons living or dead is entirely coincidental.

For information about special discounts for bulk purchases for sales promotions, corporate use, conferences or resale contact Alan at: StoriesChangeHearts@gmail.com.

This book is dedicated
to all those
who long to have
Jesus Christ
formed
in them.

CONTENTS

PREFACE

I have really enjoyed writing the Tales of Larkin series, but after five books, I thought my brain needed stretching. I may one day add to the Larkin stories, but for now I have decided to pursue something different. As I was looking for ideas, I visited a list of the adventure books that were in the public domain. That's where I found books by Joseph Altsheler. He wrote adventure stories for boys in the early 1900s. I read three of his stories, and while I thought they were interesting, I was disappointed to find that the author included views supporting evolution as well as the false idea that was common at the time that the white race was superior to all others. I also didn't like the direction he took with his character development. The bottom line is that, I used the time period, the setting, and the basic premise of Mr. Altsheler's plot as the launching point, then I wrote my own story. It took a lot work both from me as well as from my wife, Valerie, who is my editor, but I am very pleased with the end result. Since I plan to write more books about this same time period, I decided to call the series *The Flintlock Sagas.*

As with all of my books, you will find excitement, lots of adventure, fun characters, important spiritual lessons, and you might also learn what it was like to live in the wilderness of Kentucky in the turbulent late 1700s.

I want to thank my lovely and talented wife, Valerie, for all of her invaluable assistance in turning my pitiful efforts into something that can potentially be a blessing to many. It has been my goal in all my writing to create something that will encourage readers and bring glory to God and His Son, Jesus Christ. As I have done with the books in the Tales of Larkin series, I have put an appendix with chapter questions for parents or teachers to ask their children or students in the back of the book. These questions are to stimulate discussion on important spiritual lessons and character development. It has been known for some time that when teaching is incorporated with an exciting story, the lessons learned are sent straight to long-term memory. Understanding and using this amazing teaching technique will be priceless both to parents and to teachers. I believe it is the reason that Jesus in the New Testament and God in the Old Testament used stories to teach. You can read more detail about this at my website: *StoriesChangeHearts.com*

It means a lot to me that you read my books and support my work. Thank you, and may God's richest blessings be yours!

In His service,

Alan W. Harris

August 12, 2019
Lexington, South Carolina

Chapter One

AN UNEXPECTED TRIAL

In a lonely spot in the deep woods as daylight faded, a boy knelt, sobbing in anguish. His tormented mind longed for peace, but he could find none. *YOU'RE WORTHLESS, BOY!* the voice in his head screamed at him. *"ABSOLUTELY WORTHLESS! YOU COULD'VE KILLED THOSE TWO GIRLS! YOU'RE HOPELESS. . .NEVER AMOUNT TO ANYTHING. . .* With his face in his hands, the miserable boy wept bitterly. He had experienced so much hope only a few days before.

On that day thirty-seven heavy wagons sat side-by-side on a ridge of mountains overlooking the great green wilderness that the Indians called Kain-tuck-ee. The arched canvas covering of each of the transports had been bleached white over the last few months by the rains and blazing sun, causing the caravan to look like a snowdrift against the emerald carpet of the vast forest below.

As they stood gazing expectantly at the vista before them, the pioneers saw the land of hope stretched out like a beautiful, gigantic mural. The travelers were mesmerized by the wide sweep of rolling country covered with trees and canebrake. Streams of clear water, flowing here and there and shining in the distance amid the green, looked like strands of shimmering silver. The migrants examined the panorama with intense interest, because this new and unknown land was to be their home.

1

Among all of the excited pairs of eyes scanning the forest from the mountain ridge, none were more eager than William Hackett, a strong lad of fifteen standing in front of the wagons beside the trail guide, Jack Cobb. Young Will was in awe of the scout, who as a seasoned frontiersman had unerringly led them on the long journey. Jack was a tall, lean man having skin the color of well-tanned leather and carrying a rifle that seldom left his hand. Jack's strange and fascinating tales of the great wilderness had kept the boy captivated for hours. Will was also drawn to the rough trail guide because, in spite of Jack's gruff manner, he had shown a special interest in the adopted son of the Hackett family, and Jack's favors and kind efforts to encourage him had touched Will's troubled heart.

Any close observer watching young Hackett would have paused to give him a second look, seeing a tall, well-formed youth who was muscled beyond his years. By all appearances the boy seemed to fit into the picture of the wilderness. He even walked with an easy, confident bearing, but it was only a very well-played pretense that he had perfected over the last five years. It was a role that he fiercely clung to in order to suppress the nagging fears that constantly clawed at his soul.

One of the things that could be truthfully said about Will Hackett was his love for the land through which they journeyed. He was fascinated by every aspect of the wilds surrounding him. The more Jack Cobb and his good friend and associate, Dirt Gurley, told the lad about it, the more Will was convinced that this was a place where he might one day find peace.

"Is. . .is that really it?" Will asked as he stood riveted by the lush green spread before him.

"Yep," was all the answer the quiet trail guide gave.

But fortunately for the lad, the more talkative Dirt Gurley was always ready to speak his thoughts: "Yessiree, Will! You are feastin' yer young eyeballs on some of the most beautifulest woodses the Good Lord ever done sprouted from the ground! All that right there in front of you fer as far as you can see and farther is the Kentucky Territory—the best huntin', the grandest trees, and the sweetest water ever put on God's good earth! And I

2

fer one am mighty glad to be comin' back to it! Ain't 'chu glad, Jack?"

"Yep."

The long journey from their old home in Maryland had been a source of unending discovery and delight to William. There had been no painful partings. In fact, he was glad to leave their old home. He had nothing but agonizing memories of his life back there. . .except the one of being adopted by the Hackett family. The Hacketts were the best thing that ever happened to him. His adopted mother and his younger stepbrother and stepsister were in the fourth wagon from the right, and his adopted father, John Hackett, stood beside it. Further on in the same company were many of his family's relatives as well as most of the old neighbors. All of them had made the journey together. It was really the removal of a village from an old land to a new one, and with the familiar faces of kindred and friends around them, they were not lonely.

As different as this strange, new country was for them, in a way it was like coming home to Will. He had dreamed of this journey for so long that it was like he had seen it all before. The forests and the mountains beckoned to him in a friendly fashion. It wasn't the woods that he was afraid of. His sharp mind longed to discover the secrets hidden there. The closer they got to the wilderness that was to be their new home, it seemed to William that the very air grew newer and sweeter than that of the old land left behind.

The first part of their journey had been easy, relatively speaking. They had fair weather most of the way, and there had been no serious illnesses and only minor injuries. But all of that seemed to change as they drew near the Kentucky River.

The water had been low when they arrived at the Licking River several weeks before, and the crossing had been uneventful. This time, at the Kentucky River, their expectations of another easy crossing were dashed when heavy rains set in several days before they reached it. The muddy flood waters had swollen the river, and the swift current was foreboding. Jack Cobb called a meeting of all the men, and it was decided to camp until the rain stopped, in order to allow the waters time to recede.

Three weeks later, due to continued intermittent rains, not much had changed. The concern at that time was that, if they waited much longer, the caravan would arrive at their new home too late in the season to build their homes before winter hit.

After another meeting, the reluctant decision was made to attempt a crossing. Once they had a plan, things began to happen quickly. All of the men with horses herded half of the oxen into the river and swam them across to the other side. Many of the beasts were hobbled so that they couldn't wander off, but some of the strongest were used to pull the wagons across. The team of pulling oxen had two ropes attached to them, the other ends of which were carried to the east bank when men swam their horses back across. To keep from being top-heavy, the covers were taken off the wagons, and one at a time they were rolled into the waters. Several large pine trees were felled and dragged to the river to use as floats, which were roped to each side of the wagons to provide stability in the water. The ends of two ropes were tied securely to the front corners of the huge, floating carts. Separate ropes were tied to the backs, and these were looped around the trunks of nearby trees. When each wagon was ready to cross, Jack, Dirt, and several men on the opposite shore were to drive the team of oxen forward to pull the loaded vehicle through the swift-moving water. The ropes attached to the back corners were to be slowly let out as the wagons were drawn across, keeping them from being swept down the rushing river.

Because of everyone's great concern about making the dangerous crossing, John Hackett, who was looked upon as one of the leaders, offered his wagon to be the first to make the attempt. William was proud of his mother as he watched her step boldly into the make-shift boat with her two younger children.

"Do you want me to swim your horse across, Father?" Will asked hopefully.

"No, Son. I'll swim the horse. I need you to ride with your mother and the children. Keep everyone in the center of the wagon and stay as low as you can."

"Yes, sir," William returned, a little disappointed.

4

When all was ready, a signal was given, and the oxen began to drag the Hackett's Conestoga across. The trip seemed to last forever for the family, but it actually took less than fifteen minutes for the wagon wheels to touch the gravelly shore on the other side. With a great sense of relief, John Hackett helped the men untie the ropes and harness a separate team of oxen to the wagon so that it could be drawn further up the bank.

The ropes from the front and the rear of the wagon were then tied to the logs that were drawn back across the river to attach to the next wagon.

It was slow and back-breaking work, but as the day wore on, more and more of the great transports were lined up on the west side of the swollen river.

In the afternoon when the Middlebrook's wagon was rolled into position, the floatation logs were secured on either side. Mr. Middlebrook didn't own a horse, so he rode in the wagon with his wife and three children. Mrs. Middlebrook sat toward the back holding their two-year-old son, Seth, while Katherine, the oldest, and her younger sister, Grace, sat with their father toward the front. All went well until the wagon was two-thirds of the way across. Loud vibrating sounds like an out-of-tune base fiddle caused Kate's father to stand up and look for the source of the strange noise. Just then there was a sound like a gun shot, and part of the upriver rope came flying back, hitting Mr. Middlebrook between the eyes and knocking him into the bottom of the wagon like he had been hit by a hammer.

When the rope broke, there was nothing holding the right front of the wagon, and the pressure from the swift water pounding relentlessly against that side began to push the wagon over.

From the western shore Jack Cobb saw immediately what was happening and quickly whipped out his huge hunting knife, slashing the remaining rope in the front. As soon as he did so, the wagon righted itself, but since the front of the wagon was now free, it began to drift down river.

Jack tried to calm Mrs. Middlebrook, who was standing in the wagon bed screaming about their predicament. "Just sit down, madam, and be calm!" Jack yelled. "The ropes attached to the rear of yer wagon'll swing you back over to the other side, and the men there'll pull you out!"

Just then there was a loud crash as the wagon slammed against some submerged rocks. The two wheels on that side buckled under, and the wagon suddenly tilted at a forty-five degree angle. Mrs. Middlebrook managed to hang on to her baby and the side of the wagon, but Katherine and her sister were flung into the raging waters.

"GREAT SMOKIN' POLECATS!" Dirt Gurley cried out. "THEM GALS IS DONE FOR!"

Jack dashed down the bank in a panic, but the girls were quickly being washed away. Looking downstream, the scout saw Will putting the cover back on the Hackett's wagon parked at the end of the line. Jack screamed Will's name and pointed frantically at the two heads bobbing down the river.

The boy hesitated only a moment when he saw the tragedy unfolding before him. Spurred into action, he jumped from his wagon and sprinted to the shore. Several large boulders rested in the water there, and Will leaped from rock to rock, trying to get as far out into the river as he could. Katherine and her sister were almost even with him when he came to the last boulder. Without hesitation, young Hackett launched himself into the rolling red water. When he surfaced and topped a wave, he saw that he was still a good ten yards away from the girls. Marking their direction, the youth began plowing through the surging flood as fast as his strong arms could drive him. When he topped another wave, he looked again. Only five yards separated them. Again he churned the water with powerful strokes. Suddenly a large wave engulfed him, and when his head cleared the water, he heard a scream. Shaking his head to clear the water from his eyes, he saw the two terrified girls clinging tightly to each other only a few feet away. Katherine saw him too and began yelling his name. Will flipped to his back, threw his arms around both girls, and cried out, "KICK FOR ALL YOU'RE WORTH!" His legs churned the water as the three of them fought furiously for the shore. The effort to gain the bank was long and exhausting. His leg muscles screamed for rest, but still he kicked in desperation. Finally the girls' knees and hands scraped the gravelly bottom. With the last of his strength, William managed to drag them all onto the land where they collapsed in the mud and rocks.

It took until sunset to get all of the wagons, animals, and people safely to the western shore of the flooded river. The last one across was the Middlebrook's, now possessing a new set of axils and wheels. Many prayers of thanksgiving were offered to God that evening, and all felt very blessed to have escaped a serious disaster. Mr. Middlebrook, sporting a large, bruised knot in the middle of his forehead, took exception to that.

William was looked upon as a hero and was hugged mercilessly by Mrs. Middlebrook. Just as soon as the very red-faced young pioneer could slip away from the crowd, he did, finding a lonely spot in the thick forest.

Earlier in the day, when he had seen the girls in the river and realized what Jack had wanted him to do, fear had exploded in his stomach. He wasn't afraid of drowning; he was terrified that he would fail to save the girls. Even now he could hear his dead birth father's berating voice accusing him of putting those girls in greater danger because of his slowness and weakness. Being physically exhausted and emotionally spent, the tormented boy fell on his knees and sobbed.

Chapter Two

THE NIGHT STALKER

Once the wagons were drawn into line early the next morning, Jack and Dirt led them westward along the rutted wagon trail. Now that they were moving again, Will felt his hopes rising. He was eager to experience the forests and the great wilderness where his imagination had already gone. He occasionally went ahead with Jack Cobb, his hero and chosen friend. It was at these times that he dared to consider himself a man, or soon to become one, because he was exploring the unknown and leading the way for a wagon train, which to Will's way of thinking was the most important work a man could do.

As he enjoyed such thoughts, Will had to fight the familiar, nagging voices in his head that said, *Lead a wagon train? Don't make me laugh! You're worthless, boy! Do ya' hear? Worthless! You mess up everything you try! Mark my words! YOU'LL NEVER AMOUNT TO ANYTHING!* At those moments he angrily fought to push the voices back into their place and focus on what was going on around him. It helped him to listen to Jack as he answered Will's questions and taught his young friend lessons like the importance of observing and listening while traveling through the wilderness.

Whenever Will was alone, he didn't have to worry about hiding his fears from others, so he looked for every opportunity to be by himself to explore the forest. He became very familiar with the normal sounds of the woods, and if there was any new noise, the eager youth searched until he found what had made it. Looking for opportunities to watch the animals and birds, the inquisitive lad loved discovering their unique habits and traits. As for fishing, Will found it easy. He could cut a sapling to use as a rod with his pocket knife, tie a string to it, and attach a hook or sometimes even a bent pin to the end of the string. With this crude tackle, he could soon catch as many fish as he wanted in the forest creeks.

William especially liked the nights in the wilds. When the work of the day was done, the wagons were drawn up in a circle, and the horses and the oxen were tethered in a grassy place to rest under the trees. The travelers needed fires for warmth as well as cooking, so when Jack deemed it safe to do so, they built them high and long. With such large fires, everyone who wished had room to sit before the glowing red coals.

The forest was full of fallen brushwood as dry as tinder, and Will helped gather it. He appreciated the warmth of the large fire on the cool nights, but it bothered him to look at it. The crackling flames brought back terrible memories to the boy—awful memories that he wished he could forget.

It was in the evenings around the great fire that the men told stories, particularly Jack Cobb and his partner, Dirt Gurley. Both of them had spent much of their lives wandering through the forests of Kentucky. Jack called it "a fine-looking land."

"Ab-so-tively!" Dirt agreed with enthusiasm. "Wait'l you gents see it! Jus' right out there ahead of us is the finest- lookin'est land I ever did see, an' that there's a fact!"

Jack spoke of the immense forests of beech and oak and hickory and maple, the dense canebrake, and the many rivers, including the great Ohio that the Indians called the Beautiful River, which received them all. He talked about the game swarming the forests and the meadows alike: the deer, elk, bear, turkey, and buffalo. Now and then, when the smaller children were asleep in the wagons and the larger ones were nodding before the fires, the men would lower their voices and speak of the Indians. It was during these conversations that the settlers instinctively looked at their rifles and powder horns.

But William, even with all of his anxious thoughts, did not feel afraid when he heard the stories of the native tribes. He knew that savages of the most dangerous kind often came into the forests of Kentucky, but he thrilled rather than trembled at the thought. It was his great desire to not only see them, but to understand their ways as well.

Young William usually slept very lightly, even though he was on his feet nearly all day, and he also did his share of the work. Two or three times he awoke far in the night and, raising himself up, peeped out between the canvas cover and the wagon wall. He saw only the heavy darkness, in which the trees looked as thin and ghostly as shadows, and the smoldering fires, beside which two men with their rifles always watched. Often he desired to stand guard with them, but at such times the old accusing and abusive voices of failure would return, and once again he would have to struggle to bring peace back to his mind.

As the youth stared into the night shadows, his thoughts went back to what he had seen earlier. That morning as he and the others had stood on the crest of the last mountain ridge, they all felt only joy, curiosity, and excitement because before them lay the great valley of Kentucky where they were to build their future home. The long journey was almost over. The men took off their hats and caps and raised a cheer; the women joined with relief and gratitude, and the children shouted too, but mainly because their fathers and mothers did. In all the cheering crowd, Will's voice rose the loudest.

The young girl who stood beside Will also raised a shout of joy, and he smiled at her. It was his new friend, Katherine Middlebrook, two years younger than himself. Slim and tall, her dark blue eyes looked at him from under broad brows, and light-brown curls fell thick upon her shoulders.

"Oh my goodness, Will!" the wide-eyed Katherine had exclaimed excitedly. "Oh my goodness! Are we really, really here?"

"Where did you think we'd be?" chuckled William.

"Oh, I know we're here," the girl had returned, bouncing up and down, her excitement undiminished, "but even though we're here, it's just so hard to believe that we're *here* here! You know... really, really *here* here! Do you know what I mean?"

"To tell you the truth, Kate, no, I don't. But I'm glad you're happy! I'm happy too!"

"Yes, I'm very happy!" Kate had returned, still bouncing. "I'm happy that we're really *here* here. . .here where we're going to live. . .our home here! Oh, I know we haven't found the place where we are going to build our little town, but it's close, just right out in front of us, maybe not more than two or three days away. I'm happy that living out of the wagons is almost over and that we will get to live in an actual house again! I can't wait to sleep in a real bed! That's going to be exquisite!"

"What does *exquisite* mean?" Will had asked, looking down at his young friend.

"Honestly," Kate answered in a low voice, sheepishly returning Will's gaze, "I really don't know. But it's something my mother says when she's talking about something that's very good."

As they both turned to look once more at the valley spread out below them, Kate stopped bouncing, and the excited expression on her young face was chased away by a look of concern. "Will, are you afraid?" she had asked.

"Afraid of what?" replied William Hackett nervously.

"Of the forests," Kate answered. "They say that the savages often come to kill the settlers."

Will breathed a secretive sigh of relief. He wasn't ready to share his fears with anyone, especially not Kate. It was then that Will observed the worried look on the girl's face. He thought a moment before he answered her question. "There's a lot that I don't know about the Indians," William finally responded, "but I'm looking forward to learning more from Jack Cobb and Dirt Gurley. I've heard the same stories that you have, Kate. I'm sure there are plenty of dangers living on the frontier, but it seems to me that, when you consider our whole group, we are a mighty strong party. If I were an Indian, I wouldn't want to fight us, and I don't believe they will either. You don't need to be afraid, Kate."

William didn't realize it at the time, but his straightforward answer had done much to calm the younger girl's concerns. Ever since he had saved her sister and herself from the river, Kate had made William her hero. He seemed to her strong and full of ability. She stole a quick glance at him and looked away. She was glad they were friends, but she did not want to spoil their friendship by showing her admiration.

The next morning they passed into territory that sank away into low, rolling hills like the waves of the sea. Everything grew majestically, as Kate Middlebrook had declared. William had never seen such trees in the East. Here in Kentucky, beech, elm, hickory, and maple trees reached gigantic proportions, and wherever the shade was not too dense, the grass rose heavy and lush. Now and then they passed thickets of canebrake, and once at the side of a stream, they came to a salt lick. There a fountain spouted from the base of a hill and, running only a few feet, emptied into a creek. But its waters were densely saturated with salt, and all around its banks the soft soil was trodden with hundreds of footsteps.

"The wild beasts made these," said the guide to Will. "They come here at night: elk, deer, buffalo, wolves, and all the others, big and little, to get the salt. They drink the water, and they also lick up the salt from the ground."

A fierce desire laid hold of the youth at these words. He had a rifle of his own, but he was not permitted to carry it often. Will wanted so much to take it and lie beside the pool at night when the game came down to drink. There were many other fears in his young heart, but he had never been afraid of the dark. He had run out into it many times as a young boy to hide from his drunken father. The dark was a place of security and peace for William, and he needed no companionship. He also knew what to do to hunt game: remaining in the bush quietly and still for hours and choosing only the finest of deer and bear. He often daydreamed about carefully putting his rifle sights on a great buck, and the thought always excited him. Each new step into the wilderness seemed to bring him nearer to the way of life for which he deeply longed.

When they stopped to camp the next night, they built the fire higher than ever because, just after dark, they heard the howling of wolves. Later they heard a strange, long scream, like the shriek of a woman, which the men said was the cry of a panther.

"Now jus' calm down all yer frettin'," Dirt Gurley announced in his loud, nasally voice when he heard some of the women talking nervously about the large black cat. "Them pant'ers ain't gonna be stickin' their shiny black noses 'round our camp. Why, those rascals is more afeared o' us than we be o' them."

"I don't know, Mr. Gurley," Kate Middlebrook spoke up as she stood with the women, "I'm mighty afraid right now! How do you know they won't attack us?"

"Young missy," Dirt confidently returned, "yer talkin' to Solomon Gurley, frontiersman extraordinaire! I know how them thangs think. Why, I wuz raised by a pack of 'em!"

"That explains a lot," one of the women mumbled under her breath.

"Yessireee," Dirt continued, "when ya knows as much as I do about the critters what inhabitates these wilderness woodses, then ya wouldn't let one little screamin' pant'er deesturb yer slumberin's. In fact, jus' so's you ladies can rest easier tonight, yer's truly, Solomon Ambrose Gurley, is gonna personally go out thar an' have a talk with the critter."

"Have a talk with it!" one of the ladies, Amanda Wilson, exclaimed. "How can you have a talk with a wild beast?"

"Well now, Mother Wilson," Dirt responded, "wild beast it may be, but them rascals *can* be reasoned with. Why, I 'member the time I wuz trackin' a bear up in Shawnee country. I tracked that beast all day. But once it got dark, that bear done near gimme the slip. Then I spotted his eyeballs a'starin' at me in the moonlight. I raised my rifle and started to shoot, but jus' then I seen another pair of eyes to my right. An' then another pair showed up on my left. Why, it weren't no time a'tol, an' I looked around me an' realized that I done been surrounded by a whole gaggle of them critters. I never seen so many bears in one place at one time in all my born days. But then I heerd 'em, an' I realized that they weren't bears a'tol. They wuz a pack o' pant'ers, all of 'em snarlin' an' slaverin' to have ol' Dirt for their supper. That's when I learned the value of makin' a good argument. So I laid my rifle down, squared my shoulders, an' commenced to speechafyin'. Yessiree, I gave them snarlin' banshees the finest speech they ever heerd. I tol' 'em about Daniel in the den o' lions. I tol 'em to do unto others as they would have it did unto them, an' I tol' 'em that the Almighty has done made it clear as crystal in the Good Book that we gots to forgive if we wants to be forgiven ourselves."

"So what happened, Mr. Gurley?" a wide-eyed Kate Middlebrook asked.

"Wouldn't you know it, little missy?" Dirt answered, "Ain't none o' them pant'ers ever been to church, so. . .THEY KILLED ME!" As he said this, Dirt Gurley began laughing. In fact, he laughed so hard he stumbled and fell into a pile of stacked firewood. The women and girls just sniffed disdainfully and left him rolling back and forth in the wood pile, holding his stomach and roaring great sobs of laughter as tears ran down his weathered cheeks.

Aside from Dirt Gurley's efforts to calm the fretful girls and ladies, Jack Cobb assured them that there was little danger from the panthers. Even so, the cries of the creatures sounded lonesome and terrifying, and it took a big fire to bring joy back to the hearts of the travelers.

As the families sat around the campfire, the men talked more than usual that night, but they did not tell stories. Instead, they asked Cobb and Dirt many questions about the country. Only two days' journey farther on, they would reach a rich meadow that Cobb said was a perfect spot for them. Encouraged by the scout's report, all of the men were anxious get there.

"I'm tellin' you fellas the absolute truth," said Cobb. "Hand's down, it's the best land I ever laid eyes on, an' there's lots of open meadow an' canebrake, so it won't be bad to clear for farmin'. I know that area real well. Dirt an' I trapped beaver in them parts two years ago."

Jack and Dirt continued to satisfy the group's curiosity for several hours. At the end of the discussion, everyone began to realize that their long journey was soon to end. The women looked especially pleased as they left the meeting to put their children to bed. The great question settled, the men sat a while before the blazing fire, discussing among themselves what the future might bring.

Will watched them and longed to be old enough to take part in the evening talks. Like his friend Kate, he was excited by the knowledge that their journey was to end soon, and the lad was eager to see the valley where they would build their homes. Will climbed into the wagon at last but could not sleep.

By and by the men went to their bedrolls or wrapped themselves in blankets and slept before the flames. Only two remained awake and on guard. They sat on logs near the outskirts of the camp and held their rifles in their hands.

William dropped the canvas edge and sought sleep, but it would not come. Too many thoughts were in his mind. He tried to imagine the beautiful valley where they were to build their houses that Cobb had described. After a while he lifted the canvas again and saw that the fires had sunk low. Both guards were still sitting on the logs and leaning lazily against a stack of firewood. The wilderness around them was very black, and twenty yards away even the outlines of the trees were lost in the darkness.

William's young step-sister, Mary, who was sleeping at the other end of the wagon, awoke and cried for water. Mr. Hackett raised himself sleepily, but Will at once sprang up and offered to get it.

"All right," Mr. Hackett said and lay back down.

Will quickly slipped on his trousers and, taking the tin cup in his hand, climbed out of the wagon. He was barefoot and, like other pioneer boys, scorned shoes in warm weather. Stubble and pebbles did not trouble his calloused feet.

Now that William had an excuse to be outside in the middle of the night, he wanted to look around a little, so instead of getting his sister's drink from the barrel, he decided to get it from the spring, located at the edge of the woods surrounding their camp in a grassy meadow. Approaching the water, Will saw that some of the horses and oxen were tethered to stout saplings nearby. As he drew near, a horse neighed, and he noticed all of the animals were pulling on their ropes. The two careless guards were either asleep or so drowsy that they took no notice of what was happening. William was unwilling to call their attention for fear he might seem too forward. As the young pioneer walked among the animals, he was still unable to find the cause of their agitation. After traveling for so long together, Will knew every one of the animals by name and nature, and they knew him. He patted their backs and rubbed their noses and tried to soothe them. They became a little quieter, but he could not remain any longer with them since his sister was waiting at the wagon for the water. Turning, he walked quickly to the spring and, stooping down, filled his cup.

When William stood back up, his eyes happened to be turned toward the forest, and there not far away and seven or eight feet above the ground, he saw two points of light that reflected what was left of the fire. He was so startled that the cup trembled in his hand and drops of water splashed onto his feet. The young pioneer stared steadily at the red points that he now noticed moved slightly from side to side. As his sharp eyes adjusted to the darkness, he saw the dim outline of a long and large body behind the two glowing spots. He had spent over an hour pestering Jack Cobb and Dirt Gurley about the different animals that inhabited these woods, and based on their descriptions, the young pioneer was sure that it must be a panther. Either it was a very hungry or a very ignorant one to hover so boldly around a camp full of men and guns.

The beast crouched on the limb of a tree as if ready to spring, and Will was the nearest living object. He suddenly realized that he must be the great cat's intended victim. When the panther did not immediately move, the boy's courage rose, especially when he remembered Cobb telling him that, as a general rule, it was the natural impulse of all wild animals to run from man. So he began to back away, and he heard behind him the horses trampling about in alarm. The lazy guards still dozed, and all was quiet at the wagons.

Will had only taken a few steps when it dawned on him that, if he moved away, then it was likely that the big cat might attack one of their animals instead. It was at this moment that another one of Cobb's nature lessons came to the boy's mind, and he made the decision to act on it. He dropped his cup, rushed to the fire, and picked up a long brand, blazing at one end.

Swinging his torch around his head until it made a perfect circle of flame, he ran directly toward the panther, uttering a loud shout as he ran. The beast gave forth a shrieking scream of terror and, leaping from the limb, sped swiftly into the forest.

All the camp was awake in an instant, men springing out of the wagons, rifles in hand, ready for any trouble. When they saw only a boy, holding a blazing torch above his head, they began to grumble, and the two sleepy guards, seeking an excuse for themselves, laughed outright at the tale the young pioneer told. The stinging words even made William start to wonder if he really had seen the cat or if his imagination was playing tricks on him. But Mr. Hackett believed that William told the truth, and Jack, who took a lantern and quickly examined the ground near the tree, said there could be no doubt that the youth had really seen the panther. Great tracks of the beast were plainly visible in the soft earth.

"Pushed by hunger an' thinking there was no danger, he might have sprung on one of our colts or a calf," said Cobb. "No doubt the boy with his ready use of a torch saved us from a loss. It was a brave thing for him to do."

But William took no pride in their praise. He was just relieved that he hadn't messed up. It actually gave him more assurance that living on the frontier was something he could do, and although somewhat misguided, it marked the first sprouting of genuine confidence in the abused boy's heart. He began to imagine that, if he could live alone in the wilds, there would be even less of a chance that his failures could hurt others. The wilderness would be his way to escape his abusive father's prophecies of doom. He had made up his mind that he would be worthy of the challenges.

By the next morning William's troubled thoughts had drifted away. When he stepped out of the wagon, the lad found the world very beautiful. The Creator had done His part, but the lad's joy at being in that place gave the scene in Will's mind deeper and more vivid colors. Once the caravan got under way, young Hackett saw cotton-tailed hares run across their path. Squirrels chattered to one another in the tree tops and defiantly threw the shells of last year's nuts at the passing travelers. Once they saw a stag bending down to drink at a brook, and when the forest king beheld them, he raised his head and merely stared at these strange new invaders of the wilds. William admired his beautiful form and splendid antlers, but he told himself that, even if he were hunting, he would not have fired his rifle at such a magnificent animal. The buck gazed at them a few moments, turned, tossed his head, and sped away through the forest.

That evening they encamped on the crest of a range of low and grassy hills overlooking the valley they had selected to be their future home. The excitement and anticipation kept most everyone awake well into night. Men and women sat late around the fires, and even boys of William's age were allowed to stay up and listen to the plans all the grown people made. By the grace of God, theirs had not been a hard journey, but it had been long and, in some ways, tedious. Now that its end was at hand, a new and much more difficult work must begin. They would have homes to build and a living to coax from the ground.

"If it were just me," Will confided to the guide, "I wouldn't bother building a house. I'd live under the trees, and when I needed anything to eat, I'd kill game."

"A hunter might do that," replied Cobb, "but we're not all hunters, an' only a few of us can be. Sometimes the game ain't standin' right there in front of yer eyeballs waitin' to get shot just when you want it. As for sleepin' under the trees, it's all fine an' dandy in the summer if'n it don't rain, but it would be just a bit chilly in winter when the big snows come, as they do—sometimes more'n a foot deep. I'm a hunter myself, an' I've slept under trees an' in caves an' on the sheltered side of hills. But when the weather's cold, give me a wooden floor under my feet an' a solid roof over my head. Then I'll bargain to sleep to the king's taste."

William felt a little ashamed at Cobb's mild rebuke, and he decided to be quiet before he said something that confirmed his foolishness to the scout. But Will wasn't completely convinced. In his youthful inexperience, he longed to prove to himself and to the voices in his head that he could make good. It was true that he lacked knowledge and wisdom, but he had no lack of enthusiasm.

By the time the first hint of dawn blushed the eastern horizon, everyone was up and eager to move out. William had just completed hitching the oxen to his family's wagon when he saw the sun rise and shine a magnificent burst of red and gold over the valley that was to be their home. The whole camp beheld the spectacle. They had reached the crest of the hill the evening before, too late to get a look at their part of the valley, and they were all thrilled with the glorious view that met their eyes. Summer had fully come, and because of all the rain, the grass and leaves were of the most vivid and intense green. They were entering one of the richest portions of Kentucky, and the untouched topsoil was deep and fertile.

Dirt Gurley eagerly offered his learned opinion of the fruitfulness of the valley below, "Yessiree, with land as good as this, all you folks have to do is jus' tickle the ground with a hoe, and it'll laugh itself plumb into a harvest."

It was hard to doubt Dirt's prophecy, because right there in front of them was the proof of the land's productiveness in the lush grass and the gigantic trees. Down one side of the valley flowed a little river, cleaving the green like a silver band.

That morning, as the sun rose and revealed to the travelers the beautiful panorama, all their troubles and fears rolled away. Even the face of Mr. Hackett, who rarely yielded to enthusiasm, brightened at the sight and, lifting his hand, drew in the air a large circle that encompassed the valley. "There!" he said. "Right there is our home waiting for us!"

"Hurrah!" cried William, flinging aloft his cap. "We've come home."

Then, still cheering, everyone quickly climbed into their wagons, and the eager caravan started the final leg of their long journey.

Chapter Three

A FRIEND INDEED

W hen they finally arrived in the valley, they found it everything Cobb had said it would be. There was a wide, grassy meadow about a half mile from the river, and they selected that open area as the site of their new town, which they gave the name of Larkinboro, in honor of one of their leaders who had died before they left Maryland.

Although eager to begin life in their permanent homes, the travelers had to put up with living in their wagon camp a little longer while the new town was constructed. For protection they decided to build the houses in a cluster and surround it all with a log wall. The first thing the men did was to chop down trees eight to ten inches in diameter. Some of the logs were split down the center, making what are called *puncheons* for constructing the floors. Others were trimmed of their bark and were used for the walls of their homes.

After choosing the location for a house, the ground beneath was leveled. Pillars were constructed of stones mortared with mud. Two logs that were very straight and resistant to rotting, usually poplar or cedar or chestnut, were laid on the pillars as the foundation. Puncheons were then placed, flat sides up, in notches cut into the foundation logs. At this point they began constructing the walls. Tree trunks were measured and notches were cut into them near both ends. As they lifted each one, the men made sure the notches fit snugly over the ones below. When the walls were high enough, logs for the ends to hold the roof were cut progressively shorter. As these were laid in place, they formed a peak. A stout ridgepole was securely pegged into place across the top, and more poles were notched and pegged to form the rafters and supports. Some of the roofs were thatched, but most were layered with limbs, brush, and finally cut sod to form a secure, weather-proof roof.

A window was cut, and shutters were attached. A larger space was provided in the same manner for a door. The chimney was built of earth and rocks with a great, flat stone as the hearth. Some larger houses had two or three rooms to accommodate the needs of larger families.

Each house was solidly built to handle the freezing weather and the deep snows of the new land. According to Jack Cobb, the winters in Kentucky were often very cold, and at times they could be as frigid as those of New England.

Looking both pleasing and formidable, their little frontier town was composed of a group of thirty-five log homes that covered over three acres of ground. The cabins were surrounded by a double palisade that had two rows of stout, sharpened stakes planted deep into the ground and rising a full nine feet above it.

At each corner of the palisade, they built the largest and strongest of their buildings, called blockhouses. Two smaller ones were constructed on either side of the gates. They were two-story structures of heavy logs, with the second story projected over the first. Moreover, they made holes in the edge of the floor of the upper rooms so that one could look down through them upon anybody outside the fort who stood by the outer wall. Cobb went into the second story of each of the buildings, thrust the muzzle of his rifle into every one of the holes in turn, and gave a satisfied nod. "I believe that'll work," he said. "What do you think, Dirt?"

Gurley, who had joined Cobb in his inspection, eased up to the holes in the floor and ogled an eye through each one. After several minutes of careful study from all angles, he spoke his opinion. "*He, he, he!* Yessiree-bob! If any o' them reprobate aborigines attack this here fort an' tries to shelter their heathern carcasses against our walls, they's gonna find their breeches full of buckshot. Shave my head an' call me an onion if they don't!"

21

The last big project that the settlers set for themselves was to dig a well. They picked a spot in a corner of the palisade near the gate and began shoveling, striking a good supply of water at a depth of fifteen feet. With this accomplished, the work of establishing the village was complete. Now each family concentrated on furnishing their cabin and making their home as comfortable as they desired.

With William's strength and broad shoulders, he was given a man's share of the labors. But it was not all work for him. Some of the labor itself was just as good as play. What he enjoyed the most was when he was allowed to go considerable distances, scouting and hunting with Jack Cobb. For Will these journeys were full of new experiences, and he loved them. During the exploits he got to explore places no civilized boy had ever seen.

Jack Cobb and William were accompanied on many of the journeys by Dirt Gurley. Dirt was a rough frontiersman without kin in the settlement, and so, having nobody but himself to take care of, he chose to roam the country a great portion of the time. His skill in forest life and knowledge of its ways was second only to that of Cobb. Some of the men called Dirt lazy, but he defended himself: "I ain't lazy. I'm jus' what you might call, *dee-liberate*. The Great Creator made different kinds of folks, and they all live different kinds of lives," he continued. "Mine suits me and harms nobody. Besides, most folks are so busy with all their comin' an' goin' an' fixin' an' frettin' that they never get around to just enjoyin' all the beautimus creativities what the Good Lord done made. I, fer one, have decided to make time to enjoy 'em, an' I figure the Almighty appreciates that."

"Ah reckon Ah'll have to agree with you there, Dirt," Jack said with a nod. "But you know there's gonna be plenty for you and me to do, huntin' an' scoutin' for all these folks."

There was no lack of food. A lot of the provisions that they had brought with them from the other side of the mountains was stored in the bottom floor of the blockhouses, to be preserved for a possible time of need. Why should they use their stores when they could kill all the game they needed within a mile of their own chimney smoke? William tasted the delights of buffalo tongue, beaver tail, venison, wild turkey, fried squirrel, wild goose, wild duck, and a dozen kinds of fish. Never did a lad have more variety of meat morning, noon, and night. The forest was full of game. As Dirt Gurley said, "The fish are just standin' up in the river and cryin' to be caught."

William had shown so much interest and competence during their times in the woods that Jack thought it was time to teach him to hunt. Since Dirt was in full agreement, they both went to William's father to intercede for him. "The boy's getting' big and strong, an' he's most nearly a man. It's time he learned," Cobb said to John Hackett.

"I've been watchin' 'im," Dirt added. "That boy's hand is steady as a rock, an' he's got a keen eye to boot. Yessiree-bob, he's ready. . .more'n ready! An' mark my words, Will's got the makin's of a fine hunter. I know these thangs, Mr. Hackett. My momma didn't name me Solomon fer nut'in!"

After hearing these sincere words about his son, Mr. Hackett took a moment to think. He had always intended that William help farm the land until the lad was old enough to have land of his own. He saw in Will the makings of a strong community leader. But Mr. Hackett also realized that, on the frontier, a man might need to be an exceptional hunter, especially if the crops happened to be bad for a season or two. Influenced by this thought, William's father faced the two scouts and agreed to allow them to teach his son how to hunt.

Two miles away, near the bank of the river, was a spring where game often came to drink, and the hunters set out for it a little while before sundown. William, carrying his rifle, was about as excited as he had ever been. As he marched along with his friends, the young pioneer knew this hunt was a big step for him. He hoped he would finally become a man and be able to put away the nagging, condemning thoughts that plagued him. Yet despite this hope, his heart beat rapidly, and he felt his boyish nerves trembling. He grasped his precious rifle more firmly. The stock was of hard maple wood delicately carved, and the barrel was comparatively long, slender, and of blue steel. The sights were as fine-drawn as a hair. When William stood the gun beside himself, it was just as tall as he. He also carried a creamy white powder horn that had been scraped so thin that it was almost transparent, thus enabling its owner to know just how much powder it contained without taking the trouble of pouring it out. Bullets and wadding were carried in a small leather pouch by the young hunter's side.

Late that afternoon when they reached the spring, the sun was a half hour above the horizon and filled the west with a red glow. The forest was tinted by the setting sun's crimson and scarlet colors, and seen in the coming twilight, the wilderness looked very lonely and desolate. Most boys walking through the deep woods might have been apprehensive at the coming of night, but William was comforted by it.

"Wind's blowin' from the west," said Dirt, so they went to the eastern side of the spring and lay beside a fallen log at a fair distance from the water. Another log was much closer to the spring, but Jack, after a whispered conference with Dirt, chose the farther one.

"We want to teach the boy how to shoot an' be of some use to himself. We ain't out here to teach him how to slaughter," Jack explained to Dirt.

Once in position, the three remained hidden a long time and noiselessly watched the spring. Jack had determined to teach William from the beginning that the first great lesson of the forest was silence. But this was a lesson with which Will was already well acquainted. It had been his habit to sit silently in the woods alone and observe the creatures that he might find there, but the boy gave no indication to either of his friends of his past experiences. He had great respect for these men and the knowledge of the woods they possessed. All William wanted to do was to spend time with the two scouts and learn from them all their secrets.

The sun went down behind the western forest, and twilight came. A light wind began to moan among the trees. Will heard the faint babble of the water and saw beside him the forms of his two comrades. They were so still that they might have been dead. The young hunter's sight became sharper as his eyes grew more used to the dimness. There was still no game at the spring. After a few minutes Jack put his hand gently upon his arm, and William, as if by instinct, looked in the right direction. There at the far edge of the forest was a deer, a noble stag, glancing warily about him.

It was a fine enough animal to Jack and Dirt, but to William's unaccustomed eyes, he seemed gigantic, the mightiest of his kind that ever walked the face of the earth. The buck gazed cautiously, raising his great head, until his antlers looked to Will like the branching limbs of a tree. The wind blew toward his hidden foes and brought him no warning of coming danger. He stepped into the open and again glanced around the circle.

"When he stoops down to drink, aim at that spot there behind the shoulder," said Cobb in the lowest of tones.

Satisfied that no enemy was near, the stag walked to the spring. He slowly lowered the great antlers as his head approached the water. William slipped the barrel of his rifle across the log and looked down the sights. Just then the old voices began to abuse him, and he was seized with a tremor. *What a joke, YOU making a shot like that! You're going to mess this up like you do everything else. A worthless kid like you will probably gut shot the beast or more likely miss altogether.*

Will had heard these voices many, many times. His drunken, abusive father made sure that he would never forget them. The young hunter's hand continued to shake with a mixture of fear and anger at the mental torment, and a tear began to form in the corner of his eye. Jack Cobb and Dirt Gurley, with a fairness that did them credit, pretended not to notice.

With a deep breath and the resolve of a warrior who had fought these familiar enemies many times, the young hunter soon mastered the feeling. But to his great surprise, he was attacked by another emotion. He began to have pity for the stag. It too was in the great wilderness, living freely in the woods, delighting in the grass and the running streams, and had done no harm. It seemed sad that so fine a life should end without warning, just to provide food for another.

The feeling was that of a boy, the instinct of one who had not learned to hunt, and as he did with the others, he suppressed it. Here on the frontier, the killing of game was a necessity if one was to survive. So Will Hackett, after a moment's hesitation, picked the spot behind the shoulder that Cobb had mentioned, and with a steady hand gently squeezed the trigger.

There was an explosive flash, and the stag stood for a moment or two as if dazed, then leaped into the air and ran to the edge of the woods where he suddenly fell and lay still.

It was a clean shot to the heart. William was proud of his marksmanship, but he had to admit that when he looked upon his victim, he felt a little remorse as well. Yet he was eager to tell his family of his success. They skinned and cut up the deer. The Hacketts ate part of the haunch for dinner, and the antlers were fastened over the fireplace as the first important hunting trophy won by the eldest son of the house.

William did not boast of his triumph, although he noticed with secret pride the awe of the children. His best friend, Asa Whitlock, openly expressed his admiration, but Braxton Wyatt, a boy of his own age whom he did not like, sneered and counted it as nothing. Braxton knew William's past and took every opportunity to put the young hunter back in his place. The tormentor even cast doubt upon the reality of the deed, suggesting that perhaps Cobb or Gurley had fired the shot and had allowed William to claim the credit.

After his successful hunt, the work that William had to do around the house was more difficult for him because his mind constantly longed for the wilderness. He knew it would be the same when they broke ground for farming unless he could control his day dreaming. It was too late to plant crops that year, and the qualities of the soil were not yet known. The dirt was rich beyond a doubt, but they could learn only by trial what sort of seed suited it best. So they let that wait a while and continued the work of making themselves tight and warm for the winter.

The skins of deer and buffalo and beaver, slain by the hunters, were tanned and dried in the sun. They hung some of the finer ones on the walls of their rooms to make them more snug and warm. Mrs. Hackett also put two or three on the floors. William helped his father make stools and chairs. They discovered that baskets were needed, but these required longer and more tedious work, being made by cutting green withes, splitting them into strips, and weaving them together. Mrs. Hackett and her young daughter did much of that labor while William and his father made tables and a small stone oven built into the side of the fireplace.

Their main room now looked very cozy. In one corner stood a bedstead with low, square posts, and the mattress was covered with a pure white spread. At the foot was a large, heavy chest that served as bureau, sofa, and dressing case. In the center of the room stood a big walnut table, on top of which rested a nest of wooden trays, flanked on one side by a nicely folded tablecloth and on the other by a butcher knife and a Bible. In a corner a set of shelves was pegged into the logs, and on them were the blue-edged plates, blue teacups, and matching blue teapot that Mrs. Hackett had received long ago from her mother. The furniture in the remainder of the house was similar.

For the men of the village, the heaviest labor of all was enlarging the clearing, which they accomplished during most of the winter as the weather allowed. By cutting down trees and digging out stumps, they prepared the ground for planting the next spring. William had an equal share in this work, for with his broad shoulders, he was able to wield an ax blow for blow with a grown man. When he did not have to work, he went often to the river that was within sight of Larkinboro and caught fish. Nobody, except the men who were always armed and who knew how to take care of themselves, was allowed to go more than a half a mile from the palisade. William was trusted as far as the river because the watchman in the lookout on top of the highest blockhouse could see him.

The young pioneer did not hate his work, yet he could not say that he liked it. The influence of the great forests and of the vast unknown spaces was upon him. During the milder winter days, when he needed a break he could lie peacefully in the shade of a tree for an hour at a time, dreaming of rivers and mountains farther in the depths of the wilderness—anything but his past. William felt a kinship with the wild things, and one time as he lay perfectly still with his eyes almost closed, a stag, perhaps the brother to the one that he had killed, came and looked at him out of great, soft eyes. It did not seem odd at the time to him that the great animal should do so; he took it as a friendly act, and lest he should alarm this new comrade of the woods, he did not stir. The buck gazed at him a few moments, then tossing his great antlers, turned and walked off in a graceful and dignified way through the winter woods. At that moment a wave of peace swept over the lad, and it seemed to him that this was the only place on earth where he could conquer his fears and escape the tormenting thoughts.

As William lay there, he was reminded of a particular day during the journey. Because he had experienced an especially hard time battling the voices and fears, when they had finally stopped, William had slipped into the surrounding woods to find some peace. But the accusing, condemning attacks hadn't let up. They actually got worse. When William could take it no longer, he began yelling back. "I DON'T CARE WHAT YOU SAY!" he screamed to the trees. "I AM NOT WORTHLESS! YOU'RE WRONG! YOU'RE WRONG! I WILL NOT BE A FAILURE! I WON'T! I WON'T!"

William spent several long minutes venting his anger as he swung sticks powerfully into the trunks of surrounding trees, fighting his enemies. Finally he stopped to catch his breath.

"I've felt the same way."

The voice came from behind William, and he whirled to see who was there. He saw a skinny boy with a bird's nest of curly, blond hair piled on his head. It was his friend, Asa Whitlock, who had followed him into the woods. William was embarrassed, but when he looked in Asa's face, he only saw compassion.

"I mean it!" Will's young friend said again with sincerity. "I've felt the exact, same way."

"Are you serious, Asa?" Will asked hopefully. "Do you have to deal with fears of failure and worthlessness?"

"I used to. . .a lot," his friend answered with a smile. "A couple of years ago, I was kind of a mess. I didn't think that I could do anything right. My father came into my room and caught me crying, so I had to tell him what was bothering me. When I explained my fears, he told me something that caused me to look at it all differently."

"What did he say?" William asked anxiously.

"He said that everybody makes mistakes, and when I make them, I should not let that determine my worth. He told me that God had made it clear in His Word that I am worth the life of His Son. Because of that, my father told me never to say or believe that I was worthless. That's true for you too, Will."

For the first time in his life, William allowed himself to open up his heart to another person. Asa's honesty and genuine compassion convinced William that Asa was a true friend and someone with whom William could share his burdens. For the next half hour, the troubled boy told Asa all he had endured from his abusive father and the burden that he carried with him.

"It was always bad," Will admitted, "but the last night was the worst. It was late when my father came home drunk again. He jerked me out of my bed and started beating me. My mother was usually scared to death of him, but I guess when she saw how hard he was hitting me, she couldn't take it anymore. She grabbed a broom and started screaming and hitting him with it. That made him pretty mad. He threw me to the side and started after my mother. As she backed away from him, I heard her yell at me to run, so I did. I heard terrible crashing and yelling behind me. When I got about a stone's throw away from the cabin, I hid in the dark shadows and looked back. The cabin was already on fire. I figured that, as he was beating my mother, they knocked over the oil lamp on the table. When the flames touched the dry logs of our old cabin, it all went up like a match. Neither of them got out."

Asa saw large tears forming in the corners of his friend's eyes as he finished.

"You know that the Hacketts love you, don't you, Will?"

"Oh, sure, Asa," William responded as he wiped his cheeks. "They have taken me in as one of their own. They've given me a good name that I'm proud to have. I couldn't have a better family than them, but all that old stuff from before just won't leave. Even though my real father's dead, I can still hear his words. During Mr. Spebbington's sermons, I have heard him say how much Jesus loves us, an' that really sounds great, but with all this junk that keeps coming back to me, it's going to take a lot of convincing for me to put these fears away for good."

"Well then," Asa Whitlock said with a smile as he threw his arm across his friend's broad shoulders, "my job will be to remind you."

From that moment on, William and Asa were best friends.

Chapter Four

LOST IN THE WILDERNESS

One spring morning Mrs. Hackett said to her husband, "John, that boy is growing wild. All he wants is to be out in those woods."

"Yes, I've noticed that as well," her husband replied. "Exploring the forest and hunting for game can have a mighty strong pull on lads when they're young and impressionable."

The mother looked troubled, but Mr. Hackett smiled. "Don't worry about it, dear," he said. "It can be cured. We simply have to teach William duty and responsibility."

The method Mr. and Mrs. Hackett used to instruct their oldest son in important character qualities was an increase of labor. To keep William's additional work load from being too unpleasant, it also became his duty to supply the table with fish regularly. That was a job he could get excited about. When summer finally arrived, the fish became more active. He caught perch, bass, suckers, trout, sunfish, catfish, and other kinds whose names he didn't know. Once his stringer was full and the day was hot, he would take off his clothes and plunge into the deep, cool pools. Often his friend Asa Whitlock was with him. Asa was a year younger than William, and while almost as tall, was much thinner. Because of this, the larger boy felt himself Asa's protector in a certain sense, which gave William a good feeling and a desire to help his companion as much as he could.

31

During the hot summer, scarcely a day passed when the two sunburned, barefooted lads did not go to the river, quickly throw off their clothing, and jump into the clear water. For a long time they would swim, float, dive, and dunk each other, finally lying on the grass in the sun until they dried.

"Whit," said William once as they were stretched out on the bank, "wouldn't you like to have nothing to do but wander through the woods just as you pleased, sleep wherever you wanted, and kill game when you got hungry, just like the Indians?" Will Hackett's eyes were on the black line of the forest and the blue haze of the sky beyond. His heart was away in the depths of the unknown wilderness.

"Oh. . .I don't know," replied Asa. "I guess it'd be fun for a while, but that just seems kinda selfish to me. Eventually a fella has to become a man, and a man needs to provide for his family. I suppose that if I didn't have responsibilities to others, the free life in the woods would be all right, at least for a while."

"I think I could enjoy that kind of life as long as I lived," William said dreamily.

"I definitely see the need for scouts," Asa answered thoughtfully. "We couldn't have gotten here without the help of Jack Cobb and Dirt Gurley. Scouts will always be needed to help protect and hunt for us until the land is civilized. But my father says that it'll be the farmers and the settlers who'll do the real work of building the country, and those jobs can only be done with dedicated hard work."

Yet William was unconvinced, and his thoughts wandered far into the black forest and the blue haze.

The pioneer families pastured their cattle near the deepest of the swimming holes, and it often fell to the boys to bring them into the palisade at sunset. This was actually quite an important job, because if any of the cattle wandered away into the forest and were lost, they could not be replaced.

Near the end of summer, the grass and foliage were fast turning brown in the heat. Late in the afternoon on one of the very hottest days, Will and Asa went to their favorite swimming spot in the river. There had not been a breath of air stirring since morning.

The boys panted, and their clothing, wet with perspiration, clung to them. The earth was hot under their feet. Quickly they threw off their garments and sprang into the water. How cool and refreshing it felt! In fact, it felt so good that they lost track of time and did not notice the clouds that suddenly blocked the sun and darkened the southwest.

A slight wind presently sprang up, and the dry leaves and grass began to rustle. Thunder sounded in the distance, and a stroke of lightning flashed. The boys were aroused and, scrambling out of the water, jerked on their clothing.

"That storm's coming fast!" exclaimed William as he observed the darkening sky. "We've got to hurry to get the cattle in!"

The heat had been oppressive for days, and the earth was parched and thirsty. The settlers had talked the day before about rain and said how welcome it would be, but this looked like it was to be much more than a gentle soaking. It was clear that the drought was about to end, and the thirsty earth would drink deep and grow green again, but at what cost?

The rolling clouds, drawn like a great curtain over the southwest, advanced and covered all the heavens. Flashes of lightning followed each other so quickly that at times they seemed continuous. The forest groaned as it bent before the wind. Then great drops fell, and soon they were beating the earth like volleys of pistol bullets. Fragments of limbs, stripped off by the wind, swept by. The thunder and lightning came fast and continuous.

The frightened cattle were in a group, pressing close together for company and protection. The boys hurried them toward the stockade, but one yearling, driven by terror, broke from the rest and ran toward the woods. William, not willing to lose a single straggler, pursued the fugitive, and Asa, wishing to be as zealous as his friend, followed. The rest of the cattle, being so near and obeying the force of habit, continued on toward the stockade.

It was the wildest animal of the herd that made a plunge for the woods, and William, knowing her nature, expected trouble. He ran as fast as he could in pursuit of the beast. He was not aware until they were in the forest that Asa Whitlock was close behind him.

"GO BACK, WHIT!" William shouted to his friend. "I'LL BRING HER IN."

But Asa wouldn't turn back. He considered it as much his duty to help as it was William's, and he would not desert his friend.

The crazed fugitive, driven by the storm, leaped through the woods like a deer, zig-zagging and darting first one way and then another. The panting boys struggling through the brush were not able to overtake her. So on the trio went, plunging through the dark woods. They saved themselves from falls or collisions with trees only by the light from the flashes of lightning. Most boys would have given up the difficult chase and turned back, but there was a strong sense of determination in William's nature. He was driven to fight failure with every ounce of his being, so once he started something, he fought hard to complete it. Besides, the heifer was too valuable to just let her run off.

On the maddening chase went as the rain came rushing and roaring through the woods, falling in sheets, while overhead lightning blasted and thunder crashed. The boys were drenched, but they did not mind it; they did not even think about it at the time. The powerful storm continued in its fierceness for quite a while. Eventually the lightning and thunder began to lessen, and darkness fell like a great blanket over the whole forest. When it finally got too dark to see, the two boys stopped. Asa reached out and grabbed William's arm to locate him in the thick blackness as the rain still poured down heavily.

"We'll have to give up on the heifer," said Will reluctantly. "We couldn't follow a whole herd of buffalo as dark as it is."

"Maybe we can find her tomorrow," Asa returned.

"Maybe so," replied Will. "We can't do anything about it now. Let's go home."

They started back for Larkinboro, keeping close together so they wouldn't lose each other in the darkness. The rain came in sheets directly in their faces so that it half blinded them. Their bare feet sank deep in mire, and their drenched bodies began to grow cold, which motivated them to hurry. In the darkness the two boys often tripped on vines or ran into bushes. But William pressed on, searching for some kind of trail. However, he was unable to find one in the dark woods.

"We ought to be near the clearing," he said after they had walked for almost an hour.

They stopped and looked all about, hoping to see a light. They knew one would be shining from the top of the blockhouse as a guide to them. But they saw nothing. They had misjudged the distance, so they thought, and they pushed on a half hour longer, but there was still no light, nor did they come to a clearing. It was then that they paused.

"We've come the wrong way!" exclaimed Asa.

"Maybe we have," reluctantly admitted his older companion. *What a woodsman you turned out to be!* the familiar voices in William's mind yelled at him. *You lost the cow, lost yourself, and on top of all that, you have gotten Asa lost! You are totally worthless. . .worthless. . .WORTHLESS. . .*

"Asa, I'm so sorry I got us lost!" Will blurted out, almost in tears. "I should have stopped chasing that cow while it was still light enough to find our way home. But because I was so foolish, I didn't! Now I've gotten us both lost! I'm sorry, Asa! I'm so, so sorry!"

"Now just hold on a second there, partner," Asa good naturedly shot back. "Correct me if I'm wrong, O Great Guilty One, but I seem to remember that there were two of us on that chase. That means that I had as much opportunity to say something about going home as you did...and I didn't. That means that you didn't get me lost. The truth be told, we both got ourselves lost."

"But I'm older, and I should have made better decisions," William answered.

"We both should have," Asa returned.

"But *I'm the oldest!*" Will argued.

"Yeah, well, you're the ugliest too, but be that as it may, here we are. Don't beat yourself up over it, because didn't you tell me that you would love to live in the woods on your own?"

"Uh. . .yeah, I did."

"Okay then," Asa said with a chuckle, "here's your chance."

"Hey, you're right," William answered cheerfully, much encouraged by his friend's response. "But it will probably be a short adventure. I'm gonna try to get us home before midnight."

They changed their course and continued the search. The rain ceased after a while, and the clouds left the heavens. When the moon finally came out, they both hoped to see things they would recognize, but they saw nothing familiar about the surrounding forest. The great trees dripped with water, which was the only sound they heard besides the noise they made. Eventually they stopped again, worn out and discouraged. All their walking had only served to confuse them more.

At that moment William found a tree he could climb and carefully made his way to the top. He took his time staring into the darkness all around them, hoping to spot a light from Larkinboro.

"Do you see anything at all?" Asa called anxiously up to his friend.

"No," the older boy said with disappointment.

Neither lad had any idea in which direction Larkinboro lay, and to be lost in the wilderness was a most desperate matter. They might travel hundreds of miles, if their strength lasted for such a journey, and never see a single human being. They leaned against the rough bark of a great oak tree and stared blankly at each other as the moon began to break through the drifting clouds.

"What do we do now?" asked Asa.

"I'm not really sure," Will answered with concern.

The two boys stood there looking at each other in the moonlight. Finally Asa started laughing.

"What are you laughing at?" William asked irritably.

"*Ha, ha, ha.* . .I'm laughing at your face! You should see yourself. . .*ha, ha, ha.* . .You look like you're about to get scalped!"

"Well, I feel terrible about getting us lost!" William exclaimed. A smile began to involuntarily creep across his face as he looked at his laughing friend.

"*Ha, ha, ha.* . ." Asa laughed harder. "*You* didn't get us lost. *Ha, ha, ha.* . .THE COW DID!" When he said this, Asa's

36

emotional dam broke, and he fell to his knees, belly laughing uncontrollably.

Will at first began chuckling at his friend, but soon he too was laughing uncontrollably. Falling to the ground he rolled back and forth in the wet leaves, guffawing with all of his strength.

It took several long, hilarious minutes for the two boys to get control of themselves. Finally William sat up and looked at Asa, who was still giggling.

"Are you done yet?" William chuckled.

"*He, he, he. . .*I think so," Asa managed to get out in a squeaky, high-pitched voice. "You've got to feel better after a good laugh like that." As he spoke, he sat up and began to rub the tears from his eyes.

"Well, I guess I do feel better," William said with a smile as he stood and pulled his friend to his feet, "but we're still lost."

They began once more to search about them for something to give them direction. After a moment Asa put his hand on his friend's shoulder. "I think I know just what we need to do, Will."

"What's that?"

"Before we do anything else," the boy answered confidently, "we need to pray."

William recognized the wisdom in his friend's words, and they both bowed their heads while Asa offered a sincere petition to their Heavenly Father, thanking Him for protecting them through the storm and asking Him for help in getting back home.

"We don't know where we are or how to get back," Asa prayed, "but Father, we do know that we need lots of help from You and from Your Son, the Lord Jesus Christ. Please protect us, keep us alive, and show us the way home."

When Asa finished his prayer, Will said a heartfelt, "Amen."

The cold had passed with the storm, and warm winds blew up from the south. The forest began to dry, and the two friends took off their shirts and wrung the water from them. Under the influence of the southern breeze, their wet clothing began to dry. But they were so intensely sleepy that they could scarcely keep their eyes open, and now the wilderness training of both came into use.

They couldn't see far in the moonlight, but they could tell that they were among unfamiliar hills with many outcroppings of stone. The boys searched for some sort of cave in which to rest, but it was a long hunt, and they grew more tired and sleepy at every step. They were hungry too, but if they could only sleep, they would forget that. They heard again the hooting of owls, and the wind, moaning among the limbs, made strange noises. Once there was a crash in a thicket beside them, which caused them both to jump, but it was only a startled deer running through the bushes. They decided that the animal was far more scared than they were, and William was ashamed of his nervousness.

Just when they felt that their tired legs couldn't go much further, they found a sheltered ledge of dry stone in the hollow of a hill. "What do you think, Whit?" Will asked as he scrutinized the foreboding black area below the ledge.

"If there's something in there," Asa groaned as he dragged his weary legs toward the grotto, "then it's just gonna have to eat me, cause I'm too tired to care."

They crept into the hollow, and after scraping together fallen leaves to soften the hard stone, the two exhausted boys collapsed into their primitive beds. Both were asleep in less than a minute.

The hollow faced east, but tall trees shaded them from the sun's rays until it was high in the sky. When the sun climbed above the tops of the trees, the bright light shining into their eyes woke them at last. Springing up quickly, William noticed that the skies were a silky blue and had little white clouds sailing here and there. He also noticed that the forest, newly washed by the rain, had a clean, sweet smell. His enjoyment of the beauty around him was interrupted by a gnawing pain at the center of his empty stomach. When Asa sat up, his first act was to grab his own growling stomach. Ignoring his discomfort, William looked up and found that the sun was almost directly overhead, indicating noon.

As they viewed the surrounding area, nothing looked familiar. The country for as far as they could see was strange and different. It was an unbroken expanse of hill and forest, and there was not a sign of a human being anywhere. They scrutinized the horizon, but they saw no line of smoke rising from the chimneys of Larkinboro. Whether the village lay north or south or east or west of them, they did not know, and the wind that sighed so gently through the forest couldn't tell them. They were alone in the wilderness and knew that it was very vast and they were very small. But William Hackett and Asa Whitlock encouraged each other.

"I'm sorry we're in this mess, Whit," voiced William, "but at least we're in it together."

"If I have to be lost in the wilderness," Asa responded, "next to Jack Cobb and Dirt Gurley, I'd rather be lost with you."

As William studied their situation, he began to find a certain joy in it that appealed to his solitary nature and his love for adventure. After discussing their needs, the boys decided that the first thing that they should to do was to find something to eat. As a temporary cure for their hunger, each boy used his pocket knife to cut strips of the soft, inner bark of a nearby slippery-elm tree, which they chewed. It wasn't satisfying, but it eased their hunger pangs and gave them a little strength and nourishment. An hour or so later, they found ripe blackberries and some nearly ripe wild plums that they ate in small quantities. Asa wanted to devour all he could, but Will warned him against it, knowing well that if he ate too many, he might suffer worse pains than those of hunger. Even though there was not a lot to eat, the boys felt strengthened, and their spirits rose.

"We're bound to be found sooner or later," said William, "and surely we can live in the woods until then."

"If we only had our rifles and ammunition," said Asa, "we could get all the meat we wanted and live as well as if we were home."

Sadly for the lost boys, their firearms were far away, and to keep their strength up, they must obtain more solid food than wild plums and blackberries. They continued wandering until they came to a creek. Sitting for a while on its banks, they looked down at the swarming fish they could see distinctly in its clear waters.

"Oh, if we only had one of those fine fellas!" said Asa.

"Then why not have him?" exclaimed William with a gleam in his eye.

"Well sure, why not?" replied Asa with sarcasm. "I forgot to bring my fish call. I suppose that all we have to do is make a sound like a worm, and the finest of 'em will come right out here on the bank and beg us to cook and eat 'm."

"Aren't you just a ray of sunshine?" William returned. "I know we didn't bring any hooks or lines, but we can make 'em."

"Make 'em?" questioned Asa with a puzzled look on his face. "How?"

"Out of our clothes," the older boy replied.

He proceeded to demonstrate what he meant. When Asa saw what Will was doing, the younger boy was quickly taken with the idea. They drew many long strands of thread from their shirts, twisting and knotting them together until they had a line nearly ten feet long. It took them nearly two hours to complete the task. When they had finished, they were quite proud of their work. But the look of joy on Asa's face did not last long.

"We've got a line, but what in the name of common sense are we gonna do for a hook?" he asked.

"I'll furnish that," his friend answered confidently as he reached for the small metal fastening buckle in the back of his trousers. Breaking it apart, he used a rock to bend the slenderest portion of it into the shape of a hook and tied it securely to the end of his line.

"The only problem is that there's no barb on our hook, so if we get a fish to bite it, we'll have to pull hard on the line to keep the fish from slipping off," he said.

The rod and bait were easy matters. A straight, slender branch of a hickory tree cut with a pocket knife served for the first, and to get the latter, they simply had to turn up a flat stone and draw earthworms from the moist dirt beneath.

The hook was baited, and with a triumphant flourish, William swung it toward the stream. "Now," he pronounced, "for the biggest fish that ever swam in this creek."

The boys might have caught nothing with such make-shift fishing gear, but doubtless that stream had never been fished before, and its inhabitants, besides being full of a natural curiosity, did not dream of any danger coming from the air above them. The line had not been in the water half a minute before one grabbed the bait and tried to swim away.

Just as Will drew it from the water, the fish gave a flop, slipped off, and splashed back into the stream. Asa was disappointed, but William just shrugged and baited the hook again. It was not until the sixth bite that he succeeded in landing a nice perch. When they saw the fish flopping on the grassy bank, both boys gave a cry of triumph. Their joy would have been even greater if the two inexperienced youths fully understood the danger of their situation. The wilderness was indeed teeming with animal life, but it was faster and in some cases more powerful than man, and without weapons, the boys were almost helpless. To coax food from this dangerous and harsh environment was always a trial for those inexperienced in the woods.

"Now to cook him," announced young Mr. Hackett as he took from his pocket the flint and steel that he always carried. At the same time Asa began to gather dry brushwood from under the ledges that had been protected from the recent rains.

William expected that starting the fire would be the easiest of their tasks, but it proved to be one of the most difficult. As he struck the flint and steel together again and again, sparks showered down upon the small bits of dry grass they had collected but went out before setting fire to any of it. While he worked until his fingers ached, he could hear the voices from his past laughing at him, and it infuriated him. Finally with an angry snort, William tossed the fire-making implements to Asa and had him give it a try. After several minutes of hard work, a bright spark flew forth from Asa's steel and rested a moment among the lightest and driest of the grass blades. Almost immediately it began to glow and smoke. He quickly gave several gentle puffs of air on the smoldering spot, and a tiny point of flame appeared that grew and leaped up. In a few moments the great pile of brushwood was a roaring blaze, and a little later the boys cooked their fish over the coals. They ate it all with a deep sense of satisfaction, picking the bones until nothing was left.

The hunger they both still felt after they finished the fish made it clear that it was going to take a good deal more than an occasional fish to get them through their trial if it lasted longer than a few days. In order to prepare for the future, they would have to draw upon all their resources to stay alive. Their hook and line was but a make-shift device, and they might not have such luck with it again, especially after the fish got wise to it. Asa suggested that they make a fish trap of sticks tied together with vines and strips cut from their clothing and put it in the creek. William thought it was a good idea as well. They agreed to try it the next day, if they were not found, and spent the next hour talking about the best way to construct it.

Noticing the undergrowth was swarming with rabbits, they decided that they would also make very tasty food. After a short discussion William selected a small, clear spot near the thick undergrowth where a rabbit would naturally love to make its nest. He drove in a number of smooth pegs in a circle about twelve inches in diameter. Then he tied a cord made of thin strips from the tails of their shirts to one end of a stout bush that he bent over until it curved in a semicircle. The other end of the cord was formed into a sliding loop around the pegs and was attached to a little wooden trigger that held it in place in the center of the enclosure.

The slightest pressure upon the trigger released it, causing the noose to slip off the pegs and close with a jerk around the neck of anything that might have its head thrust into the enclosure. The bush would fly back into its place, and the intruder would be left hanging by the loop.

Will and Asa made four of the ingenious little devices and baited them with bruised pieces of small plantain leaves that rabbits loved. As they viewed their work, both felt a strong sense of satisfaction.

But Asa suddenly began to look worried. "I don't like the way this is going," he said with concern. "If it costs us some of our clothes every time we get a dinner, we soon won't have any left."

Will only laughed.

It was near sunset, and as they had worked hard, they would have been thankful for supper, but there was none to be thankful for, and they were too tired to fish again. So they determined to go to sleep, which their hard work made very easy, and dreamed of the wonderful meals back home.

They gathered armfuls of fallen brushwood that littered the forest floor, dried by the sun and the breeze, and built a heap as high as their heads. When lit, it blazed and roared wonderfully, sending up a column of smoke that rose far above the trees and trailed off in the blue sky. They wanted it to be a signal for any of their friends who might be searching for them, as well as being a comfort to them during the dark, lonely night.

Lying beside his friend on the soft turf, Will watched the red sun sink behind the black forest in the west. The strange longing to understand and explore the wilderness again came into his mind. He thought once more of the mysterious regions that lay beyond the line where the black and red met. *I really could live in the woods,* he told himself. He was actually doing so now without weapons. If he only had his rifle and ammunition, he could provide all he needed. Then he would be able to experience the wonderful excitement of exploring new and unseen lands! That old thought came to him with renewed force. His heart longed to roam the wilderness and see things that civilized man had never seen. He would make a canoe and float down the great rivers to their mouths. He would wander far out on the vast plains that was said to lie beyond the hundreds of miles of forest and see millions of buffalo go thundering by. These were William's thoughts before he finally drifted off to sleep.

Chapter Five

A FIERY WALL OF DEATH

Will was suddenly awakened by a long, wailing shriek that was answered a moment later by a similar cry. Once he would have been alarmed by the sound but now knew it was one panther calling to another. Though the castaways were unarmed, they had something as effective as guns against panthers: the great bonfire roaring and blazing near them. He was glad that they had built it high. Again hearing the panther's eerie cry sent a chill down his back. He looked at Asa, but his comrade still slept soundly. Remembering the words of Jack Cobb that, as a general rule, no wild animal would trouble man if man did not trouble him, and rolling a little nearer to Asa, he shut his eyes and sought sleep.

But it would not come, and presently he heard the cry of the panther again but much nearer. Rising upon his elbow, Will gazed into the darkness. He could just make out a dim form moving with flowing motion, and slowly from the night shadows, it took the shape of a great, cat-like animal. Then he saw behind it another one, slightly larger, and he knew that they were the two panthers whose cries he had heard.

William was not frightened by the cats, although there was something strange and mysterious in the spectacle of the two powerful beasts of prey stealing about the fire so near to the unarmed boys. He knew, however, that they were drawn not so much by the desire to attack as by curiosity. The fire was to them

44

a magnet, like a snake is to a fascinated bird. He longed for his gun, the faithful rifle that rested on the hooks over his bed in his father's house. *If I had my rifle, I'd make you cry for something,* he said to himself, looking at the largest of the panthers.

The animals lingered, glaring at the boys and the fire with red eyes. Their boldness irritated William, so he rose to his feet, snatched up a blazing torch, and rushed at them, shouting furiously.

In their eagerness to get away from the terrible, flaming vision that raced toward them, the panthers dashed headlong through the undergrowth. Their flight was so quick that they disappeared in an instant, and Will knew they would not venture near the site of the fire again for a long time. With a snort of satisfaction, he turned back and found Asa surprised and alarmed, standing erect and rubbing his eyes.

"What in the name of sour pickles are you *doing?*" cried his drowsy friend anxiously.

"Calm down," Will returned with a smile. "It's nothing to worry about." Then he told his younger companion about the panthers.

To Asa there was a lot to worry about. He did not share his friend's attraction for the wilderness, and he wished again for the strong, log walls and comfortable roofs of Larkinboro. But Will reassured him that both Jack Cobb and Dirt Gurley had told him the wild beasts were, as a rule, quite shy of man, although they were curious about things like fire. Comforted by his words, Asa lay back down and eventually went to sleep again, but William wasn't sleepy and decided to keep watch for a while.

Almost an hour later the young frontiersman noticed the fire dying. After throwing fresh fuel on the flames, he tried to sleep again. Gradually weariness mastered him. The woods grew dim, his heavy eyelids closed, and he was asleep.

Will awoke, with a strong tug at his shoulder. He instantly thought that one of the panthers had grabbed him, and he sprang up quickly to defend himself.

"No, Will! It's me. . .Asa!" cried a boyish voice. When William saw that his *panther* was really his friend, he relaxed and began rubbing the sleep from his eyes. The sun again was high in the heavens. The fire was still burning, though it had somewhat diminished. "You're beauty sleep doesn't seem to be working," Asa added, "so get up and let's go check the traps. I'm hungry."

"MY BREAKFAST!" cried William as he felt an uncomfortable emptiness in his mid-section.

With a burst of energy, they took off for the snares. The first had not been touched, nor had the second. The bait was gone from the third, and the loop sprung, but there was nothing in it. The hearts of the boys sank, and they thought again of wild plums and blackberries which, while tasty, were not satisfying. But when they came to the fourth snare, Asa threw up his arms and gave a shout of triumph. A fat rabbit, caught in the loop, hung beside the bush.

"It's a good thing that the forest is so full of game that at least some of it falls into our trap," Will said with a laugh.

"What!" Asa exclaimed in mock hurt. "Shame on you, William Hackett. That wasn't an accident. That, young sir, is the result of our *in-gen-nuitive idears*, as Dirt Gurley would say."

"Well," Will responded with a chuckle, "our *in-gen-nuitive idears* may have helped, but I think the Almighty felt sorry for us and decided to answer your prayer."

They cooked the rabbit immediately and ate it all. Will saved the entrails to make cordage for more snares and fishing tackle. Taking the intestines to the creek, he washed and laid them out on a flat rock. Asa took one end, and Will took the other. They trimmed off all the fat, just like Jack Cobb had showed him. With the length of the rabbit gut cut open, William took them back to the creek to clean again. Spreading the intestines flat on the rock, the boys took their knives and very gently scrapped the soft inside away so that only a long, thin sheet of muscle remained. Will took a small green stick and tied one end of the gut to it. He had Asa hold it while he tied the other end to another stick. When done, Will began to pull and twist his stick while his friend held the other end. When Will had the gut twisted tightly, he and Asa both stuck the ends of their sticks in the ground, the twisted gut stretched between them.

"In a day or two, once the sun dries it out, we'll have about eight feet of really nice cord to use," Will announced.

After finishing that, they used more thread from their clothing and the buckle in the back of Asa's pants to improvise another set of fishing tackle. By the middle of the afternoon, both boys began to fish. Because their most pressing problem was finding enough to eat, they decided for the present not to leave the creek that seemed to be their best source of food. So instead of searching for Larkinboro and risk not being able to find their way back, they decided to stay and keep their fire burning high as a signal to searchers.

Either the fish had learned that the curiously shaped thing with the tempting bait upon it was dangerous, or they had gone to visit friends in distant parts of the creek because over two hours passed without either boy getting a bite. When finally the fish did hit the bait, it was usually to slip off the rude hooks.

"OH. . .OH. . .OH. . .I GOT ONE!" Asa yelled as he saw his pole bend almost double.

"Don't let him get away!" Will cried.

Asa yanked hard on his pole, and suddenly a large sunfish flew out of the water and landed soggily in the grass behind him.

They kept fishing until sundown when William also made a catch. To add to their meager supper, they gathered more plums and berries. They also found and dug up the root of a plant called an Indian turnip. Jack Cobb had told Will that, if it was eaten raw, it burnt the mouth like fire, but it could be used for food if it was soaked in water for a few hours. After their supper that night, both boys agreed that they should have soaked it longer. . .a lot longer.

"You know, Will," Asa said the next morning, "I'm still convinced that we could save ourselves a lot of time if we built a fish trap."

"You're probably right," William returned, "but let me ask you this—if you had your choice, would you rather eat fish or rabbit?"

"Well," Asa answered, "as hungry as I am, I'd take both, but if I had to choose, I'd pick rabbit."

"Me too," William agreed, "so why don't we spend today putting together two more rabbit snares and setting them, and tomorrow we'll work on your fish trap?"

Will walked over to check the dried gut and decided that it was cured enough to use for one of the snares. The other they made out of more of their clothing.

After the new snares were set and they were resting beside the creek, Asa found himself thinking about home, and a deep sigh gave away his feelings. "Will, do you think we will ever get out of this mess we've gotten ourselves into?" he finally asked.

William looked at his despondent friend and a wave of compassion filled his heart. But then another thought came to the older boy, prompted by the presence of his spiritual companion. "Whit, you're always preachin' at me to trust God. Well, I'm ready to do it. Last Sunday during his sermon, Mr. Spebbington read out of the Holy Book that James said, *If anyone lacks wisdom, he should ask God, Who gives to all generously.* We, my friend, lack wisdom. So let's ask Him for some and trust His generosity to get us back home."

"An excellent idea, Mr. Hackett!" Asa said, bouncing back to his usual enthusiasm. "Let's do it right now!"

For the next half hour, the two lost boys humbly poured out their hearts to their Father in heaven. When they had finished, Asa spent several more minutes thanking Him for how He was going to answer their prayers.

After the last *amen* was said, there was quiet for a few moments until Asa spoke up. "Alright, Mr. Hackett. We have asked the Father in heaven for wisdom, and if we're going to trust Him, then we need to start looking for His answer. So what has He given us?"

Will couldn't discern any new thoughts in his head, so he started to look around. "Well, He's given us this creek."

"How can the creek get us home?" Asa asked with a blank look.

"We could. . .uh. . .follow it."

"Follow it?"

"YES," Will answered enthusiastically, "WE'LL FOLLOW IT!"

"Why?" Asa asked again with the same questioning look.

"Because it's eventually going to flow into a river. . .most likely the same river that flows by Larkinboro. We just need to collect a few days' worth of food and start following the creek."

"Will, that's brilliant!"

"Well, it did come from God," the older boy chuckled.

That evening they discussed their plan in more detail as they lay beside their large, roaring fire. The nearness of the panthers motivated the boys to take turns during the night to watch for enemies and to keep the flames built up.

The next day they devoted to the construction of a fish trap that, by the end of the afternoon, was successfully completed and positioned in the deepest part of the creek. After a meal of roasted rabbit and plums, the lost lads took their places on the turf beside the campfire for the fourth night.

When morning arrived, it was clear that it was going to be as hot as the day before. All traces of the great rain were gone. Forest and earth were again as dry as tinder. The heat kept the forest creatures bedded down in the shade, so no rabbits were found in the snares. In spite of this, the youthful scavengers managed to eat well because they found three large fish in their trap.

After the sun set, it was still uncomfortably warm, so they refreshed themselves with a swim in the creek before lying down to sleep. Even so, they were soon panting with the heat that seemed to hang in heavy clouds. The forest shut out any breeze that might be moving higher up in the trees.

Despite the discomfort, the friends built the fire as high as usual, both for protection and as a signal to those who might be looking for them. They knew that those searching would never cease so long as there was hope of success. But to escape the unwelcome warmth from the large fire, they moved away from it and into the shadow of the woods where it was a little cooler.

"If only the wind would blow!" said William. "This heat is stifling!"

"I'd be willing to stand a storm like the last one if it would just rain," agreed Asa.

But neither rain nor wind came. Eventually tiredness overcame their distress, and they fell asleep. Sometime in the middle of the night, William was startled awake by a roaring in his ears. At first he thought that Asa was about to have his storm, but then he was dazzled by a great flash of light, and he sprang to his feet in sudden alarm.

"GET UP, WHIT!" he cried, grasping his comrade by the shoulder. "THE WOODS ARE ON FIRE!"

Asa was on his feet in an instant. Sparks flew in their faces, and flames twisting into spirals and columns leaped from tree to tree with a sound like thunder. Limbs that burned through fell to the ground with a crash. Millions of sparks blasted into the air, igniting more tinder.

The terrified boys ran at full speed toward the creek with the great fire roaring and rushing after them. Will looked back once, but the sight horrified him, and sparks scorched his face. He realized that the inferno had been set by their own bonfire and must have been fanned by rising wind as they slept, but it was no time to lament. Feeding upon the dry forest and gathering strength as it advanced, the rush of the flames was terrific. It sounded like thunder in the ears of the frightened lads, and they fairly skimmed over the ground in the effort to escape. They could feel the firestorm's hot breath on their necks while smoke and sparks flew over their heads. Dashing into the creek, each slid under the cool and refreshing water.

"Let's stay here!" Asa cried as he surfaced.

"We'll die if we do!" replied his friend. "The water's not deep enough to protect us from that terrible heat. We've got to keep going! COME ON!"

The boys sprang out of the shallow creek and ran up the opposite hill. William paused a moment at its crest and looked back again at the frightful scene. The flames leaped higher than the tops of the tallest trees and thrust out long, red, twisting arms like coiling serpents. The roar was deafening.

"Asa!" exclaimed William, seizing his comrade's arm. "We've got to run as we've never run before! It's to save our lives!"

Tucking their heads to protect them from the blast of sparks, the two boys raced through the forest with the ruthless pursuer thundering after them. As he ran, Will glanced back once more and saw the fire gaining on them. The serpents of flame were coming nearer and nearer, and the sparks flew over their heads in greater showers. Asa panted and, being the younger and smaller of the two, his strength began to fail. Will felt his comrade start to lag behind, so he grabbed Asa's arm and pulled him along. It was clear to Will that his younger friend was tiring quickly. If he let go, Will knew that he could run faster. It was just then that the hated voices returned. *What makes you think a chump like you can save Asa? You can't even save yourself. Give up! You're done for! Worthless. . .worthless. . .*

"NO-O-O!" Will roared in response, and he remembered his promise to get Asa back home. Regardless of what was to happen, Will could never quit on his friend at such a moment. So he pulled on his young companion to hasten his speed, and together the boys went on.

The two soon noticed that they were not alone in their flight. Deer and rabbits also raced before the inferno. The deer were in a panic of terror, and a great stag ran for a few moments beside the boys, having lost his fear of humans in the face of the fiery death behind. In addition, four buffalo presently joined the frightened herd. One was a great bull, running with his head down and blowing great blasts of steam from his nostrils.

Asa suddenly sank to his knees and gasped, "I can't go on! Let me stay here, and you save yourself, Will!"

William Hackett looked back at the great, fiery wall that swept over the ground, roaring like a storm. It was very near now, and the smoke almost blinded him. A boy with a spirit less determined than his might well have fled in a panic, leaving his companion to his death. But the nearer the danger came, the more resolute the young frontiersman grew. He saw too that he must do something drastic to motivate Asa to start running again.

"GET UP!" he ordered, and he jerked the fainting boy to his feet. Snatching a stick, he struck Asa several smart blows on his back.

"Ow!" Asa cried. "What are you doing?"

"RUN, ASA! RUN!" Will yelled sternly at his friend and gave him another hard blow with his stick.

Asa cried out again with the sharp pain and, stimulated by it into physical action, began to sprint with renewed speed.

"That's right, Whit!" cried Will supportively, dropping his stick and seizing his comrade again by the arm. "Keep going! We'll make it! Just over this hill!

"O Lord," William shouted a desperate prayer to God, "we are done for without Your help!"

"Please help us, Lord Jesus!" Asa wheezed as they ran.

Both were gasping for breath when they reached the brow of the hill, but what they saw caused them to give a shout of delight. There was no forest for perhaps a quarter of a mile beyond, and down the center of the meadow was a wide, silver streak glittering in the moonlight.

William was so excited that he cried out again. "See, Whit! See!" he exclaimed. "The Lord heard us! That's a river! Now RUN!"

Using all their remaining strength, the boys charged forward, the sight of the water motivating them to keep going. They shot out of the terrible forest and across the short, dry grass, burnt brown by late summer days, running for their lives toward the flowing current. When they reached the bank, they plunged at once into its depths.

William sank with a mighty splash and went down for nearly twelve feet. Touching a hard, rocky bottom, he pushed off and shot back to the surface, spluttering and blowing water out of his mouth and nostrils. He saw Asa bobbing beside him.

SPLASH!

A heavy body struck the water nearby with a crash too great for that of a man. It was a stag that had leaped into the river for safety. He began to swim about, looking at the boys with great, pathetic eyes, as if he would ask them what he ought to do next.

Splash! Splash! Whoosh!

The water resounded like the beating of a bass drum. Three more deer, a buffalo, and lots of smaller animals sprang into the river and remained, swimming or wading.

"Here, Whit! I've found a sandbar that we can stand on," Will called to his friend when he had found a footing. At the same time he grasped Asa by the wrist and drew him to the submerged bar. They stood in the water to their necks and watched the great fire as it divided at the little prairie and swept across the dry grass towards them. At the river's edge the flames passed to left and right, consuming the trees along the bank. It was a grim sight. All the heavens seemed ablaze, and the clouds of smoke were suffocating. Even in the water, the heat was most oppressive, and at times the faces of the boys were almost scorched. They thrust their heads under the surface and kept them there as long as they could hold their breath.

"It's a good thing for us the river is here," said William. "Another half mile, and we'd have been ashes."

"God led us here, Will!" Asa responded with a grateful heart, "and we need to thank Him right now."

As Asa led them in prayer, they watched the fire with anxious eyes. It swept away from them in a great red cloud that ate all in its path.

It wasn't long at all before the blaze was on the far side of the prairie and began to grow smaller in the distance. The huge inferno remained visible a long time, dying at last in a red band under the horizon. Even then the air was filled with drifting smoke and ashes.

The boys looked back at the path over which they had come, and although the joy of escape was still upon them, it was with real grief that they gazed at the stricken forest that had been so grand and stately. It was now just a desolate and blackened ruin. Here and there charred trunks stood like chimneys of burned houses, and others lay upon the ground like fallen and smoking rafters. Scattered about were great beds of living coals where the brush had been thickest, and smoke rose in columns from the burned grass and hot earth.

"We started that fire," Asa said humbly.

"I guess we did," responded William, "but we didn't know our campfire would grow into so great a blaze."

"I just hope no people are hurt by it," Asa answered earnestly.

They swam back to the bank and walked toward the remains of the forest. But the ground was still hot to their feet, and the smoke troubled them. Near the edge of the wood, they found a deer still alive but badly burned and with a broken leg. It had tripped in its panic-stricken flight or had been hit by a falling tree. Now in shock, it barely clung to life. Will Hackett felt pity as he looked at the dying animal, but they were two hungry boys, and they must have a food supply if they were to continue to survive. He approached the suffering animal cautiously and quickly killed it with his pocket knife.

They cleaned and dressed it and found that the carcass was as much as they could carry. With great effort they lifted it over the hot ground and across another little meadow until they came to woods in a low damp area that was only partially burned. There they hung the meat on the limb of one of the standing trees, out of the reach of beasts of prey.

When the sun finally rose, the tired, hungry lads gathered still glowing coals and dry limbs and soon had a modest fire burning. Over it they cooked two very large deer steaks for their breakfast.

When their stomachs were no longer demanding attention, the two lost friends began to relax from the stress of their escape. They resolved to spend the day under the shade of the trees because, for the present, they were too exhausted to do anything other than rest. As they did so, they skinned the deer and scrapped the fleshy side, after which they draped it over the fire to both dry it and to let the smoke cure it.

When William examined the skin later that afternoon, he turned to Asa. "I don't know about you, Whit, but I've got cuts all over the bottoms of my feet from running away from that fire. I think we should use this deer skin to make foot coverings for ourselves."

"That's a great idea," the younger boy agreed. "We'll make moccasins."

"Well, probably nothing as grand as that," Will returned, "since we don't have an awl or anything to sew with. I'm thinking something more like foot bags."

"We could use our pocket knives as awls," Asa suggested.

"You're right," Will agreed, "we could, but it will still take some time to cut thread out of the skin and then cut and sew the moccasins. My poor feet can't wait that long. Let's just cut the skin into large enough patches that we can wrap our feet and tie the skin up around our ankles."

Later that afternoon, as Asa worked on his deerskin shoes, he felt a great longing for home. The fire and their narrow escape stayed on his mind. Their hardships were beginning to weigh upon him, and he longed for the comfortable little log houses and his mother's home-cooked food.

William knew what Asa was thinking. He was also remembering home, and he pitied the grief of their families and friends, who must now be mourning them as lost forever.

"Whit, I believe this is the river we hoped we'd find," William announced encouragingly, "the one that runs by Larkinboro."

"Do you really think so, Will?"

"It's got to be," the older boy replied confidently. "I never heard Jack or Dirt or any of the men speak of another large river near enough for us to have reached it since we've been wandering around, so it must be the same one. What I don't know is whether we're above Larkinboro or below it. We'll just have to guess on that point and hope for the best. We shouldn't have too much trouble making a decent raft; the fire's put a lot of trees on the ground that we can use. All we've got to do is roll some logs into the river, tie 'em together with vines, and float with the stream until we come to Larkinboro."

"But what if we never come to it?" Asa asked with concern.

"Then we'll get off the raft and travel back up river along the bank. Eventually we're sure to reach home."

The more Asa thought about William's plan to float down the river, the more excited he got.

Chapter Six

TERROR IN THE NIGHT

Will and Asa were so full of excitement about their new idea that they couldn't stop talking about it. They finally had a plan, and tomorrow for the first time since their ordeal started, they would be actually doing something to get themselves back home. They celebrated that evening with plenty of roasted deer meat and discussed the construction of their raft until the fire began to fade.

For protection that night the two boys stacked a pile of wood in a circle about their small camp. With most of the burnable debris cluttering the forest floor consumed, there seemed little chance of them causing another inferno, but just to be sure, they made their camp a safe distance away from the nearby patch of woods. When they were ready to go to sleep, they lit their circle of brush wood and, except for a small opening, surrounded themselves in a wall of flames. William felt that they needed a little extra security because most of the game had been run off by the fire, and any predators left in the area would be more likely to consider humans as a suitable alternative.

"You know, Will," said Asa sometime later as he reflected on their recent escape, "God has been very good to us. It was only by His grace that we got out of that fire alive."

William nodded his agreement with his friend's convictions.

"My point is that, if you doubted your worth to the Heavenly Father, then all that He has done for us should convince you,"

Asa continued, locking eyes with his friend. "He didn't have to do that. That fire was our own doing. He could have let us experience the full consequences of our irresponsibility, and He would have been just to do it. But out of His great love for us, He showed us mercy once again. He let us live, not just because He loves us, but because He has plans for us. He has plans for you, Will. I believe that God will use all of the horrible experiences of your past as well as the blessings He has brought into your life now to shape you into the man He has called you to be. But you've got to let Him. You must trust Him with your life."

"But how do I do that?" Will asked. "I try to escape my past, but it just won't leave."

"Do what I had to do," Asa returned. "Give those horrible memories and accusing thoughts to King Jesus. Just offer them to Him, and He'll take them and redeem them into something precious and valuable."

"That sounds way too simple," William shot back skeptically. "How do you know that Jesus even does stuff like that?"

"Because when you read the stories in the Bible, the nature of Jesus is on display. You can clearly see what He's like and what He does! He redeems things. That means He takes the messes we make and creates something useful and beautiful out of them to bring Him glory," Asa answered enthusiastically. "He did it for me. He took my fears and even made something good come out of them.

"What do you mean?"

"What I mean is that God took my fears and used them to help you."

"Well, that's true," William had to admit.

"He also did it for the Apostle Paul in the Bible," Asa continued. "You remember the Bible story. . .Paul's original name was Saul, and he hated Jesus and his followers so much that he persecuted them and even killed some of them. But Jesus had other plans for Saul, revealing Himself to him and winning his heart. That's when Saul came to be called Paul. While he wasn't proud of his ugly past, Paul willingly told others about it to show people that, if Jesus could love him and use his broken life for good, then He could love and use them as well. There was also Peter and Nicodemus and Matthew and Simon the Zealot and..."

"Okay, okay!" Will said cutting him off. "I get it. I just don't know if I've got the strength to change."

"That's the whole point, my friend," Asa said smiling, "you don't and never will. . .and neither will I. That's why we need a powerful King Who does it for us. We just need to trust that He can and that He will."

"You mean Jesus will change me?"

"Of course," Asa answered confidently. "That's what grace is!"

"I thought grace was just forgiveness," the older boy returned.

"Oh, no!" Asa countered with a smile. "Grace is much more than that! The Bible says that we are to grow in grace. You can't grow in forgiveness. You're either forgiven or you're not. Grace is God's strength in us to accomplish His will. It is also God's power in us to do what we are powerless to do ourselves."

"Don't we have to do something for His grace to work in us?" Will asked.

"You have to believe," Asa returned. "If you believe that Jesus is God's Son and that He came to earth to give His life to pay the full price for your sins, and if you are willing to make Jesus your Lord and King, then God's grace is yours, along with forgiveness, worth, heaven, the best life possible that continues forever, and everything else Christ has. It is all ours in Christ."

William was quiet for some time, thinking on all that had been said. He was very grateful for Asa, and he realized that God was using his friend to give him hope to at last find peace. Asa was right. His dream of living alone in rough country was selfish, but he couldn't escape the powerful pull that the wilderness had on him. Like Asa said, the settlers depended on those who knew the secrets of the forest. Maybe God was calling him to be a frontiersman for the benefit of others. If so, that would be a noble calling indeed.

"Whit," William said at last, "I've been thinking about all that you've said. I believe that Jesus is God's Son and that He died for me. I want to make Him my King, but I'm not sure I know how."

"Making Jesus your King simply means that you do what He says from now on and not what you want."

"Okay," the older boy said thoughtfully, "so what does He want me to do?"

"Well, I know He wants you to repent of your sins. Have you done that?"

"I think so," Will returned. "I know that I'm short-tempered and selfish, and I've asked God to forgive me of those."

"William, are you willing to forgive your birth father for all the abuse he put you and your mother through?"

"I don't know if I can do that, Asa!"

"You have to, Will. If you aren't willing to forgive others who have hurt you, then God can't forgive you. That's pretty clear in the Bible. Just think about who Jesus had to forgive. He asked God to forgive the very people standing at the foot of His cross who had put Him there."

"I don't know," the older boy returned.

"Will, think about this," Asa said, grabbing his friend's arm. "Your father did some terrible things to you, and he's now having to answer to God for them, but don't let him keep abusing you. He is not worth losing heaven for. Don't forgive him for him; he's in God's hands now. Forgive him for you. By forgiving him, you will tear his claws off you once and for all. Forgiving him brings *you* freedom! Besides, if you ask Jesus, He will give you the forgiveness for your father that you need."

"You know. . .you're right!" Will said with resolve. "That man ruined my childhood. I will not let him ruin my future.

"Oh, Father in heaven," William began a prayer, "You have done so much for me! You've given me a wonderful family who loves me, my good friend Asa who is like a brother to me, and You've given me Jesus as a wonderful, faithful King Who will lead me. I want to be right with You, Father! I don't want anything to stand between us, so I willingly forgive my father of all the evil he did to me and my mother. I put all of that in Your hands and ask You to give me freedom from it all.

"Wow!" Will said with a smile as he finished his prayer. "I feel light as a feather right now.

"So what else does the King want me to do?"

Asa was thoughtful for a moment. "I know He wants us to confess our faith in Him before others."

"I believe I've just done that."

"Oh, yeah," Asa laughed. "So you have. Well then, the only other thing that Jesus said for his followers to do is for you to be baptized. Have you ever done that?"

"No, I haven't," his friend answered. "Is getting baptized really that important?"

"It's where you get a chance to express your commitment to follow Jesus in a public way. You're putting your faith into action, so to speak. The Apostle Paul said in the book of Romans that it symbolizes our death, burial, and resurrection with Jesus.

"If he were here, we could have Mr. Spebbington baptize you in the river," Asa said his thoughts out loud.

"But he's not here," the older boy responded. "Should I wait until we get back home?"

"In the book of Acts, when the Philippian jailer believed in Jesus, he was baptized right then, and it was after midnight."

"Alright then," William said with conviction. "Let's do it now, and you can stand in for Mr. Spebbington."

Both jumped to their feet, hurried through the small gap in the fire ring, and raced down to the river. In the moonlight they waded out into the slowly moving flow, and Asa Whitlock baptized his friend into the name of the Father, the Son, and the Holy Spirit. As the two wet friends walked back to their fire, they joined all the angels in heaven who were rejoicing as a new child was born into the family of God.

"Have you eaten enough?" William asked about an hour later as the two finished their supper of roasted deer steaks.

"In honor of this celebratory occasion," Asa said pompously, "I would dearly love to imbibe in a greater preponderance of our delectable provisions, but due to my over-stuffed state of affairs, I'm afraid I can't find a place for it."

"Mr. Spebbington couldn't have said it better," William laughed.

The two sat awhile on the soft, warm earth, watching the moon creep across the night sky. William was wondering how

God could possibly love them so much when he heard a faint sighing, like someone lightly plucking the strings of a guitar, and he knew that it was the breeze wandering among the burned tree limbs. Then he heard a distant thud and knew that it was the fall of a tree, into whose trunk the flames had bit deeply. As he lay under the starry sky, his sharp ears were alert to the faintest rustle in the surrounding brush. But he had no fear because the fire they had built was like a ring of steel about them.

Asa heard few of these sounds, or if he heard them, he paid little attention to them. The wilderness was not talking to him. He was merely in the woods, and he was very glad indeed to have his strong and faithful comrade beside him.

The scorched tree trunks that curved like columns in a circle around them became misty and unreal. Despite himself, Asa Whitlock began to feel a little fear. He was a brave boy, but this was the wilderness—the wilderness in the dark—inhabited by wild animals and perhaps by wilder men, and they were lost in it. He moved a little closer to his companion. But William, into whose mind no such thoughts had come, rose presently and heaped more wood on the fire. When he finished the task, he spotted the serious look on Asa's face and decided to try to lighten his friend's mood.

"I say, Mr. Whitlock," he said in a high, lofty tone, similar to the one Asa had used earlier, "it seems to me that two worthy gentlemen like ourselves, who have had a day of hard toil, should retire for the night and seek the repose that we so deservedly have earned."

"Bless me," Asa responded with a twinkle in his eye and with the same lofty voice. "What you say is certainly true, Mr. Hackett. Correct me if I'm wrong, old fellow, but it appears that we have happened upon an inn, worthy of our great merits and high positions. This, you see, Mr. Hackett, is the Kain-tuck-ee Inn, a most spacious place, noted for its pure air and the great abundance of it. In truth, Mr. Hackett, I may assert to you that the ventilation is perfect."

"So I see, Mr. Whitlock," said William as he clasped his hands behind his back and strode pompously back and forth, viewing their surroundings. "It is indeed a noble place. We are not troubled by any boorish guests, nor are we crowded by any fellow lodgers."

"Quite true, good fellow! Quite True!" agreed Asa as he fought to suppress a laugh. "We seem to have the whole place to ourselves. And, if I may be so bold, it is a most noble apartment that we have chosen. I have seldom been in one more spacious. My eyes are good, but good as they are, I cannot see the ceiling, it is so high. I look to right and left, and the walls are so far away that they are hidden in the dark."

"Correctly spoken, Mr. Whitlock," William returned, "and our inn has more than size to speak for it. It is furnished most beautifully as well. In addition, I do not know of another that has in it so good a pantry. Its great specialty is game, both numerous and of wide variety. It has too a most wonderful and plenteous supply of pure, fresh water."

"Undeniably, Mr. Hackett! You are indubitably incontestable in your assessment."

"Do you even know what you just said?" Will giggled at his friend.

"Uh. . .I think so," Asa snickered back.

"Well then, Mr. Whitlock," William responded, once again taking up the lofty tone, "That being said, I propose that we get a drink and go to bed."

"Here, here!" agreed Asa with enthusiasm.

The two boys again slipped through their wall of flame, went to a nearby brook that ran into the river, and drank heartily. They then returned within the ring of fire and piled more wood in the opening.

Being thoroughly tired and sleepy, the friends quickly threw themselves down upon the soft, warm earth, pillowing their heads on their arms, and the great Kain-tuck-ee Inn bent over them a roof of soft summer skies.

But the wilderness never sleeps, and its inhabitants knew that two strangers were among them. Finally the last cinder left behind by the forest fire died, the earth cooled, and the forest creatures began to stir in the woodland clearings where the inferno had passed. The disaster had come and gone, and perhaps it was already out of their memories forever. Rabbits timidly sought their old nests. A wild cat climbed a tree, scarcely yet cool beneath his claws, and stared at the ring of fire that formed a circle of light in the forest and at the two unusual beings that slept within its shelter. A deer came to the brook to drink and snorted at the sight of the red gleam among the trees. When the strange odor of man came to its nostrils on the wind, it fled through the forest.

The wild cat crawled far out on the bare limb and stared, half afraid, half curious, and also angry at the intrusion. He could look over the red blaze and see the boys stretched upon the ground, their faces upturned to the sky. To human gaze they would have seemed as still as two dead, but the keen eyes of the wild cat saw their chests rising and falling with deep, regular breaths.

Time passed, and the red ring of fire about Asa and William sank. Hasty and tired, they had not collected enough wood to last out the night, and now the flames died one by one. Eventually the coals smoldered, and after a while they too began to go out. The fiery circle of protection that enclosed the two lads slowly faded away.

Light clouds came up from the west and were drawn like a veil across the sky. The night darkened, and the wild cat, keen though his eyes were, could scarcely see the two strange beings lying in the night shadows. The wild things, still full of curiosity, pressed nearer. The terrible red light that filled their souls with dread was gone. Instead of fire, there was a ring of eyes about William and Asa, but the boys remained in the bonds of glorious sleep, peaceful and happy.

Suddenly a new faraway sound echoed through the wilderness, and it made the timid creatures tremble with dread. It was faint and more like a high pitched moan brought down upon the wind, but the ring of eyes drew back into the forest. When the sound came a second time, the rabbits and deer fled, not to return. The wild cat gave a snarl, but his courage lasted only a moment before he also scampered away and did not stop until he had gone a full mile. Then he swiftly climbed the tallest tree that he could find and hid in its top.

The ring of eyes was gone, and though danger was near, William and Asa slept on. A long, distant howl came again on the wind. It was like a whine but with something uniquely ferocious in its note. Far away, a score of forms, phantom and shadowy in the gloom of night, ran quickly with low, slim bodies and outstretched nostrils that had in them the odor of prey soon to be devoured.

God had blessed Will Hackett with a physical body of great strength but also as delicate as that of a watch. Any jar to the wheels or springs was registered at once by the minute hand of his brain. He stirred in his sleep and moved one arm in a troubled way. He was not yet awake, but his mental minute hand quivered, and from the depths of his soul an alarm sounded. He stirred again and abruptly sat up, his eyes wide open, his whole frame tense, and his mind focused and alert. He saw the dead coals where the fire had been. The long, quavering, and ferocious whine came to his ears, and in an instant he understood. He sprang to his feet and, with one sweeping motion, pulled Asa to his also. "Up, Whit! Get up!" he cried. "The fire is out, and wolves are coming!"

Asa's physical senses were less sharp than his friend's, and he did not understand at first. He was dazed and confused, but William gave him no time.

"It's our lives, Asa!" he cried. "Another enemy as bad as the fire is after us!"

Not thirty feet away grew a giant beech, spreading out low and mighty limbs, and William shoved his friend up its trunk until Asa could wrap his arms around the first branch.

"Now, Whit, hang on with all of your strength while I climb up your body."

Fortunately for both of them, Asa was awake enough to understand their peril, and he gave the limb a deadly grip. William sprang up and grabbed Asa around the thighs, and with powerful arms pulled himself over Whit's form until he reached the limb. Turning around, he drew Asa up to join him.

"We may not be safe yet!" Will cried. "Up you go! Keep climbing!" Asa, though not yet thinking with a clear head, instinctively obeyed the fierce command. William scrambled after him, and as they rose higher among the limbs, the ferocious whine burst into a long, dreadful howl, and grey forms shot from the forest and hurled themselves at the beech tree. In that instant the moon slid from behind a cloud, illuminating the terrifying creatures.

William, despite all his courage, shuddered involuntarily. Clutching a limb tightly with one hand, he put the other on his comrade to see that he did not fall. He could feel Asa trembling in his grasp. The two looked down upon rage-filled eyes, cruelly sharp, white teeth, and slobbering mouths. Although the boys still panted from their climb, each breathed a silent prayer of thankfulness. They had been just in time to escape a hungry pack of wolves. The terrible animals howled horribly for a while, then sat on their haunches, staring silently up at the sweet, new food that they believed would fall at last into their mouths.

Once he got his breath back, Asa said weakly, "Will, I'm mighty glad you're a light sleeper. If it had been left to me to wake up first, I'd have found myself right in the middle of the stomach of one of those wolves."

"Well, we're here, and we're safe for the present," said William, "and I, for one, think this is a mighty fine beech tree. I'm reasonably sure that you and I will never see another one as good, friendly, or as loved as this one."

Asa laughed now with more heart. "That's exactly right!" he said. "You are a mighty good friend, Mr. Big Beech Tree, and as a mark of gratitude, I shall kiss you right in the middle of your wonderful, barky, old forehead," and he touched his lips lightly to the great trunk. The sight of Asa kissing the tree made Will laugh.

"I think it's past midnight," said the older boy as he studied the position of the stars, "In spite of our rough night, we've at least had several hours sleep. That's better than nothing."

"But they'll go away as soon as they realize they can't get us," said Asa. "Then we can climb down and build a new and bigger ring of fire about us."

Will shook his head. "They don't realize it," he replied. "It's not how they think. They expect just the opposite. They're as sure as a wolf can be that we'll be theirs before the night is over. Look at that old fellow with his forepaws on the tree! Did you ever see such confidence?"

Asa looked down fearfully, and the eyes of the biggest of the threatening creatures met his. So fascinated was he at the terrifying features of the fierce old wolf so near to them that he almost lost his balance.

"ASA!" William cried sharply and grabbed for his friend.

The younger boy jerked his eyes away as he regained his balance, shuddering from head to foot. "Sakes alive!" he gasped. "I almost joined him!"

"Yes, and you can bet he would have given you a warm welcome too," Will replied sharply. "Remember that your best friend just now is not Mr. Big Wolf, but Mr. Big Beech Tree, and it's wise to stick to your best friend."

"I'm not likely to forget it," said Asa as he grasped even more tightly to the limb of the tree.

William looked down at their besiegers, who were sitting in a solemn circle, gazing at the two lads and at the venison hanging from the limb of another tree very near. In the dusk and the shadows, they were a terrible company, gaunt, ghostly, grey, and grim.

For a long time the wolves neither moved nor uttered a sound; they merely sat on their haunches and stared upward at the living prey that they felt would surely be theirs. Time passed, dragging slowly for the boys in the tree, but the wolves, though hungry, were patient. Strong when they were in a pack, they were lords of the forest and felt no fear. A large black bear, lumbering through the woods nearby, suddenly threw up his nose in the wind, caught the strong, pungent odor of the wolves, and wheeled abruptly, trotting off on another course.

It was a new kind of prey that the wolves had scented and driven to the limbs, but the odor was very sweet and pleasant in their nostrils. It was a tidbit they must have, and they stared at the two strange, tender-looking creatures who stirred now and then in the tree, making odd sounds to each other. When they heard these occasional noises, the wolves would reply with a long, ferocious whine that gave back echoes from every point of the compass. Then the leader, the largest and most terrible of the pack, would stretch himself upon the tree trunk and claw at the scorched bark, but the food he craved was still out of reach.

The savage pack of hunters noticed that the strange creatures above them began to move more often and to draw their limbs up as if they were growing stiff. Then the wolves' howls grew longer and more ferocious than ever. As the night continued to advance, the moon dropped below the horizon, and the dark hours that came before dawn were at hand. The forest became black and misty like a haunted wood, and the dim forms of the wolves were the ghosts that lived in it.

When the darkness was thickest, the wolves grew hot with impatience. Already they smelled the dawn, and their hunger begged to be satisfied. Could it be that the food they coveted would not fall into their mouths? The old leader vented his frustration with a long, terrible howl. The pack took up the note, and the lonely forest became alive with its echoes. But the two creatures in the tree stirred only a little and made very few sounds. They seemed to be safe and content, and the wolves raged back and forth, leaping and howling.

The old leader was not only frustrated but angry. They had spent the entire night waiting for these victims without success, and his hunger wore out his patience. Finally to the relief of Will and Asa, the sun broke the horizon, and the world was bathed in a luminous, golden glow. The alpha wolf cast one last, longing look at the inaccessible food in the tree, then uttering an angry howl fled headlong through the forest with the rest of the pack close behind. Their gaunt bodies were gone in a moment, like ghosts that vanish at the coming of the day.

"They're gone, Whit!" cried William. "They all ran off! It's finally safe for us to climb down."

"Are you sure? Where'd they go?"

"They went looking for easier prey," Will answered. "Did you see how thin they were? They haven't had a good meal in a day or two. It took most of the night, but they finally got tired of waiting on us. Listen, you can hear their howls are getting farther away."

"That's mighty good news to me!" said Asa with relief. "The great Inn of Kaintuckee was not so hospitable after all, or at least some of our fellow guests were too hungry."

"It's because we were careless and let our fire die out," explained Will. "We'll have to do better next time. Jump down, Whit! I need out of this tree!"

When they were both safely on the ground once again, the two stiff and sore lads began to bend, stretch, and rub their legs and arms vigorously to get the blood flow to return to their limbs.

"Now for breakfast," Will announced after they had gotten the feeling back in their limbs. "It will be easy, as Mr. Landlord has kept the venison hanging in the tree for us, out of reach from our hungry fellow guests."

As he stood beside the tree, holding the venison and preparing to untie the rope, William stopped to enjoy the morning. He stretched once more, taking in a chest full of the sweet morning air. He was back in his element. Now that the terror of the night had passed, he easily cast aside all thought of fear.

Asa, on the other hand, was still troubled. "Will," he said, "I really don't want to stay here any longer. The danger of almost being eaten while we slept, barely making it up the tree before those horrible creatures arrived to kill us, and me almost falling into that big wolf's mouth. . .I've had it with this place! Let's get away from here as soon as we can!"

"Sure, Whit," William responded encouragingly, "whatever you want. There are many rooms in the Kaintuckee Inn, and if the one we have doesn't suit us, we'll just find another. Wait till I get our venison down, and we'll move without paying our bill."

"We almost paid that to the wolves," said Asa, smiling a little.

William lowered the venison and divided it to make it easier to carry. Then each took his share, and they moved swiftly away among the trees, still following the flow of the river. Eventually they came to a large area of unburned forest, thick with leaves and undergrowth, and without hesitation they plunged into it. As Will led the way, suddenly a sound came to his keen ears that he knew was not one of the natural noises of the forest. He stopped and listened intently. It was a beat—faint, but regular and steady. He knew that it was made by footfalls, and he knew too, that in the wilderness, everyone was an enemy until proven to be a friend.

"Down, Whit! Sink down!" he hissed urgently, and grasping his companion by the shoulder, Will pulled him low among the thick bushes, dropping with him. "Don't move for your life!" he whispered. "Someone's coming, and they may not be friends!"

Asa at once became as still as death. The two boys crouched close together, their heads below the tops of the brush, although they could see between the leaves and twigs. Neither moved a hair.

Suddenly, out of the foliage in front of them and to their right, came a line of Indian warriors. In single file and at a long-distance trot, the grim-faced braves passed the two hiding youths.

The sudden appearance of so many braves so close caused Asa to gasp, but William quickly clamped a hand over his mouth. Fortunately the members of the hunting party seemed not to notice as they hurried on through the woods.

The boys stared through the leaves and twigs, afraid but fascinated. There were fourteen Indians in all—William counted them—but not one of the warriors spoke a word. They were there for only a moment; then they were gone, though their dark, painted faces long remained engraved like portraits on the minds of both lads. The leaves of the bushes rustled a little when they passed, then stilled.

After the Indians disappeared from view, Will leaned close to Asa and whispered, "It's a good thing you wanted to leave our last camp site. Those fellas are headed straight for it."

"I knew nothing good would come of us staying there any longer," the wide-eyed Asa whispered in response.

"You were right," Will quietly agreed. "They are most likely from the southern tribes of Cherokee who come up here now and then to hunt. But they seldom stay long for fear of the more warlike and powerful northern Indians who come down to Kentucky for the same purpose. At least that's what I heard Jack and Dirt say."

"Well, they did seem to be traveling fast," breathed Asa, "and I'm mighty glad of it. Do you think they could have done any harm at Larkinboro?"

Will shook his head. "I doubt it," he said. "Jack has always said that little danger was to be dreaded from the south. Besides, I didn't see those warriors carrying any plunder."

"I guess you're right," said Asa with deep relief, "but I think that you and I ought to go down to the river's bank and build that raft as soon as we can."

"All right," said Will calmly, "but let's put some more distance between us and that hunting party."

After walking through the woods for another half hour, William stopped and suggested that they eat something. The lads both set to work gathering the driest wood they could find. Once lit, it made a small fire that produced almost no smoke. After cooking venison for their breakfast, they took the time to roast several more large pieces of meat to eat as they worked. With their stomachs full of deer steaks, life looked much better.

Chapter Seven

THE QUEEN A' SHEBER'S BARGE

Strengthened by a good meal, the two friends lost no time in beginning construction on their raft. They carefully retraced their steps till they reached the edge of the burned area where they found plenty of fallen timber from the fire. The problem was finding the right-sized logs. They had to be big enough to use for their raft but small enough for the two of them to carry or roll to the river bank. Not bothering to search for food, they simply ate what they had already cooked and kept working. They used vines, of which there were plenty, to lash the tree trunks together. It was clear as they assembled the raft that it wasn't going to look like much, especially with branches sticking out of some of the logs. But as long as they made it large enough to hold them and their supply of food, it would be good enough to suit their needs.

They finished at the end of the second day and spent the evening cooking more deer meat to take with them. After handling so much burned wood, the two friends were nearly black from the soot. As one of them watched the steaks being cooked, the other would jump in the river and scrub himself with sand to get as much of the soot off as possible.

Early the next morning, the two navigators launched the clumsy craft into the muddy brown river and began drifting toward the unknown. Each of the boys carried a slender hickory pole for steering. They securely fastened the cooked meat on the raft, wrapped in one of their shirts, as well as the remainder of the deer, their most precious possession.

It was a fine little river, running in a deep channel, and William felt more confident than ever that it was the one that flowed by Larkinboro. They drifted on for hours, rarely using their poles, and eventually they entered a gorge between cliffs of considerable height. The forest was very dense. Mighty oaks and hickories grew right to the water's edge, throwing out their limbs so far that often the whole stream was in the shade. Will enjoyed it. This was one of the things that he had always longed to do. He was now floating down an unknown river through unknown lands, and it was possible that his and Asa's might be the first settlers' eyes that had ever looked upon these hills and splendid forests. Resting now after hard work and danger, he breathed again the scent of the wilderness. He loved it—the silence, the magnificent spaces, and the majesty—and was glad that he had come to Kentucky where life was so much grander than it was back in the old Eastern regions. Life was an adventure in the wilderness.

They ate their dinner on the raft, still floating peacefully, and tried to guess how far they had come, but neither was able to judge the speed of the slow current. Asa fitted himself into a snug place on their odd craft and drifted off to sleep. William, while also keeping an eye out for other things, watched him lest he roll over and fall into the water.

The young explorer was still watching when, in about the middle of the afternoon, he saw a thin, dark line lying like a thread against the blue skies. He studied it long and came to a conclusion. *Smoke!* he said to himself. *That could mean Larkinboro. . .or Indians.*

They drifted on, and the spire of smoke broadened and grew. The look of the river became more and more familiar. Asa still slept, and William would not awaken him. He looked at the face of his comrade as he slumbered and noticed for the first time that he was thin and pale. Life in the woods had been hard upon Asa. The older boy did not realize until this moment how very hard it had been for him.

Just then there was a shout from the bank, followed by the crash of bodies among the undergrowth. "MY NEKED HEAD!"

exclaimed a nasally voice from the left bank. "Thar they be, a-floatin' down the river on their own barge, as comfy as the Queen a' Sheber!" It was the voice of Dirt Gurley, and his face, side by side with that of Jack Cobb, appeared among the trees at the river's edge.

William felt a great flush of joy when he saw them and waved his hands. Asa, awakened by the shouts, looked up groggily, but when he beheld old friends again, joy burst from his heart as well. William thrust a pole against the bottom and shoved the raft to the bank. Then he and Asa sprang ashore and shook hands again and again with their two friends. Jack told of the long search for the two boys. He, Mr. Hackett, Dirt Gurley, and a half dozen others had never ceased to seek them. They feared at one time that they had been carried off by savages, but nowhere could they find signs of Indians. Then their dread was of starvation or death by wild animals, and they had begun to lose hope.

Both boys were deeply moved by the story of the grief at Larkinboro. While William actually enjoyed their adventure, it broke his heart to hear of the sorrow they had caused. Guided by Jack and Dirt, they proceeded to the palisade, which was indeed at the bottom of the smoky spire. As they approached the gates side-by-side with the two scouts, shouts were heard from the tops of the blockhouses. At first a few, then quickly a cheering crowd, hurried from the fort to greet the lost lads. The Hacketts and the Whitlocks pushed their way through the excited throng to be the first to hug their missing children. The heifer, the original cause of the trouble, had wandered back home long ago.

"How did you survive alone in the forest?" Mr. Hackett asked William, after the celebration began to settle down.

"It was hard at first, but we were beginning to learn," replied the lad. "If we'd only had our rifles, it would have been a lot easier. Father, the wilderness is wonderful!"

Mr. Hackett noticed the expression on his son's face and thought to himself, *I must not let the yoke of the farm bear too heavy upon the boy. He's going to need to regularly spend time in the woods.*

But Asa's joy was complete. He was home and very glad to be there, preferring to live in Larkinboro, where survival was hard enough. In his mind, wilderness existence was one of continuous hardships.

Later, when William's family hosted a great dinner to celebrate the return of the wanderers, Asa felt at that moment that life could get no better. All of the residents of Larkinboro brought food that was spread out on make-shift tables in the open area near the gate. Jack Cobb and Dirt Gurley were present, and with them too was Charles Wingfield Spebbington.

On that occasion, theirs was in truth a table fit for a king. In fact, few kings could duplicate it without sending to the uttermost parts of the earth. Meat was the main dish. They had wild duck, wild goose, wild turkey, deer, elk, beaver tail, and a half dozen kinds of fish. But the great delicacy was buffalo hump cooked in a special way—rubbed with salt, stuffed with wild ginger leaves, and baked in an earthen oven. It was served in the hide of a buffalo from which the hair had been singed off. Cobb, who had learned the recipe from the Indians, showed them how to do it, and they all agreed that it was indeed quite tasty. When dinner was over, William and Asa had to answer many questions about their wanderings, and they were quite willing to do so.

A look of concern showed on the faces of some of the men at the mention of the Indians whom the boys had seen, but Jack agreed with Will that they were surely from the south, coming to hunt, and so their presence in the forest was soon dismissed.

After a couple of days rest and lots of good food, both boys found themselves back in their normal daily routines. William's work included helping to dig out stumps from felled trees to provide more land to farm, but his labor was not always hard. On several occasions he was asked by Jack and Dirt to accompany them on hunting expeditions, as game was always needed. William's love of the wilderness did nothing but increase when he ranged through it with the scouts. The young frontiersman took every opportunity to observe and understand its ways. The times he spent alone in the woods also helped him put the accusing voices in their proper place. When he had chosen to walk with King Jesus, William had hoped that the mental attacks would go away, but they were still there, just waiting for an opportunity to leap on him again. Even so, he felt much more at peace because he had the Lord to fight for him now.

One morning when William went out to dig more stumps, he noticed that the air was much cooler. That evening the temperature dropped even more. Frost covered the ground the following morning, and the settlers knew that autumn was near. The air grew crisp and cool, and the foliage of the forest turned to wonderful reds, yellows, and browns. From the summit of the blockhouse tower, William saw a great blaze of varied color, and he decided that he liked this part of the year best.

The autumn and its beauty deepened. The colors of the foliage grew more intense and burned in the distance like flame. Mr. Hackett and a few others, anxious to test the qualities of the soil, plowed up newly cleared land to be sown in wheat, but William was compelled to devote only a portion of his time to that work. In the remaining hours, when not sleeping, he was usually seeking game in the forest.

Once the fields were finally prepared for next spring's planting, all of Larkinboro's inhabitants turned their attention to hunting. With winter coming, the settlers began to accumulate a great supply of game. Elk, deer, bear, buffalo, as well as smaller animals, were jerked and smoked at every house. Each pantry was filled to the brim. The settlers agreed that there must be no lack of food for the coming winter.

On one fine fall day, William and Asa took to the forest with Dirt Gurley to hunt for deer. As soon as they entered the woods surrounding the village, Dirt turned to face the boys. "Now look-a-here, fellers," the scout said, addressing the two youths. "It ain't no use us nosin' around these woods close to the fort. With ever'body an' his sister Ruth out lookin' fer game, we've got about as much chance of findin' a beached whale as a deer. So if'n we're gonna bring meat home with us, we're gonna have to travel a ways to find it, savvy?"

Both boys nodded their understanding.

"Alrightee then," Dirt began again, "hitch up yer breeches, an' let's make tracks."

The scout led them on a long distance run through the forest. The frontiersman set a pace that was between a sprint and a trot. It was an easy, loping stride that all Indians and most woodsmen could keep up for hours. Dirt led them northwest of the settlement, a fact that both boys made sure to note since they didn't want to lose themselves in the wilderness again.

Over an hour later Dirt held up his hand, stopping his small procession. Calling the boys close, he spoke to them in a whisper. "Okay fellers, here's the plan: Less than a quarter of a mile directly in front of where we are right now is a small, grassy meadow. That's where I figure there might be a deer or two grazin'. Asa, I'm sending you a hundred paces through the woods to the right. I'll do the same to the left. Will, you stay here an' count to a hundred. That should give us time to get in position. Then we'll all start walking toward the meadow. If you see a deer, take good aim and drop 'em. But listen here, you two—only shoot deer that are out in front of you! No shootin' sideways toward any of the rest of us. You got me? I mean it now! I ain't taken either of you two home with a bullet hole in yer carcass! Why, yer mothers would skin me fer sure! An' don't ferget, them critters can smell ya from a long ways off. . .so keep quiet. Alright then, let's go."

After exchanging a confused look with William, Asa began moving through the thick woods to his right, counting his steps as he went. He took his time in order to make as little noise as possible. He was only on step eighty-two when he heard a noise in front of him and to his right. The young hunter froze. He couldn't tell what it was, but it was big and moving straight towards him. Quietly Asa cocked his rifle and prepared to take aim.

Suddenly the thick brush just five paces in front of him was crushed down as a massive, wooly head pushed through. The buffalo bull spotted Asa at the same moment and let out a bellowing roar. The boy jumped, and his rifle went off. The upper half of the buffalo's left horn suddenly splintered where Asa's rifle ball had struck it.

Furious and now hurting, the angry bull shook its bleeding head and charged at the young hunter. Asa gave a yell, dropped his useless rifle, and turned to escape. To keep the bull from trampling him, he began weaving around trees as he ran. The crazed beast was determined to kill the boy, but his size and long body made it harder for him to maneuver around the trunks, and Asa managed to stay ahead of him.

Panic stricken, the sprinting boy knew he couldn't keep away from the bull forever. Looking ahead, he spotted a tree small enough to climb. After rounding another trunk, he dashed to his potential refuge and sprang up, wrapping his arms and his legs around it. Asa snaked his way up as fast as he could. The buffalo saw what he was doing and charged. Just as the boy managed to pull himself up about ten feet, the attacking bull rammed into the tree trunk. The violent blow knocked Asa loose from his grasp, and he fell, landing on the back of the enraged buffalo. As soon as the boy hit the broad back of the great beast, the bison roared and began kicking and bucking. Asa didn't have the presence of mind to hang on, and he was thrown several feet into the air and into another tree nearby. As soon as his body slammed against it, pain shot through his side as three of his ribs snapped.

Knowing that the furious beast would soon stomp him, the injured boy painfully pulled himself to his feet and tried to stagger away. He heard the bull roar again and took a quick look behind him. The raging buffalo spotted him once more and charged. There was a limb just above Asa's head, and he instinctively reached for it, but as he did so, paralyzing pain shot through his injured side. Turning to face the charging beast, he realized there was no escape.

"Lord Jesus, help me!" he breathed as he looked certain death in the face. Just then two rifle shots sounded. The charging bull seemed unaffected for two more strides, then suddenly collapsed. The force of his charge caused his body to slide into Asa, knocking him over.

"Whit! Whit!" William cried as he ran to his prostrate friend. "Are you hurt?"

Asa groaned as his head and shoulders were lifted. "I think my ribs are broken," he answered through clenched teeth.

William and Dirt, after hearing Asa's gun go off, had rushed forward and arrived just in time to save his life. They gently lifted the boy and carried him to a bed of soft leaves a short distance away from the dead buffalo. William took off his coat, rolled it up, and placed it under his injured companion's head. Then he gave Asa a drink from the wooden canteen Dirt handed him.

The scout leaned down and listened to Asa's chest. Finally he sat up with a smile on his scraggly face. "Well, young one," he began, "it appears to me the Almighty was lookin' out fer ya today. Not only did Will an' myself show up right smack in the Nicholas of time to snatch you from the horns of dee-struction, so to speak, but also the Good Lord has done kept ya from puncturin' yer lungs when ya broke yer ribs. You'll hurt fer a spell, an' it ain't gonna be no pleasant journey back to the fort fer ya neither, but you'll heal up good as new in a few weeks. And just look at all this fine meat you done scared up fer us! Ya know, it was right nice of ya to sacrifice yerse'f so's Will and I could have such a handy target."

"Don't mention it," Asa groaned.

"So what do we do now, Dirt?" William asked, looking at the dead bull and back at his injured friend.

"Well, the way I sees it, we'll let this big buff lay right here for the time bein' whilest you an' yours truly get ol' Asa back to the fort where he can get hisself took care of. After that we'll bring several of the men back with us to skin and cut up this monster."

"Will," Asa groaned painfully, "when I had to run from that bull, I dropped my rifle over there to the right where all that brush is crushed. Can you go find it for me?"

"I'm sorry, Whit," William said a few minutes later as he returned with the rifle, "but it looks like the buffalo stepped on it as he charged you and broke the stock." He held the barrel and lock of the rifle in one hand and part of the broken stock in the other.

"Well," Asa said sadly and with a little sarcasm, "at least I won't be bored while I'm waiting for my ribs to heal; I'll be carving a new gun stock. Whoopee."

The days grew shorter as the autumn waned. Every morning the wilderness gleamed and sparkled beneath a beautiful covering of white frost. In a few days autumn came to an abrupt end with a cold rain that soon turned to snow.

Winter, which was very early that year, came roaring down on the settlement. Wind swept out of the northwest, bitter and chilly, and the desolate forest, with every limb stripped of its leaves, moaned before the blast. But it was cheerful in the settlers' warm log homes. When the sleet and icy rain beat upon the roof and the cold wind rattled the rude shutters, the families sat before their big fires and praised God that they were snug and safe.

There was one aspect of the coming winter that William Hackett was not looking forward to. It was during the winter that the teacher, Charles Spebbington, opened his school, and it was necessary for William to attend. Many of the pioneers who crossed the mountains from the eastern states and founded the great western outpost of the nation in Kentucky were men of education and cultivation with a knowledge of books and the world. They did not intend that their children grow up ignorant. They wished their daughters to have wisdom, grace, and manners and their sons to become men of courage, knowledge, and character. So one of their first duties in the wilderness was to found schools, and this they did.

Master Charles Wingfield Spebbington was a man of fine girth and stature, with a red face as round as the full moon, a quick laugh, and the mellowest voice in the colony. He was by reputation a man of learning who could at once give the chapter and text of any verse in the Bible and had twice read through the ponderous history of the French gentleman, M. Charles du Fresne. The teacher was a favorite in the settlement with both men and women. The sight of his cheerful face seemed to bless all who met him. He was also an expert hand with both ax and rifle, and his services in Larkinboro were not merely mental and spiritual. He was at all times able and willing to earn his bread with his own strong hands, though the others seldom permitted him to do so.

William entered school with some reluctance. Being sixteen and with an unusually powerful frame developed by a frontier life, he was as large as an ordinary man and quite as strong or stronger. He preferred that his schooling be over and that he be considered one of the men of the settlement, but his adopted

79

father insisted upon another winter under Mr. Spebbington's care, and William yielded.

Thirty boys and girls sat on rough wooden benches and received instruction. Mr. Spebbington did not undertake to guide them through all branches of learning, but what he taught, he taught well. He too had the feeling that these boys and girls were to be the men and women who would hold the future of the West in their hands, and he intended that they should be fit. Among the red-faced boys and girls who sat on the benches were young people of promise who could change the course of a country, and he tried to teach them their duty as the heirs of a wilderness, soon to be the home of a great nation.

One of his favorite pupils was Asa, who did not have William's skill in the forest, but who loved books and the knowledge of men. He could follow the difficult lines of history when William would much rather have been following the difficult trail of a deer. Nevertheless, Will persisted in his studies, encouraged by Asa, as well as the knowledge that this was his last winter in school.

Chapter Eight

THE CALL OF THE FOREST

Studying books had always been difficult for William, not because he wasn't intelligent, but because the learning he got from books didn't excite him like the learning he got from being in the forest. Now that his father had agreed to let this be his last year in classes, it was all William could do to stay focused on his studies. It had been easier for him to find food when he and Asa were lost in the wilderness than it was for him to labor at his daily lessons. The walls of the little log building in which he sat enclosed him like a prison cell, the air was heavy, and the space seemed to grow narrower and narrower. The young frontiersman was sick of solving mathematical problems, studying the world's geography, and memorizing the history of England. Just when he felt like he couldn't do it anymore, he would look across the room and see the studious face of Asa bent over the big text of ancient history. Watching his friend's diligence shamed William and gave him the motivation and encouragement he needed to continue his work.

Mr. Spebbington would neither praise nor blame, but often when the boy did not notice, the teacher looked thoughtfully at William. "I mean no disrespect to you or to William, but I believe it is fair to say that your son will not be a great scholar," he said once to Mr. Hackett. "Oh, the lad's intelligent enough, to be sure, but it's just not in him to devote himself to books. It is clear to me that the Almighty has formed this boy for different work.

81

He will be like Nimrod in the book of Genesis, a mighty hunter before the Lord, a man of action, and a leader of men. And that's a good thing, John, for out here in the wilderness, his is the kind that we will need the most, I dare say."

"I can see the truth in what you say," replied Mr. Hackett with a nod of understanding. "With all of the trouble they're having back in the colonies, we'll be getting no help from that direction for some time. We will need to fend for ourselves."

Involuntarily he looked toward the east, and Mr. Spebbington's eyes followed his. Both remained silent upon that portion of their thoughts.

"Another fine trait that the boy possesses is his sense of duty," added the teacher. "In spite of the difficulties of his early life, you can count on that young man to be loyal and true."

A few days later William shot a magnificent stag with great antlers that he mounted and presented to Mr. Spebbington, who was thrilled at the trophy.

The next morning was a quite a long one for William. He had before him a map of the Empire of Muscovy, but he saw little there. Instead he let his mind wander to the beaver dam he had seen the day before and the pool above it where the stag he had shot had come to drink.

The master looked very grave that day, and he seemed to have his mind on other things as well. William and Asa tried to guess the cause. Will heard that Jack Cobb had arrived the night before from the nearest settlement, which was a hundred miles away, but had left again, going to their second nearest neighbor one hundred and fifty miles south of them. Cobb brought news of some kind which only Mr. Hackett, Mr. Middlebrook, the teacher, and three or four others knew. So far these men had chosen to keep the information to themselves.

Without warning the school master turned to face the class and suddenly brought the long measuring stick he held down upon his desk with a loud crack, getting everyone's immediate attention. The teacher's face grew graver than ever as he spoke. He told them that when they left the East, there had been great trouble brewing between the colonies and the mother country.

They had hoped that it would pass, but now for the first time in many months, news had come across the mountains from their old home. The troubles were not gone. On the contrary, they had become worse. There had been fighting, a battle in which a number had been killed, and a great war was begun. The colonies had decided that they would all stand together to fight for their independence, and no man could tell what the times would bring forth.

Everyone was stunned by this heavy news. Though divided from their countrymen by hundreds of miles of mountain and forest, the patriotism of the settlers in the wilderness burned strongly. More than one young heart in that log room longed to be beside their fellow brethren in the far-off east, rifle in hand.

But Mr. Spebbington spoke again. He said that there was now a greater duty upon them to hold the west for the union of the colonies. There were rumors that the British would use the savages against them. If the Indians from the North came down in force against them, it would take all of them to defend their little village. He said no more but adjourned school for the rest of the day.

Rather than walk to their homes, the boys stood together and discussed the life-changing news. "Will! Asa!" a voice called from a short distance away. Looking up, they saw Katherine Middlebrook and her friend, Gardenia Leavenworth, approaching. "What do you think all this means for us?" Katherine questioned.

"Yes!" Gardenia added. "Are the Redcoats coming to kill us?"

"Don't be so dramatic, Gardenia," her friend returned.

"Kate, I asked you to call me Louise," Gardenia whined.

"But your name is Gardenia," Asa returned with a confused look.

"I know," the girl responded, "but I don't like Gardenia. Ever since I read in my European history book about this princess named Louise, I fell in love with that name. So I've decided that I want to be Louise now."

"Gardenia," Kate snapped, "we have more important things to talk about than what you want to be called!" Katherine turned and looked expectantly at the two boys.

"Well, as far as being attacked by the British," Asa began. "I don't figure they'd march an army way out here just to attack our little fort, but I'm sure that they don't want us controlling the wilderness."

"If they do anything," William added, "they'll most likely send agents to stir up the northern Indian tribes against us. At least that's what the schoolmaster said."

"I think I would rather us be fighting the British than the Indians," Kate returned.

"Eventually we will most likely have to fight the Indians whether the British stir them up against us or not," the older boy answered. "What I want to do is to head back East and help with the real fighting that's going on now."

"No, Will!" Asa shot back. "If the British use the Indians to attack our settlements like Mr. Spebbington said, it'll take all of us to protect Larkinboro. We will need you here."

"If you go back East, William, would you take me with you?" Gardenia asked. "It would be so much easier to be a princess back there than out here in the wilderness."

"I'm not going back East, Gardenia," Will answered. "I just said that I wanted to go."

"Louise! Call me Louise!"

After the message from Jack Cobb, no more news came to the little settlement about the war, nor was it likely to for some time. They might be fighting great battles back on the Atlantic coast, but no word came through the wall of woods. With the cold winter and deep snows, they were not likely to hear anything more until spring.

Although the settlers at Larkinboro were but a small outpost of civilization hemmed in by the vast and frozen wilderness, theirs was not an unhappy life by any means. The men and boys, trying to save their powder and ball, still set traps for small game and were not without reward. Often they found elk and deer and, once or twice, a buffalo floundering in the deep snowdrifts. These they added to the winter store. Breaking holes in the ice on the river, they caught fish in abundance, as much for the enjoyment of doing so as for the food. They also worked about the houses, making more tables, benches, chairs, and shelves to add to the comforts of their homes.

The excessive snow lasted about a month, then a change in the weather brought a heavy rain that melted all the snow but not much of the ice. Although the river rose rapidly and overflowed its banks, the flood waters did not reach Larkinboro. Warm winds followed the rain, and the melting snow turned great portions of the forest into lakes. The trees stood in water a yard deep, and the appearance of the wilderness was gloomy and desolate. During these times hunting and trapping came to a stop.

Eventually the winds from the south grew warmer and warmer, all the snow and ice had melted long ago, faint touches of green and pink appeared on grass and foliage, and the young buds began to swell. Will heard the whisper of the winds, and every one of them seemed to call to him. They were not like the voice of his abusive father, which still occasionally tormented him. These were restoring voices of peace and quietness. He longed to go alone into the wilderness, to see the deer steal among the trees, and to hear the beaver dive into the deep waters.

The boy grew slow in his tasks; he dragged his feet, and there were even times when he was not hungry. When his mother noticed his behavior, she became concerned and said something to her husband. She was afraid that William was getting sick.

After hearing his wife's concerns, John Hackett began to observe his son more carefully. Finally, with a smile of understanding as well as remembering his son's deep attachment to the woods, he called William to him. "Son, spring has come. Take your rifle and bring us some fresh venison."

A smile quickly spread across William's face, and without a moment's hesitation, he snatched up his rifle, powder horn, and ammunition pouch and hurried into the forest. He didn't even bother to take Asa with him. It was not human companionship that he needed that day, so he did not stop until he was deep in the wilderness. Looking around at the majesty of the woods, he filled his lungs with fresh air and felt the glory of living! Blood was flushing through his veins just as sap was rising in the trees around him. He saw all about him signs of new life: tender young grass in shades of delicate green, opening buds on the branches, and a subtle perfume that came on the edge of the southern wind. Beyond him the wild turkeys on the hill called to each other. William, excited to be back in the forest again, ran up the slope and watched as the large birds took flight through the trees, their brilliant plumage gleaming in the sunshine.

As he walked on, rabbits sprang out of the grass and raced away into the thickets. Birds in plumage of scarlet and blue and gold shot like a flame from tree to tree. The forest was filled with the melody of their voices, and William took it all in.

He paused a while at the edge of a brook to watch the sunfish play in the shallows until he noticed something different. He could hear birds in the distance to his right, but there were no woods' sounds to his left. The young frontiersman had listened so intently to the voice of the forest, as he called it, that not hearing those familiar sounds distracted him.

His curiosity peeked, William moved cautiously in the direction of the silence. He was completely focused. Practicing the lessons Jack Cobb had taught him, the youth crept stealthily through the woods, placing his feet in the spots that would make the least amount of sound. Cobb and Dirt had been amazed at how quickly Will had picked up the art of moving silently through the forest. Not only was William good at it, but his eye was so sharp in selecting just the right places to step that he could do it at a pace faster than a person would walk.

The lad glided along like a ghost, following the unnatural quiet. A slight noise not far away alerted him, and he froze. He waited in complete stillness for several minutes, hearing nothing more, but the light breeze brought to his nostrils a very faint hint of man-smell.

Checking the direction of the wind, the boy once again moved silently forward but with much more caution. He halted again when he spotted a movement just ahead. Through the small stems and leaves, he clearly saw seven Indian warriors crouched low in the brush, looking away from him. They were interested in something beyond them, but Will didn't dare move to see what it was. He studied their clothing and weapons. Most were bare-chested with leather leggings and leather moccasins. One wore a buckskin hunting shirt, and the one who seemed in charge had on a faded, French military jacket. He carefully studied the bead patterns on their belts when he could see them. The inexperienced young hunter thought they were Shawnee warriors, but Cobb would know when he described them to him. William realized that, if they indeed were Shawnee, they would scalp him in a heartbeat, so he remained motionless.

Soon another warrior joined them and began making signs to the others. It wasn't long before the leader in the French coat motioned toward the west, and they immediately grabbed their weapons and crept away.

When they were gone, Will straightened and caught a glimpse of the last of the warriors as they disappeared into the brush and grass. Looking to the west, the young hunter spotted a large herd of deer grazing in the distance.

Grateful that he had not been noticed, William carefully retraced his steps to Larkinboro. He had traveled a quarter of a mile when suddenly a great stag sprang up and stood for a few moments, gazing at him with expanding and startled eyes. William, standing quite still, returned the look, seeking to read the expression in the eyes of the deer. They confronted each other a half minute, then the stag turned and fled through the woods. Because there was no undergrowth, for a long time William watched the deer fleeing through the trees as it became smaller and smaller until it disappeared.

All the forest was glowing red in the setting sun when he returned home. There was no little excitement among the men when Will told them what he saw. Once he described them, Jack Cobb confirmed that the Indians were Shawnee. Will eased their concerns somewhat when he assured them that the warriors never saw him. Even so, the guards were doubled in the blockhouses for the next week.

"By the way, Son," John Hackett asked when they got back to their house, "where's the deer I sent you to get?"

"Why. . .I forgot to shoot one!" William responded with a look of confusion.

"With the Indians nearby, that was a good thing," Mr. Hackett returned.

"Yes, Sir," Will answered with a sheepish grin, "it was."

Chapter Nine

BIG BONE LICK

W hen the warmth of spring had arrived in earnest, many of the people in Larkinboro began to complain of weariness and lack of appetite. A number of the children and a few of the women began to experience painful muscle cramps. Jack Cobb identified the problem almost immediately: it was the lack of salt. They had run out of this precious mineral early in the winter and were now experiencing the effects of their bodies' great need for it.

To the settlers of Kentucky, salt was as precious as gold. There were only two ways to obtain it on the frontier: either by bringing it hundreds of miles over the mountains from Virginia in wagons or on pack horses, or by boiling it out at the salt springs in the Indian-haunted woods.

They had neither the time nor the men for the long journey to Virginia and so prepared at once for obtaining it from one of the salt springs that Jack and Dirt knew about. A small amount had been gathered from a salt spring close by, but the supply was not nearly enough for all the village. It was decided to go a considerable distance northward to the famous Big Bone Lick. Nothing had been heard of Indian war parties in the area since William spotted the Shawnee hunters weeks before, and Jack and Dirt believed that this would be the best time to attempt such an expedition. Besides, with the amount of salt present at Big Bone

Lick, they could bring back enough of the needed mineral to last more than a year.

When they first heard of the proposed journey, Asa Whitlock pulled William to one side. The two boys were just outside the palisade, and it was a beautiful spring day. "Do you know what the Big Bone Lick is, Will?" asked Asa eagerly.

"I know there's supposed to be a lot of salt there," replied William, a little confused at his friend's excitement.

"Oh, it's so much more than that! Why, it's the most wonderful place in all the world!" said Asa excitedly, his blond bird's nest of curly hair bouncing with his movements. "When that hunter came through Larkinboro this past winter, Mr. Duncan, he spoke to me about it. I didn't believe him then, it sounded so amazing, but Mr. Spebbington thinks it's all true. There's a great salt spring boiling out of the ground in the middle of a kind of marsh, and all around it for a long distance are piled hundreds of large bones, the bones of gigantic animals, bigger than any that walk the earth today."

"See here, Whit," said William scornfully, "you can't stuff my ears with mush like that!"

"It's true, every word of it!"

"Then if there were such big animals, why don't we see 'em running through the forest?"

"Because they've all been dead thousands of years. But somehow their bones have been preserved there in the marsh. According to the teacher, they lived in a time when animals as tall as trees strolled up and down over the land and were the lords of creation."

William puckered his lips and snorted. "I still think you're trying to hoo-doo me."

But Asa was not offended at his friend's disbelief. "Mr. Spebbington believes it to be true," Will's younger friend argued, "and I trust him. Just think about it. . .all of those ancient bones of such amazing creatures. Very few people get to see wonders like that. I want to go so badly that I can't stand it! Why don't we both ask to go with the saltmakers? Then you can see for yourself."

Big Bone Lick

William thought on this for a moment. "It does sound like an interesting adventure, and even if it's not, it's still a great excuse to be out in the forest. Alright, I'll see if I can get permission."

That night in both the Hackett and Whitlock homes, excited sons made their most persuasive arguments as to why they should go with the band.

"Father," said William, "I know it's planting season, but we've already gotten a good start on that. You and the other men have said that getting salt is critical to our survival. They'll want me up at Big Bone Lick, helping to boil the salt and a lot of things."

Mr. Hackett smiled. His son, like most boys, seldom showed much zeal for manual labor.

But William went on undaunted. "Jack Cobb says that they'll be taking enough men to defend themselves against any Indian hunting parties, and, Father, I want to go awfully bad."

John Hackett smiled again at the closing declaration, which was so frank.

Just at that moment in another home, another lad was saying almost exactly the same things, and another father gave the same answer that Mr. Hackett did.

"The planting will not be hard to finish," Mr. Whitlock said thoughtfully. "Since it's to be a good, strong company of careful and experienced men who will not let you get into any mischief, you can go along. But a trip like this is no place for boys on holiday. Getting that salt is going to be hard work, and if you're going to go, I expect you to do your fair share of it."

The party was to number a dozen skilled foresters, and they were to lead twenty horses, all carrying huge pack saddles for the needed utensils and for the precious salt on the return trip. Mr. Charles Spebbington, who was a man of his own will, announced that he was going too. He puffed out his ruddy cheeks and said emphatically, "I've heard from hunters of that place. It is one of the great curiosities of the country, and for the sake of learning, I'm bound to see it. Just think of all the gigantic skeletons of the ancient monsters that roamed this land lying there on the ground for ages!"

William and Asa were glad that Mr. Spebbington was to be with them as he was always an enjoyable traveling companion, and with his great knowledge of the world, he was continually teaching them something interesting and new.

They departed in the grey dawn of a fine spring morning, and almost all Larkinboro saw them off. It was an impressive-looking little caravan. The pack horses with their heads up, sniffing the breeze, seemed eager to make the journey. The men also, excited to be on a new adventure, strode with purpose from the gate of the palisade. Everyone carried a long, slender-barreled Kentucky rifle on his shoulder. Most of them also wore fringed, deerskin hunting shirts falling almost to their knees, and below that were deerskin pants and moccasins. It was a striking picture of the young West, so strong and full of life and confidence.

At the edge of the forest, all of them stopped again, as if by an involuntary impulse, and waved their hands in a last good-by to the watchers at the fort. Then they plunged into the vast wilderness that surrounded them for unknown hundreds, if not thousands, of miles.

They talked for a while of the journey and the things that they might see on the way, but before long conversation ceased. The spell of the dark and limitless woods in whose shade they marched fell upon them, and there was no noise but the sound of breathing and the tread of men and horses. Due to the narrowness of the path through the undergrowth, they dropped into Indian file, one behind the other.

William was near the rear of the line, the determined schoolmaster just in front of him, and his comrade Asa just behind. Young Hackett was full of thankfulness that he had been allowed to go. It all appealed to him: the tale that Asa told of the giant bones and the great salt spring, the dark woods full of mystery and delightful danger, and his own place among the trusted band sent to bring back the salt. His heart swelled with pride and pleasure, and he walked with a light, springy step and with the endurance equal to that of any of the men before him. He looked over his shoulder at Asa, whose face also was touched with enthusiasm. "Aren't you glad to be along?" he asked in a whisper.

"As glad as I can be!" replied Asa in the same whisper.

The new sun finally broke the horizon, showering golden beams of light upon the forest. The air grew warmer, but the little band did not cease its rapid pace northward until noon. Then at a word from Jack Cobb, all halted at a beautiful glade, across which ran a little brook of cold water. Dirt Gurley gathered three of the men, and the four of them went in different directions, scouting for signs of enemies.

The horses were tethered at the edge of the forest but were allowed to graze on the young grass that was already beginning to appear. The men gathered the makings of last year's fallen brushwood for a small fire at the center of the glade on the bank of the brook.

"We won't build the fire high and will use dry wood so it don't smoke much," said Jack, who was captain as well as guide. "That way nobody in the forest will be able to spot it. There may not be a single Indian south of the Ohio, but the fellow that's never caught is the fellow that never sticks his head in the trap."

"Sound philosophy!" the schoolmaster spoke up enthusiastically. "Yes, indeed, sound philosophy! Your logic is irrefutable, Mr. Cobb!"

Jack's weathered face broke into a grin. He did not know what *irrefutable* meant, but he was reasonably sure that Mr. Spebbington had intended to compliment him.

William and Asa eagerly assisted with the fire. In fact, they did a large portion of the labor, each wishing to make good on his commitment to work hard on the journey. It didn't take long to gather the wood. Then one of the men lit some tinder with a flint and steel that, when flaming, was placed under carefully stacked dry branches. The fire was tended carefully to keep the blaze low and the smoke almost nonexistent. Even so, it gave plenty of heat, and in a few minutes they cooked their venison and corn bread, serving coffee in tin cups. William and Asa ate with the ferocious appetites that the march had given them. Nobody restricted them because the forest was full of game, and such skillful hunters and riflemen could never lack for a food supply.

It wasn't long before Dirt and the scouts returned with a good report. Even so, the ever cautious Jack Cobb had two of the men who finished eating first to stand watch while the rest completed their meal.

Mr. Spebbington leaned with an air of satisfaction against the large stump of a fallen oak. "Ah, friends, it's a wonderful world that the Creator has given us," he said, looking at the tall trees surrounding them, "and just think, we're among the first pioneers to find out what it contains."

"All right!" Jack announced after all had eaten, the small fire had been put out, and everything was packed up, "We need to push on. We've got no time fer lollygaggin' in the woods. They need that salt at Larkinboro."

Once more they resumed the march, traveling in single file amid the silence of the woods. About the middle of the afternoon, Jack invited Mr. Spebbington and the two boys to ride three of the pack horses. William at first declined, not willing to be considered soft and pampered. But as the schoolmaster promptly accepted, and Asa, who was obviously tired, did the same, he changed his mind. Will wasn't tired, but he didn't want his younger friend to feel badly about taking the ride.

In this way they marched steadily northward, Jack leading and Dirt covering the rear. Both of the accomplished frontiersmen watched every movement of the forest about him and listened for any sound. They knew from years of experience what was natural in the forest, and if anything not belonging to the usual order of things should occur, either Jack or Dirt would detect it in a moment. But this day they saw and heard nothing that was not according to nature: only the wind among the limbs or the stamp of an elk's hooves as it fled, startled at the scent of man. The hostile tribes from north and south, fearful of the presence of each other, seemed to have deserted the great wilderness of Kentucky.

William studied the beauty of the country as they passed along: the gently rolling hills, the rich dark soil, and the clear streams. Once they came to a river too deep to wade, and all of them except the schoolmaster promptly took off their clothing and swam it.

"My age and my calling forbid my doing as the rest of you do," said the schoolmaster, "and I think I shall stick to my horse." He rode the biggest of the pack horses, and when the strong animal began to swim, Mr. Spebbington thrust out his legs until they were almost parallel with the animal's neck. The scholar was nearly dry when they reached the opposite bank.

William and Asa did not envy the schoolmaster. They thought he had too great a weight of dignity to maintain, and they enjoyed swimming through the clear current of the river. The two boys did not remount after the crossing but, fresh and full of life, walked on with the others at a pace so swift that the miles dropped rapidly behind them. They were passing through a country rarely trodden even by the Indians, which William concluded by the great quantities of game they saw. The deer seemed to look from every thicket, and occasionally a magnificent elk went crashing by. Once a bear lumbered away, and twice small groups of buffalo stampeded in the glades and rushed off, snorting through the undergrowth.

"They say that far to the westward, on plains that seem to have no end, those animals are to be seen in the millions," said Mr. Spebbington.

"It's so," confirmed Jack Cobb, who was walking nearby. "I've heard it from the Indians."

They stopped a little while before sundown, and as the game was so plentiful all around them, Cobb said he would shoot a deer. "You come with me while the others are making the camp," he said to Will.

The boy flushed with pride and gratification, and taking his rifle, plunged at once into the forest with the guide. He said nothing, knowing that Jack Cobb would appreciate silence far more than words, and took care to make no noise as he followed. As the two glided quietly through the brush and undergrowth, Jack regarded him with silent approval. *A born woodsman,* he thought to himself.

A mile from the camp, they stopped at the crest of a little hill that was thickly clad with forest and undergrowth and looked down into the glade beyond. They saw several deer grazing, and as the wind blew from them toward the hunters, the animals had taken no alarm.

"Pick the fat buck there on the right," whispered the scout to his young companion.

William did not say a word. He had learned the quietness of the woods and, leveling his rifle, took sure aim. There was no buck fever about him now, and the old voices that plagued him seemed to be in the distant past. When his rifle cracked, the deer bounded into the air, then fell almost immediately. Jack was all business as he began to cut up and clean the game, and with Will's aid, he did it so skillfully and rapidly that they returned to the camp loaded with the juicy deer meat by the time the fire and everything else was ready for them.

William and Asa ate with eager appetites, and when supper was over, they wrapped themselves in their blankets and lay before the remnants of the fire. Asa went to sleep at once, but Will did not close his eyes so soon. Far in the west he saw the last red bar of light cast by the sinking sun and the deep ruddy glow over the fringe of the forest. Then it suddenly passed, as if whisked away by the hand of God. Twilight came and gradually covered the wilderness with darkness. The last thing he heard before sleep took him was the south wind singing a small, sweet song among the branches above his head. He did not awaken until he heard Dirt Gurley and the others cooking breakfast.

Four days later they reached the wonderful Big Bone Lick, but they approached it with the greatest caution. The scouts were concerned that an errand similar to theirs might have drawn hostile Indians to the great salt spring. But as they made a wide circle around the desired goal, they saw no Indian sign. With a sense of relief, Jack Cobb led them through the marsh to the source of the salt.

William opened his eyes in amazement. All that the schoolmaster and Asa had told him was true. Acres and acres of the marsh lands were fairly littered with bones, some small, some large, and some gigantic. Will stood some of the bones on end and found that they were very heavy. Others he could not lift.

"Why do they weigh so much?" he asked.

"Because they have been in the ground for so many years that they have become mineralized." said Mr. Spebbington, bubbling with delight. "They have turned into stone, my lads!

"Look at them all! Great, monstrous creatures! William, you and Asa are looking upon the remains of animals thousands of years old, killed perhaps in fights with others of their kind over these very salt springs, or quite possibly drowned during Noah's flood itself! What a wonder!"

For the first day or two, Mr. Spebbington was absolutely no help at all in making the salt because he was far too excited about the bones.

"I can understand," said William, "why the animals should come here after the salt, since they crave salt just as we do. But it seems strange to me that salt water should be running out of the ground hundreds of miles from the sea."

"It's the sea itself that's coming up right at our feet," replied the schoolmaster thoughtfully. "Away back yonder, during Noah's time, the sea covered the whole earth. When it receded or the ground rose, vast subterranean reservoirs of salt water were left, and now when the rain sinks down into the full reservoirs, a portion of the salt water is forced to the surface, which makes the salt springs that are scattered over this part of the country. It is a process that is going on continually. At least, that's my theory."

But most of the salt-makers did not bother themselves about causes and accepted the giant bones as facts without curiosity about their origin. Nor did they neglect to put them to use. By sticking them in the ground, they made tripods on which to hang their kettles for boiling the salt water. Other bones were used to devise comfortable seats. But to the schoolmaster and Asa, the bones were an unending source of interest. They were ever prowling in the swamp for a bone bigger than any that they had found before.

All the while the salt-making progressed rapidly. The kettles were kept boiling day and night, and sack after sack was filled with the precious crystals. At night wild animals, eager for the salt, came down to the springs despite the known presence of the men. The settlers rarely molested them. Only a deer now and then was shot for food. William and Asa lay awake one night watching two big bull buffalo not fifty yards away fighting for the best place at the spring.

Jack and Dirt did not do much of the work at the salt-boiling but kept themselves busy scouting the surrounding forest for signs of enemies. Wishing to give William more experience, the scouts often took the youth with them on these silent trips through the woods. The first time Will went, he felt badly on Asa's account because his comrade was not chosen also. But when he returned, he found that his sympathy was wasted. His younger friend and the master were deeply absorbed in the task of trying to fit together some of the gigantic bones in order to re-create the animal to which they thought the bones belonged. Will discovered that Asa was far happier with the scholar than he would have been scouting or hunting.

The day's work ended, and all the others sat around the campfire with the dying glow of the setting sun reflecting off the springs and marshes. But Asa and the master toiled zealously at the gigantic figure that they had constructed, supported partly with stakes and bearing a remote resemblance to some animal that lived a few thousand years ago. Mr. Spebbington had tied together some of the bones with vines, and he and Asa were hard at work trying to fit a section of vertebrae into place.

After they had returned from scouting, Dirt Gurley sat down by the fire, stuffed a piece of juicy venison into his mouth, and looked with eyes of wonder at the two workers in the cause of natural history. "Great land o' Goshen! You two fellers has been constructifyin' on them bones all day long. Even if'n you managed to get that there former critter all put back together, he's still gonna be dead. It seems to me that you two fellers is makin' a whole heap o' trouble fer yerselves over some ex-beasty what's been pushin' up daisies so long he's become part of the landscape. Now if'n you two wants to get all frothed up about some bones, there's some right over here that's got lots of dee-licious, fresh cooked, deer meat wrapped around 'em just waitin' an' beggin' to be et up. Yessiree, *these* here bones is some I can get mighty excited about!"

Asa and the schoolmaster ignored Dirt's teasing and continued their project. Just at that moment one of the vines snapped, and their attempt to reconstruct a prehistoric beast collapsed. The master stared at them in disgust and exclaimed, "It's no use, Asa! We can't put them together away out here in the wilderness!"

"Well, one thing's for sure," his young apprentice observed as he viewed the pile of bones, "Whatever that thing was, it was huge!"

"And dead!" called Dirt with a mouthful of meat.

With an irritated snort the schoolmaster stalked over to the fire and, taking a deer steak, ate hungrily. The steak was very tender, and gradually a look of contentment and peace stole over Charles Spebbington's face. "It may be hard to be a scholar here in these wilds, constantly beleaguered by contented ignoramuses," he murmured, cutting his eyes at Dirt, "but one can have a glorious appetite, and it is most pleasant to gratify it."

"Now yer talkin', Perfesser!" Dirt Gurley agreed with emphasis as grease from the deer meat he chewed ran down his scraggly beard.

When the darkness settled upon them, Jack announced that, in one day more, they ought to have all the salt the horses could carry, and it would be best to leave immediately, hurrying back to Larkinboro as swiftly as possible. A half hour later all were asleep except the sentinels and those on salt-making duty.

Chapter Ten

A DANGEROUS TURKEY

William had conducted himself so well and had shown such skill on his first scouting trip that Jack Cobb decided to take him again the next day. The news thrilled the young woodsman. He was no longer worried about Asa because he saw that his friend's interests and desires were not the same as his own. The heaps of "old bones" were a mere curiosity to Will, but he respected Asa and the master if they found them worthy of study and close attention.

When it was time, Jack and William slipped away into the undergrowth, and the young scout soon noticed that the guide's face, which was tense and preoccupied, seemed graver than usual. The boy was too wise to ask questions, but after they had searched through the forest for several hours, Jack remarked in the most casual way, "I heard the gobble of a wild turkey away off last night."

"Yes," said William, "there're quite a few of 'em around here. You remember the one I shot Tuesday?"

Jack did not reply just then, but in about five minutes, he spoke again, "I'm looking for the particular wild turkey I heard last night."

"Why that one, when there are so many, and how would you know him from the others if you found him?" asked William quickly, and then a deep burning flush of shame broke through the tan of his cheeks. He, William Hackett, a rover of the wilderness, to ask such foolish questions! A child of the towns would have shown as much sense.

The scout, who was looking covertly at him out of the corner of his eye, saw the mounting blush and was pleased. The boy had spoken impulsively, but he knew better. "You understand, I guess," Jack probed.

"Yes," replied Will humbly, "I understand why you want to find that wild turkey, and I know why you said last night we ought to leave the salt springs just as soon as we can."

The smile on the face of the scout brightened. Here was the most promising pupil who had ever sat at his feet for instruction. Now they redoubled their caution as their soundless bodies slipped through the undergrowth. Everywhere they looked for the trail of that particular wild turkey. Time passed; noon and part of the afternoon were gone. They were still curving in a great circle about the camp when Jack suddenly stopped beside a small creek and pointed to the soft soil at the edge of the water.

His young apprentice followed the long finger and saw the outline of a moccasin print. "Our turkey has passed here," William observed in a low voice.

"Most likely," the guide answered with a nod, "and if not ours, then one of the same flock. But that footprint is three or four hours old. Come on, we'll follow this trail until it grows too warm."

The footsteps led down the side of the brook, and when they curved away from it, Jack was able to trace them on the turf and through the undergrowth. A half mile from the start, other footsteps joined them, and these were obviously made by many men, perhaps a score of warriors.

"You see," said the scout, "I guess they've just come across the Ohio, or we wouldn't a been left all these days b'il'n salt so peaceful like as if there wasn't an Indian in the whole world."

William drew a deep breath. Like all who ventured into the West, he had expected some day to be exposed to Indian danger and attack, but it had been a vague thought. Even when they had come north to the Big Bone Lick, Indian trouble seemed like a dim, far-away affair. But now he stood almost in its presence. The fierce Shawnee, whose very name inspired terror in new settlements, were probably not a mile away. He felt tremors of fear at the nearness of such danger, as he had when he spotted the hunting party before, but this time the enemy warriors most likely knew they were at the salt spring.

He approached this emotion the same way he dealt with the voices and the fear of failure: he faced it head-on. *Lord, help me now!* He prayed in his heart as Asa had taught him. *This is not fear of failure. This is fear for my life and the lives of my friends. I do not want this fear to control me any more than the other fears I've always had to deal with. I may feel afraid, but Lord, please give me Your strength so that I will not allow fear of any kind to make decisions for me!* As soon as he finished, he felt his heart begin to calm, and his mind cleared.

"Step lighter than you ever did afore in your life," said the guide. "Keep low an' stay right on my tail, and don't you let a single twig nor nothin' snap as you pass."

Jack had spoken in a sharp, emphatic whisper, and William knew that he considered the enemy near. Will bent far down and, holding his rifle before him in such a position that it could be used at a moment's warning, followed behind Jack so silently that the guide, hearing no sound, took an instant's backward glance. When he saw the boy, he permitted another faint smile of approval to pass over his weathered face.

They advanced about three-quarters of a mile. Then at the crest of a hill thickly clothed in tall undergrowth, the guide sank down and pointed with a long, ominous forefinger. "Look," he whispered.

His young companion peered through the interlacing bushes and, for the third time in his life, gazed upon a band of red men. As he looked, his blood for a moment turned cold. Perhaps forty in number, they were sitting in a glade around a small fire. All had blankets of red or blue about them, and they carried rifles. Their faces were hideous with war paint, and their coarse, black hair rose in the defiant scalp lock.

"I'm figurin' they don't think we know they're here," Jack whispered his thoughts out loud. "If it were me leadin' that bunch, I'd wait til midnight and attack our people while we wuz sleepin'."

The guide's theory seemed reasonable to William, but he said nothing. It was no business of his to venture opinions before one who knew so much about the wilderness.

"It can't be more'n two o'clock," whispered Cobb after he glanced up at the sun's position, "an' they'd attack about midnight. That gives us ten hours. Will, the Lord is with us. Come on."

He slid away through the bushes, and his young companion followed him. When they were a half mile from the Indian camp, they increased their speed to an astonishing gait and in a half hour were at the Big Bone Lick.

"Have 'em load up all the salt right now!" Jack called to Dirt Gurley. "We've got to skeedaddle back to Larkinboro like our feet was greased."

Dirt shot him a questioning look, and Cobb nodded, which sent Dirt to work with extraordinary diligence, and the others imitated his speed. To the schoolmaster the guide breathed the one word "Shawnee," and William in a few sentences told Asa what he had seen.

They had no intention of deserting the salt, however close the danger. Fortunately the precious mineral was already packed, and it was quickly transferred to the backs of the horses, along with food for the trip home. In less than a half hour, they were fleeing southward with Dirt Gurley leading the way. Cobb was at the rear, his eyes and ears noticing everything, and his every nerve attuned to danger.

The master cast back one regretful glance at his beloved giant bones, then with resignation turned his face permanently toward the south and the line of retreat.

"Will," whispered Asa, half in delight, half in terror, "did you really see them?"

"Yep," replied his friend, "nearly forty of 'em, and an ugly lot they were too, with their faces all painted up. Whit, it'll be tough if it comes to a stand-up fight. They're three to our one, and they know more of these woods than we do. Then there's the salt. We can't run as fast as we'd like to because we've got to save what we've come for."

Asa swallowed hard and nodded his head in agreement.

The men took care with the heavily laden horses. Nobody was allowed to ride except as a last resort. Southward they went in Indian file, as they had come, only much faster. Will Hackett glanced around him and saw nothing threatening danger. It was a beautiful spring afternoon. The forest radiated life as the new leaves grew, and the clear sky above was a brilliant blue. Never did the world look more attractive or more harmless, and it seemed incredible that these woods should contain men who were thirsting for the lives of others. But he knew differently. He could not forget that circle of painted faces in the glade that he and Jack had seen.

"Do you think they'll follow us?" asked Asa.

"I don't know," his young friend replied, "but Jack seems to think so. At the very least they'll hang on our trail for a long time."

"And if they catch us, I guess there'll be a fight."

"You can count on it," William returned confidently.

Hackett studied Asa's face and saw him grow pale. He knew his younger friend was fighting his fears, as Will also had to do. The bigger and stronger lad also knew his comrade's courage and tenacity, and he respected him all the more for it, because Asa was perhaps less fitted physically for the wild and dangerous life of the frontier than some of the others.

After these few words they sank again into silence. As the day wore on, the sun grew very hot. It was poised at a convenient angle in the heavens and poured its fiery rays directly upon them. Mr. Spebbington began to gasp. His was not a body built to hurry. Jack Cobb's keen eye fell upon him.

"I think you'd better mount one of the horses," he said to the teacher. "The big bay there can carry his salt and you too for a while until you are rested."

"What! I ride, when everybody else is afoot!" exclaimed Mr. Spebbington, indignantly.

"We cain't afford to lose you," said Cobb with a straight face. "Why, if somethin' wuz to happen to you, we'd lose both our preacher *and* our schoolmaster."

Mr. Spebbington looked at him, but he could not detect any change of countenance.

"Hop up," continued the scout, "it ain't any time to be bashful. Others of us may have to do it 'afore long."

The winded schoolmaster yielded with a sigh and climbed upon the horse. He was immediately glad that he had done so as he enjoyed the luxury of a rest. Asa and one or two others took to the horses' backs later on, but William continued the march on foot with long, easy strides and no sign of weakening. Jack noticed him more than once, but he never made any suggestion to Will that he ride. Instead the faint smile of approval appeared once more on the guide's face.

The sun began to sink; the twilight came, followed by the night. Jack called a halt, and clustered in the thickest shadows of the forest, they ate their supper and rested their tired limbs. No fire was lit, but they sat under the trees, hungrily eating the dried venison they had brought with them from Larkinboro and talking in the lowest of whispers.

Mr. Spebbington was vexed. He had been troubled by their hasty flight, and his dignity suffered. "It is not fitting that civilized men should run away from danger," he said.

"Wel-l-l, I see yer point, Perfesser," Dirt responded knowingly. "I shorely do. An' maybe it ain't fittin', so to speak, but it's safe."

"At least we are far enough away now," continued the master, "that we might rest here comfortably until dawn. We haven't seen or heard a sign of pursuit."

"When it comes to book-learnin', Perfesser," Dirt continued, "you're about the smartest gent I ever laid my eyeballs on. But with due respect to that astutified brain o' yours, you don't know the nature of Shawnee warriors. When them rascals make the least noise is when they're most dangerous. Both me an' Jack are certain sure that they struck our trail not long after we left Big Bone Lick, an' we need to make our plans like they're a'follerin' close behind. In these woods the man that takes the fewest risks is the one who lives the longest."

They rested half an hour, with no sound save the shuffling feet of the horses; then they started on again. They travelled more cautiously because the night was dark, and they wished to make as little noise as possible threshing about in the undergrowth.

Asa pressed up by the side of William. "Do you think we shall have to go on this way all night?" he asked. "Wasn't Mr. Spebbington right when he said we were out of danger?"

"No, the schoolmaster was wrong," replied Will. "Jack and Dirt know more about the woods and what is likely to happen in them than Mr. Spebbington could know in all his life. It's every man to his own trade, and it's Jack Cobb's and Dirt Gurley's trade that we need now."

After hearing these sage words, Asa asked no more questions, but he and William walked side by side throughout the night, except when they were riding. To avoid stopping for rests, they all took turns on horseback. Twice they crossed small streams and once a larger one, where they exercised the utmost caution to keep their precious salt from getting wet. Fortunately the great pack saddles were a protection, and they emerged on the other side with both salt and powder dry.

When the night was thickest, in the long, dark hour just before the dawn, the two boys, who were again side by side, heard a faint, distant cry. It was a low, wailing note that echoed eerily from the darkness. It seemed to be far behind them but inclining from the right, and after a few moments there came another faint cry just like it, also behind them but far to the left.

Despite the soft, wailing note, both William and Asa felt a shiver run through them. The strange, low sound, coming in the utter silence of the night, had in it something ominous.

"It was the cry of a wolf," said Asa.

"And his brother wolf answered," said his older friend.

Dirt Gurley was just behind them, and they heard him laugh.

Asa wheeled about at once, his pride aflame at the insinuation that he did not know the wolf's long whine. "Well, wasn't it a wolf that called, and a wolf that answered?" he asked.

"Well, I suppose from a certain point o' view, you might say that it were a couple of wolves," replied Dirt. "But them two wolves only had four legs between 'em. That there was signal cries of the Shawnees, an' as me an' Jack has been tellin' you this whole time, they're hot on our trail. Whoo-wee! It's a mighty good thang fer us we didn't stay all night back there where we stopped, or we'd a' all woke up without our top knot."

Asa turned pale again, but his courage, as usual, came back. "Thank God it will be daylight soon," he murmured to himself. "Then if they overtake us, we can at least see them."

Faint and far away but ominous and full of threat came the howl of the wolf again, first from the right and then from the left, and then from points between. William noticed that Jack and Dirt were tense and alert, and his eyes shifted to Mr. Spebbington. Seeing the clueless expression on the scholar's face, he knew at once that the master did not understand. He had not heard the words of Dirt Gurley.

"It seems that we are pursued by a pack of wolves instead of a war party," said Mr. Spebbington. "At least we are numerous enough to beat off a lot of cowardly, four-footed assailants."

"Those are not wolves, Mr. Spebbington," William said, "those are the Shawnee calling to one another."

"Then why in heaven's name don't they speak their own language?" exclaimed the exasperated schoolmaster.

William, despite himself, was forced to smile, but he turned his face. He would not offend the schoolmaster, whom he held in high esteem.

The dawn began to brighten. The sun, a flaming red sword, split the gray sky and poured down a flood of golden beams upon the vast green wilderness.

Jack Cobb gave the word to halt, and again they ate their cold food. While the others sat on fallen timber or leaned against tree trunks, Jack and Dirt talked in low tones. Will could see that their words were marked by the deepest earnestness.

Cobb presently turned to the men. "You heard the howlin' just afore dawn, an' I guess all of you know it was not made by real wolves but by Shawnee callin' to each other an' directin' the chase after us. We've come fast, but they've come faster, an' I know that by noon we'll have to fight."

The schoolmaster's eyes opened in wonder. "Do you really mean to say that they are overhauling us?" he asked.

"I shore do," replied Jack. "You see, they're better skilled at travelin' through the woods, an' they ain't hampered by hauling hundreds of pounds of salt like we are."

Mr. Spebbington said nothing more, but his lips suddenly closed tightly, and his eyes flashed. Charles was a man of learning and a man of peace, but when it was time to fight, he was as ready as anyone else.

The two guides again consulted, then Cobb said, "We think that, since we'll have to fight, it would be better to face it when we are fresh and steady and in the best place we can find."

All the men nodded. They were tired of running. The questioning eyes of both guides roamed round the forest, and finally the two uttered a low cry of pleasure. Before they halted, the group had been climbing a hill with a rather steep ascent that dropped off steeply on three sides.

"We won't find a better place than this," Jack said loud enough for all to hear. "It looks like a fort just made for us."

"But there is no line of retreat," objected the schoolmaster.

"We had a line of a retreat last night and all this mornin', an' we've been followin' it the whole time," rejoined the leader. "Now we don't need it no more, but what we do need to do is to make a stan'-up fight an' lick them fellers."

"And save our salt," added the schoolmaster.

"Now yer talkin', Perfesser!" Dirt Gurley agreed emphatically. "We didn't come all these miles an' work all these days just to lose our hard-earned goods to a bunch a' salt-stealin' polecats!"

They climbed rapidly upon the great, jutting peninsula of rocky soil. It fortunately was covered with a good growth of trees, and they tethered the horses in a thick grove nearby.

"Now we'll just unload our salt an' make a wall," directed Cobb. "They can shoot our full sacks as much as they please, just so they don't touch us."

The thick bags were laid in the most exposed place across the narrowest neck of the peninsula, and the settlers also drug up all the fallen tree trunks and heavy limbs that they could find to build up their primitive fortification. When done, they sat down to wait, a hard task for men, but hardest of all for two boys like William and Asa.

A couple of the men took the horses to the back side of their hill and tethered them where they could watch over the animals and guard against any possible attempt to scale the slope in their rear. The other defenders lay close behind the wall of salt and brushwood.

The great red eye of the sun, centered in the heavens, looked down at the frontiersmen crouched close to the earth behind their low defense. It also shone into the forest at the savage warriors creeping silently from tree to tree, eager to destroy their enemies.

The two boys behind the wall saw nothing and heard nothing but the breathing of those near. They fingered their rifles and, through the crevices between the bags, studied intently the woods in front of them. But no trace of their enemies was spotted. Looking from tree to tree, William's sharp eye couldn't detect any unnatural movement at all. Where the patches of grass grew, it moved only with the regular sweep of the breeze. Beginning to think that Jack and Dirt must be mistaken and that the warriors had abandoned the pursuit, he glanced at Cobb a dozen feet away. The leader's face was so tense, so eager, and so earnest that William ceased to doubt. The man's whole appearance indicated the knowledge of danger, present and terrible.

Even as Will looked, a rifle flashed from the woods in front of them, the ball whizzing through some nearby limbs. Jack Cobb suddenly threw up his rifle and quickly pulled the trigger. A flash of fire leaped from the long, slender muzzle of blue steel. There was a sharp report like the swift lash of a whip, then a painful cry.

"They've started their attack, but Jack dropped one of 'em," William whispered breathlessly to Asa.

Asa, who was noticeably trembling, nodded his understanding.

The master crouched nearer to the boys. He was one of the bravest of the men, and in that hour of danger and suspense, his heart went to these two lads, his pupils, each a good boy in his own way. He felt that it was a part of his duty to get them safely back to Larkinboro and their parents, and he meant to accomplish it.

"Keep down, lads," he said, touching William on his arm. "Don't expose yourselves. You are not called upon to do anything unless it comes to the last resort."

"We are going to do our best!" replied William with determination. He resented the suggestion that he and Asa hide while the others fight for them. Mr. Spebbington, seeing that his feelings were touched, said no more.

A foreboding silence followed the opening shots, but the brilliant sunshine poured down on the woods just as if it were a glorious summer afternoon. William again searched the forest in front of them, and although he could see nothing, he was not deceived by the silence and peace. He knew that their foes were there, more thirsty than ever for blood.

More than an hour passed, then the forest in front of them burst into life. Muzzles blasted from many points, the sharp reports blending into one continuous, ominous rattle. Little puffs of white smoke arose; whistling bullets passed over-head or buried themselves with a sighing sound in the bags of salt. High above all rang the fierce war whoop of the Shawnee, the last sound that many a Kentucky pioneer would ever hear.

The terrible tumult sent a thrill of terror through the two boys, but their disciplined minds and the grace of God held their bodies firm, and they remained crouched by the primitive breastwork, ready to do their part.

"Steady, everybody! Steady!" exclaimed Cobb in a loud, sharp voice, every syllable of which cut through the tumult. "Don't shoot until you see something to shoot at, an' then make your aim true!"

Through the smoke William began to see dusky figures leaping from tree to tree but always coming toward them. It was his impulse to fire the moment a flitting figure flashed briefly into view, but he remembered Jack's caution and their terrible need. Will restrained himself, although his finger already lay caressingly on the trigger. Around him the rifles began to crack. Cobb and Dirt fired with slow, deliberate aim, then reloaded with incredible swiftness. Down the line the others did likewise. Bullets spattered into trunks and limbs or buried themselves in the salt, but William could not tell if anyone was hurt.

He suddenly saw a dark figure passing from one tree to another, and the passage was long enough for him to take a good aim. He pulled the trigger and involuntarily shut his eyes. He was a hunter, but he had never hunted men before. When he looked again, he saw a blur upon the ground, and despite himself, he shuddered.

Beside him, Asa was in a state of wild excitement. The younger boy's nerves were not so steady, and he loaded and fired almost at random. In the excitement of the moment, Will's young friend stood up almost unconsciously to his full height, but he was dragged down the next instant as if he had been seized from below by a bear.

"ASA WHITLOCK!" the schoolmaster exclaimed fiercely, all the instincts of a schoolteacher rising within him, "if you jump up that way again, exposing yourself to their bullets, I'll turn you over my knee right here, big as you are, and give you a licking that you'll remember all your life!"

The master was savagely in earnest, and Asa, with wide eyes, did not dare disobey. Will fired once more and a third time, and the roar of the battle seemed to reach a fever pitch. Then suddenly the terrible racket ceased. So sudden and so absolute was the silence that it was startling. A light breeze blew the smoke away, revealing a few dark objects lying close to the ground among the trees before them, but nothing else. Not a sound came from the forest, and no flitting form could be seen.

Chapter Eleven

SHOWERS OF BLESSING

William and Asa stared intently at the woods before them, but where a large war party of Shawnee had just been, not a living soul could be seen. The boys heard again the peaceful wind blowing among the trees. The savage army had melted away as if it had never been. The only evidence that a battle had just taken place was the smoke still drifting up into the leafy branches and the fallen enemy fighters.

"Well, don't that jus' make you wanna kiss yer sister!" exclaimed Dirt Gurley jubilantly. "We done scorched their britches that time, an' nobody on our side has more'n a scratch,"

"That's so," said Cobb, casting a critical eye down the line. "It's because we took the time to find ourselves a good position an' made ready. There's nothin' like havin' time to prepare when you're facin' a fight. How're you, boys?"

"All right, I guess," Asa replied shakily, "but I've been pretty badly scared, I'll have to admit. But we're not hurt, right, Will?"

"Thank the Almighty," murmured the schoolmaster under his breath, and then he said aloud to the scout, "I suppose they'll leave us alone now."

Cobb shook his head. "I wish I could say it," he replied, "but I cain't. We've laid out four of 'em, an' the Shawnee, like all other Indians, ain't got much stomach for a straightaway attack on folks behind breastworks. I doubt if they'll try that again, but you can bet yer moccasins they'll be up to new mischief soon. Our job

112

right now is to keep a sharp eye out for tricks. Them rascals is sly, so we has to be slyer."

Taking advantage of the lull in the action, Jack Cobb had his men get something to eat but cautioned them to stay behind cover at all times. Two or three bullets were fired from the forest, but they whistled over their heads and did no damage. The frontiersmen seemed to have control of the situation at the moment, but Cobb was troubled. He knew that, when night fell, the Shawnee would be able to take advantage of the darkness, creep up to within a few yards of their fortifications, and attack them at many points.

William had heard enough about Indian fighting from Jack and Dirt to understand the danger they now faced. He, along with most of the others, hoped that the two scouts would come up with a plan. As the young frontiersman observed closely, he noticed that the guide stared at the heavens. William, following his intent gaze, detected for the first time a change in the appearance of the clouds and also that the atmosphere began to have a different feel. There seemed to be a slight heaviness to the air. He had been so focused on the excitement of the battle that he had forgotten such things as sky, clouds, and air. As he did so now, he began to guess at the guide's plan.

Over the next half hour, clouds began to roll in, and the sunlight began to fade. Very quickly the skies became a vast dome of dull, lowering gray, and the breeze had a chilly edge. Heavy, dark clouds came over the brink of the horizon in the southwest and crept threateningly towards them. The sky steadily darkened, and suddenly the dim horizon in the far southwest was cut by a vivid flash of lightning. Low thunder grumbled over the distant hills.

"Whoo-wee!" exclaimed Dirt Gurley. "There's a storm a comin', an' it's gonna be a whopper!"

"Ay," returned Jack, who had been back among the horses, "an' it just might save our scalps. When this thing hits, all you fellas be sure to keep your powder dry."

"It's a good thang we packed our salt in deerskin bags. That'll keep the rain from getting' to it."

"One of the men," Cobb continued, "has found a big gully runnin' down the back end of our hill, an' I think if we're keerful, we can lead the horses to the valley that way. But fer now we'll jus' wait a spell. How about some of you fellas plug up the bullet holes in the bags when it gets a little darker."

The two boys watched the on-coming squall in fascination. In the past they had seen great storms that sometimes swept the wilderness, but the one coming seemed to be charged with a deadly power. It rushed forward with terrible swiftness. The thunder, at first a mere rumble, rose rapidly to crash repeatedly, stunning their ears. The livid flashes of lightning split the southwest like flaming swords, appearing and reappearing with such intensity that they seemed never to leave. The wind rose, and the forest groaned. From afar came a sullen roar, and then the great gale rushed down upon them.

"LIE FLAT!" shouted Cobb.

All except the four who held the struggling and frightened horses threw themselves upon the ground, and although William and Asa hugged the earth, their ears were filled with the roar and scream of the wind and the crackle of limbs and whole tree trunks snapping through, like the rattle of rifle fire. Trees crashed all around them, and fragments whistled over their heads. Fortunately they were untouched.

The great volley of wind was gone in a few moments, as if it were a single, huge cannon shot. It whistled off to the eastward but left in its path a trail of torn and fallen trees. Then came the sweep of the great cloudburst. The air grew darker, thunder ceased to crash, lightning died away, and water poured down in sheets over the black and mangled forest.

"We'll start now," Cobb announced. "Them Shawnee had to hunt fer cover. With 'em all hunkered down, they won't be able to see what we're a doin'. So up with them bags of salt, an' let's skedaddle!"

In an incredibly short time, the sacks were loaded on the pack horses. Sharpened sticks had been shoved into the bullet holes to protect the precious mineral from the rain. Immediately Cobb got the men moving, and they picked their way carefully down the steep, slick, and dangerous gully in the side of the hill. Will, Asa, and the master locked hands in the dark and driving rain to save each other from falls. Jack and Dirt seemed to have the eyes of cats in the dark and showed the way.

"Merciful heavens!" gasped Mr. Spebbington, "I could not have dreamed ten years ago that I should ever take part in such a scene as this!"

After much difficulty and some danger in the terrible storm, they reached the bottom of the hill unhurt, at which point they sped across a fairly level country as quickly as they dared. Jack led, and Dirt brought up the rear to keep everyone close together and to make sure no one would be lost in the darkness and rain. Now and then the two men called the names of the others to see that all were present, but beyond this precaution, no word was spoken save in whispers.

Both boys felt a deep and devout thankfulness for the storm that had saved them from a long siege and possible death. In their gratitude for God's protection, they for the moment did not concern themselves with the fact that they were soaked to the skin, cold, tired, and still tramping through the lone wilderness far from Larkinboro.

On they marched through the darkness, taking only brief stops to rest. The pouring rain continued through most of the night and only began to lessen as dawn approached. Suddenly the downpour stopped, and the heavy clouds began to disperse. Stars appeared in the openings in the sky, and trees emerged from the mist and gloom. All the salt-workers felt their spirits rise. They knew that they had escaped from the conflict wonderfully well. Tired as they all were, fresh strength came to them when they saw the dawn break in the east and the last shower of rain whisk away to the north. As the sunlight illumined the world around them, they saw a wet path with drops of water sparkling here and there like millions of crystal beads.

Jack Cobb drew a deep breath of relief and ordered a halt. As the men and animals rested from the difficult forced march, Jack stared anxiously at the rear of their column. After several minutes he saw Dirt come trotting up to join them.

"Did you see anything?" Jack called with concern to his friend.

"Not nary a single sign of them painted varments," Dirt called back. "They either lost our trail in the storm, or give up an' went home to mamma. I reckon they could foller us again, but they know now that they bit off somethin' a heap too tough for 'em to chaw. I don't figure they'll try it again, 'specially after havin' been beat up by the storm."

"And to think we got away with our scalps and brought our salt with us too!" Mr. Spebbington exclaimed. "HA HAA, what a triumph! The Good Lord has indeed blessed us!" The beloved teacher then had them all bow their heads as he led them in a heartfelt prayer of thanksgiving to God.

The party of salt-makers continued their steady march south until past sunset, when the guide called a halt. Just as dark arrived, Dirt returned from scouting their back trail. His report was a happy one. He had neither seen nor heard any evidence of the Shawnee following them. Based on that confident report, Jack allowed a fire to be lit, but they kept the blaze small.

It was no easy matter to start a fire, but the two scouts at last accomplished it with flint, steel, and dry splinters cut from the underside of fallen logs. When the flames had taken good hold, they placed more brushwood upon it, and never were heat and warmth more appreciated by tired travelers.

Until then the two boys did not realize how weary and how very wet they were. They basked in the glow of the fire and watched beds of coals form with delight. Taking off part of their clothing, they hung it close to the heat, and when it was dry and warm, put it on again.

"I guess two such terrible fighters as you," Jack said to William and Asa, "wouldn't mind a bite to eat, would you? I've heard tell as how the Romans, after they fought a good fight with them Carthagians or Mastadoonians or whoever they was, would sit down, take in a little grub, an' then be ready to go at it again."

"Food sounds wonderful," Asa exclaimed, speaking for both of them, "but we'll pass on another fight."

"Hear, hear!" Mr Spebbington joined in. "A bit of sustenance would be quite apropos!"

With a hesitant nod and a confused smile on his face, Jack Cobb returned to the fire.

After so much danger and suffering, the sense of safety and warmth penetrating the bones of the two boys prompted an emotional release, and they seized each other in a friendly scuffle. It terminated only when they were about to roll into the fire. Then they ate venison as if they had been famished. Afterwards, when they were asleep on their blankets before the fire, Jack said to the schoolmaster, "They did well for their age."

"They most certainly did, Mr. Cobb," said the teacher with some pride. "This has been a difficult march, and yet the lads handled the hardships of the wet, dreary trek like true legionnaires."

Jack Cobb smiled a little, and then his face quickly became grave. "It's what comes with livin' on the frontier," he said. "Every settlement will have to stand the troubles that come—and come they will, but it's encouragin' to see lads like these growin' into men."

A vigilant watch was kept all the long night, but there was no sign of a second attack. Dirt Gurley had reckoned truly when he thought the Shawnee would not care to risk further pursuit, and the next day they resumed their journey under a drying sun.

They were not troubled any more by Indians, but the rest of the way was not without other dangers. The rivers were swollen by the spring rains, and they had great trouble in carrying the salt across on the swimming horses. Once Asa was swept down by a swift and powerful current, but William managed to seize and hold him until others came to the rescue.

They were passing through the region that would come to be known in later days as the Garden of Kentucky. As they traveled through magnificent forests and threaded their way through dense canebrakes, squirrels chattered in every tree top, deer swarmed in the woods, and buffalo were found in almost every glen.

"Mark my words," Mr. Spebbington announced to William and Asa as they marched along through the vast wilderness, "one day all of this will be settled and civilized."

But William, with only the thoughts of youth, could not conceive of a time when the thick forests should be cut down and the game would go. He was concerned only with the present, and the words of the schoolmaster made no impression on him.

At last on a sunny afternoon, whole, well fed, and with their treasure preserved, they approached Larkinboro. The hearts of the two boys thrilled at signs of habitation. They saw where an ax had bitten through a tree and came upon broad trails that could be made only by pioneers going to their work or hunting their cattle.

Asa showed the most excitement at returning home. Larkinboro was the only spot on earth for him. But William turned his back on the wilderness with a certain reluctance. A love for the beauties and fascinations of God's amazing wild lands and all they contained had been fully awakened in him. He had been forced to face his old fears and some new ones, and he had found God to be faithful. The danger of the battle had revealed to the young man more of what was in him. His fears and self-doubts were certainly present, but there was something else that he didn't expect. He discovered that, at the moment of truth, when the battle was raging, a powerful sense of duty and a zeal to protect those he cared about had gripped his heart, shoved his fears aside, and moved him to action, and he thanked God for it.

It wasn't until the battle was over and he was alone with his thoughts that the old, nagging voices began to ask all of the *what if* questions that attacked his confidence. As William marched beside Asa when they approached Larkinboro, he forced himself to admit that the *what if's* had not occurred and that the Lord had clearly been with him. Then he remembered a Bible verse that the schoolmaster had quoted to him and to Asa around the fire the night before, "When I am afraid, I will trust in God." *That's a verse I better keep handy,* he told himself.

Mr. Spebbington was visibly joyful as they drew closer to home. The wilderness appealed to him in a way, but he considered himself essentially a man who enjoyed the pleasures of home, and Larkinboro was becoming quite comfortable to him.

"I have had my great adventure," the schoolmaster said as he clapped a hand on Asa's shoulder. "I have helped to fight the wild men, and in the days to come, I can sit around the hearth and tell exaggerated tales of our exploits together just as the ancient Greeks did. But once is enough for this old scholar. I would fain wage the battles of learning rather than those of arms."

"Why, them ol' Greeks ain't got nothin' on you, Perfesser," Dirt Gurley announced when he heard Mr. Spebbington's words. "When you had to do it, you reared back and fought like a she badger!"

The teacher shook his head and replied gravely, "Dirt, my good man, you are categorically correct to say *when I had to do it*, and I do not begrudge my portion in our recent skirmish. But I mean that, unless a conflict is thrust upon me, I shall endeavor to circumvent any more of the same."

Dirt Gurley just stared at the scholar with an open mouth. "Perfesser," the scout finally answered, "I ain't got no idear what you jus' said."

From a hill they saw a thin, blue column of smoke rising, hanging like a streamer across the clear blue sky.

"That comes from the chimneys of Larkinboro," Jack called to the rest, "an' I guess she's all right. That there smoke looks kind a' quiet, like good smoke: the kind a smoke you see when nothin' out of the way has happened."

They pressed forward with renewed speed, and presently a shout came from the forest. Two men ran to meet them and rejoiced at the sight of the caravan returning unharmed and with every horse heavily loaded. The salt gatherers triumphantly marched into Larkinboro, with the crowd about them thickening as they neared the gates. William's mother threw her arms about his neck, and his father grasped him by the hand. Asa was in the center of his own family, completely engulfed, and all the space within the palisade resounded with joyous greetings and laughter that became all the more heartfelt when some of the men told of the great danger through which they had passed.

That evening when they sat around the low fire in his father's home, William had to repeat the story of the big bones, the salt-making, and the great adventure with the Shawnee. He grew excited as he told of the battle and the storm, his face flushed, and his eyes shot sparks. As Mrs. Hackett looked at him, she

119

realized, half in pride, half in terror, that she was the mother of a hunter and a warrior.

Chapter Twelve

CAVE DUST

With the large supply of salt brought to the village, the settlement now had enough to last for over a year. Mr. Spebbington also pointed out that, by frequenting the smaller salt springs closer to their fort, they could easily add to their supply and make it last even longer. All of this greatly eased many of the concerns among the citizens of Larkinboro. But the news that a Shawnee war party was in Kentucky and had chased them far southward caused John Hackett and leading men of the village to hold several councils.

After much discussion the men decided to strengthen the walls of their fort with another row of log stakes. Several weeks were dedicated to the work, as well as to making the gates thicker and heavier. When all the labor was finally accomplished and they took the time to inspect their supply of ammunition, it was discovered that, although there was plenty of lead, the amount of gunpowder was frighteningly low. A fresh supply had been expected with a new band of settlers from Virginia, but the settlers had failed to come.

As the town leaders stared gravely into the barrel containing the remnants of their gunpowder, Mr. Middlebrook said what they were all thinking: "If the Shawnee decide to attack us now, we don't have enough powder to defend ourselves!"

"It will take months to send a party back East to purchase more and haul it here," another man added.

121

"That's if you could even make a trip like that with the Indians and the war with England," said another.

"I had forgotten the war," Mr. Middlebrook spoke again. "There might not be any powder available for us if it's all being used for the patriot army."

The effect of this conversation was that the faces around the storeroom were creased heavily with concern. It was just at this moment that Mr. Spebbington spoke up. "Gentlemen," the scholar began, "I have a suggestion that might get us out of this predicament. You will recall that some of our hunters have reported the existence of great caves to the southwest. I had an idea that I wanted to pursue, so when I heard that Jim Hart was headed back that direction, I asked him to bring some samples of dirt from the cave floors. I suspected that this dust might be strongly impregnated with niter. Last week Mr. Hart returned and brought with him my samples. As it turned out, there are indeed large amounts of niter present in the dust from the centuries of bat droppings that have accumulated there. It is from niter that we obtain saltpeter, and with sufficient amounts of saltpeter, sulfur, and charcoal, we will be able to make gunpowder. We need not send to Virginia for our powder; we can make it here in Kentucky for ourselves!"

"Do you truly think that's possible, Mr. Spebbington?" asked John Hackett doubtfully.

"Indeed I do!" replied the schoolmaster confidently. "Situated as we are in this wild land, powder is the most precious thing on earth to us. If we were able to produce it right here, it would certainly be worth the effort, wouldn't it?"

"Yes! Yes, it would!" said Mr. Hackett with hasty emphasis. "Without powder we are absolutely helpless before the attacks of our enemies. Are you sure that this cave dust contains saltpeter?"

"I have the utmost confidence!" Mr. Spebbington returned excitedly.

"Then you must go for it. Jack Cobb, Dirt Gurley, Jim Hart, and a strong party must go with you as well. We cannot run the risk of losing any of you through another run in with the Indians."

"I believe that the risk of Indian attack is very small," said the scholar. "The greater risk is with the northern tribes, and these caves are a good ways south of Larkinboro. Southern Indians, who are less bold than the northern tribes, don't venture into Kentucky very often. The hunters say that they have seen no signs of Indians in that particular region for quite some time."

"Yes, I believe I've heard that as well," said Mr. Hackett, "but we need to be careful all the same."

When William heard of the new expedition, he was wild to go, but his parents, remembering the great danger of the journey to the salt lick, were reluctant to give their permission.

Then Jack Cobb interceded for the boy. "Will is just fitted for this sort of work," he said. "He's a born woodsman and is quickly becoming a fine hunter. Even as young as he is, he's about as strong as any man in the village, and he'll work hard."

The scout saw the less-than-convinced look on John Hackett's face, so he tried again: "Mr. Hackett, I know you and the misses have got grand plans for Will, but I've never seen a lad, or a growed man, fer that matter, as quick to learn the ways of the woods as your son! That's a gift put in him from the Almighty Hisself! Now you might want him to be farmer or maybe even a statesman, but all I know is that God has designed him to be a woodsman. . .a really good one. If that's what he's to be, he needs all the experience he can get. This here trip we're about to take is as safe a way for him to get that experience as there is around these parts. So I think you should let him go with us. But that will be up to you."

John Hackett had no reply to such an argument, and after a moments' reflection, he gave his consent.

When Asa heard that William was to go, he gave his parents no rest, and when Mr. Spebbington, whose favorite he was, seconded his request on the ground that he would need a scholar with him, the permission had to be granted.

Before sunrise on the appointed day, two excited youths set forth with the others, the dangers and terrors of the Shawnee encounter already gone from their minds. Neither Jack nor Dirt believed that they would meet up with Indians on the trip, but each member of the party was cautioned to be constantly alert.

The summer was now at hand, and the forests were an unbroken mass of brilliant green. In the little spaces where the sunlight broke through, wild flowers—red, blue, pink, and purple—peeped up and nodded gaily when the light winds blew. The members of the expedition saw plenty of game, but they killed only enough for their needs. Around the campfire the first night, a lively discussion arose regarding their individual hunting skills. After several minutes, Jack Cobb made it clear to all that he believed it was against the will of God to shoot deer, elk, or buffalo and leave the carcass to rot merely for the pleasure of the killing.

As the scout finished his short sermon, Dirt Gurley called out, "PREACH IT, BROTHER!"

After traveling through the woods for a week, they forded a large river, left the forests, and came into a great, open region. They decided to call this area the Barrens, not because it was a desert, but because it was bare of large trees, having mostly grass and shrubs. William at first thought it was the land of prairies, but Jack said that, if left to nature, it would be forested eventually. "I think this must have been burned off by successive forest fires," Jack Cobb said his thoughts out loud. "Maybe hunting parties of Indians put the torch to it in order to drive the game."

Whether his supposition was true or not, the Barrens were covered with buffalo, elk, and deer. In fact, they saw buffalo in comparatively large numbers for the first time. Once they looked upon a herd of more than a hundred grazing in the rich and open meadows. Panthers, attracted by the quantity of game upon which they could prey, screamed horribly at night, but the flaming campfires of the travelers were sufficient to scare them away.

All these things the frontiersmen saw only in passing. They knew the value of time, and being unsure of how long it might be before the northern Indians decided to attack Larkinboro, or of how long the process of collecting the saltpeter would take, they hastened on to the region of the great caves. Jack Cobb, who was in overall command of the expedition, had asked Jim Hart to be their guide because he had spent several months hunting in the great cave region and knew the area quite well. Hart was a hunter, trapper, and a woodsman who made Larkinboro his occasional home.

"I think there are caves all over, or should I say, *under* this country that the Indians call Kaintuckee," he declared, "but down in this part, they're the biggest I've ever seen. . .uh, the caves, not the Indians."

"I know the caves are there," Jack agreed. "I've been through that region before. The thing that I want to know is whether this saltpeter dirt will be there."

"We'll find it and plenty of it," replied Mr. Spebbington confidently. "That sample that I examined was full of niter, and when we leach it in our tubs, we shall have genuine saltpeter, the explosive dust that is the first ingredient for making gunpowder."

They passed on through the Barrens and entered a region of high, rough hills and narrow, little valleys. The hills and valleys alike were densely clothed with forest. Hart pointed to several large holes in the sides of the hills, always at or near the base, and said they were the mouths of caves. "But the big one in which I got the peter dirt is farther on," he said.

They came to the place he had in mind just as twilight was falling. In the middle of a small valley surrounded by thick forest, Hart led them into the woods on their right. They traveled nearly a quarter of a mile until they came to a place where the ground had formed a large, sunken area. Water dripping from moss-covered rocks fell into a gaping hole in the bottom of the depression. William and Asa looked curiously at the black mouth, and they felt some tremors at the knowledge that they were to go in there and remain inside the earth for a long time, shut from the light of day. It was the dark unknown, not the fear of anything visible that frightened them.

The travelers made no attempt to enter that evening, although night would be the same as day in the cave. Instead they made a comfortable camp because the horses and a couple of guards would have to remain outside. The valley itself was an excellent place, containing lush grass for grazing. At the far end was a little stream flowing out of the hill and trickling away through a cleft into another and slightly lower valley. After tethering the horses, they built a fire near the cave mouth and sat down to cook, eat, rest, and talk.

125

"Ain't there danger from bad air in there?" asked Jack. "I've heard tell that, sometimes in the ground, air will blow all up when fire is touched to it, just like a bar'l o' gunpowder."

"Well, I've been in thar before with a torch, an' I didn't get blowed up," Hart answered. "Tha air's fine when ya' first go in. It gets a mite musty when ya' go back a ways, but we won't have to go in too far. It'll be better in thar than it'll be out here, 'cuz durin' tha day when it gets hot out here, it'll be nice an' cool in thar."

"That's true," said the master meditatively. "Most caves have fresh, pure air. Although where there are a large number of active bats, there will be a strong odor."

That night they found a large, fallen pine tree and cut long torches from the resinous heartwood. Early the next morning all except two, who were left to guard the horses, entered the cave. Since he had been there before, Jim Hart, a fearless man with an inquiring mind, led them into the dark cavern. Everyone carried a torch as they followed their guide down the rocky, damp slope and into the mouth of the cave. Once inside they came to a perfectly dry passage, all the time breathing delightfully cool and fresh air.

After walking for a few minutes, Asa and Will looked back. They had come far enough into the cavern that the light of day from the cave mouth could no longer reach them. As they viewed the way they had come, all they saw was thick blackness. Before them where the light of the torches didn't reach was the same black wall, and they found themselves in a small island of light. With each step they took, the huge cave continued to open up before them as if it were a vaulted, subterranean gallery hewn out of stone by the hands of many giants!

William held up his torch, and from the roof twenty feet above his head, he saw thousands of tiny, glittering flashes of light. "Are those jewels?" he gasped as he pointed above him.

"They look like it, don't they?" Mr. Spebbington chuckled. "They are actually minerals that have formed into crystals along the cave's ceiling."

Asa's eyes followed Will's, and the gleaming roof fascinated him. "Why, it's all a great, underground palace!" he exclaimed.

Hart heard the boy's enthusiastic words and smiled. "Come here, Asa," he said, "I want to show you somethin'."

When the youth arrived at his side, Hart swung the light of his torch into a dark opening.

"I see some dim shapes lying on the floor in there, but I can't tell exactly what they are," said Asa.

"Take a look inside," Hart prompted, lifting the torch so that its light revealed the contents of the room.

"*AIIIII!*" Asa cried and leaped backward, almost knocking William down.

"*Hee, hee, hee!*" Jim Hart chuckled. "Yep, that's about the same reaction I had the first time I stepped in thar."

They each took turns looking and discovered three figures long dead, lying in solemn repose. When Asa calmed down enough to view the crypt once more, he saw the dark, withered faces of Indians that seemed to him a thousand years old.

"God only knows how long they've been a-layin' here where their friends brought 'em for burial," Hart said after they all had viewed the bodies. "See the bows an' arrows beside 'em? They ain't like any that the Indians use now. If'n you look close, you can tell they're made different."

"And the cool, dry air in this part of the cave has preserved them for hundreds of years," said the schoolmaster beside them.

"Y'er right," agreed Dirt when he stepped in the crypt. "Their dress and weapons don't look like those of any Indians I've seen."

"I'm for stepping out of here and leaving them just as they are," said Asa.

"O' course," Hart returned, "it wouldn't be right to disturb 'em. I jus' thought that it'd be interestin' to introduce 'em to you. *Hee, hee, hee!* It wuz!"

Exiting the tomb, they went deeper into the cave and found that, the farther they traveled, the more beautiful and grand it became. The walls glittered with the light of the torches. The ceiling rose higher and became a great, vaulted dome with fantastic formations hanging down. From the floor equally fantastic stalagmites shot up to meet the stalactites. Water slowly fell drop by drop from the point of the one upon the tip of the other.

"This dripping has been going on for thousands of years," said the schoolmaster, "and the same drop of water that leaves some of its substance to create the stalactite hanging from the roof goes on to form the stalagmite jutting up from the floor. They grow faster or slower over time, depending on how quickly the water flows. Look over here, Asa, there's a seat for you. Sit here and rest a bit."

Beside them was a rock formation that looked almost like a chair, and Asa plopped down and found it adequate, but a little harder and a little colder than he preferred. They paused only a moment and passed on, devoting their attention to the cave dust that was getting thicker under their feet.

Scooping up a handful of it, the school master studied it carefully by the close light of his torch. He held it close to his face and sniffed the dust. "*HA!*" he exclaimed exultantly. "It's the genuine article, my friends! You can smell the niter!"

"You are sure of it, Scholar?" asked Jack Cobb anxiously.

"Sure of it?" Mr. Spebbington replied. "Why, I *know* it! Look at how much peter dust is lying on the floor of this cavern. If we stayed here long enough, we could make a thousand barrels of saltpeter and, with that, make all of the gunpowder we will ever need."

Cobb breathed a deep sigh of relief. He had had his doubts to the last, and none knew better than he how much depended on the correctness of the schoolmaster's assertion. "There seems to be acres of dirt covering the floor of this huge cavern," Jack observed. "Based on what you jus' said, I reckon there's nothin' left to do but start makin' saltpeter."

They went no farther for the present, but began scooping the dirt with spades, loading it into sacks, then carrying them to the mouth of the cave. At the scholar's direction, they leached the dust by putting it in wooden tubs and pouring water over it. Stirring the mix until the niter dissolved into the water, the solution was then strained through a piece of cloth into a large copper pot. The liquid was boiled off, and what was left was saltpeter. Mixing it with sulfur and charcoal would produce gunpowder, without which no settlement in Kentucky could exist.

The little valley became a scene of great activity. Fires always burned, and sack after sack of saltpeter was laid safely away in a dry place. William and Asa worked hard along with the others, but they never passed the crypt containing the mummies without a little shudder.

During one of their times of rest, the two inquisitive boys decided that they wanted to explore the cave. When they asked Jim Hart about doing so, he wanted to talk to them. Jim began telling them about the first time he went through the cave and some of the things he did. As he continued to talk, Will's mind began to wander. Maybe it was one of Jim's facial expressions, or maybe it was the way his voice reminded the boy of his abusive father's, but as Jim talked about the cave, all Will heard was his abusive father's mocking words.

You're wrong, Father! the troubled boy argued in his mind. *You said I was no good and would never amount to anything. Well, look at me now! I'm here with the men of my village on an important mission. And I'm doing my part! I'm not worthless! I'm responsible. Jim Hart, Jack Cobb, and Dirt Gurley say so! Now Asa and I are going by ourselves to explore this cave! You're wrong! You're wrong!"*

Just about then Will heard Asa say, "Thanks, Mr. Hart! We will!"

Glad to be on their own, the boys each grabbed a torch and walked deeper into the mysterious cavern. With a new and more serious view of his responsibility, William led the way, taking his time at every new twist and turn in the cave's tunnels. He noticed that Asa seemed to be lagging behind. "Hurry, slow poke!" William called back.

Asa hastened to catch up, and off they went again. After several more minutes, William lost track of Asa once more and spotted his torch almost a stone's throw behind. "Whit!" William called, this time more firmly. "We need to stay together!"

Once again his friend hurried to catch up. As Will led them deeper, the passageway they followed narrowed into a tunnel that was just tall enough for them to stand in. Eventually it opened into another large room. They hadn't walked far when William gave a little gasp of fear and came to a sudden stop. Not five feet in front of them appeared the mouth of a great, perpendicular well. It was nearly round, about ten feet across, and when the boys held their torches over the edge, they could not see the bottom. Will shouted down the hole, but only a dull, distant echo came back. "We'll call that the Bottomless Pit," he said with a nervous little laugh.

"Bottomless or not, it's a good thing to keep out of," said Asa. "It gives me the shudders. To be honest with you, I'm starting to get nervous about this. I've done about all the cave exploring I want to do. Why don't we head back?"

With a nod of agreement, William turned and began leading them back the way they had come. Reaching the end of the room they had entered, he suddenly stopped. Three separate passages exited the room, and William had no idea which one led back to their friends. He stood staring at the three openings as panic began to build. *You no good kid! Just look at the mess you've gotten into now! Not only have you gotten yourself lost, you've gotten Asa lost with you—the person you were supposed to protect. You really are worthless! You're worse than worthless! You're so far back in this cave, nobody can hear you. Now you and your friend are going to die in here, and it will be your fault. . .your fault. . .YOUR FAULT!*

The old voices beat him mercilessly. Suddenly Asa pushed past him and started into the opening on the far right.

"WHIT, WAIT!" Will cried in a panic. "We can't just wander around in here, or we'll never get out!"

"I'm not wandering around," his friend answered casually. "I'm going back to the entrance."

"NO, WAIT!" Will yelled as Asa once again started into the passage. "How can we be sure this is the way out?"

"Because I've been doing what Jim Hart told us to do. Weren't you listening to him?"

"Well," William answered sheepishly, "I guess I wasn't. What did he say?"

"He said that, to keep from getting lost, we needed to stop every few feet and look behind us because a cave always looks different when you look backward than when you look at it forward. That way we can recognize the rock formations when we retrace our steps. That's what I've been doing."

"That's why you've been lagging behind," Will said, finally understanding.

"Yep," Asa answered, "and that's why I know this is the way out." Turning, the younger boy marched confidently through the right hand passage, and a much humbler William followed. Will didn't notice much of the cave on the way out. He spent most of his time thanking God for His faithfulness and for Asa.

As it turned out, saltpeter-making did not give them any more opportunities to go exploring, and both lads were content with what they had already seen. The cave had many wonders, but the sunshine outside was glorious, and the vast panorama of green forest was very restful to the eyes. There was hunting to be done too, and in this William bore a good part. He and Jack or Dirt went regularly into the woods to supply the fresh meat for their meals.

A large creek flowed less than a mile away, and Asa volunteered himself to be chief fisherman, bringing them quite a few large fish that turned out to be delicious when smoked over the fire.

When not hunting, Jack Cobb and Dirt Gurley spent most of their time roaming far through the woods, searching for signs of Indians. They returned from their most recent scouting trip, and Mr. Spebbington was one of the first to meet them. "Are we still safe from the savages, gentlemen?"

"We saw nothing to be concerned about, Scholar," Jack answered with a reassuring smile.

"That's right, Perfesser," Dirt added with confidence. "Yer as safe as in yer mommy's arms."

"How about that other item I asked you gentlemen to look for?" Mr. Spebbington asked again.

In answer to this question, Jack reached into the pouch at his side and pulled out a shiny black rock. "Is this what you wanted?"

When he saw the stone, the scholar's eyes got large, and he gave a little gasp. Snatching the offered prize, he looked closely at its surface. Then he held the rock closely to his nose and inhaled deeply. "Bless my soul!" he finally exclaimed. "This might be it!"

Quickly the teacher knelt beside the fire and held a corner of the stone in its heat. In a moment he noticed a blue flame roll across its surface and go out. Once again he smelled the now burned surface of the rock. A broad smile began spreading across the scholar's very round face. "How much of this is there?" he asked excitedly.

"Over the years the rains have exposed a huge ledge of the stuff," Cobb answered. "It's about as tall as three men and over a hundred paces long."

"Is it easy to get to?"

"Why, Perfesser," Dirt spoke up, "You could walk right up an' kiss it if'n ya wanted to."

"CAPITAL, MY LADS!" Mr. Spebbington exclaimed, rubbing his hands together vigorously. "CAPITAL INDEED!

When the work at the cave was finished, everything was packed up, and Jack led them half a day's journey to the eroded area on a hillside where a large vein of coal had revealed itself.

"What are we doing here?" William asked as he and Asa stood beside the schoolmaster.

"Follow me," Mr Spebbington said excitedly as he led them to stand beside the wide layer of black mineral.

"*AH HA!*" the master exclaimed as he closely examined the surface of the coal. "I was hoping for this. Do you see that layer of yellow crystals covering the face of the black rocks? The rain, which our heavenly Father used to expose this vast amount of coal for us, has also leached out some of the sulfur contained inside, and it has formed this delightful layer of crystals over the rocks' surface. All we have to do is scrape it off, and we will have plenty of the second ingredient for our gunpowder."

"Then all we will need is charcoal," Asa added excitedly, "and we can make plenty of that at home!"

"Precisely!" the schoolmaster agreed, smiling at the young scholar.

As Jack and Dirt scouted the area for signs of enemies, the rest diligently worked to fill the remaining sacks with sulfur crystals. Again the scouts found no evidence of Indians in the surrounding forest. After several more days of industrious labor, the sulfur had been gathered in sufficient amounts. When the sacks that were filled with saltpeter and sulfur were loaded on the pack horses, the group set out for home. Everything had gone much better than any of them had expected, and all of them were eager to return safely with their treasures.

Upon their arrival at Larkinboro, Mr. Spebbington wasted no time in organizing the production of the desperately needed gunpowder, and he had plenty of volunteers to help. The scholar put Asa in charge of slow-burning the wood to make charcoal while he directed the actual mixing of the final product. In a short time the barrels of black powder that had been almost empty began to be refilled, giving a great sense of relief to everyone. With the successful completion of the schoolmaster's brilliant idea, the people now felt that they could hold their village against even a strongly sustained attack.

The learned scholar had shown them how to make gunpowder, which was almost as necessary to them as the air they breathed. Not only that, they knew where they could always get the materials needed for making more of it. Knowledge was truly a great thing to have, and they respected it. As a show of their extreme gratitude for what Charles Spebbington had done, almost every family in Larkinboro invited the scholar for a special dinner to express their thanks to him personally.

"*Gaff, gaff, gaff!*" the scholar chuckled to Asa and William one day as he sat in his chair, patting his protruding paunch. "What a reward! I have never eaten so many fine meals in a row in all my life! I've feasted every night for two weeks, and there's more to come! I'm telling you boys, this is worth more to me than a chest of gold!

Chapter Thirteen

A SHEEP IN WOLF'S CLOTHING

As the ground warmed and the first seeds that had been planted in hope pushed their leaves out of the soil, an atmosphere of excited anticipation spread through the little frontier town. The settlement's entire future depended on the success of their crops, and close observation of the emerging plants was accompanied by a lot of prayer. While there was obvious concern, the settlers were confident. All their lives had been spent close to the soil, and they knew what good ground looked like. When they came over the mountains searching for land richer than any they had tilled before, they all believed that they had found it in this little valley. They had seen the blackness of the dirt and, digging down with the spade, had tested its depth. For thousands of years, vegetation falling upon the soil had decayed and increased the land's fertility, so each of them eagerly anticipated the first crop.

The young green shoots of the wheat were the first to break the ground, and everyone in Larkinboro old enough to know the importance of their appearance went out to examine them. Mr. Hackett, Mr. Middlebrook, and Mr. Spebbington held a serious discussion about what they found, and the final verdict was given by the schoolmaster. "The stalks are at least a third heavier than those in Maryland or Virginia at the same age," he said, "and we can fairly infer that the grain will show the same proportion of increase. I take a third as a most conservative estimate; it is really

134

nearer a half. If the Lord blesses us with rain and good weather, Larkinboro can count on twenty-five bushels of wheat to the acre, and it is likely to go higher."

This news was received by the citizens of Larkinboro with a great deal of excitement and thanksgiving.

"Did you hear, Will? Did you hear?" Kate exclaimed with wide eyes as she bounced up and down uncontrollably. "The wheat is better than any we've ever had back East!"

"It sure looks like it," William returned.

"And aren't they just the cutest things!" Gardenia gushed as she bounced beside Kate.

Will, Asa, and Kate turned to look at their friend with expressions of confusion. "What are you talking about, Gardenia?" Asa asked what they were all thinking.

"Why, the baby wheat, of course. They look so cute, poking their little heads out of the ground and waving at everybody."

"It's just wheat," Will added. "It's not like they're people."

"To other plants they are!" Gardenia said defensively. "I know all about plants and where they come from. My momma told me about it."

"So where did she say they come from?" Asa asked guardedly.

"Oh, well, first there's a momma wheat and a daddy wheat and then. . ."

"HOLD IT!" Kate said, her face turning red. "Gardenia, I don't think your mother was talking about wheat!"

"Actually. . .she wasn't," Gardenia answered. "But I figure it's basically the same thing."

"I think you had better go back and talk to your mother again," William advised. Kate and Asa vigorously nodded their agreement.

When the ground was nice and warm, it was time to plant corn, which was to be one of their chief crops. The settlers began to cultivate the land they had cleared the autumn before. Their handmade plows were crude, made of strong, heavy wood, and finished with a single iron point.

Doing his share of the plowing, Will Hackett's body became sore from head to foot as his plow point repeatedly slammed into roots in the virgin soil. When the spring advanced and the sun grew hotter, he looked longingly at the shade of the forest and thought of the deep, cool pools with silver fish leaping up and of the stags with large antlers coming down to drink. About that time Will's plow point would run into another root, slamming the wooden frame back into his hip, painfully prompting him to stay focused on his task.

In addition to clearing land for fields, the men plowed the space close around the fort for the vegetable and herb gardens the women and girls wanted to plant. When the heavy work of planting and cultivating was over, the long wait for the harvest began.

The weather that summer seemed to be especially blessed. The heat wasn't oppressive, and rains came at just the right times. All that the pioneers planted burst from the ground in abundance. The soil, so kind to the wheat, was equally so to the corn and the gardens. William surveyed with pride the field of corn he had cultivated himself, in which the stalks were now almost a foot high, looking in the distance like a green veil spread over the earth. His satisfaction was shared by all the villagers. Each one felt confident about their future in this place.

Just after planting, a small group of scouts had arrived at Larkinboro, sent by General George Rogers Clark. The general was recruiting an army to bring into the western territory to defend the settlements against the British use of the Indian tribes. The commander sent a message to the village leaders, asking them to send out scouting parties to explore the land around them in order to prepare maps for him to use. The pioneers at Larkinboro already knew a lot about the land to the north and the south of their fort, so the leaders decided that it was important to learn what the territory was like to the west. In order to acquire that information, a small expedition was organized to explore. It would be the scholar's job, with Asa's help, to gather enough knowledge about the unknown area to draw reliable maps when they returned.

Since his strength wasn't going to be needed until ingathering, William was given permission to go on a special scouting trip to the Mississippi. In the party were Jack Cobb, Dirt Gurley, the schoolmaster, Will, and Asa.

Larkinboro had no civilized neighbor near, and all the settlements lay to the south or east. Beyond them, across the Ohio, was a formidable host of Indian tribes, the terror of which always overhung the settlers. West of them was a vast waste of forest spreading away far beyond the Mississippi and inhabited, it was supposed, by wild animals.

Each member of the party of explorers carried a rifle, a hunting knife, and ammunition. Both scouts also carried steel-headed tomahawks tucked in their belts. In addition, they led three pack horses bearing more ammunition, their ground meal, jerked venison, and buffalo meat. This small group expected to live off the land but took the extra food stores as a precaution.

They started early one bright summer morning, and almost immediately William found all his old love of the wilderness returning. He was really looking forward to the trip because it wasn't to be a short trek. They could be gone perhaps two months and would pass through regions wholly unknown. Even though he had worked long and hard plowing, William felt that this holiday more than made up for it.

When the explorers set out, it required but a few minutes to pass through the cleared ground and the new fields and reach the forest. As they looked back, they saw what a slight impression they had made on the wilderness. Larkinboro was but a bit of human life, nothing more than a tiny island of civilization in a vast sea of trees.

Five minutes more of walking, and both Larkinboro and the newly opened country around it were lost to view. They saw only the spire of smoke rising high until it trailed off to the south with the wind, where it lay like a whiplash across the sky. It too was soon lost as they traveled further. Then they were alone in the wilderness.

"Since we were able to survive in the woods without arms or ammunition, it's not likely that we'll suffer now, is it?" asked Asa.

"Suffer!" exclaimed Will. "Whit, you couldn't pay me to miss this trip."

"It ought to be enjoyable, lads," said Mr. Spebbington with a straight face, "unless, of course, our relatives find it necessary to send into the northwest and try to buy back our scalps from the Indian tribes." As soon as he said this, the scholar started his peculiar laugh that sounded like someone coughing, "*Gaff gaff gaff gaff. . .*"

William smiled more at his friend's bouncing double chin than at the joke. Asa could see nothing funny in the scholar's comment.

They camped that night about fifteen miles west of Larkinboro under the shadow of a great, overhanging rock where they cooked squirrels that Dirt had shot out of a nearby tall tree. The schoolmaster upon this occasion elected himself cook. "It is widely thought," he said when he asserted his place, "that a man of books is of no practical use in the world. I hereby intend to give a living demonstration to the contrary."

Jack built the fire, and while the schoolmaster set himself to his task, Will and Asa took their fish hooks and lines and went down to the creek that flowed nearby. It was so easy to catch perch and sun fish that there was no sport in it, and as soon as they had enough for supper and breakfast, they went back to the camp where the delicious smells that arose indicated the truth of the schoolmaster's claim. The squirrels were done to a golden brown, and no doubt of his ability remained.

"Ahhh!" sighed the scholar as he savored the aroma of his creation. "There you have it my good friends. . .Squirrel ala Spebbington."

"Land o' Goshen, Perfesser!" Dirt exclaimed impatiently. "Quit sniffin' 'em an' serve 'em up! I'm about to drown in my own slobber over here!"

When the friends had finished their tasty supper, they made themselves beds of leaves and tender branches under the shadow of the rock where the horses were tethered. The two tired boys sank into dreamless sleep until the schoolmaster woke them the next morning.

That day they marched into magnificent woods with mighty oak, hickory, and beech trees so ancient and a canopy of leaves above so thick that the forest floor was almost clear of undergrowth. As they passed through, it was like walking under the lofty roof of an immense cathedral. The large masses of foliage met overhead and shut out the sun, making the space beneath dim and shadowy.

William remarked to Asa as they walked along that he was glad that they had not built Larkinboro here. "Can you imagine what it would take to cut down these massive trees and then try to clear this land to plow?"

Asa's mouth dropped open at the thought, and all he could say in response was, "Oh, my!"

After they passed out of the great forest, they entered the widest stretch of open country that they had yet seen in Kentucky. The thick grass of the vast area was only broken by occasional patches of brush and shrubs. Whatever caused the great prairie, animals certainly appreciated it. Because of recent rains, the grass was fresh, green, and thick everywhere. Climbing a low hill and looking across the plain, the explorers saw buffalo, elk, and common deer grazing or browsing on the bushes.

Retreating into the edge of the woods, the friends found a clear spot under the spreading limbs of a massive oak to make their camp. Just as they lowered their packs, Dirt made an announcement, "Bein's that there's more game out on that grassy plain than you can shake a stick at, I propose that we send Asa out there all by his lonesome self to bring back supper."

"You can do it, Whit!" William cheered his friend.

Jack smiled and nodded at his young friend.

"Get us a nice, fat deer, Asa!" Mr. Spebbington said excitedly, rubbing his hands together.

"Well. . .okay," Asa answered reluctantly as he hefted his rifle and began walking in the direction of the grassland. "I'll do my best."

"An' don't be draggin' in no puny runt," Dirt ordered. "Bring us back a man-size critter."

With a nod of his head, Asa walked away.

After Asa disappeared, Dirt giggled and began digging through his pack.

"Alright, Dirt, let's have it," Jack said firmly. "You've got somethin' goin' on. I've seen that look on your face before."

"*Hee, hee, hee!*" Dirt chuckled. "I've been waitin' two whole months to do this." From his pack the scout pulled out a bundle of grey fur. When he unrolled it and shook it out, everyone could see that it was a large wolf skin.

"I kilt this critter three months ago. It took me two days, but I skint out the whole beast. . .head, ears, legs, and tail." Dirt draped the skin over his head and stood looking out the space where the eyes had been, appearing very much like a wolf. "*Hee, hee, hee!*" Dirt giggled again. "While Asa's out there huntin, I'm gonna slip up behind him an' scare the liver out of him!"

"Dirt, have you lost your mind?" Jack said with a roll of his eyes. "You're gonna get yourself shot!"

"No, I ain't," Dirt said defensively from under the skin. "I've done thunk this out. I'm gonna hide in the grass until he fires at somethin', THEN I'll slip up on him. *Hee, hee, hee!* I'm gonna give that kid an adventure he'll never forget! *Hee, hee, hee!*"

As the giggling scout began to sneak after Asa, he stopped and turned to the others. "*Hee, hee, hee!* I'm a sheep in wolf's clothing. *Hee, hee, hee!*"

After Dirt reached the edge of the woods that opened up onto the vast meadow, he searched until he spotted his young friend slipping through the tall grass further ahead. Bending low and still giggling, the scout in his disguise slipped stealthily through the weeds, stalking Asa. Dirt went on for several minutes until he noticed that the youth had stopped and intently watched something in front of him. The prankster couldn't tell what it was, but it absorbed his victim's attention, allowing the scout to creep nearer. When he thought he was close enough to spring his surprise, Dirt squatted down in the grass to stay hidden until the right moment.

Unaware of what was happening behind him, Asa was fascinated by a dramatic battle taking place a short distance in front of him. In a slight depression two huge bull elks were in a fierce battle. They threw their great bodies and massive racks into each other again and again, neither giving an inch. The smaller of the two was getting the worst of it, and Asa began to feel sorry for him. With a sudden impulse Asa raised his rifle and fired. For several more long seconds, they fought on, oblivious to the noise of the blast. Then suddenly, the larger of the two collapsed, shot through the heart.

"You're welcome!" Asa called cheerfully to the surviving bull.

With a trumpeting bellow, the remaining elk snorted angrily at Asa, stomped the ground, and charged.

With wide, terrified eyes, the young hunter gave a cry of panic and sprinted back the way he had come.

As Dirt in his wolf suit prepared to spring his surprise, he saw Asa suddenly flash past him. The stunned scout quickly rose to his feet, staring at the rapidly retreating youth. "What in the name of Bertha's bunions got into him?" the scout said out loud. Suddenly, a trumpet call blasted from behind. Dirt turned and saw the raging bull elk top the low hill and charge straight for him.

Staring at the rapidly approaching beast, the scout muttered, "Oh, stink!" He then turned and sprinted after the speeding Asa.

As Dirt entered the edge of the woods and raced for their camp, he could hear the snorting and heavy hooves of the great beast thundering behind him. Just in front of him was the low limb of an oak tree on which were perched Jack, Will, and Asa. With his and William's arms reaching down towards him, Jack cried, "JUMP!"

Without slowing down, Dirt ran to the base of the tree and pushed off one of the massive roots, launching himself towards the waiting arms of his friends. The elk arrived as the scout was in midair and lunged at his enemy. Instead of piercing Dirt, the antlers got entangled in the wolf skin. The skin was suddenly jerked from Dirt's head, flipping him in the air. Jack managed to catch one leg and Will quickly grabbed the other to keep their friend from falling back to the ground. The enraged elk bellowed his anger and slung his great rack from side to side, trying to dislodge the hide.

When Jack and Will finally seated Dirt on their limb, the rescued scout took a moment to look around with wild eyes. Finally he asked, "Where's the Perfesser?"

"He refused to try to climb the tree," Will volunteered, "so he's hiding in some brush to the left."

"Are you okay?" Jack asked with a smile.

"That rascal almost had me," Dirt wheezed as he watched the crazed elk charge off through the woods with the skin still caught on his antlers. "There goes my wolf hide." Dirt sighed with disappointment.

Finally looking over and spotting Asa smiling at him, Dirt almost shouted, "WHAT DID YOU DO?"

"Well," Asa began with a twinkle in his eye, "you said you didn't want a puny one. When I spotted that big fellow, I thought I'd bring him back so you could tell me if he was 'man-size' enough."

"Listen here, I'm about as fair-minded as a man can be," Dirt responded, still breathing hard, "'specially when it comes to wantin' to give critters a sportin' chance an' all. But great granny's garters, Asa, next time, shoot them thangs afore you bring 'em into camp!"

Chapter Fourteen

A FAINT SOUND IN THE DARKNESS

For a number of days, their journey west was fairly easy except when they came to rivers. Some of them were too deep to ford, but Jack and Dirt were prepared. Perched upon one of the horses was a stout buffalo hide they had sewn into the shape of a canoe. To actually form a small boat, all that was needed was to construct a framework out of saplings and stretch the skin over it. Two or three trips carried them and all their equipment over the stream while the horses swam behind.

Using their small craft, they managed to cross the Barren River, and many days later they used it to cross the wide Tennessee. Even on a slow moving river, great care had to be taken when using the canoe. It was small enough that, with a load, any careless movement might tip it over, and while they were all good swimmers, the loss of their precious ammunition would be a disaster.

As the explorers continued their journey west, they observed the country changing before them. The hills sank. The streams flowed with a deep, sluggish current and always to the west. Marshes spread out for great distances, and they were thronged with millions of wild fowl. The air grew heavier, hotter, and damper.

"We must be approaching the Mississippi," William remarked as he noticed the changes in their surroundings.

"It can't be far," replied Jack, "'cause we're in low country now."

The wet, marshy ground made traveling much slower. There were so many deep creeks and lagoons to cross and so many marshes to pass around that they could not make many miles in a day. Needing rest, they camped for several days on the highest hill they could find and fished and hunted.

"Storm's a'brewin'," Dirt Gurley announced as he scanned the sky on their second day on the hill.

"Yep," Cobb agreed. "I felt the change."

"There ain't no good shelter about," Dirt added. "It might help our cause if'n we spent today puttin' one together."

Instead of answering, the scout just nodded his agreement.

"Okay, feller's," Dirt called to the others. "Plans have changed a might. There's a big storm headed straight for us, an' there ain't no cave around here we can lay low in. That means that, unless you fellers don't mind gettin' blowed clear to Chinie, me an' Jack figure our best bet is to constructify us some kind a shelter. So let's spread out an' find as many logs and branches as we can. The big ones we'll drag up here with the horses."

The storm appeared to be coming from the southwest, so they decided to build their lodge on the northeast side, just below the brow of their hill. Once enough material had been dragged in, Cobb and Dirt set to work with their tomahawks, trimming branches and notching logs. To save time, the experienced scouts constructed a three sided lean-to, with the open side facing the northeast. Limbs woven back and forth across the top formed a strong roof. Dark clouds were rolling in, and the wind was picking up as Dirt called everyone to gather sod to cover the roof. The last of it was just being packed into place when the rain began.

"Here she comes!" Dirt shouted as he stood up from his work on the roof. "Perfesser, have you got all our packs stored in the shelter?"

"William is handing me the last one as we speak," the scholar called back.

Rain drops and bits of blown debris hit the scout in the back as he jumped off the roof and ducked into the opening of the lean-to, joining his companions. Not seeing Cobb or Asa in the lodge, Dirt looked out and saw the two missing explorers running up the hill through a heavy rain.

"*Hee, hee, heeeee!*" Dirt laughed loudly at the two. "You took yer own sweet time picketing the horses, an' now you're gettin' soaked. RUN, RUUUN. . .*he, he, heeee!*"

With a soggy thud Asa and Cobb dove into the opening. Jack took an extra step to make sure he landed on top of Dirt.

"Get off me, you wet swamp rat!" the scout cried as he shoved his snickering friend to the side.

"It's a good thing we built this when we did," William observed as he viewed the downpour through the lodge opening. "Look at all that rain! You can't even see the woods at the bottom of the hill anymore!"

"Well, it looks like ol' Dirt come through again," the scout said pompously as he hooked his thumbs under his armpits. "All a' you poor ducks are jus' fortunate that yers truly decided to make this here trip with you. I pity to think what you rascals would look like if. . .HEY!"

Jack Cobb chose this moment to throw his sopping wet form back on top of his mouthy friend.

"GET YOUR SMELLY CARCASS OFF A ME, YOU WORTHLESS, WET POLECAT!"

The fierce storm continued most of the day, flooding the country and swelling all the creeks and lagoons. The friends were in no hurry, so it was decided to stay put until the sun dried out the land again. The break would also allow their horses to rest up after so long a journey carrying the packs.

When it was finally dry enough to travel, the friends renewed their westward march. Two days later they stood on the low banks of the Mississippi and looked at its vast yellow current flowing in a mile-wide channel. It was not beautiful; it was not even picturesque. But its size, its loneliness, and its desolation gave it a somber grandeur that all the travelers felt.

"We know where it goes to, for the sea receives them all," said Mr. Spebbington, "but no man knows from where it comes."

"And to find out the answer to that question, Perfesser, would take a mighty long trip," said Dirt.

"Yes, indeed," agreed the scholar, "and while I would greatly desire to obtain that knowledge, the acquiring of it would too greatly tax the extent of our originally proposed strategy."

"Uh. . .yeah," agreed a confused Dirt, "an' besides, we ain't got the time to make a trip like that."

"I believe that's what I said," huffed Mr. Spebbington.

"Well, I guess I'll jus' have to take your word on that, Perfesser," Dirt said, smiling as he turned and walked over to check on the horses. As the scout passed William and Asa, they heard him mumble to himself, ". . .got no idear *what* you said. . ."

They followed the banks of the great river to the north for many days, sweltering in the heat and humidity. At last they reached a wide expanse of low country overgrown with bushes and cut with a broad yellow band coming down from the northeast.

"The Ohio River!" Jack Cobb announced to the rest of the group. "The Indians call this the Beautiful River, although it don't look so beautiful right now since the rains have filled it full of runoff mud."

"So this is where the Ohio joins the Great Mississippi!" Asa said with awe. "I never thought I'd see all this."

"Few civilized people have," agreed Cobb.

"We are all getting quite an education on this trip," the scholar spoke up. "Asa, are you keeping up with your journal as I asked you to?"

"Yes, sir," the boy answered quickly. "I write in it every evening."

"Excellent!" Mr. Spebbington returned. "It is imperative that we return with accurate descriptions of all we've seen."

They made a camp on a hill overlooking the rivers, and while Asa and the scholar explored and documented the land close around them, the two scouts took Will with them in the canoe to look at the area on the other side of both rivers.

Jack and Dirt were constantly impressed with how quickly William picked up insights and understanding of the natural world. The lad was always watching, observing, and studying what was happening around them. It seemed to the two seasoned scouts that the woods seemed to unfold their secrets to him. With the experience he was gaining on the trip, William was becoming as skillful with the canoe as either the guide or Dirt. Both scouts taught the boy everything they knew about tracking, and William absorbed their instruction like a sponge.

He was in his element and wanted to understand it thoroughly. William was actually disappointed when Jack announced that they needed to paddle back across the river and rejoin their friends. They faithfully reported to the scholar and Asa all they had seen so that it could be recorded in their journals.

The night was cold that evening, but the circling wall of trees provided shelter, and the fire radiated a gratifying heat that warmed them. Mr. Spebbington sat with his back to a log, keeping watch over the camp while Asa, Dirt, and Jack dozed. But the scholar's mind was far away as he dreamily stared into the fire.

William neither slept nor wished to do so. His gaze shifted from the red coals to the bright moon in the sky. The world seemed to him very beautiful and very intimate. These limitless expanses of forest seemed peaceful. It was here in the wilderness that his mind was at rest. The horrible, accusing, and condemning voices seemed far away at the moment.

The scholar, despite his best efforts, began to nod, then he too soon fell fast asleep. Will alone was awake, enjoying the beauty of the night and its lonely peace. He strained his ears to hear every sound, listening to the chirp of the crickets and the high-pitched drone of the frogs. There was also the light, airy brush of the leaves swaying in the gentle breeze above his head. Young Hackett recognized the sound of a squirrel as it clawed its way along a limb in the darkness, never seeing it but knowing it was there.

Hours passed, and the boy was yet awake. The firelight died down, and only a few smoldering coals were left. The blackness of the night, coming ever closer and closer, hovered over his companions and hid their faces from him. The great trunks of the trees grew shadowy and dim. Out of the darkness came a sound slight, but one not in harmony with the ordinary noises of the forest. Will's acute senses noticed at once that something was amiss. The peaceful, contented look on his face instantly transformed, and his eyes became alert, watchful, and intent.

For five minutes he lay perfectly still. Then the discordant note among the familiar sounds of the forest came again, and he glanced at his comrades. They slept peacefully. His first thought was to awaken the others to his concerns, but then the voices began: *You don't know what you're doing! You're going to wake your friends from a sound sleep just because you heard a squirrel jump in the leaves. That's exactly what a no-good worthless kid would do. . .completely worthless. . .*

William gritted his teeth against the mental assault. *I am not worthless,* he told himself, and he would prove it. He decided that he would make sure before he woke anyone.

Moving his hand forward, the alert young scout grasped his rifle and powder horn, then very quietly slipped away from the clearing and into the forest. The cautious lad moved not by walking, nor altogether by crawling, but by a curious, almost noiseless, gliding motion that he had practiced and taught himself. He clung to the shadows where his shifting body blended with the dark. All the while his comrades slept by the fire, and even the trained foresters slumbered in peace.

The youth reached the wall of the woods, and his form was completely swallowed up by the blackness. He lay a while in the bushes, motionless, all his senses alert, and for the third time the curious sound came to his ears. The maker of it was on his right and, as he judged, perhaps fifty yards away. Proceeding at once to that point, he determined to identify the source and find out for sure if there was a threat that could endanger the lives of his friends.

Raising his head slightly, his keen eyes could see nothing in the forest save ghostly and shapeless trunks and branches. After a few moments of intent listening, William heard a faint sighing sound on the wind like a distant bird, but he knew that it was not. Convinced that the sound was made by human lips, a light shiver passed over his frame. Realizing that it might be a signal concerning his comrades and himself, he considered returning to warn his companions. But that nagging, accusing voice spoke again. Without considering the consequences, he once more decided that he would identify the threat before alerting the others.

He resumed his cautious passage through the undergrowth. Not a sound marked his advance. The forest fell silently behind him, and he went towards the spot from which the sounds had come. As he crept forward, he reached another opening among the trees, similar to the one where his friends now slept. William lay very low amongst the undergrowth when he spotted for the first time the object of his search. Before him a fearsome group of warriors appeared in the night shadows, some sitting, others standing, and though there was no fire and the moonlight was slight, he could make out the hardness of their faces. At this moment Will thought of his comrades whom he must save. Once again the cruel voices belittled him for wasting so much time and not warning his friends sooner.

The older of the warriors talked in a low voice, saying unknown words in a harsh, guttural tongue, and the young frontiersman could only guess at their meaning. But they seemed to be awaiting a signal, and presently the low, thrilling note was heard again. Then the warriors turned as if this were the command to do so and came directly toward the boy who lay in the darkest shadows of the undergrowth.

William was surprised and startled, but only for a moment. Swiftly he sank away in the bushes in front of them as before, no sound marking his passage. His mind raced for a plan, not for himself, but for what he could do to save his friends.

When he had gone about fifty yards, he put his idea into effect. Shouting at the top of his lungs, he gave a call that was long and full of warning to his friends at the camp. As soon as he finished, he turned to his right and crashed through the undergrowth, purposely making noise that the pursuing warriors could not fail to hear. Cobb and the others, he knew, would be aroused instantly by his cry and would take measures to protect themselves. William recognized that the Indians would understand this as well and therefore would likely give up their surprise attack and pursue him instead. As he stopped to listen, the brave lad heard sounds indicating that the warriors had indeed turned aside and were now on his trail.

At that moment Will's only thought was to get the Indians as far away from his friends as possible. He ran swiftly and directly more than a mile away from his companions' camp. Suddenly he burst out of the forest and found himself standing on the bank of a deep little river flowing straight across his path. He was ready to drop down in its waters but saw that, before the farther shore could be reached, the moonlight would make him a clear target for his pursuers. He hesitated and was about to turn at a sharp angle, but the warriors emerged from the forest. It was too late.

The savages whooped a shout of triumph and charged forward. William was raising his rifle to fire when the swiftest of the warriors hurled themselves upon him in a brown mass. He felt a stunning blow upon the head, sparks flew before his eyes, and the world reeled away into darkness.

Chapter Fifteen

A NEW LIFE

When William began to regain his senses, the first thing
he became aware of was throbbing pain in the side of his head.
With a low moan, he slowly opened his eyes and discovered that
he was lying on the ground with his head propped against a log.
Surrounding him was a circle of brown faces—cold, hard,
expressionless, and seemingly devoid of human feeling. Fully
realizing his situation, the captured youth calmed his heart,
breathed a prayer for courage, and raising his head, met them
with a gaze as steady as their own. Taking a quick glance around
the circle, he saw that there were no other prisoners, and he saw
no scalps. This told him that his comrades had escaped, and with
deep satisfaction in his heart, he eased his sore head back upon
the log.

It wasn't long before Will saw three more warriors glide
silently out of the woods to join them. Taking a better look
around, he saw that he was still near the river on whose banks he
had been struck down. He lifted his bound hands to his head
where it ached and saw blood on his fingers when he took it away.
He concluded that one of the warriors must have hit him with the
flat side of a tomahawk. Remembering the lessons Jack Cobb had
taught him about Indians, William showed no outward sign of
pain but made his face expressionless. One of the warriors,
apparently a chief, watched carefully the captured lad's response,
and he muttered something that seemed to have the note of

approval. Will rose to his feet, and the chief still regarded him, noting the boy's courage and the hint of surpassing physical powers soon to come. Confronting the prisoner, the leader said some words and, tapping Will's chest, pointed toward the north and west. William understood his meaning. His life was to be spared for at least the present, and he was to go with them into the northwest. To what fate he knew not.

One of the braves bathed William's head wound and wrapped it in a poultice of leaves from the feverfew plant, which eventually dulled the pain. The fact that they were taking care of him was proof to Will that he was to be a slave. The youth endured these attentions with indifference, making no comment and showing no interest.

At a word from the leader, they took up their silent march, skirting the river for a while until they came to a wide, shallow place where they forded it and again buried themselves in the dark forest. The Indians passed among its shades swiftly, silently, and in single file, with William near the middle of the column. He had completely recovered his strength and was able to keep up with the warriors with ease. As the captive youth marched along, he offered a sincere prayer of thanks to God for sparing his life and the lives of his friends. He realized that, since God had saved him, it must be for some good, and he determined to submit himself to whatever trial God brought to him. Just then another more interesting thought come to him. It seemed to him that, without any will of his own, he was about to begin the vast wanderings that he had selfishly longed for.

Hour after hour through the night, the silent line of warriors trod swiftly into the northwest, no one speaking, their footfalls making little or no sound on the soft earth. When the moon set, it grew darker, and they had to move more slowly. They kept traveling until, out of the blackness, came the first glow of dawn. A shaft of pale light appeared in the east, bringing in its trail the red and gold of the rising sun.

They continued their journey through the forest in the cold, dawn air. Here and there in the open spaces and on the edges of the brown leaves, the white gleam of frost appeared. But William worked to show no sign of fatigue, and the vigorous march kept him warm. He traveled with a step as easy and as tireless as that of the other warriors in the band, and he kept his head up as if he were one of them, not their prisoner.

About an hour after dawn, the party, numbering fifteen men, halted at a signal from the chief and began to eat dried buffalo meat taken from their pouches. They gave William a good supply of food, and he found it tough but savory. As hungry as he was, anything would have tasted good. As he contentedly ate his meal, he studied his captors with the advantage of daylight. Full sunshine disclosed no more softness or mercy than the night had shown. The features were immobile and the eyes fixed and hard, but when the gaze of any one of them, even the chief's, met the youth's, it was quickly turned away. As William studied the bead patterns of their moccasins and belts, he thought they looked like what Jack had drawn representing the Miami Indians. Seeing these warriors up close did not stir fear in William—instead they interested him.

After eating, they rested for a while. During this time the chief said some words to William, but the lad could understand none of them, and he shook his head. Then the chief took the rifle that had belonged to the captive, tapped it on the barrel, and pointed toward the southeast. Will nodded to indicate that he had come from that point. Next the chief pointed to the young captive and his rifle, then pointed firmly to the northwestern horizon. Remembering more advice that Jack had given him about dealing with Indians, William nodded and held out both of his hands palms up to the chief. He meant to say that he would go with them without resistance, at least for the present, and the chief seemed to understand, as his face relaxed into a look of comprehension and even of good nature.

Resuming their march, they passed out of the forest, crossed the Ohio in hidden canoes, and entered a region of small but beautiful prairies. Along the way they came to several shallow streams that they hurriedly waded. William began to suspect that the band came from some very distant country and was hastening in order not to be caught on the hunting grounds of rival tribes.

The northwesterly direction that they followed confirmed him in this belief.

They continued their hurried march all day. When night finally came, they ate more of the jerked meat and lay down in a thicket. Will was very tired, quickly falling into a sleep that was deep, sweet, and dreamless. He did not know then that, shortly after he slept, the chief took a robe of tanned deerskin and threw it over him, shielding his body from the chill autumn night. In the morning shortly before he awoke, the chief took away the robe.

That day they came to a mighty river, and William knew that the yellow waterway was the Mississippi. The Indians dragged two canoes from the sheltering undergrowth, and the whole party paddled up stream until nightfall. When they landed, they hid the crafts in thick foliage on the western shore and encamped on a crest above the river. They seemed to feel that they were out of danger as they built a fine fire, and the captive basked in its warmth.

William had not made the slightest effort to escape, nor had he indicated any wish to do so, finding his reward in the increased freedom the warriors gave him. The leather straps were removed from his wrists, and he could have walked as he chose in a limited area about the camp. But he did not avail himself of the privilege for the present, preferring to sit by the fire, where he thought of Larkinboro and those whom he loved. Then he had a swift twinge of conscience. When they heard, they would grieve deeply and for a long time, and one, his loving stepmother, would never forget him. He felt that he should have sought more eagerly to escape. Moved by these thoughts, he glanced quickly about him, but there was no chance. However careless the warriors might seem, there was always one between him and the forest. He resigned himself with a sigh. Though the night was bitingly cold, he comforted himself by the warmth of the glorious fire.

William was still sitting when a young Miami warrior walked over and shoved him away. Without a word Will stood up and shoved him back and resumed his original position. The warrior yelled angrily at William, who rose to face him. When the angry Indian saw no emotional response from the muscular youth, he jerked out his tomahawk and advanced threateningly. The warrior paused only a moment, then threw himself at William. Grabbing the Indian by the wrist, the strong youth ducked under his attacker and used his shoulder to launch the warrior over his back and onto the ground. The twisting motion on the Indian's wrist as he flipped allowed William to remain in possession of the tomahawk. All of the Indians grabbed for their weapons when they saw their slave was armed. Still with no expression, William tossed the tomahawk at the feet of the chief and motioned to his opponent that he was ready to continue wrestling. The young Indian whom Will had thrown lay on the ground appraising the captive and rubbing his wrist. Finally he stood up and, with a slight smile, pointed at William and then to the coveted spot beside the fire. The victorious prisoner returned the gesture with a smile of his own and resumed his spot by the fire. The chief, Black Cloud, bestowed on both a look of approval but uttered no comment.

Presently Black Cloud gave orders to his men, and they lay down to sleep, but the chief took the deerskin robe and handed it to William. The young captive received the robe and thanked the chief in words, whose meaning the chief understood by their tone. Then he lay down and slept as before, a dreamless slumber all through the night.

They traveled for several more days before arriving at a fairly large village. William was viewed by all of the Indians as an oddity, but Black Cloud made it clear that their captive was not to be harmed. As stories began to circulate of his courage and boldness, respect for the young captive grew.

The chief took a special interest in William. As he saw the prisoner work hard at his chores and seem content with his life in the village, the youth was given more and more freedom. For Will's part, he relished the opportunity to learn about the Indian culture, and with the quickness of an eager student, he soon picked up enough words of their dialect to make himself understood. Hunting parties took him with them when they made expeditions, and he was permitted now and then to use his own rifle. Only six men in the band had guns, and two of them were rifles, the other four being muskets. William soon showed that he was the best marksman among them, and respect for him grew even more. On one trip the Indian he had knocked down was gored in the side by a wounded stag when only young Hackett was near. The captive slew the stag, bound up the Miami's wound, and stayed by him until the others came. The warrior, Gray Fox, quickly became one of William's best friends.

Hackett's knowledge of forest lore grew rapidly. His new friends taught him how to trail like one of them, to take advantage of every shred of cover, and to make signals by imitating the cry of bird or beast. The universal way to communicate among Indian nations was sign language. William relentlessly pestered Gray Fox until he taught him to sign.

The climate was colder than that from where Will had come, and winter, with fierce winds from the Great Plains, was soon upon them. But the camp, which was to remain in its current place until spring, was well chosen, and the steep hills around it fended off the worst of the blasts. Yet snow came soon in great, whirling flakes. The next morning William saw the world blanketed in white and thought it was absolutely beautiful. He did not mind the snow, as clothing of dressed skins had been given to him, and he had a warm buffalo robe for a blanket. Because of his accuracy with his rifle, he was regularly asked to join the bands of hunters searching the hills for game, and the young captive seldom disappointed them.

His fame in the village grew quickly, and Will found himself enjoying it. The wild, rough life appealed to every instinct in him, and his new fame as a tireless and skillful hunter encouraged him greatly. He thought of his people and Larkinboro, it is true, but he consoled himself again with the belief that they were well and that he would return to them when the opportunity arose.

Meanwhile, his body matured at an impressive rate. Soon there was not a warrior in the village who could match his physical strength. His face darkened in the wind and sun, and his features grew stronger and more masculine. Clothed wholly in deerskin, it would have taken more than a casual glance to discover that he was not an Indian.

The winter deepened. The snow was continuous. Fierce blasts blew in from the distant western plains and even searched out their sheltered valley. Game grew scarce about them, and the hunters went far westward in search of buffalo.

William was with a party that had traveled farthest from camp toward the setting sun, and they were gone for many days. Winter was at its height, and when they came out of the forest into the Great Plains, all things were hidden by the snow.

From the summit of a small hill, William saw before him an expanse as mighty as the sea. His companions told him that it rolled westward, *no man knew how far*, as none of them had ever come to the end of it. In summer it was covered with life. Here the grass grew thick, and buffalo passed in the millions.

The day after their arrival on this wide, snow-covered plain, they were caught in an immense storm of wind and hail. The cold was bitter, and the wind cut to the bone. They were saved from freezing to death only by digging a rude shelter through the snow into the side of a hill. There they were forced to huddle for days with little food left in their knapsacks. Their situation became desperate, and they knew that, if the cold did not get them first, without game they would starve. The most experienced hunters went forth during lulls in the blizzard but returned with nothing, thankful to find their way back to the shelter.

In desperation William turned to God in prayer: "O Great Father in heaven, You know our desperate need. We will all die if we don't find food, and I'm about the only one left strong enough to go look for it. Black Cloud and his tribe have been good to me, and now I ask you in the name of King Jesus to be good to them. Please, Heavenly Father, let me find food where there should be none, that we might live, and show them all that there is a God in heaven."

Taking his rifle, he ventured out alone, the others being too listless to stop him. Before the noon hour he found a lone buffalo bull struggling in the snow. William concluded that he must have been some outcast from a herd that had gone southward. Saying a prayer of deep gratitude to God, the young hunter sent two rifle balls into the great beast. William then cut out a large chunk of meat and hurried back to the others with the life-saving news of his successful hunt. The starving warriors expressed their most sincere gratitude, but the young hunter would not receive any recognition. He made it clear that he had asked the Gitche Manitou, their Father in heaven, and His Son, Great Chief Jesus, for the meat. It was to their heavenly Father and His Son that they must give their thanks.

When the storm ceased, they renewed their journey toward the south with a plentiful supply of food. In a few days they ran into the buffalo herd, a mighty black mass of moving millions. The earth rumbled hollowly under the tread of innumerable feet, and the plain was black with bodies to the horizon and beyond.

They killed as many buffalo as they needed. Then making litters out of poles and buffalo skins, they loaded them with as much meat as they could carry and began the swift journey homeward.

Although a captive, William was regarded in a sense as one of the leaders of the hunting party. The Indians knew that it was the young hunter's skill, courage, and endurance that had saved them all from death, and they each respected him for it. But Will took little interest in their favors. He knew that they were alive only by the grace of God, and with his limited understanding of their language, he set about to explain that fact to them.

When they returned, they found the village at the edge of starvation. Their supply of meat arrived just in time to relieve the crisis. As word of William's part in the hunt spread, he soon perceived that he was a hero to them all, and it made him uncomfortable. He wanted them to understand that it was God who had saved them. William explained to Gray Fox that, before he went out and killed the old buffalo, he had prayed to the Great Spirit to lead him to game.

"The Gitche Manitou listens to you?" Gray Fox questioned suspiciously.

"Why would He not?" Will returned. "He is our heavenly Father."

"How can you call the Manitou *Father*?"

"The Gitchie Manitou, our Heavenly Father, made us all," William answered, "and He loves the children He has made. He has told us this."

"The Great Spirit speaks to your face?" Gray Fox asked again.

"Not to my face, but He spoke to others who marked down the signs of the Heavenly Father's words. We keep these signs and read them to remember what our Heavenly Father's will is. They tell us that the Gitchie Manitou wants to be our Heavenly Father. To prove His love for us, our Heavenly Father sent His Son to walk with us and to show the Father's love for us."

"Who is this One Who is the Son of the Gitchie Manitou?" William's Indian friend asked. "I have not heard of the Manitou's Son."

"He is Great Chief Jesus," William answered in terms Gray Fox could understand.

"Jesus," Gray Fox repeated the name, "and He is a chief?"

"Yes, He is a great chief."

The Indian thought about this for a moment and asked, "Is this Jesus a war chief or a peace chief?"

"He is both," returned Will with a smile.

"How can he be both?" said Gray Fox skeptically. "No man can be war chief *and* peace chief."

"He is the Son of the Gitchie Manitou, Gray Fox. He has the wisdom of a sage, but he also has the heart of a warrior. He is both."

"My brother," Gray Fox probed further, "you said that the Son of the Manitou came to show us His Father's great love for us. How did He do that?"

William was silent for a few moments as he thought how to explain God's grace to his friend. Finally he said, "All of us do things that the Manitou does not like. These bad things are called *sins*, and the Gitchie Manitou is so pure and good and just that He must withdraw Himself and punish these sins. These sins are so bad that He must stand against the ones who commit them. Not only do the sins offend the Manitou, but He wants us to stop them because sins harm us and they harm others. Now, Gray Fox, this is where His great love comes in. He loves His children so much that He sent His Son, Great Chief Jesus, to come to this world and take the punishment for us. Jesus came into our world and told those who walked with Him about the great love of His Heavenly Father. Then with the greatest of courage, He showed how much the Father loves us by letting His enemies put Him to the worst of tortures until He died. In doing this, He took the punishment for our sins so that those who choose to walk with Him will not have to be punished. But that is not the end of the story, Gray Fox. After Jesus had been dead and buried for three days, the Great Spirit gave life back to His Son and brought Him out of the grave. Those who followed Him saw Jesus alive again. The Gitchie Manitou did this to show that those of us who walk with Jesus as our Great Chief will also be raised from the dead when the Manitou's Son returns for us, and we will live forever with Jesus and with the Father in Heaven. He gained victory over our worst enemy—death

"I have chosen to walk with the Great Chief Jesus. That is why I do not fear death. When I die, I will be taken into the presence of the Great Chief where I will stay with Him and with my Father in Heaven."

Gray Fox seemed to understand and was very thoughtful. Eventually the young warrior told William that he would explain the message to the village—that the Great Spirit had given the people of the tribe their lives as a gift, and He had used William to do it.

When the tribe understood that William talked with the Gitchie Manitou and that the Manitou answered him, all of the people felt that the young hunter's presence in their village brought them special protection, and they watched him incessantly, lest he should take it into his head to flee to the people who were once his own. In response to this frustration, Will began to pray for God to show him what he was to do. Trusting that his heavenly Father would faithfully answer his prayer at the proper time, William felt some peace.

Chapter Sixteen

STRANGERS

When the sad scouting party returned home with the news that William had been taken by Indians, the Hackett family and the rest of the village were crushed. Mr. and Mrs. Hackett refused to blame anyone for their son's capture, but Jack Cobb and Dirt Gurley took it especially hard since they both felt responsible for the lad. A few days after they came back, Cobb, carrying his rifle and a loaded pack, walked up to Dirt. "I won't be back for a while," Jack said with no expression.

"You goin' lookin' for Will?" Dirt asked. "With winter comin' on, you know it's gonna be tough."

"I know, but I have to go."

"I understand," Dirt returned. "Can I go with you?"

Jack paused for a moment, looking out of the gate at the forest in the distance. Finally he responded, "I think it'd be best if one of us stays here. . .just to look after things, if you know what I mean."

"Naw, you're right," Dirt agreed. "These are good folks an' all, but they ain't too savvy yet about lookin' out fer Injuns."

"After what happened to Will, I'm beginning to think that I'm not too savvy either," Jack shot back.

"Now listen here, Jack, you cain't blame yerself. You saw as well as I did that, when we scouted that area during the day light, there was no sign that Injuns had come into our camp. There was only his footprints a slippin' away into the woods. Obviously the boy heard somethin' durin' the night, and he went to check it out."

"He should have said something to us!" Jack barked.

"I know, I know," Dirt returned. "He should have! But he's just a kid. . .a really big kid. . .who's smarter'n most folks about woods stuff. He just made a bad decision."

"Yeah," Jack agreed, still agitated, "a bad decision that may have cost him his life!"

"But he saved ours."

"That's what kills me, Dirt!" Jack said through clenched teeth and with fire in his eyes. "We should have been the ones savin' his, not the other way around!"

Dirt Gurley dropped his eyes and nodded his head in agreement. "How long you figure you'll be gone?" Dirt finally asked.

Jack again paused and look toward the forest. "I don't know," he finally answered. "Two, maybe three months. I figure I'll cross the Ohio and scout north."

"Well, if ya go north of the Ohio, ya know ya ain't gonna be walkin' into no villages askin' fer directions," Dirt warned. "We got no friends north of the Ohio! Any Injun up there'll take yer top knot faster'n you can say howdy."

"Don't worry, Dirt," Jack said with a smile, placing his hand on the scout's shoulder, "I plan on keepin' my hair."

"Well, ya better," Dirt said firmly. "Usually ya got me there a watchin' yer back!"

"It'll be alright, partner," Jack returned comfortingly. "We both need me to do this."

"Yeah. . .well. . .I jus' wish I was goin' with ya."

With a smile Jack patted his friend on the back and turned toward the beckoning forest. "I'll see you in a few months," Jack called over his shoulder as he marched purposefully toward the west.

Dirt watched until Jack's form was swallowed by the green of the thick woods in the distance. As the lone scout turned, he caught the eye of Mr. Spebbington approaching the gate. "I saw the scout leaving with his pack," the scholar began. "Where's he off to?"

"Well, Perfesser," he replied with a sigh, "losin' young Will just about kilt Jack. He's done fretted hisself plum sick over it. We never found the boy's carcass, which means that he might have been took as a slave. Anyway, sittin' around here stewin' about it was mor'n Jack could take, an' he's gone off to look fer signs of the boy. He left me here to keep an eye on thangs 'til he gets back. Ol' Jack figures he can move faster an' cover more ground by hisself."

"Do you think he will find the lad?" the scholar asked as he stared at the western woods.

"I'd love for him to, Perfesser! Honest I would. But I don't see it happenin'. To be factical, I figure this trip is more for Jack than it is for Will. I jus' couldn't tell him that."

As days passed, the pain of losing William was dulled by the constant load of hard work that it took to carve a home out of the wilderness. After spring had arrived, on one warm afternoon near sunset, two strangers walked out of the woods and approached the gates of Larkinboro. They wore wide brimmed hats, carried long rifles, and had packs slung on their shoulders.

"What do ya think, Dirt?" one of the guards in the blockhouse above the gate said to the scout as they both studied the approaching travelers.

"Hmmm," Dirt Gurley mused thoughtfully, "I ain't quite shore. They's dressed like trappers, but I don't see no traps. The one on the left carries hisself like a woodsman, but the other one don't."

When the two were quite near, they halted in front of the gate. "Hello the fort!" the one on the right called to the guards.

"Hello, yerself!" Dirt called back from a window of the blockhouse, making no move to open the gate. "Who are you fellers, an' what'cha doin' in our neck o' the woods?"

"My name is Edmond Trask," the man on the right answered, "and this is my companion, Simon Girty. We carry a message to your leaders from the colonial military."

"Should we open the gate?" the guard asked Dirt.

"Well, now, let's be a little bit cautious afore we do that," Dirt returned. "Maybe they's friends an' maybe they ain't. How about

163

we scan that tree line in the distance real careful like, just to be sure there ain't nobody hidin' out there waitin' for us to let down our guard?"

Dirt and the other lookouts stared hard at the woods, looking for any suspicious movement.

"Well, can we come in?" the one named Trask persisted.

After seeing no one else, the order was given to open the gate. Water was drawn from the well, and the travelers were offered as many dippers full as they wanted.

By the time they finished quenching their thirst, Mr. Hackett, Mr. Middlebrook, and several of the other leading men arrived, and introductions were made. When Trask informed them that he had news and an important message from General Clark of the Virginia militia, John Hackett called a young man standing nearby and asked him to tell all the men to assemble in the school house immediately. That announcement spread quickly through the small fort, and within minutes the settlers gathered into the small building that was used both for school and worship.

"What's this message you have for us?" Mr. Hackett asked loudly when everyone had arrived. "And what can you tell us about the war back east?"

Edmond Trask took off his hat and stood before the men. "When we left Williamsburg several weeks ago," Trask answered, "the news was that General Washington and his army occupied the high ground around the city of New York. He was besieging the British troops there. We also heard that a British attack was made on the south. British war ships sailed into the Charleston harbor, but General Charles Lee and his men were able to fight them off and keep them from landing. The last report was that the frustrated British commanders finally ordered their ships to turn around and sail away."

Murmurs of approval were heard around the small room at this news.

"At least for the time being, gentlemen, it sounds like the colonies are holding their own," Trask said with a smile. This was met with nods of agreement.

"And that brings me to the subject of our mission," Trask said, tilting his head toward Girty, who stood expressionless

164

beside him. "At this moment General George Clark is gathering troops in Virginia. When all is ready, he will lead his army into the western wilderness. His goal is drive all the Indian tribes further north before the British can stir them against our frontier towns." More expressions of appreciation and thankfulness could be heard at this announcement.

"When can we expect the troops to arrive?" Mr. Spebbington asked what they were all thinking.

"It will be a few weeks yet," Trask returned. "The general will be waiting for our report in order to complete his plans. Girty and I have been given the task of scouting the Indian tribes throughout the territory and letting General Clark know where he can find them."

"And have you done that?" another voice asked. "Have you identified the locations of many of the tribes?"

A smile slowly spread across Trask's face. "Indeed we have," he returned confidently as he cut a glance at his companion. "I really don't think the general's army is going to have much to do. It seems that rumors have already reached many of the tribes, and they have begun moving their villages to the north...quite rapidly, I might add."

When the settlers looked at Simon Girty for confirmation of this, he simply nodded his head in agreement.

"Ah!" exclaimed Mr. Middlebrook. "Sir, that is the best possible news you could bring us!" Several quickly spoke up in agreement.

"Girty and I thought you'd enjoy hearing that," Trask chuckled. "Every Indian in the territory is running away from you as fast as they can. Since they don't know when the general will actually be coming, they likely won't be back for a while."

"Maybe never," the stoic Girty added.

"Yes, that's right," Trask agreed. "The Indians don't mind coming against a few settlers, but they sure don't want to tangle with an army! This should be the end of your Indian problems for quite some time!"

The atmosphere was quite cheerful at the Middlebrook home that evening where Trask and Girty were welcomed as the guests of honor. Mrs. Middlebrook and her daughters bustled busily around the house, finishing preparations for a special meal of roast goose for the men who had brought them such wonderful news.

As seventeen-year-old Katherine finished setting the table, her fourteen-year-old sister, Grace, brought mugs of warm cider to their guests.

"Why thank you, my dear," Edmond Trask said with a charming smile as he received the mug from Grace. "It's quite an honor for the two of us to be served by such lovely ladies as you and your sister."

With an embarrassed smile the blond haired Grace lowered her blue eyes and took the second mug to Simon Girty.

Girty leaned forward to move closer to the girl and gave her a big, toothy smile. "You know somethin', darlin'?" Girty said, taking the mug from the shy girl. "Yer just about as purdy as a picture. *Hee, hee, hee!*"

Cutting his eyes over to Katherine as she set the plates on the table, he added, "That sister o' yer's is quite a looker too." After saying this, Girty's eyes lingered for some time on the older girl as she moved around the room.

Several times during the meal, Katherine looked up to see Girty staring at her, and it made her very uncomfortable. When the meal was finished, she excused herself early from the table and asked Grace to help her clean the kitchen. She wasn't exactly sure what it was, but she had decided that she didn't want herself or her sister to be anywhere near that man.

The next morning as the two scouts were getting ready, Trask walked up to Silas Middlebrook. "See here, my good fellow, before we leave, I was wondering if I could ask you a favor. Girty and I have been living off the land for some time now, and with all the hunting we've had to do, both of our powder horns are almost empty. Would you be willing to sell us some gun powder to get us safely back home?"

"Of course," Mr. Middlebrook responded confidently. "That's no problem. We have plenty to spare. Come with me."

The scouts were escorted across the courtyard to one of the blockhouses. Once the heavy door to the lower storeroom was opened, the two travelers were led into it. Several barrels rested near the outer wall. Walking to the closest one, Mr. Middlebrook pried open the lid and invited the scouts to look inside. Girty and Trask noted that the large barrel was almost full of black powder.

"There you go, friends," Silas said cheerfully. "Help yourselves to all you need."

As Girty began filling both of their powder horns, Trask took a moment to look around the room. "Are all these barrels gunpowder, Mr. Middlebrook?" the scout asked off-handedly.

"Oh, no," Silas returned. "The barrel beside this one is powder, but the rest contain mostly dry goods, except for those boxes beside the powder barrels. They contain led shot. As you can see, we are more than able to defend ourselves."

"Well, I must admit that you do have a nice supply of powder and shot. That's always good out here on the frontier," Trask returned pleasantly. "But it seems to me that all you're going to need it for is hunting."

"Yes, indeed!" Silas Middlebrook smiled broadly and nodded his head knowingly. "Quite right!"

When Girty had their horns full, Trask drew a pouch from his pocket and pulled out a gold coin, handing this to Mr. Middlebrook. "This should cover the cost of the powder."

"I should say so!" answered Silas as he studied the coin. "I haven't seen one of these in quite some time. How did you come by a British crown?"

"Oh. . .uh. . .before we left, General Clark gave us a purse for our expenses. I assumed it was gold that he must have collected on his last raid," Trask answered.

"Well, as much as we have enjoyed ourselves here, Girty and I must be on our way. The general is waiting for our report, and we have a long way to go. Farewell, friends!"

The whole village turned out to watch the two scouts depart. Trask smiled and waved at the crowd as they marched out the gate. Girty spotted Katherine Middlebrook on the edge of the well-wishers and gave her a long, approving look. As soon as Kate spotted his piercing gaze, she turned quickly and hurried away.

As they watched the two scouts disappear into the forest, Mr. Middlebrook said to the scholar standing beside him, "Now that was some excellent news! All of the Indian tribes are moving away from us."

"Does that mean we won't need as many men on guard duty each night?" the scholar asked hopefully.

"I believe it does," Mr. Middlebrook said with a chuckle. "Are you looking forward to a little more sleep, Scholar?"

"Oh, absolutely, my dear fellow!" Charles Spebbington exclaimed. "Absolutely!"

Chapter Seventeen

THE FIGHT FOR PEACE

Shortly after William was brought to the tribe, Black Cloud called him *Otoahnocto,* or Bull Bear, because he was so strong as a young man. But later, when he revealed his superior hunting skills, Will was given the name *Kajika,* or Walks Without Sound.

After the harsh winter had ended, a time of blessing seemed to come to the village. The spring leaped suddenly into full bloom, and the woods began to swarm with game. It was the most plentiful season that even the oldest man in the tribe could recall. There was no hunter so lazy or so slow that he could not find buffalo and deer.

It was then that the band decided to take down its lodges and travel slowly into the north, farther and farther from the little settlement down in Kentucky, much to William's frustration. At that time there was peace among the tribes, and they could go where they chose. They came at last to the shores of a mighty lake called Superior, and when William looked out upon an expanse of water as limitless to the eyes as the sea, he felt the same thrill of awe that had passed through his veins when the Great Plains lay outspread before him.

As it was now midsummer and the dry forests crackled in the heat, they lingered long by the deep, cool waters of the lake.

On a particularly hot day, Will, Gray Fox, and several others were trying to spear fish while wading in the lake. William stepped up beside the unsuspecting Gray Fox and shoved him good-naturedly into the deeper water. The Indian came up, thrashing in a panic. When Will realized that his friend could not swim, he quickly dove in and pulled him closer to shore.

"Gray Fox," Will said with emotion, "I am so sorry! I never meant to hurt you. I thought you could swim."

"We are Miami, not fish!" Gray Fox shot back. "If the Gitche Manitou wanted the Miami to swim, He would have given us fins and a tail."

"He gave you arms and legs," Will returned. "Use them to swim—like this. . ." Will turned and dove into the water, swimming back and forth on the surface. Then he went under and popped up some distance away, smiling and waving to his shocked friends.

After several minutes William swam to shore and began to coax his friends to let him teach them to swim. The only one to agree was Gray Fox.

"If Kajika can swim, Gray Fox can swim," the young warrior declared. For the next hour William patiently showed Gray Fox how to stay afloat and move through the water. By the end of the day, the two were sporting about the lake like two large fish.

A few weeks later French traders arrived at their camp, speaking a tongue unknown to William. They came with rifles, ammunition, and bright-colored blankets to trade for furs. More than one of them saw and admired the tall, powerful young warrior with the singularly watchful eyes, but none of them knew that, under his paint and tan, he was not an Indian. Instead they took him to be a great warrior of the tribe and showed him respect. William observed enough of the traders' dealings with the Indians and their manners with each other that he realized that the French men were not to be trusted, and he warned Chief Black Cloud about them.

In the late summer the chief gave the word for them to move south again. He let it be known that he wanted to return to their old valley to camp for the winter. So as not to wear out the women and children, they traveled for a day, then camped for two or three days to rest and allow the men to hunt.

On one of the rest days, several braves went out to search for game. About midday several of the party returned in a panic, carrying one of their companions who had been killed, a cousin of Gray Fox.

"It was the Shawnee!" Gray Fox said with contempt to William a short time later. "They killed Growling Bear but were driven back by Miami arrows."

"Why did they attack?" William wanted to know.

"The men said the Shawnee claimed these hunting grounds as theirs," Gray Fox answered, "and when they ran away, they warned that they would be back with more warriors."

"What will Black Cloud do?" William asked with concern. "Will we go back north?"

"Kajika, if you knew better the heart of Black Cloud, you would know that he will not do that. If we go back north, then when winter comes, it will bring death to many of us. Black Cloud will not let the Shawnee force us to die. He will fight!"

A drum sounded from the center of the camp, calling everyone together, and all gathered in haste.

"It is decided!" Black Cloud announced loudly when he saw the assembled people. "The Shawnee are angry with the Miami for hunting here, though all Indians hunt here when they pass through. It has always been this way. But the Shawnee now claim this land as their own. The Miami do not claim this land. We only claim the right to pass through to our valley and hunt what we need on our way.

"I do not want war, but I will not let the Shawnee or anyone else push us back north to the harsh winters and death. We will take what we need and continue to travel south. If the Shawnee attack us, then the Maimi will fight, and Charging Elk, our war chief, will lead us!"

As Black Cloud finished his speech, a runner broke out of the forest and hurried to the chief. "The Shawnee are coming!" he called loudly enough for all to hear. "A large band of fighters painted for war is headed this way through the woods!"

The chief reached into his teepee and pulled out William's rifle, powder horn, and ammunition pouch. He handed them to Charging Elk, who took them and walked straight to the young

171

captive. The war chief held the weapon in front of him and said "Kajika, will you fight with us?"

William looked around and saw every eye in the village looking straight at him. As Will searched his heart for the answer, he remembered the strong trust in God that his friend Asa possessed. Immediately lifting his hands and eyes to heaven, he loudly spoke his thoughts to God. "Oh Gitchie Manitou, my Father in Heaven, I come to You in the name of Your Son, Great Chief Jesus. Chief Black Cloud has said that the Miami want peace, but the Shawnee are coming to fight against us. Please protect us, Great Father! The Miami only want to pass through in peace, and I know You love peace. If we must fight, then I ask that you give us strength and courage to end this battle quickly. Show the Miami *and* the Shawnee that there is a Great Manitou in Heaven Who wants His children to live together in peace."

When he finished, William dropped his hands and looked at Black Cloud and then at Charging Elk. "Kajika will fight with the Miami to protect the village." As he said this, the young hunter took the rifle, horn, and pouch.

Charging Elk ordered all the braves to grab their weapons. He had the old men, boys, and young women arm themselves and hide in the woods to the north until they were called back.

In less than three minutes, the men were ready, and the war chief led them on a run to the east to meet the attacking warriors. Led by their scouts, the war party loped through the forest. After running at a long distance pace for over an hour, the leaders called a halt when another Miami scout suddenly appeared in front of them. He quickly reported that the Shawnee fighters were coming rapidly through the woods and would arrive soon.

"We will run straight at them," Charging Elk called to all of his warriors, "and show the Shawnee how the Miami fight!"

"Chief Charging Elk!" a voice called from the group. It was William. "May I speak a different plan to you?"

"What council do you have, Kajika? Has the Manitou spoken to you?"

"I think He has," the youth answered confidently.

Ten minutes later the leaders of the Shawnee war party came racing through the woods and saw, standing confidently before them, Peace Chief Black Cloud and four of his braves. The brave standing beside Black Cloud held an evergreen branch as a sign to talk. The large band of enemy fighters stopped a little less than a bowshot away from the Miami. The Shawnee war chief stepped in front of his warriors and with an angry expression signed, *Speak, dog!*

Black Cloud signed his speech. He said that the Miami had no desire to harm any of their Shawnee brothers and only wished to feed their families as they passed through peacefully.

With the same angry expression, the Shawnee leader signed his answer. *You are dogs AND cowards! The Shawnee is brother to neither!* The enemy chief then raised his war cry, and all of the warriors charged for Black Cloud. But the Miami leader and his braves were already sprinting toward fallen logs behind them. With the attacking enemy fighters chasing furiously after them, Black Cloud and his men leaped over the barrier. As they did so, Charging Elk gave the signal, and almost a hundred Miami warriors stood up from behind the logs and launched arrows or fired rifles at the oncoming attackers. Several of Shawnee fell. The ambush caught the enemy fighters by surprise and stopped their charge. A few with rifles fired back at the Miami as the rest, in confusion, looked for cover. Several more Shawnee fell.

From behind the logs Chief Charging Elk looked to his left down the line of fighters. He saw William reloading his rifle. "Kajika!"

On hearing his name, Will looked up and spotted the war chief, who quickly gave William the agreed upon hand signal. The young hunter nodded his understanding as he replaced the ramrod of his rifle. Dropping low behind the logs so as not to be seen by the enemy fighters, Will moved along the line of defenders to his left. He gathered ten warriors he had previously chosen and led them to the dry creek bed behind their fighting line. Once everyone was in the gully, Will guided them quickly to the north.

After Charging Elk saw William collecting his men, the chief turned toward the other end of the line of defenders and signaled

Gray Fox. When the Miami warrior received the message, he summoned his ten fighters and, crawling back to the creek bed, hurried away to the south.

The Shawnee recovered from their shock of the surprise attack by the Miami and began creeping forward. Charging Elk knew the enemy fighters were trying to get close enough to rush their defensive line. He yelled to his warriors to continue sending arrows and rifle shots into the advancing Shawnee. The battle went on for several more minutes. Finally, when the Shawnee war chief thought they were close enough, he screamed his war cry, and all of the crawling warriors leaped to their feet and charged the defended logs.

The Miami launched their arrows and then, at Charging Elk's cry, pulled out their tomahawks and knives, leaped the logs, and rushed to meet their enemy.

The hand to hand battle was fierce and loud. Several warriors dropped on both sides. The furious Shawnee pressed their attack and began to push the Miami back. The enemy war chief saw that they were winning, and from behind his fighters, he screamed at his men to fight harder and finish the Miami.

Just then savage yells blasted from the woods behind the Shawnee, and out rushed William and Gray Fox, leading their braves into the fight. Completely caught off guard by the fierce attack from their rear, the Shawnee yelled in fear and began running in every direction to get away.

Gray Fox tackled the Shawnee war chief, and William, who was fighting nearby, clubbed his adversary with the butt of his rifle and quickly stepped on the Shawnee chief's tomahawk before he could swing it at Gray Fox. When the remaining enemy fighters saw that their war chief had been captured, they stopped fighting and dropped their weapons.

As soon as the battle ended, Black Cloud, who was standing near Charging Elk, walked over to William and Gray Fox. Seeing their chief approaching, the two warriors lifted the captured war chief to his feet and turned him to face Black Cloud. The Miami leader stood in front of the captured Shawnee, who would not look Black Cloud in the eyes. *We are your slaves,* the defeated Shawnee signed.

The Miami are not cowards, the Miami chief signed back. *The Miami are not dogs. The Miami are your brothers. Take your wounded and go home. The Miami will feed our families and pass through peacefully.*

The Shawnee chief's mouth dropped open when he saw the message. William smiled and nodded respectfully to Black Cloud, then he and Gray Fox released their captive, and Will handed him back his tomahawk. The freed Shawnee stared at the tomahawk in his hand with a shocked look on his face. Finally he looked at the Miami chief, lifted his hand in a sign of friendship, and walked away.

The battle with the Shawnee had cost the Miami three killed and fourteen injured, most of which were minor wounds. Everyone in the tribe was pleased with the outcome. When they arrived back at their camp and called in the women, children, and elderly, a great celebration broke out. There was much dancing around the fire that evening, and the story of the battle had to be retold many times.

The next day Black Cloud called the tribe together. When everyone had arrived, the chief stood up and began to speak. "The Miami did not fight to take land. The Miami did not fight to conquer. The Miami did not fight to take the Shawnee teepees or their women or anything that is theirs. The Miami fought for peace! The Miami fought bravely and did not run before our enemies. Yesterday War Chief Charging Elk and our warriors won a great victory, but blood was spilled. We lost three more of those we love. As I call the names of the four who died, remember them. They died fighting for all of us. . .Growling Bear. . .Swift Eagle. . .He Keeps Watch. . .Blackbird. Paint their symbols on your teepees. They must be remembered.

"We must also honor the warrior whose counsel led us to victory. . .Walks Without Sound! Kajika, come here and stand beside me."

Reluctantly William made his way to the chief's side.

"Kajika," Black Cloud began as he looked at William, "though you are young, you have shown yourself to be a strong warrior, a great hunter, and a possessor of wisdom. Yesterday you taught us a new way to defeat our enemies. You came to us as a captive, but you have proven yourself to be one of us. I have spoken with Chief Charging Elk and the elders, and we have agreed that, from this day forward, you are no longer a captive. You are Miami!"

Nods and grunts of approval were heard across the crowd of Indians. Gray Fox and many of the other young warriors shouted whoops of celebration.

William turned to the chief and asked, "Chief Black Cloud, may I speak?"

The Miami leader nodded his permission, and William raised his hands to quiet the crowd. When everyone had settled down and all were looking at the tall, broad-shouldered youth, Will began, "I thank Chief Black Cloud, Chief Charging Elk, and the elders. It is a great honor to be accepted by you as Miami. But I want all of you to know that the victory was not because of me. You heard my prayer before we left to fight the Shawnee. I asked the Gitchie Manitou in the name of Great Chief Jesus to help us, and He did. The Manitou was with us and helped each of us in the fight. The Manitou loves peace and moved the heart of Chief Black Cloud to seek it.

"The Manitou gave our chief the courage to confront the army of enemies and give them one last chance to leave us in peace, but their hearts were bad. They had not listened to the Gitchie Manitou. Their ears were open to the devil, the evil one, and they wanted war. So we fought them. The Manitou and His Son Jesus smiled on the Maimi and gave Chief Charging Elk and us victory. The honor belongs to the Gitchie Manitou and His Son Jesus, not to me."

Chapter Eighteen

THE CALL OF DUTY

As the Miami continued their journey south, they were left alone by the other tribes. Apparently word traveled ahead of Black Cloud's people that they were not to be trifled with. Once they arrived in their familiar valley, everyone busily set up the winter camp.

As William observed the tribe's work, he saw things that concerned him. He noticed that very little planning was being made for the possibility of another hard winter. When he was still in Larkinboro, William recalled the conversations he and his father had about the important decisions and work that should be done to insure the village was protected and cared for when the weather was harsh. "Son, we must prepare like every winter will be worse than the one before," he remembered his father saying.

Except for last year, which was extremely harsh, the Miami had always been able to find plenty of game in this valley during the coldest months. Now everyone seemed to have forgotten the severity of the previous winter and was expecting a milder one like the ones they were used to.

Realizing the danger of this attitude, William believed that better preparations needed to be made. He explained carefully his concerns to Black Cloud and the elders until he convinced them of the tribe's needs. Under his constant suggestions, advice, and pressure, they stored so much food for the winter that there was no chance of another famine, whatever might happen to the game.

As it turned out, while the winter was not as severe as the last one, it was still very cold, and hunting was scarce. Due to the preparations that had been made, dangerous hunting expeditions in the freezing temperatures did not have to be made. Needless to say, everyone was very grateful for the large amount of food that had been stored.

Once again the chief and the tribal elders expressed public gratitude for William's counsel and forethought. The young warrior thanked them for the honor and respect they showed him, but again made it very clear that the blessings and abundant provisions the tribe enjoyed were not his doing, but came from the Gitchie Manitou, or, as Will called Him, the Great Father in Heaven.

When the long winter finally came to an end and the buds burst from the limbs, the tribe traveled southeastward, eventually arriving at the Mississippi. The sight of the vast body of flowing water brought back to William thoughts of those with whom he had first seen it, and he felt a pang of homesickness.

A number of canoes were constructed by making frames of green limbs and stretching tanned skins over them. This allowed the village to cross the great river and advance into a green and rich land, pleasant to the eye and full of game. They wandered and hunted as they drifted slowly to the east.

It was late in the afternoon when William, Black Cloud, Charging Elk, and Gray Fox traveled several miles east of their camp and came upon a large Chickasaw encampment. When the village learned that Black Cloud's tribe were the ones who had defeated their mortal enemies, the Shawnee, the Miami chiefs and the others were received as heroes and welcomed as guests for as long as they chose to stay.

William noticed the Chickasaw warriors were painted for battle. At least a thousand warriors were in hideous varieties of war paint, and in the fading light, the scene was weird and ominous. The war songs in their very monotony were chilling and full of ferocity.

Long glances were cast at William, but even the keen eyes of the Chickasaw failed to notice that he was not an Indian, and he stood watching them, his face impassive but his interest aroused. A dozen warriors, naked to the waist and hideously painted, sang a war song while they capered and jumped to its rhythmic tune. In their dances the warriors playacted the horrible things they intended to do to their victims. It made William sick to think about, and he started to leave. Suddenly there was a loud cry, and the drums stopped. All the dancers ceased their wild gyrations and turned toward the one who had shouted.

William moved closer so he could see what was happening. The Chickasaw chief stood at the entrance to his lodge, and beside him were two white men. One appeared to William to be a hunter with a long rifle and wearing a wide brimmed hat, but the other was striking in his appearance. He was shorter but looked magnificent in his bright red coat and flashing gold buttons.

William made every effort to let no expression cross his face, even though he was stunned to see a British officer so far into the wilderness. The Indian chief held up his hands to quiet the rowdy band. Speaking to his warriors in their native tongue, which William didn't understand, the chief then pointed to the officer. The tall hunter by his side leaned over and spoke something in the officer's ear. With a big smile the British military leader stepped forward and addressed the tribe, "My brave friends of the Chickasaw nation, I bring you greetings from your good friend, Great King George of England!"

At this point the officer stopped and looked over to his companion, who immediately interpreted what he had said to the crowd in the Chickasaw language. When the interpreter stopped, he looked back at the officer, who began again, "I am Major Edmond Trask, an officer in King George's army, and this is my associate, Simon Girty."

As Trask gave his speech, he always paused long enough after each sentence to allow Girty to translate. "Your friend, Great King George, has heard of the brave and fierce fighters of the Chickasaw nation, and his heart is sad for the insults his children, the Chickasaw, have had to endure. For too long the American settlers have torn up the land and destroyed the hunting grounds that King George wants to give to the Chickasaw. The Americans dishonor you by their presence and show no respect to the proud and fierce Chickasaw warriors."

William had heard from Jack Cobb and Dirt Gurley that the British were trying to stir up the Indians against them, but he had never expected to actually witness it. The major continued his rant, blaming the Americans for everything he could think of that would upset the Indians, and it worked. After several minutes the warriors were so angry that they could scarcely be calmed down enough to listen to the rest of the major's speech.

"King George wants his Chickasaw children to claim the land that he has given them. To help you in this great work, he has sent a gift to you. Girty and I have brought the great Chickasaw warriors guns to use against their enemies, as well as powder and bullets."

As Girty interpreted this last statement, Trask nodded to the chief, who walked over to several long boxes lying nearby. Throwing open the top box, the chief snatched up a brown musket and held it over his head. A thousand warriors suddenly screamed their war cries at the top of their lungs, and all was bedlam. More boxes were opened, and Trask and Girty joined the chief in handing out muskets, full powder horns, and bullet pouches.

An hour later one of the Chickasaw warriors that William had met earlier came up to him and talked to him in sign language. He told him that the British major had heard that great warriors from one of the Miami tribes were visiting the Chickasaw and wanted to speak with them. When William reported this to Black Cloud, the Miami chief had a question for his young friend, "Kajika, you are of his people. Do you trust this man?"

"No!" William answered emphatically.

"You do not trust one of your own, Kajika?" Charging Elk asked with some surprise.

"I do not trust this man, Chief Charging Elk," William returned. "I know where he comes from and what he is trying to do."

"Then Black Cloud and Charging Elk will not speak with him," the war chief declared. "Let us leave and return to our village."

"May I speak further?" William asked as the chiefs started to turn away.

Turning back to face the young warrior, Black Cloud nodded.

"The Great Manitou loves peace," William began. "The Miami have listened to the Manitou and love peace as well. This Red Coat, he does not listen to the Manitou. Instead he is for war. He is stirring the Chickasaw to fight against people who have not harmed them. No good can come of this.

"I think it would be wise to meet with this man and hear his words. Let us find out if his plans may bring harm to the Miami."

Black Cloud and Charging Elk spoke with each other for a moment, then with a grunt and a nod Black Cloud said, "Once again Kajika has given wise council. We will not go, but you go for us, since you understand his tongue, and track this Red Coat's heart."

A few minutes later William stood inside the Chickasaw chief's lodge in the presence of Trask and Girty.

When Trask saw William enter, he gave a nod of approval and turned to his companion, "Would you look at this young buck, Girty! He's a powerful lookin' Indian!"

"If all the Miami look like him," Girty answered, "I wouldn't want to tangle with 'em!"

"So you speak Miami?" Trask asked.

"Just a little," Girty answered. "It'd probably be better if I just sign to him."

"Well, welcome him and tell him we've heard that the Miami are brave and fierce fighters. That's usually what they want to hear. Tell him that we will bring more guns for all the Miami if they will join the Chickasaw and kill the Americans."

Acting ignorant of what Trask had said, William watched as Girty signed the message. When he had finished William responded by asking where the attack would be made.

"Tell him that it's a little over a hundred miles southeast of here, or however you say that in Indian," Trask answered as he pulled out a roll of soft leather and spread it on the dirt floor. "I'll show him on this map. What's his name?"

"He says his name is Walks Without Sound," Girty translated.

"Okay, Walks Without Sound, come over here and look at this map."

William allowed Girty to sign it to him before he stepped over beside the major. As Trask showed where they were on his hand-drawn map, then dropped his finger down to the picture of a walled fort near a river, Will came to a startling realization: the major was pointing at Larkinboro. He had armed these warriors and was sending them to attack William's family and friends.

"Does he understand?" Trask asked Girty, when the Miami made no response after staring at the map for two minutes.

"Well, I think so," Girty answered as he got William's attention and signed again that they wanted the Indians to attack this fort.

Finally Will forced himself to look at Girty once more, willing himself to show no emotion. He signed a question and waited in dread for the answer.

"He wants to know what they're to do with the people once they take the fort," Girty related.

"Kill them," Trask answered. "Kill them all!"

"Not all of them," Girty protested. "You promised."

"Oh yeah, I forgot. You can have the two sisters from the Middlebrook family, but why a man needs two squaws is beyond me. Just tell him what I said."

The young warrior struggled hard to control himself as he finished the conversation with Girty and excused himself to go talk to his chief. As Will made his way back through the Chickasaw village, the chill of horror that had seized him at the sight of the blood-thirsty dancers passed over him again—deeper, stronger, and longer than before. He knew Larkinboro would fall! There could be no doubt of it! Nothing could save it! The hideous band, raging with musket, bow and arrow, tomahawk, and knife would dash without a word of warning, like a bolt from the sky, upon Larkinboro, so long sheltered and peaceful in its valley. He could see all the phases of the savage triumph: the surprise, the swift attack and ferocious yells, the rapid volleys of rifles, the flashing of knife blades, the burning buildings, the shouts, the cries, and men, women, and children in one red slaughter. In another year the forest would spring up where Larkinboro had been, and the wolf and the fox would prowl among the charred timbers. Among the bleaching bones would be those of his own family, as well as Asa, and Kate Middlebrook—if they were not taken away for a worse fate.

In that moment the agony the vision conjured in his mind was worse than anything he had ever had to cope with. All his old life, the dear, familiar ties surged up and were hot upon his brain. His place was there! With them! Not here! Suddenly the voices so long silent screamed at him again. *You failed them! You could have found some way to escape these Indians and have been there to help them, but you didn't! Worthless. . .no good. . .never amount to anything. . .*

In that moment of agony and fear for his friends and family, the sense of helplessness crushed him. In a few hours or less the war party would start, and it would flit southward like the wind, just as silent but far more deadly. No, nothing could save the innocent people at Larkinboro; they were as surely doomed as if their destruction had already taken place.

After leaving the meeting, William rejoined Black Cloud and the others at the edge of the encampment. They said farewell to the Chickasaw, then began walking back toward their own camp.

With a great surge of determination, William made a decision. It was so sudden, so transforming, that the whole world changed at once. The blood-red tint thrown by the sunken sun was gone from the forest, but instead, the silver sickle of the moon rose and shed a faint, radiant light of hope.

Drawing Black Cloud aside, Will spoke to him with words full of firmness and feeling. He explained that the Chickasaw attack was against his own family and friends. Insisting that he must go to warn his people, he would leave at once.

Black Cloud was silent for a moment, and Will saw the faintest quiver in his eyes. He knew that he held a certain place in the affections of the chief.

"I was a captive of the tribe," said William, "but it has made me its son. I respect this great honor, but my family and dearest friends are in the gravest danger, and I must save my people. The Chickasaw march south tonight against them, and I go to give warning. It is better that I go in peace." He spoke simply but with dignity and looked straight into the eyes of the chief, where he saw that slight, pathetic quiver come again.

"I will not keep you if you would go," said Black Cloud. "I could not do that to one who has done so much for us. But when you are far away, it may be that the memory of those with whom you have lived and hunted these few seasons will call to you, and you will hear and return to us."

William was moved by these words, yet the voice of love and duty called to him with a much more powerful voice. He had to go, and there must be no delay.

"Farewell, Chief Black Cloud," he said with the same simplicity. "I will think often of you who have been so good to me."

The chief called the other warriors and told them their comrade was going far to the south, and they might never see him again. Their faces expressed nothing, whatever they may have felt. William repeated the farewell, then with no more hesitation, he plunged into the forest. He stopped when he was thirty or forty yards away and looked back. The chief and the warriors stood side by side as he had left them, motionless and gazing after him. It was night, and to eyes less keen than Will's, their forms would have melted into the dusk, but he could still make out their outline. Hoping they could still see him, he waved his hand in a final farewell and resumed his flight, not looking back again.

Chapter Nineteen

THE LONG WAY HOME

It was a dark night, and the forest stretched on, black and endless. The trunks of the trees stood in rows like phantoms of the dusk. Whenever he came to an opening in the woods, Will Hackett looked up at the moon and the few stars he could see and reckoned his course. Larkinboro lay well over a hundred miles away, chiefly to the south. He had a general idea of the direction from the map Trask had shown him, but the war party would know exactly. That thought motivated him to move as swiftly as he could through the moon shadows.

Though fear of the disaster that loomed over his friends was constantly clawing at his heart, William, for the present, would not allow himself to even consider the possibility of failing to reach the fort in time to warn them. He prayed as he ran, thanking God that he had found out about the danger while there was still a chance to tell his loved ones of the approaching army. He also asked his heavenly Father to show him the way home. William wasn't sure that, even with warning and time to prepare, the village could defeat such a large party of hostile warriors, but he very much wanted to be with his family and friends in this desperate time and do what he could when the attack came.

Once he had made the decision to go, a strong feeling surged through him. William felt that he was now about to make atonement for his long neglect. *But maybe there was more to it*, he thought to himself as he ran. *Perhaps God had ordained long*

185

ago that he should be with the Indians at this critical moment, see the danger, and bring Larkinboro a warning that could save them, like Esther in the Bible. Young Hackett found consolation in the thought.

The desperate runner increased his pace and sped southward in the easy trot he had learned from his red friends, a gait he could maintain for many hours and with which he could put ground behind him at a remarkable rate. He carried his rifle by his side, his head was bent slightly forward, and he listened intently to every sound of the forest as he passed. So focused was he on the dangers in front and behind that nothing escaped his ear, whether it was a raccoon stirring among the branches, a deer startled from its hiding place, or merely the wind rustling the leaves. Instinct also told him that, for the moment, the forest was at peace, and he kept moving.

To the ordinary man the darkness of the night, the wilderness with its ghostly tree trunks, and the silence would have been full of strangeness and awe, dark with omens and warnings. Few travelers, when alone in the wilds at night, would not have felt fear's icy claws, but to William it brought only hope and the thrill of achieving his goal. He had no sense of loneliness; the forest hid no secrets from him. It was like home, and he was merely passing through on a great quest.

As the young frontiersman glided from under the dark canopy, he looked up at the moon and stars and confirmed his course, though he never slackened speed. He found himself running across a prairie where the moonlight was brighter, painting the crests of the swells with silver light. A dozen buffalo rose up and snorted as he flitted by, but he scarcely bestowed a passing glance upon the massive black animals. The small prairie was only two or three miles across, and at the far edge flowed a shallow creek that he crossed rapidly before entering the forest again. The land began to change as he came to rough country with steep little hills, a dense undergrowth of interlacing bushes, and twining, thorny vines. Though the trail was more challenging, he made his way through in a manner that only one forest-bred could accomplish and pressed on, hardly slackening his speed.

When the night became darkest, he lay down in the deepest shadow of a thicket, his hand upon his rifle, and in a few minutes was slumbering soundly. It was a matter of training with him to sleep whenever he needed it. He knew too, despite his haste, that he must save his strength.

It was his will that he should rest about four hours, and his system obeyed the wish, awakening him close to the appointed time. The sun was just rising over the vast green wilderness, lighting up a world seemingly as lonely and deserted as it had been the night before. The unbroken forest, touched with the rich green of new leaves and bathed in the pure light of dawn, bent gently to a west wind.

William stood and inhaled the sweet air. He was a striking figure, yet a few yards away he would have been visible only to the trained eye. His Indian garb of tanned deerskin blended with the colors of the forest. Before he moved, he examined the woods around him, listening intently as he searched. He was then neither savage nor civilized man, but having acquired many of the qualities of both, he used his trained senses and his reason to study his surroundings. Everything seemed peaceful, but the young frontiersman knew that, as he tried to outrace the Chickasaw war party, he must consider that danger was always near.

The slight swaying motion of his body ceased suddenly, and he remained as still as a rock. He seemed to be a part of the green bushes that grew around him, yet he was never more watchful, never more alert. The indefinable sixth sense, developed by most who lived their lives under the constant perils of the wilderness, had given him an alarm. Something was not as it should be. He was aware that there was a presence in the forest that was foreign in its nature. He could not tell what had alerted him to its being there—maybe a sound or a faint smell—but he was sure someone was near, and he was certain that whoever it might be was not friendly.

William reasoned with himself that, if he had been the Chickasaw chief, he would have sent out braves ahead of the main war party to scout the way. With this insight his senses became even more attuned to his surroundings. As anxious as he was to reach his friends and warn them, he knew that their only chance of survival rested on his ability to get there safely. To give in to impatience or to make a thoughtless decision now would get him and, therefore, all those in Larkinboro, killed.

Presently he sank down in the undergrowth so gently that not a bush rustled; there was no displacement of the stems or leaves around him. The grass and the foliage were just as they had been. But the figure, visible before to the trained eye, could not be seen at all. Then he began to creep silently through the grass and brush. Examining the ground and the forest around him as he traveled, he stopped and slowly rose to study his surroundings. William made sure that his face was hidden by the bushes, although his eyes still searched every part of the forest.

The expression on his face now completely changed. He might be the hunted, but he bore himself as the hunter. Those who wished to kill him were stalking him, and he would fiercely defend himself. His thin lips were slightly drawn back, showing the line of white teeth, the eyes were narrowed, and in them was the cold glitter of expected conflict. Brown hands, lean but big-boned and powerful, clasped a rifle having a long, slender barrel and a beautifully carved stock.

Sinking down again, he moved in a small circle to the right. Will stopped behind a large tree and, sheltering himself, riveted his eyes on an area in the forest about thirty yards away. He had spotted the unnatural movement of a branch and suspected his possible adversary was there.

As his sharp eyes stared at the suspicious point, a leaf moved, but not in the way it should have swayed before the gentle wind. He noticed that there was a passing spot of brown in the green of the bushes. It was visible only for a moment, but Will had detected it.

He had to get his enemy to show himself, without allowing the warrior to know exactly where his own hiding spot was. It was not going to be easy because the young frontiersman knew his adversary was watching for him as well. Spotting a dead branch at his feet that was several feet long, William slowly picked it up and used it to move the limb of a bush as far as he could reach to his right. Then dropping the dead branch, Will raised his rifle to his shoulder and continued watching the spot where he was sure his opponent hid. Suddenly a rifle flashed from the leaves where he was looking, the ball passing through the brush to William's right.

Before the passing spot of brown was gone, the rifle at William's shoulder spat a stream of fire from its slender muzzle, and its sharp, cracking report, like the lashing of a whip, was blended with a distant grunt of pain.

The bullet had scarcely left his gun before William fell back almost flat against the ground, and an answering shot crashed through the spot where his head had been. While the sound of that last gunshot was still echoing through the woods, William sprang to his feet and rushed forward, drawing his tomahawk and uttering a fierce war cry.

He had known there were two enemies stalking him. As Will had made his searching course through the forest, he had passed directly over their trail and read the signs. He even recognized the moccasin prints as Chickasaw. The young warrior knew that one of the war party's advance scouts would give him no further trouble, and the other, like himself, had an unloaded rifle.

Just at that moment the second savage uttered his war cry and sprang forward from the bushes. William might well have recoiled at the terrible figure that rushed to meet him, but he did not have time to think before he was set upon by his fierce enemy. The fight only lasted a few moments. As the charging Indian drew near, he threw his tomahawk, but William parried the blade upon the barrel of his rifle still in his left hand. The enemy was close enough to leap on his prey, his knife flashing in his hand. Dropping his rifle, Will grabbed the wrist gripping the descending knife and let the weight of the hurtling Indian drive him over the young frontiersman and flip him onto the ground. The savage landed hard on his back but rolled quickly to his feet and turned to plunge his knife into his enemy. Suddenly another gunshot sounded from behind William, and the Chickasaw grabbed his chest and collapsed.

Still breathing hard from the battle, Will quickly turned, tomahawk in hand, to face the unknown rifleman. Trotting confidently out of the woods and with a faint smile spreading across his face was Gray Fox.

The young frontiersman smiled when he saw his friend and quickly reloaded his rifle, offering a prayer of thanksgiving for his deliverance at the same time.

"I'm sorry to end your fight, Kajika," Gray Fox said as he stopped beside his friend. "I think you would have defeated him, but you didn't have time. The Chickasaw are near."

"Thank you, Gray Fox," Will returned, "but you shouldn't have followed me. You saw how many warriors they have. I could be going to my death."

"Then Gray Fox will die with his brother." As the Miami warrior said this, he reached out his right hand, and William grasped his friend's forearm warmly.

Knowing that other enemy scouts were close enough to have heard the rifle shots, the two needed to leave quickly. They took a moment to snatch dried venison from the pouches of their vanquished foes to eat as they traveled. The sun was shooting up higher and higher in the east and bathed the forest in a shimmering, golden light. Confident of his direction, William Hackett turned and led them swiftly and silently to the south, praising God for their protection and desperately asking for more.

When they had gone a half mile in their noiseless flight, Will halted and, listening intently, heard the faint echo of a long-drawn, whining cry from behind. After that came silence, heavy and ominous. The cry did not surprise either of them. They had known that the larger party of enemy fighters to whom the two Chickasaw warriors had belonged would find their dead comrades and seek to pursue the ones who defeated them. He realized just how accurate Gray Fox's scouting report was. The Chickasaw army was very close behind them, and that realization caused the intelligent youth to consider another plan.

"They are close to us, Kajika," the Miami observed.

"Yes," William agreed, "I've been thinking about that. They are traveling much faster than I thought they would. They will get to my friends the same time we do, and there will be no time to warn them."

"Now that they have found their dead warriors, the Chickasaw know that they have enemies just ahead of them," Gray Fox said. "Maybe we make them chase us."

"Exactly," Will agreed. "We'll go east and make noise and leave enough signs to draw them after us. We'll let them get close enough to think they're about to catch us, then slip around them and run to my home."

"That will delay the Chickasaw enough to let you warn your people, and they will have time to get ready," the Miami replied.

The young warrior immediately decided to implement their daring plan. He threw back his head and gave a full-throated yell of his own war cry, a long piercing shout that trailed off in distant echoes. It was at the same time an act of defiance of the army of Chickasaw fighters, as well as a suggestion to them where they might find him. William and his friend then resumed their flight but not at full speed. The shrewd young woodsman wanted the enemy army to get closer.

All day the two friends led their enemies in sustained flight toward the east, and at no time were the young woodsman and his companion more than a little beyond their enemy's reach. Often the Chickasaw thought their hands were about to close down upon their prey, but always the evasive enemy slipped away, usually giving another challenging war cry after their escape. The attacking warriors' savage hearts were furious with rage at the constant taunting.

At the coming of the twilight, one of the Chickasaws' best warriors was chasing their quarry at some distance ahead of the main band when suddenly he was slain by a rifle shot from some bushes. Then came that defiant war cry again, faint but full of challenge. For several hours the army of furious warriors scoured the woods from where the shot had come but found nothing. The ones they pursued were now traveling with speed, and darkness soon covered all sign of their flight. When the two friends were half a mile from their enemies, William gave another piercing yell of victory.

The young frontiersman felt a sense of satisfaction as he drew the Chickasaw army eastward. So far everything had occurred as he had wished, and with the night at hand, it was time that he and

Gray Fox shake them off. He said as much to his friend. Checking the stars, Will turned to the south and headed swiftly toward Larkinboro.

Throughout the day they had eaten dried venison they carried and felt no need to stop for food. They did not rest until after midnight when they lay down in a thicket and slept soundly until daylight. William opened his eyes just as the dawn was breaking. Touching the shoulder of his sleeping friend to wake him, they rose again, refreshed, and faster than ever sped on their swift way toward Will's family and friends.

Chapter Twenty

THE RETURN

Larkinboro lay quietly and peacefully in its pleasant valley, never suspecting the disaster that was approaching. Instead, the settlers rejoiced in the nice weather. The men of the village foresaw a great season for their crops. Smoke rose from many chimneys, and now and then the red or yellow homemade linsey-woolsey dress of a girl gleamed in the sunlight. To the left were fields cleared for Indian corn, and near the fort were gardens. Beyond both were hills and unbroken forest.

Occasionally a man, carrying on his shoulder the inevitable Kentucky rifle, long and slender-barreled, passed through the palisade. Everything about the scene seemed peaceful. The town was prospering, and all of its citizens were confident about their future.

In the Hackett house was a silent sadness—silent because they were people who were familiar with the hardships of life, and it was their custom to hide their grief. The oldest son was gone, lost to the wilderness, and whether he had perished or not, nobody knew.

John Hackett was not an emotional man; feelings rarely showed on his face. His wife alone knew how hard the blow had been to him because she had suffered the same stroke. But the children—the younger brother, Jay, and the sister, Mary—because of their youth, would not always remember as clearly, and with them the impression of the one who was gone would grow dimmer in time. The wilderness always seemed to demand a certain percentage of loss in human life. It was one of the facts of the frontier that had to be accepted by the pioneers, and thus the name of William Hackett was rarely spoken.

Today was especially beautiful, with not a cloud in the sky. Last summer new emigrants had come across the mountains, adding welcome strength to the colony and extending the size of the village. Danger had seemed to pass them by. They had heard once or twice more of the great war in the far-away east, but it was so distant and vague that most of them had forgotten it. They had seen no evidence of the coming army of General Clark, but neither had they had problems with the Indians. The tribes across the Ohio had apparently decided to stay in the north, and so far Will Hackett was the only toll they had paid. Because of this, there was reason for happiness for most of the villagers.

A slim girl, bearing in her hand a wooden pail, came through the gate of the palisade. She was bare-headed, but her light-brown hair, coiled in a shining mass, was touched here and there with golden gleams where the sunshine fell upon it. Her face, browned somewhat, was yet very white on the forehead, and the cheeks had the crimson flush of health. Wearing a dress of homemade linsey-woolsey dyed red, she walked with strong step toward the spring that gushed from a hillside, forming a pool a short distance from its source.

It was Kate Middlebrook, looking more like a young lady. Instead of drawing water from the well in the fort, she spotted her teacher, Charles Spebbington, sitting by the spring in the distance, and she chose to stroll out to join him for some fresh air and quietness. "Good day, Mr. Spebbington," she said pleasantly as she arrived at the spring. "I hope I'm not disturbing you."

"Not atoll, Katherine! Not atoll! The morning is lovely, and our little spring and its pool are especially captivating today!"

Kate set her wooden pail on the bank and looked down at the cool, flowing stream. It did seem to be inviting her, and she ran her arm through it, making curves and oblongs. "You're right," the girl said, answering the scholar. "The sweet song the water sings as it flows over the rocks is very pleasant."

She was in a thoughtful mood. Once or twice she looked at the forest, and each time it was, to her, like looking at a thick wall of green behind which lurked unknown mysteries.

Charles Spebbington, the schoolmaster, watched her gazing into the trees and understood her thoughts. The two had become great friends and had talked together on many occasions. Unchanged by time, the teacher was the same strong, gray-haired man with the ruddy face. He was not unhappy in Larkinboro, even though he was by nature not a frontiersman. Although considered the intellectual leader of the colony, the wilderness also appealed to him. "The new leaves are bursting forth, Katherine," he said, "and it has been an easier winter. We should be thankful that we have fared so well."

"I think most of us are," she replied, letting her gaze swing back upon their growing settlement. "We'll soon be a big town, you know."

"Yes, indeed!" the scholar answered enthusiastically and launched into one of his favorite lectures. He liked to predict how the colony would grow, and already he saw that one day their little village would be a great city. He found a ready listener in Kate. This too appealed at times to her imagination, and if at other times interest was lacking, she was too fond of the old scholar to let him know. Presently she filled the pail and stood up, straight and strong.

"I will carry it for you," said the schoolmaster.

"That's sweet of you, Mr. Spebbington," Kate said with a chuckle, "but I've done this so many times that my arm wouldn't know what to do without this bucket hanging from it."

"Well, alright," the scholar chuckled in return. "But if you will not let me carry the water, at least let me walk with you?"

But the girl did not reply, and Charles Spebbington was startled by the sudden change that came over her. First a look of wonder showed on her face, then she turned white, every particle of color leaving her cheeks. The master could not tell what her expression meant, and he followed her eyes, which were turned toward the forest.

From the trees came two figures, both very strange to Charles Spebbington. One was clearly an Indian warrior, proud and strong. The other was a tall youth with a powerful frame, his face so brown that it might belong to either the white or the red race, but with fine, clean features. His long hair was pulled back and tied with a thin leather strap, and he was clad in buckskins. He had a tomahawk and a knife in his belt and carried a long-barreled rifle over his shoulder. Spotting the scholar and the girl, he came forward with swift, soundless steps.

The master recoiled in alarm at the approach of the strange and ominous figure, but as the red flooded back into the girl's cheeks, she put her hand upon the scholar's arm. "It's him!" she said in an intense, nervous whisper. "I knew he wasn't dead!"

As soon as she said the words, the master realized whom she meant, and his heart surged with joy, followed by confusion and astonishment. It was clearly William Hackett who was standing before them, but he had changed remarkably.

The young warrior quickly stepped forward and, with a big smile, seized the hand of the scholar. "Mr. Spebbington, it's me, William Hackett! It is so good to see you!" he said excitedly. In stunned amazement the scholar stood pumping his long lost friend's hand, unable to find the words to respond.

Then William turned to Kate, who extended her much smaller hand to him. As William took her hand in his, Katherine spoke first. "I knew you were still alive! I just knew it!"

"Where have you been for so long, my lad?" the scholar blurted out, finding his voice. "Most of us thought you were killed by the Indians!"

"The Indians did have me," William answered as he turned and looked at Gray Fox. "I was captured by the Miami, and to be honest, I wasn't sure I would ever see any of you again, but God saw fit to allow me to return home, thanks to the help of my friend here."

The master, recovering from his momentary shock, threw his arms around his former pupil and welcomed him with many words.

"I have much to tell you all," William replied, "but there is no time to spare! The entire village is in grave danger! The Chickasaw are coming with a thousand warriors, and I have raced ahead of them to warn you."

His manner and his intense concern convinced them of his sincerity. Will quickly snatched the full water bucket as if it weighed nothing and, calling to Gray Fox to follow, hurried them back towards the palisade.

As they drew near, Charles Spebbington yelled the exciting news of William's return to the guards at the gate and, by the time the four of them entered, word had spread throughout the village. The gate guards and a few others quickly gathered around William and his companion, but these were suddenly pushed aside as Will's stepmother forced her way to her missing son. Flinging her arms around his neck, she cried great tears of joy. The others in William's family were right behind her.

When it was Asa Whitlock's turn to welcome his long lost friend, he just stood there in amazement. Finally he said, "Oh my goodness, Will, is it really you? You've changed so much!"

"So have you!" Will shot back. "Just look at you, Whit! You're as tall as your father now!"

"What happened to you?" Asa asked as his curious gaze went from his friend to the intimidating Miami warrior behind him.

"ALL OF YOU, LISTEN TO ME," William said loudly enough for everyone to hear, "I KNOW SOME OF YOU ARE CONCERNED ABOUT THE INDIAN WHO CAME IN WITH ME. HIS NAME IS GRAY FOX, AND HE IS A GOOD FRIEND OF MINE. HE SAVED MY LIFE, AND HE RISKED HIS OWN TO COME WITH ME. THERE IS SO MUCH I WANT TO TELL YOU, BUT I WILL HAVE TO DO THAT LATER. RIGHT NOW WE ARE ALL IN GRAVE DANGER!"

In a few words he told how he won his freedom from a far northwestern tribe, of the coming of the Chickasaw war party, and of the need to take every precaution for defense. "There's no time to spare," he added. "Very soon a thousand enemy fighters will be here to kill us. Everyone outside the fort must be called in at once, and we must prepare to fight for our lives."

Charles Spebbington relayed William's warning to a guard on top of the blockhouse. The fellow immediately lifted a cow's horn to his lips and blew a long, loud blast, calling those at work in the fields and the forest to hasten to the fort.

John Hackett, Will's step-father, hurried in with the others from the fields. When he realized it was his son standing in front of him, he fell on Will's neck and cried almost as hard as his wife had.

The last to come running through the gates were Jack Cobb and Dirt Gurley, on their way back from a hunt. They had been carrying a large stag between them, but on hearing the horn blast, they dropped the deer and raced to the fort.

When all were inside the palisade, the gates were barred, and the best marksmen were sent to watch in the upper story of the blockhouses. The women and girls were sent to the homes to begin melting lead and molding bullets.

"What in tarnation happened to you?" Dirt Gurley asked William after he and Jack welcomed him back home. "And who in the world is this?" he added when he saw Gray Fox standing near.

"This is my good friend Gray Fox," Will answered, nodding toward the Miami. "He saved my life. The rest of my story will take too long to explain right now. If we make it through this, I'll tell you all about it."

Turning to Gray Fox, Will said, "This is Cobb and Gurley. They are good men and taught me much of what I know about the forest."

The young Miami warrior nodded his understanding and signed a greeting to the two scouts, who both signed back a friendly response.

"Did I hear you say that there's an army of Chickasaw headed for us?" Jack asked William with a look of confusion. "I thought the Chickasaw were way west and north of here."

"Normally they are," Will answered confidently, "but they're being sent down here specifically to kill everyone in Larkinboro and burn it to the ground."

"Sent here!" Jack shot back angrily. "By who?"

"By two British agents: a Major Trask and another guy named Girty."

"That sounds like the two fellas you said showed up here," Jack said as he turned to Dirt Gurley.

"MAJOR Trask?" Dirt exclaimed. "He didn't say he was a major. He just said he and Girty was scouts fer General Clark of the Virginia militia."

"That may have been what he told you," William returned, "but when I saw him, he was wearing a British uniform, red coat and all. He told the Chickasaw that King George loved them and was giving them this land. All they had to do was to kill all of us and take it. He and Girty even gave them the muskets and powder to do it. He offered to do the same for the Miami who had captured me."

"So the Miami have joined the Chickasaw in this attack?" Jack asked with concern.

"No," Will answered. "At least our tribe hasn't. Since he knew I could speak their language, the Miami chief asked me to talk to them, but I never let Trask and Girty know I spoke English. As far as they understood, I was just another Indian."

"Well, the truth be told, it's kinda scary how much you look like one," Dirt agreed.

"I thought they might be freer with their words if they didn't think I could understand them," Will explained, "and as it turned out, I was right. Whenever I spoke to them, I only used sign language, which Girty knew. But the whole time they were talking to each other, I was listening to them. Trask pulled out a map and showed me what settlement they wanted to attack. That's when I figured out that they were going to destroy Larkinboro, and I knew I had to get away and warn you."

"But why didn't the Miami join them?" Jack asked.

"I told the chief that Trask and Girty couldn't be trusted, and he believed me. Besides, Chief Black Cloud of the Miami is a man of peace. He will fight. . .but only when he has to."

"If Trask and Girty came here, that explains how they knew so much about Larkinboro," Will added. "He told the Chickasaw it would be an easy village to take because the people here weren't prepared and wouldn't be expecting an attack."

"YEAH," Dirt shot back angrily, "because that no good pile o' pond scum tol' us there weren't no Injuns within two hundred miles of us. . .AN' WE BELIEVED HIM!"

"Well, with the warnin' Will has given us, we at least have time to get ready," Jack said as he turned and strode quickly to the nearest blockhouse.

"Amen to that," Dirt called after his friend.

"Thanks fer comin' back, Will," the scout said sincerely to his young friend. "You've givin' us a fightin' chance!"

"Come on, lad!" Dirt called as he followed after Jack. "And bring yer friend. We got's lots to do. Let's give them Chickeesaws a fight they'll long remember."

"That's why we're here," William returned with a smile.

"Jus' wait till I gets my peep sights on that rascal Trask!" Dirt Gurley growled loudly. "I sure do hope he's got on that purdy red coat o' his, 'cause I'm gonna shoot them shiny gold buttons clean off it!"

With a chuckle Will translated the scout's words to Gray Fox, who gave a slight smile and snort.

Chapter Twenty-One

WHO TO TRUST

When Jack Cobb understood the danger, he immediately doubled the guards on top of the blockhouses and gave them orders to watch for signs of the approaching enemies. He also assigned men to check the storerooms below the blockhouses to be sure they had plenty of powder and ammunition in each one.

Empty barrels were placed strategically around the village, and everyone who was free to do so was put to work filling them with water from the well. Once it was done, extra buckets were placed near each of them.

William Hackett was constantly busy, helping with the preparations and telling those who must soon fight the great battle everything he knew about the enemy coming against them. He made sure they were aware that most of the Chickasaw warriors with fire arms would be using muskets. While he had been in their village, he had only seen a few rifles. That meant that the warriors with muskets would have to get close to the fort before their shots would be effective.

As Katherine watched all of the preparations, she paid particular attention to William. He was no longer the boy she had known two years ago. Not only did he look different, he acted differently. There was a confidence and a mature seriousness in his bearing as he worked to get ready for battle. She could tell by his behavior that he was no stranger to fighting, and he obviously knew how to win. The others seemed to recognize this in him as well.

The only one who seemed to question William's knowledge and advice was Braxton Wyatt. Several times Kate was close enough to hear Wyatt utter his doubts about William and his Indian friend to others. Braxton had never liked Will and had been secretly glad when he didn't come back with the others two years ago.

"Don't it seem strange that Hackett should come back so suddenly when he might have come before?" he remarked with apparent carelessness to Kate Middlebrook. "You know he's been gone almost two years."

She looked at him sharply, admitting to herself that the same thought had occurred to her. But she didn't like the way Braxton Wyatt said it. "Regardless of what kept him away," she said defensively, "he returned in time to save us from a great danger."

Wyatt laughed at this, but his mouth was curled back in an ugly sneer. "It's probably just some made-up tale to impress us, or more likely, to cover up something else," he replied. "There's not an Indian within two hundred miles of us, except the one he brought. I know! I've been through those woods, and there is no sign."

She turned away, not liking his words and liking his manner even less. Presently she stopped by a corner of a house on a slight elevation where she could see a long distance beyond the palisade. Viewing the forest in several directions, Kate had to admit that everything seemed to agree with Braxton Wyatt's words. The spring day was full of golden sunshine; the fresh new green of the forest was as peaceful and quiet as it always was. She could see no evidence of the extreme danger Will had spoken of. Grudgingly she had to acknowledge that Wyatt might have grounds for his suspicion, but why should William Hackett sound a false alarm? The words *perhaps to cover up something else* returned to her mind, but she dismissed them angrily.

Kate went to the Hackett house and rejoiced with Mrs. Hackett, whose son had come back from the dead. According to her mother's heart, a miracle had been performed, and she openly praised God for it, accepting it as a special gift from heaven.

The blockhouses and the walls of the little village were soon brisling with rifles held by determined and eager defenders. With all of their preparations accomplished, there was nothing to do but wait for an attack to come. William Hackett's warning had scared the settlers enough to make them extremely vigilant, and yet there was some distrust. Braxton Wyatt, a clever youth, had craftily sowed his seeds of suspicion, and it was beginning to have an effect. Subtly he had called attention to the strange appearance of the returned wanderer, the Indian-like air that he possessed, and his new ways that were unlike their own.

As the beautiful day continued peacefully with no evidence of danger, it began to appear that Wyatt was right and that William, for some hidden purpose of his own, perhaps to hide the secret of his long absence, had deceived them. The sun continued to slowly creep across the sky until it touched the western horizon, but still no sign of an enemy appeared.

If Will Hackett was aware of the discontent, he did not show it. The fire of the approaching battle was still in his eyes, and his thoughts were chiefly of the great conflict to come. After the work was done, William took Gray Fox and went to his home and recounted to his family all that had happened during his long absence. While he told the story, his mother praised God repeatedly, thankful for the Father in Heaven's great mercy for returning her son to her. When she heard him speak of his friendship with Gray Fox and all he had done to help William get home, she went over to the Indian, took his hand, and thanked him profusely. When Will interpreted his mother's words, the young frontiersman admitted to himself that Gray Fox showed more emotion than he had ever seen in an Indian.

"She's a good mother," the Miami declared in his native tongue, clearing his throat as he turned to William. "She love you very much!"

"She got to you, didn't she?" William asked with a smile.

Expressionless, the Miami looked at his friend and just snorted. Finally he said to William, "You tell her, Kajika's mother is Gray Fox's mother."

"She *did* get to you," Will returned, still smiling. "I will tell her, and she will be honored."

When Will relayed Gray Fox's words, his mother gave the Miami a sweet smile and patted his arm. Gray Fox cleared his throat again and turned to the side.

"*He, he,*" Will chuckled, "That's Indian for 'I like you too,'. *He, he.*

"Now, Mother, there's something I need to tell you and Father!" he said at last. "I have done all that I can do to make sure that the settlement is as prepared as it can be to face the Chickasaw. I don't want you to worry, but I am not going to be here when they attack. I am going outside."

"Outside!" she gasped. "You mean outside the palisade? But you are safe here!"

He smiled and shook his head. "Please trust me," the confident young warrior returned. "I know how to take care of myself out there. I know the forest as you know the rooms of this house."

"Are you sure about this, Son?" his father asked with concern. "We will need every rifle we can get to hold off so many Indians!"

"That is true, Father, but I can do so much more out there than I can in here. I will blend with them and attack them secretly when they aren't looking. I know how they will attack and what strategies they will use. If I need to, I can slip into the fort and warn you in time for you to prepare for their tricks. It will be best for all of us if I fight out there."

John Hackett finally had to nod his head in resignation. He saw changes in his step-son that he did not understand, but he also saw a mature confidence that he felt compelled to trust.

William turned and explained to his Indian friend what he had just told his parents.

"Gray Fox fights where Kajika fights," was all he said.

William kissed his mother quickly and turned away.

"Gray Fox!" Mrs. Hackett called as they started to leave. The Miami turned to face her. "Please look after my son!" she said with imploring eyes.

William started to interpret, but the Miami cut him off. "Gray Fox knows what she said," the Indian responded. "Tell her that Gray Fox will give his life for you if he needs to."

As William and his friend passed from the house into the little square, Katherine Middlebrook overtook them. "William, are you going to defend the walls?" she asked.

"Actually, Kate, I think I can be of more help out there than in here," he replied, pointing toward the forest.

"It would be better for you to stay," she said with concern.

"I can take care of myself."

"It's not that. Do you know what some of them are saying about you? They are saying that you are not one of us anymore, that it's looking like you made all of this up, and that no attack is coming! If you leave now, it will just confirm to them that they're right."

His dark eyes flashed with anger, but he soon got control of his emotions. "Gray Fox and I will be able to do much more good for the settlement out there than in here," he said, pointing again toward the dark line of the forest, "and we're going to go. Whether I'm telling the truth or not will soon be known. The doubters will only have to wait a little longer. But you believe me, don't you, Kate?"

She looked deep into his steady eyes, and she read there only truth. But she had known even before she looked that William Hackett could never be guilty of treachery. "Oh, yes, I believe you," she replied, "but I want the others to believe you as well."

"They will," he said with a reassuring smile.

No sooner had Will and Gray Fox left the fort than the slanderous tongues began to wag again. Braxton Wyatt said that it was some kind of a trap, though no one could tell how. A sly report was then started that Will had become the worst of all creatures in his time: a renegade, a pioneer who allied himself with the Indians to make war upon his own people. The fact that he had brought an Indian with him was sighted as proof of this. This gossip came to the ears of Asa Whitlock, and the heart of the loyal youth grew hot within him. Asa was not fond of war or fighting of any kind, but he had plenty of courage, and he and

William had been through danger together. "He is changed, I will admit," Asa said loudly when he heard Wyatt discussing this newest charge with his friends, "but if Will says we are going to be attacked, we shall be. I wish that all of us were as true as he."

He checked the powder in the pan of his rifle and flipped the frizzen shut with an ominous *snap* as he stared hard at the mouthy Wyatt. The gossipers said no more in his presence.

But as the day ended, and the sun sank below the distant horizon, still no attack came. The nerves of the villagers became more strained, and more discussions could be heard among the defenders about the possibility of the warning being a hoax. They spoke of going about their regular pursuits: there was work that could be done on the outside in the twilight, and enough time had already been lost through a false alarm. But some of the older men with cautious wisdom advised them to wait, and their counsel was taken. Night finally came, thick and black.

The forest faded away in the darkness. Nothing was visible even fifty yards from the palisade, and in the log houses, few lights burned. The little colony, a tiny oasis of light, was alone in the vast and circling wilderness. In all directions the forest curved away for hundreds of miles. It would be a journey of days to any other settlements; they were hemmed in everywhere by silence and loneliness. Whatever happened, they must depend upon themselves, because there was no one else who could bring them help. Their small village could be completely wiped out, and the rest of the world would not hear of it until long afterwards.

A moaning wind came up and sighed over the log houses. The younger children fell asleep at last, but the rest who understood the possible danger could not find such solace. In this black darkness their fears became real.

There was little noise inside the fort. By the low fires in the houses, the women steadily cast rifle balls. They seldom spoke to each other as they poured the melted lead into the molds. By the walls the men too, rifles in hand, were silent as they sought with intent eyes to mark what was passing in the forest.

Katherine Middlebrook worked in her father's house, melting lead at a bed of coals in the wide fireplace. Her face was flushed as she bent over the fire, and her sleeves were rolled back, showing her strong arms. She hated the thought of war, but she was resolved to do her part to the last. As she labored beside her mother and sister, she let her mind return to Will. She tried to tell herself that he had confidently assured her that he was at home in the dark forest and knew very well how to take care of himself, but her fears for his safety wouldn't go away.

When she finished her task, she went to the door of the log home and stepped out into the cool of the night. Drawn by curiosity, she continued her walk until it brought her near the palisade. There she watched the men on guard, their dusky figures touched by the pale light that came from the half moon. Asa Whitlock, who was on duty beside the gate, saw his friend and approached her.

"You had better go back," he said. "We may be attacked at any time, and a ball or arrow could reach you here."

"So you believe Will like I do—that an attack is coming?"

"Of course I do," replied Asa with emphasis. "There are some things about Will Hackett that will never change. If he tells you something, you can count on it!"

Just then they were interrupted by the approach of several men talking loudly. Braxton Wyatt was with them, and Katherine saw at once that it was the group of complainers.

"I'm telling you, this whole thing is a made up nothing!" said Seth Lowndes, a loud, arrogant man, the boaster of the colony. "That 'Half-Indian' Hackett is a fool or a liar!" As he said this, he glared straight at Asa. Kate stood close enough to smell the liquor on his breath. "There ain't no Indians in these parts, and I'm gonna prove it."

He stood in the center of a ray of moonlight as he spoke, and it lit his red, sneering face. Kate and Asa were both disgusted with this tipsy braggart, but neither said anything.

"I'm going outside," repeated Lowndes in a yet more noisy tone, "and if I run across anything more than a deer, I'll eat my hat!"

"Well, you aren't going through the gate," Asa said firmly. "We've been ordered to keep it barred shut tonight."

One or two uttered words of protest, but Braxton Wyatt kept pushing him to go on, joining him in words of contempt for the alleged danger.

With a snort of disdain, Lowndes walked to the palisade and ascended the ladder that led to the narrow walkway where the guards stood. Climbing onto the top of the innermost row of logs forming the upright wall, he balanced himself unsteadily with one foot on the second row of sharpened logs. He stood straight and tall like he was the king of the world, lord of all that was before him. Lowndes wobbled slightly, breathing hard and red-faced from the exertion of the climb. His eyes gleaming triumphantly as, from his high perch, he looked toward the forest. "YA SEE!" the arrogant Lowndes called loudly so that all on the wall could hear. "NOTHIN'. . .NOTHIN' ATOLL! I'M TELLIN' ALL OF YOU, THERE'S NOT. . ." But the words were cut short. From the forest came a sharp report, echoing in the still night, and the puffy man grabbed his chest and fell from the palisade back into the enclosure, dead before he touched the ground.

Kate let out a scream as his body landed just in front of her. Her cry was immediately joined by a chorus of fierce yell and war whoops bursting from the forest. The shrieks, so full of menace and fury, was more terrible than that of the rifle. Then came other shots—a rapid, pattering volley—and bullets struck with a low, sighing sound against the walls of the blockhouse. Long, quavering cries from the voices of many Indian warriors rose again, echoing in the black forest.

As all of it happened, Kate stood like stone, paralyzed in fear. The terrible cries outside rang in her ears, and it seemed to numb her mind. But Asa grasped her by the arm and drew her back. "Go into your house!" he cried. "A rifle ball could reach you here!"

Once Asa got Kate moving, he quickly hurried back to the wall. Obedient to his duty, the young defender rushed to do his part in the defense of the fort. Climbing to the top of the palisade, Asa leveled his rifle and aimed carefully at the muzzle flashes in the darkness. He and the other guards continued to load and fire at the multitude of rifle blasts for several long minutes.

Kate retreated to the nearest log house but felt compelled to stop and watch the anxious defenders as they blasted their weapons at the invisible warriors in the distance. She stood in the darkness for several minutes, unable to take her eyes off the battle.

After the initial shock of horror at the death of Lowndes, she was able to get control of the paralyzing terror that had gripped her. Fear was certainly still present, but taking courage from Asa, Kate realized that she could be afraid, but that fear didn't have to control her. As she began to take stock of her feelings, she was also conscious of another emotion. It took her a moment to identify it, but she finally realized that it was a feeling of relief. Will Hackett had told the truth. He knew what he was talking about when he brought his warning. He had risked his life to warn his friends and family at Larkinboro, and he and his friend were out there risking their lives right now, trying to save them from this army of savage fighters. In Katherine's mind they were heroes.

Chapter Twenty-Two

THE SIEGE

The instant the first volley of musket and rifle fire blasted from the surrounding forest, everyone in Larkinboro knew that William had spoken the truth. Immediately the entire village exploded with activity. Men who had not been manning the walls burst from their homes, each with rifle in hand, and raced to join the fight. Children were left safely inside with their older siblings while many of the women rushed to the base of the wall where, illuminated by torches and lanterns, they reloaded empty rifles with powder and shot. Ready-to-use fire arms were quickly passed back to the defenders above.

Most of the Indians who were firing at the settlers were using smooth-bore muskets, which were more of a nuisance than a real danger due to their inaccuracy at the distance from which they were firing. The Indians soon figured this out, and they changed the nature of their attacks. A group of warriors would make a dash toward the fort in the darkness and fire irregular volleys, then rush back to the safety of the forest before the riflemen on the wall could target their muzzle blasts and pick them off.

A small number of the enemy fighters had rifles, and they used them to try to pick off settlers whenever the shape of a head appeared above the wall. After a while rifle balls began to hit the north wall of the fort, and the defenders on that side noticed the flash of rifles from the area of a small hill half way between the woods and the fort. The attackers were hidden by darkness, but when they fired their guns, the muzzle blast revealed their location, and sharpshooters on the wall then saturated the area with lead. Clouds soon blew in, covering the light from the moon, and the savages were able to crawl nearer, making the enemy's less accurate muskets a greater threat. As the Indians began to fire in mass from their closer positions, splinters and large chunks of wood were blasted off the tops of the log posts forming the walls of the fort. So much lead flew that the defenders had to duck behind the palisade for protection. Few of the pioneers were brave enough to keep firing in the face of the new onslaught. Of those who did, several were wounded.

Suddenly a war cry was heard in the darkness, and at that moment a thousand ferocious warriors took up the yell and, leaping to their feet, charged the fort.

"HERE THEY COME!" the voice of Jack Cobb called out firmly. "STAND YER GROUND, AN' MAKE EVERY SHOT COUNT!"

"Lord Jesus, help us!" cried a terrified Betsy Middlebrook, Katherine's mother, as she loaded rifles below the wall. The prayer was immediately repeated by every voice in the court yard.

Just at that moment clouds that had been covering the moon separated. The illumination that fell on the open fields in front of the walls was dim indeed, but it was enough. The shapes of the charging Chickasaw warriors were revealed, and the determined pioneers could now see their targets. The muzzles of the defending rifles belched a chorus of death and destruction into the mass of blood-thirsty attackers.

When many of the Indians in the front line suddenly fell, it caused the rest to waver in their attack. Just as the leaders screamed for their braves to renew the assault, the loaded rifles that had been passed up to the defenders on the wall released another devastating blast. When the smoke cleared, the pioneers saw the remainder of the Chickasaw army flee back to the safety of the forest shadows.

A feeling of exaltation rushed through the hearts of the men on the wall as they saw the Indians running away. A cheer broke out, but it was short lived. Even as the defenders congratulated themselves, a steady volley of rifle and musket fire erupted from the edge of the woods, and bullets began to splinter the top edge of the wall again.

Small bits of wood showered down on the crouching Asa Whitlock as a bullet struck the wall where he had just been standing. Blowing away the bits of wood dust that had fallen on his nose and eyes, Asa jumped back to his feet and, lining his sites carefully on a tiny flash in the distance, fired his rifle.

Just as the defenders grew confident in their ability to keep their enemies pinned down in the distant forest, the wind would blow in some new clouds to cover the moon, and before long the enemies' muzzle blasts would be much closer and more effective. When the Chickasaw warriors decided that the moon-covered darkness would last, they made another rush at the walls.

"PRAY, LADIES! PRAY!" Charles Spebbington called down as his skin crawled with the sound of screaming Indians charging at them again.

This time the darkness was so thick that none of the advancing forms were visible. Some of the defenders discharged their rifles into the darkness, hoping to accidentally hit a target, but most were disciplined and held their fire until the enemy was close enough to see. Several more braves dropped when the rifle fire commenced, but the Chickasaw tasted victory and pressed their attack. During this fight, six Indians ran up carrying a small log and began battering the gates. They had only made three strong blows when suddenly two blasts of buckshot from the holes in floor of the blockhouses dropped two and scattered the rest of those wielding the log. Many of the fighters ran away, yelling in pain and fear, and as more lead rained down on the rest, the remaining attackers began to lose their nerve. Soon another race for the safety of the dark woods broke out, met by more cheers from the relieved defenders.

After this the Indians seemed to settle for blasting away at the pioneers from the edge of the forest. This continued for the rest of the night. Just as the first glimmer of dawn appeared in the east, the Indians stopped shooting. Not a sound was heard from the dark woods in the distance.

Surprised at the sudden, abrupt ending of the fight, Asa Whitlock took a careful look over the wall, ready to drop back down at the first report of a gun. Asa stared hard at the edge of the woods that became clearer in the dawning light, but he could see nothing. The forest rose up like a solid, dark wall, and in the cleared space between the fort and the woods, not a blade of grass stirred. The savage army seemed to have vanished like smoke melting into the air. Asa wasn't the only one who was dismayed.

"Asa! Asa! What do you see?" called Kate from below, upon whose ears the sudden silence was almost as terrifying as the noise of battle.

"Nothing!" the young defender called back. "It's like they all just disappeared!"

"They're gone!" another man called down to the anxious ladies below. "There ain't a single Injun is sight! They must of all turned tail an' run off!"

"WE LICKED 'EM!" another defender cried as cheers began to go up among all the villagers.

"Yeah, we licked 'em alright," Braxton Wyatt said loudly, "but no thanks to that Will Hackett!"

"HEY!" called Asa angrily. "You've got no call to. . ." but Wyatt cut him off.

"I've got all the call I need!" the youth shot back. "That no good Hackett ran off like a coward before the fightin' even started! Why, he was probably one of them out there shootin' at us!"

As soon as the words left his mouth, Asa's fist landed solidly on Wyatt's nose, knocking him flat on his back.

"WHAT DO YOU MEAN, HITTIN' ME LIKE THAT?" Wyatt yelled up at Asa as he held his red, swollen nose.

"I had to, Braxton," Asa returned calmly. "You see, I didn't have time to reload my rifle *so I could shoot you!*"

Braxton Wyatt's eyes got big, and he began scooting away from Asa. "Keep him away from me!" the bully called to those around him. "That guy's crazy!"

Asa stepped forward and bent over his injured victim. "Will Hackett speaks the truth! He risked his life to bring us warning about this attack, and it saved all of us. He also said that he was going out in the woods to help us beat these Chickasaw, and that's exactly what he's doing! You better watch what you say about Will Hackett. Do you understand me, Wyatt?"

"Jus' get away from me!" Braxton said again. "You're crazy!

"Did all of you see what that crazy Asa Whitlock did to me?" Braxton said to those standing around. "All I did was speak my mind. A man's got a right to speak his mind. Asa should be locked up for what he did!"

"Just calm down, Wyatt," Jack Cobb said in his slow, calm voice. "Asa actually saved your life."

"What are you talkin' about? He didn't save my life!"

"Sure he did," Jack persisted. "After what you said about Will Hackett, if Asa hadn't hit you, I was gonna throw you over the wall and let the Indians have you!"

"You're. . .you're crazy too!" Braxton said as he rose to his feet and backed away. "They're both crazy! Keep them away from me!"

A report ran through the village that the defeated savage army had gone, and the women and the men with little experience believed it, but the veterans rebuked such premature rejoicing. Jack Cobb told all of the men on the walls to keep watch with more vigilance than ever. "It may look purdy lonesome out there," he announced to the men on guard duty, "but you can bet your britches those rascals ain't done with us yet."

Then long hours of waiting began, and those who could, slept. All morning no sign of the Chickasaw army could be seen or heard.

Katherine Middlebrook went back to her house, ate a little, and spread a buffalo robe over herself, trying to sleep. But as tired as she was, Kate found it hard to drop off. All the stress and the terror of the recent battle kept her agitated thoughts from settling into peace. The night's events kept replaying in her mind over and over again. Eventually weariness had its way, and she dozed, but only for a short time. When she awoke, Kate immediately hurried out to find what was happening.

"Are they still there?" was her first question when she walked up to the wall.

"Who knows?" one of the guards called down. "Nobody's seen any of them since the fight, but no one's gone out there lookin' for 'em either."

Even though it was a bright, sunny day, the watchful eyes of the guards observed nothing save what had been there before the savages came. They could actually see a little ways into the forest, but it looked like empty woods as far as their eyes could reach. They saw no encampment, and not a single warrior could be seen passing through the undergrowth.

Kate hoped that the danger was over, and she turned and started walking back to her house. Looking up, she saw Asa coming towards her. She lifted her hand to wave at him when she heard a distant report, and Asa's fur cap, pierced by a bullet, flew from his head to the earth. Asa himself stood in amazement, reaching for the top of his head where his cap had been. He was still standing, looking for his cap, when Kate screamed at him drop to the ground. Suddenly awakened to the danger, the youth bent low and moved quickly to the shelter of one of the log houses. His pace quickened as two more rifle balls struck the ground near him.

Once more the alarm went through the fort. This was a new danger, and the defenders were at a loss as to how to meet it. It was evident that the firing came from a high point, one commanding a view inside the walls. Bullets pattered among the houses and in the open spaces enclosed by the walls, wounding two of the men. The threat had become serious.

At risk to his own life, Jack Cobb made several trips back and forth across the open area between the houses and the wall to draw the fire of the Indian sharpshooters. As he did so, Dirt Gurley and several other men watched in the general area where the suspected snipers were. Several shots were fired at Jack. All came close, and one tore a hole through the tail of his hunting shirt.

"Well?" Jack called urgently when he finally made it to shelter. "You aren't gonna make me do that again, are you, Dirt?"

"Don't get your feathers all ruffled," Gurley called back. "I think we got 'em spotted!"

"Where are they?" Jack asked eagerly.

"Me an' Mace Wilson both spotted some puffs of gun smoke from that big oak at the edge of the forest northwest of the stockade." Dirt answered. "Looks to be several of them weasels up in them branches shootin' at us." Dirt could see the disgusted look on his friend's face.

"Yeah," Dirt spoke again, "it's the same tree me an' you tried to get everybody to cut down last year for this very reason, but they all voted against it 'cuz it was gonna take too much time away from their field work. I'm wonderin' how they all feel about it now?"

The fire of the Indian riflemen in the tree was so accurate that the north wall of the palisade could not be manned. It had even become extremely dangerous to pass from house to house. The terrors of the night were gone, but the day had brought with it a menace just as deadly.

On the sheltered side of one house, the leaders of the village held a desperate conference. The schoolmaster, Jack, Dirt, John Hackett, and Silas Middlebrook faced each other.

"Don't even say it," the later said as he looked anxiously at the two scouts. "We should have followed your advice and cut that tree down last year, but we didn't, and now we're in a fix!"

"Any ideas, gentlemen?" John Hackett asked, looking around at all of them.

"It is profoundly evident that those savages have in some manner procured a number of our long-range Kentucky rifles," the schoolmaster began. "But they are no better than ours, nor is it any farther from us to that tree than it is from that tree to us. Why can't our best marksmen pick them off?" He looked questioningly at Jack and Dirt, who shook their heads without changing their expressions.

"It ain't dat easy, Perfesser," Dirt said. "There's a bit of difference betwixt our sitchee-ations."

The scholar gave the scout a blank look.

"He means they're too well sheltered behind all those leaves," replied Jack Cobb, "while we would not be if we should try to fire at them."

"That's right, Perfesser," Dirt agreed. "Our riflemen would be stickin' their heads up, just beggin' the Injuns to put a bullet through 'em, whilst the best our fellers could do would be to just guess where to aim their shots."

"But we *must* solve this problem! We have to get rid of them somehow!" exclaimed Mr. Hackett.

"John's right," agreed Mr. Middlebrook, and as he spoke, they heard a bullet thud against the wall of the house. From the forest came a wild, quavering yell of triumph, full of the most merciless menace. Mr. Hackett and Mr. Middlebrook shuddered as they both thought of their wives and children and what might happen to them if the Indians managed to enter the fort.

"Maybe you fellers have already figured this out, but if those rascals in that tree keep on driving us from the palisade," explained Dirt, setting his face in the grim manner of one who forces himself to tell the truth, "there's nothin' to prevent the main war party of them scum-suckin' marsh rats from makin' an attack. While their sharpshooters keep all of us pinned down, the rest of them cut-throats will be climbing over the wall."

They stared at each other in silent despair as Jack Cobb went to the corner of the house and very carefully took a glance at the fatal tree. No one was firing then, and he could see nothing among its branches. In the fresh green of its young foliage, it looked like a huge, leafy ball set upon a giant stem, and Cobb growled at it in futile anger. Nor was a foe visible elsewhere. The entire savage army lay hidden in the forest, and nothing fluttered or moved but the leaves and the grass.

The schoolmaster, led by the same interest, followed Cobb, and keeping to the safety of the walls, stole glances at the tree. As they looked, they heard the faint report of a shot. Just then a brown body was seen to tumble out and crash to the ground, where it lay very still.

"Ha!" cried the scholar in exultation. "There is at least one marksman among us who can beat them at their own trick! Who did it? Who fired that shot, Jack?"

Cobb did not answer. A look of surprise passed across his face, then he began to study the forest. But he could discern no movement. The faint sound of a second shot came, and another brown body dropped to the ground.

The master cried out once more in exultation and wished to know why others within the palisade did not imitate the skillful sharpshooter.

But Jack Cobb shook his head slowly. "It ain't what you think, Mr. Spebbington. Them shots never come from any of our men. We've got friends outside, an' they's apickin' off them murderers one by one. Right now the savages think we're doin' it, but they'll soon figure out the difference."

There was a third shot, and the tree ejected a third body.

"Three shots an' three hits. It appears to me that whomsomever's doin' that shootin' is mighty good at it!" exclaimed Dirt Gurley with a tone of admiration.

"There, they've figured it out," Jack said when a terrific yell full of anger came from the forest. "But they ain't got him. They'd shout in a different way if they had."

"Well, I know one thang fer sure," Dirt Gurley added. "Them murderin' reperbates still stuck up in that tree are lookin' at life a whole heap different than they did a few minutes ago! Let me tell you, I'd hate to be wearin' their moccasins right now!"

An hour later a fourth Indian was shot from the tree, and less than fifteen minutes afterwards, a fifth fell victim to the terrible rifle. At that moment the last two survivors dropped from the limbs and ran for the forest. Cobb, Dirt, and Asa were watching together and saw the flight.

"I reckon that's about all they could do," voiced Dirt Gurley as he watched the two Indians run, "but them two is in fer it now."

"You don't think they'll make it?" Asa asked.

"Well, let me put it this way: based on how our friend out there's been shootin', if both of them two weasels reach the woods safely, you can call me a skunk cabbage."

At that moment another shot rang out, and the foremost savage fell just at the edge of the forest. The other one, the sole survivor of the tree, escaped behind the sheltering trunks. Asa quickly turned to look at Dirt, who only smiled in return.

The furious Chickasaw, angry at having lost their snipers, vented their frustration in a loud chorus of ferocious yells and rifle balls fired against the stockade. This was answered by a strong volley of rifle shots from the walls of the fort. When the short exchange ended, peace settled down upon the little valley once again.

Chapter Twenty-Three

NIGHT ATTACK

For the rest of the afternoon, the guards on the wall kept a sharp eye on the edge of the forest, but nothing more of the enemy army was seen. When the sun had set and night finally came, the sentinels continued their vigil on high alert. Two hours later a steady breeze blew in clouds that blocked the stars and the light from the moon, and the night became very dark. Only being able to see a short distance past the wall caused a dramatic increase in the guards' alertness. A tense watch was kept, anticipating another night attack, but none came.

In the quietness of the night, Katherine Middlebrook, Lizzy Blake, and Gardenia Leavenworth climbed the ladder to the walkway behind the northeast wall where Asa Whitlock was on watch. They found Asa with his rifle beside him, leaning against the outside wall, scanning the outer darkness. Hearing his name whispered behind him, he turned to see his three friends. "You're just in time," he said cheerfully.

"In time for what?" Gardenia answered back.

"To keep me from nodding off because it's so boring up here."

"Are the Indians still there?" Gardenia asked as she stood on her tiptoes and gazed into the darkness.

"I expect so," Asa answered, "but so far no one has seen or heard anything of them."

"Then how do you know they are still there?"

"Because, Gardenia, there's no reason for them not to be," Asa returned. "If we were just being attacked by a small war party, then their losses so far might be enough to discourage them and send them home. But this is an army of them, and they're here to destroy our home. It just makes sense to expect them to try a few more attacks against us."

"A FEW MORE ATTACKS!" Lizzy exclaimed. "How in the world are we supposed to survive a few more attacks? I thought we were all going to be shot to kingdom come when they had all of those people up in that tree just firing away at us!"

"Yeah," Asa nodded his agreement, "for a little while today we were in big trouble. Fortunately for us, we have friends out there who were able to stop them." As he said this, he looked over at Kate and winked.

"Well, I think," Gardenia announced firmly, "that someone should go out there and tell those Indians that we don't appreciate what they're doing!"

"We should give them a piece of our mind!" Lizzy agreed.

"That's right!" Gardenia agreed with feeling.

"Are you two serious?" Katherine asked with a confused look on her face.

"Of course we're serious," Lizzy shot back.

"Kate, we can't let those Indians push us around!" Gardenia said with fire in her eyes. "We've got to let them know we aren't going to stand for all their shenanigans! Don't you agree, Asa?"

"Sure I do," Asa answered, "but we've, sort of, been telling them that all day, except we've been speaking with our rifles at a nice, safe distance.

Just then one of the older men held up his hand in a warning.

"What is it, Tom?" one of the other men on guard duty whispered.

"I ain't sure, but I thought I saw something move in the dark below the wall."

Asa gave a hand sign to the girls that they should move toward the ladder as he and the other guards prepared to fire their rifles.

Just then there was a slight noise on the outside, so faint that only keen ears could hear it. "Don't shoot!" they heard a voice whisper from below. "It's a friend!" Then came the sound of scratching, and as they watched the edge of the wall, a hideously painted face rose above it.

A scream escaped the lips of the terrified Lizzy Blake, and one of the older men threw his rifle to his shoulder, but quick as a flash, Asa pushed the rifle barrel to the side. "Don't fire!" he cried out with a smile. "It's Will! Will Hackett!"

"Are you sure?" Tom said as he stared in amazement at the savage face before him. Suddenly that painted face spread into a wide grin.

"Hey, Mr. Mason," it said in a friendly greeting. "It's really me, Will Hackett."

"Thunder an' lightening, boy!" Tom exclaimed when he finally recognized John Hackett's son. "What in the name of common sense are you doin' dressed up like one of them wild men? You could have gotten your head blown off, an' then what would I have said to your pa an' ma?"

"Well, I am grateful to all of you for not shooting me," William said, still smiling, "but by dressing like this and painting our faces, Gray Fox and I have been able to sneak into the Chickasaw camp and learn their plans.

"Oh, hello ladies," Will said politely when he saw the girls standing near the ladder.

None of the three responded. They all had their mouths open and a look of astonishment on their faces. As he climbed over the wall and stood among them, Will gave a low soft laugh at the girls' expressions. "Well, aren't you going to say hello to your old friend?" Will said with a chuckle.

"I. . .I didn't recognize you," Kate finally blurted out.

"Land sakes, William," Gardenia exclaimed, "you look more like the Indians than the Indians do."

"You scared me silly!" Lizzy added, still clasping her hands to her chest.

"I'm sorry I scared you," Will returned genuinely, "but I needed the Chickasaw to think that I'm one of them. There are actually a couple of different tribes of them together, and they all don't know each other, so that helped us blend in."

As soon as word got down to the guards that William had returned, Jack Cobb, who had been standing at the gate, hurried to the northeast wall. "Glad you made it back in with all your hair," the scout said without expression.

"Me too," William returned with a smile.

"Where's your friend?" Jack asked.

"We thought it might be too dangerous for both of us to try to sneak back, so he stayed in their camp to keep an eye on the Chickasaw while I came to report in."

"It was you who shot the Indians in the tree," Jack announced matter-of-factly.

"You're not complaining about it, are you?" he said with a sly smile.

"No, we're definitely not complaining," replied Cobb. "In fact, we're all pretty excited about it! You saved our bacon that time, and that's fer sure."

"That's actually the reason I came back tonight," Will said more seriously. "You're in trouble again, and I came to warn you."

Jack quickly stepped over to the ladder and waved to Dirt Gurley to come up. When the scout arrived, Jack turned to face the young frontiersman. "Alright, Will, what did you come to warn us about?"

"Well, we could tell something was up," William began. "There was a lot of discussion among the braves earlier this evening. The problem is that neither Gray Fox nor I speak Chickasaw, and we couldn't tell exactly what they were planning. We do understand their sign language, but if we used it in camp, they would wonder why we weren't speaking their language, so we decided to wait. Later, when all their warriors started moving off in different directions, I had an idea. I followed some of their scouts sent farthest out to watch the fort. I knew they would want to be as quiet as possible, so I asked them in sign language what was going on."

"So what in the name of Amos Bosworth IS goin' on?" Dirt asked impatiently.

"In less than an hour, they're going to send archers up as close as they can to the north and south walls and shoot fire arrows into the fort to set the homes on fire. While you're fighting the flames, they're planning on sending a quarter of their fighters against the gate. The rest will attack from the east against the rear wall of the fort."

"Oh squash!" Dirt groaned. "We cain't fight fires an' Injuns at the same time!"

"I think that's their point, Mr. Dirt," said Gardenia sincerely.

"I know that's their stinkin' point!" the scout snapped in frustration as he held his head in his hands.

"MR. DIRT!" Gardenia gasped. "WATCH YOUR LANGUAGE! THERE ARE LADIES PRESENT.

"Beggin' yer pardon," the scout growled under his breath.

He turned to his friend. "What are we gonna do, Jack?" the scout asked with concern. "I'm afeared them reprobates may have us this time!"

"Well, we can get everyone to form bucket brigades and soak the roofs of the homes closest to the north and south walls so them fire arrows get quenched when they hit."

"But if they get close enough, them murderin' rascals can shoot 'em all over the fort!" Dirt pointed out anxiously.

"I think I have an idea that may keep the archers from getting that close," Will spoke up.

"There ain't no moon tonight, an' it's as dark as pitch out there," Dirt shot back, "so we sure as death ain't gonna see 'em! If'n you got some genius idear to solve that little problem, well, I'm all ears!"

"I'll tell you while we get everyone busy with the water buckets," Will answered. "We don't have much time. This thing's supposed to start soon."

Jack sent the alarm through the fort and quickly got both men and women passing buckets of water from the barrels to men standing on ladders set against the houses. The ones with sod roofs were ignored, trusting in the sod to quench the flames, but the thatch roofs were soaked thoroughly. The women proved to be so eager and efficient at the task that Jack was able to send most of the men back to the walls to watch for the coming attack.

The children were hustled into several central houses, and a few mothers stayed with them while the rest grabbed blankets and stood with their backs to the north and south walls, ready to fight fires if needed.

When Jack completed the plans to his satisfaction, he hurried back to the gate. Arriving at the top of the west wall, he found William and another guard finishing up tying unlit torches to long poles.

"You think this is gonna work?" the skeptical guard asked Jack when the scout arrived.

"It made sense to me when Will explained it," Jack returned confidently. "When the time comes, we'll light the torches, stand 'em up, an' tie the long poles to the wall in several spots. That way the light from the torches will shine out far enough to let our sharp shooters see the Chickasaw before they can get very close."

"The torches high on the poles," Will added, "will keep the light out of our eyes and prevent it from spoiling our aim."

Jack looked around and saw Dirt on the north wall, the scholar on the east wall, and John Hackett on the south wall, all looking intently at him. Each had helpers holding their prepared torches.

"Hey, what's that?" one of the guards asked, pointing into the night.

A tiny pinpoint of light moved quickly through the darkness from the woods toward the fort.

"That's it!" exclaimed William. "They're running torches out to light the fire arrows!"

'LIGHT 'EM UP!" Jack yelled and turned, giving a loud, shrill whistle back into the fort.

Immediately fire was applied to all the torches, and workers began tying the tall poles against the walls. The area in front of each of the walls was suddenly illuminated by the radiating light.

"I SEE 'EM!" one of the guards near Dirt Gurley yelled as he scanned the lighted plain in front of them.

Standing only fifty yards away from the wall was a line of ten Chickasaw warriors holding bows and arrows.

"LET 'EM HAVE IT!" Dirt yelled as he raised his rifle to his shoulder. "DRIVE 'EM BACK TO THE WOODS!"

Fifty rifles fired almost simultaneously from both the north and the south walls as the Indian archers came into view. With yells of panic, many of the enemy archers dove for cover or ran away as bullets began to strike the earth all around them.

After several had fallen to the rifle fire from the fort, the Indian archers had to retreat further into the darkness to hide from the settlers' accurately aimed long guns. That's when the Chickasaw were able to initiate their plan.

"HERE THEY COME!" Dirt shouted to the others as he saw the flaming arrows arching through the night sky straight for them. The guards on the north and south walls ducked as the arrows flew over them. The water soaked thatch roofs did their job as the fiery missiles struck, sizzled, and went out. Unfortunately not all of the fire arrows hit the roofs. A few fell short and embedded in the wooden sides of the houses. As flames began to take hold in the dry bark of the logs, women standing against the walls quickly went into action. They took blankets, dunked them into the water barrels, and rushed forward to slap the fire with the sopping wet covers.

Frustrated at not seeing the hated fort burst into flames, the Chickasaw leaders screamed their war cries, and suddenly nearly a thousand warriors charged, yelling like demons.

Unfortunately for the Indians, the bright, raised torches revealed their running forms fifty or sixty yards before they got to the fort. The gunfire from the walls was relentless and accurate. As the attacking warriors saw more and more of their comrades drop from the accurately aimed long rifles, they began to have second thoughts. Those in front staggered as more bullets flew. When the muzzle blasts from the wall continued furiously, those leading the charge suddenly turned and raced back into the night, leading the rest with them.

Jack quickly turned to see if the defenders on the other walls needed help, but in each case the attackers were retreating. Yelling below the north wall drew Jack's attention, and he saw a persistent flame running under the eaves of one of the log homes that the ladies with their wet blankets could not reach.

"DIRT!" Jack yelled to his celebrating friend on the north wall. "Quit dancing around like a yahoo an' help those ladies put out that fire!"

For the next hour all was quiet. William had Jack put out the torches but told the men be ready to light them back up at a moment's notice. When all was dark again, Will slipped over the wall and disappeared into the night. Jack kept a strong guard at their posts for the next three hours as they waited anxiously.

It was well past midnight when a whispered voice was heard below the west wall. "Don't shoot! It's me, Will Hackett! I'm coming up."

Jack was waiting on him when the young scout climbed over the top of the wall. "What'd you find out?" Jack asked anxiously.

"*Hee, hee,*" Will chuckled. "It looks like they think the Great Spirit's mad at them. They can't figure out why their plan failed so miserably."

"Are they givin' up?" one of the guards wanted to know.

"They're done for tonight," William answered confidently, "but Trask won't let them quit. I heard him and Girty talking. They are bound and determined to burn down this fort."

"That's bad," another guard spoke his thoughts.

"It may not be as bad as it seems," the youthful scout answered with a smile. "I saw some of the looks a few of the young braves gave Trask and Girty when they weren't looking. If the Great Spirit gets much madder at the Chickasaw, those two British agents may have an army of angry Indians after *their* hair."

"So do you think the Great Spirit might get madder at them?" Jack asked as a faint smile spread across his weathered face.

"We'll have to talk to Him and see," William smiled in return, "but I'm thinking there's a really good chance that He might."

Chapter Twenty-Four

STRIKE THE ROCK

"So I guess you'll be going out again?" Asa asked his friend after William gave his report to Jack.

"As long as Trask and his army of cut-throats are out there scheming to take our scalps, that's where I need to be." Will answered. "I won't be going back out tonight though. I need some rest and some of my mother's good food."

"Do you think you should go get Gray Fox?" Asa asked with concern.

"I asked him if he wanted to come with me," Will answered, "but he showed me a big deer roast he had stolen from the Chickasaw, and he's going to eat it in a warm spot he built under some thick brush to the west of their camp. I think he'll be fine."

"Well, if you're going to go see your mother, I think you better do something about how you look," Asa suggested.

"What's wrong with the way I look?" William asked with mock hurt.

"Well, for one thing, you look like you've come to scalp us all!" Asa shot back, laughing. "If Gardenia was here, she'd say 'Glory be! It gives me the heeby jeebies just looking at you!'"

All of the guards on top of the blockhouse laughed at that last statement.

"Well, I don't want everybody getting the *heeby jeebies*," Will laughed. "I'll go wash this paint off my face. Then, Whit, if I could get you and Jack to escort this wild man to his home, you can let folks know who I am until I can get out of my Chickasaw suit."

Everyone in the village knew that William Hackett had returned and brought them warning of the fire arrow attack just in time. Because of this, all the doubts about William's loyalty were cast aside, and everyone began to appreciate that John Hackett's oldest son had come back and was fighting for them...everyone accept Braxton Wyatt. Nothing was going to change his mind about William.

The exhaustion of her step-son became apparent to Betsy Hackett the next day when William slept till noon. She had to skip the breakfast she had planned for him and instead go straight to the big dinner.

"What's that amazing smell?" Will said groggily as he leaned his head over the edge of the loft where he slept and looked down on his mother's meal preparations.

"I'm cooking a roast," his mother called up.

"That doesn't smell like deer," Will returned.

"It's not. It's a beef roast."

"How did you get a beef roast?" Will asked again as he got dressed.

"Well, when we knew the Indians were coming, we brought many of the oxen into the fort for protection," she answered, "but now we're running out of grass to feed them. It was decided to kill a few to thin their numbers. That's how we got the roast."

"I hate to see us lose the oxen," her step-son returned as he climbed down the ladder from the loft.

"All of us do," agreed his mother, "but this way we can try to keep some of them alive."

William enjoyed the delicious meal with his family. He tried to answer all of their remaining questions about his last two years with the Miami as well as what he had learned while spying on the Chickasaw. John Hackett was amazed at the knowledge and skill his step-son had acquired during the time he had been gone.

When night came, William once again said goodbye to his family and friends, resumed his Indian garb and paint, and strode across the courtyard to where Jack and Dirt stood near the gate.

Jack saw William walking up, but Dirt, who had his back turned, jumped in surprise when he discovered an Indian warrior standing beside him. "GREAT SMOKIN' POLE CATS, BOY!" Dirt Gurley exclaimed. "You need to warn a feller when you're sneakin' up behind him in that heathern outfit a' yorn! I thought I'd lost my hair fer sure!"

Will good-naturedly reached over and lifted up the wide brimmed hat his friend was wearing. "I don't think you've got enough up there to worry about," Will said with a chuckle.

Dirt quickly grabbed his hat and tugged it back on. "I'd *have* more hair if I didn't have to fret so much about yer worthless hide!"

Will reached over and put a hand on his friend's shoulder and gave him a smile.

"I appreciate what your doin' for us, Will!" Dirt said again, more seriously. "We'd all be dead right now if it weren't for you. I jus' want you to be as careful as ya can, savvy?"

"You can count on it," the young scout returned. "Gray Fox and I will be trying to figure out what their next move will be, and when we do, I'll let you know. In the meantime we'll be making life as miserable for them as we can."

"Without getting caught!" Jack added firmly.

"Right," the youth agreed. "I think it's dark enough. How about cracking the gate open for me, and I'll slip out of here and get back to work."

William lost no time putting his plans into effect. He silently crept across the open area between the fort and the woods. The adopted Miami warrior, Walks Without Sound, found each of the Chickasaw sentinels that watched the fort and quietly put an end to their murderous careers. He then crept quietly around the Indian camp until he came to the western edge. At the base of a large sweet gum tree, the young frontiersman gave the soft whistle of a whippoorwill. In a moment an answering call sounded from up in the tree. Shortly after, Gray Fox dropped lightly to the ground beside his friend. They spoke briefly in whispers, then separated. Each crept toward the Chickasaw camp from a different direction to watch what was happening.

Over the next few days, the savage army that besieged the colony now found that it was itself assailed by a mysterious enemy. Try as they might, they could not catch him or even find signs of his passing. Each night they lost warrior after warrior, and all the deaths were baffling. It was usually those who were sent out to stand guard. They blamed the loss of the lookouts positioned closest to the fort on settlers who must have been sneaking out and attacking the sentinels. But the Chickasaw guards watching the north, west, and south sides of the camp were slain as well.

Some were found under trees with large, broken limbs having fallen on their heads. Others were found drowned in the creek. Several were found hanging from tree limbs with vines wrapped around their necks. But in each case no evidence could be found of another human presence. The Chickasaw began to believe that the forest was fighting for the settlers.

One evening after he and Gray Fox had made their rounds to eliminate the Indian lookouts, William casually strolled into the Chickasaw camp with an armload of firewood. After depositing it beside the central fire, he sat down, pretending to warm himself, all the while carefully observing those around him.

He had only been there a few minutes when two Indians came running in and stopped in front of the large teepee that Trask and Girty used. They yelled something, and suddenly Girty stepped out. He had an animated discussion with the two warriors, who were soon joined by several others, all voicing their angry opinions. After several minutes Girty turned and darted back inside the teepee.

William stood up and casually walked into the shadows beside the tent. When he reached a place where the Indians near the fire could not see him, he squatted down and listened carefully to what was being said inside the teepee.

"That's what I told 'em, Trask, but they don't believe me, and you're not listening!"

"Calm down!" Trask shot back. "I heard everything you said, but there are no ghosts in the woods killing their braves! Somebody's out there, and the sooner they find him, the sooner all this stops! Most likely it's one or both of the scouts the settlers mentioned."

"Yeah, I remember that," Girty agreed. "Those scouts would be the only ones who could pull off something like this."

"Exactly," Trask returned. "You said Little Turtle and his brother just found the west lookout dead. That means the assassins are still out there, probably heading for the other scouts. So have the chief send out braves to scour the woods north and south of us. Also have someone check on the lookouts toward the fort."

"I'll tell him," Girty answered, "but they're all so spooked, I don't think they will go alone."

"THEN SEND THEM IN GROUPS, BUT FIND THE KILLERS!"

When William heard Girty rush out of the teepee, the youth began to move away from the back wall of Trask's headquarters. He smiled to himself as he moved silently through the woods.

To keep from being noticed, Will joined one of the search parties. He picked the one that Girty led and stayed near the rear. They traveled north of the camp a short ways and eventually found the body of another sentinel. Girty kept everyone back as he used the torch he was carrying to search the area. Soon he started yelling and pointing to the ground. When the rest of the party arrived, Girty's yelling and anger soon got them all yelling. As near as Will could tell, Girty was telling them that he had found footprints of the assassin, but they were in a place where Will knew he hadn't left any. When it came his turn to look at the discovered prints, he saw that they were larger than his feet. He realized that Girty had made them to convince the Indians that the killer was not a ghost, and based on the reaction of the Indians, it seemed to have worked.

From then on the Chickasaw sent out two or three warriors for lookout duty. That made it too difficult for Will and Gray Fox to attack the guards, but they still managed to find an individual victim every so often.

Trask had hoped to defeat the fort quickly by stealth, but none of his plans had worked. He was determined to utterly destroy the American settlement, so he decided on the only plan left to him. He directed the Indians to no longer make direct attacks on the walls, but instead to form a complete circle around the fort and wait for thirst and famine to weaken them.

Jack Cobb had foreseen this danger and early on had given directions to prepare the fort for a siege. A large supply of dried or salted food stores had always been kept in one of the blockhouse storage rooms, and they had completed the well just inside the gate. Unfortunately for the settlers, the one thing they couldn't prepare for happened. For several weeks before the attack, no rain had fallen, and now the days became hot. The leaves curled, the grass turned brown, and the ground began to crack as the drought became severe.

What made the lack of rainfall especially difficult for the settlers was that the well inside the fort dried up. It was John Hackett himself who first saw the coming danger. He got several men to try to dig the well deeper, but after dropping the depth six more feet, there was still very little water in the bottom.

Rationing became necessary, so the supply for each person was cut down one half and then reduced again. They all knew that even that small portion of water would soon be shrunk even more unless the rains came. Intense prayers were offered, and desperate eyes searched the skies daily, but no clouds appeared.

Men who feared no physical danger saw their family members growing pale and weak before their eyes, and they did not know what to do but pray. It seemed that, unless God intervened, the fort must fall without another blow from the enemy.

It was on one of these hot, dry mornings that Katherine Middlebrook stepped out of her home and walked toward the gate. She reached the spot where, if she looked to the northwest, she could look over the palisade and see the ground outside the fort sloping gradually up to meet the forest several hundred yards away. Stopping in this favorite spot of hers, she let her eyes fall on all that was before her. She saw the sea of dry brown grass waving in the light breeze. She saw the stately trees in the far distance, and those leaves that had not already turned brown definitely had a yellowish tint to them. Then she let her eyes drop slightly, and she noticed the sunlight glinting off the surface of the deep pool formed below the spring that flowed out of a rocky outcropping not quite a hundred yards north and west of the fort. She remembered the lovely mornings when she had strolled out to the pool and sat beside it, bathing her feet in its coolness and enjoying its sweet song as the water ran over the rocks.

As Kate looked longingly at the pool so temptingly near, she was deeply moved by their desperate situation and began to pray. After several long moments of impassioned pleas for help, the girl stopped and looked once again at the light flashing off the water in the distant creek. All at once a thought came to her. It was actually more of a familiar memory, and it seized her imagination. She wasn't sure what it meant, but it wasn't a thought that she could put aside. It obsessed her so much that she felt she had to tell someone. She went to the gate where her father, John Hackett, Jack, Dirt, and the scholar were in conference with several others.

"Father," she exclaimed, "I was just asking the Lord how we could get water, and a thought suddenly came to me that I believe is from Him, but I don't know what it means!"

"What did you hear, child?" the schoolmaster asked with interest.

"I didn't actually hear anything, but I remembered a Bible story about what God did when his people needed water in the desert. God told Moses to strike a large rock, and water gushed out—so much that they were all satisfied."

"I'm not sure what that has to do with our situation," her father stated in confusion.

"I remember the story well," Dirt spoke up. "The Good Lord give ever'one o' them thirsty Isrealites all the drinkin' they could do from the river of water that flowed outta that rock. Yessiree Bob, a rock like that would sure fix our sitcheeation, little missy. The only problem is that we ain't got no rock to strike."

"Maybe we do," Charles Spebbington said thoughtfully. "The nearest water to us right now is the spring with its deep pool. What if God wants us to strike the ground between us and the spring? Is there a way to dig a channel from that pool of water to us?"

"Not without gettin' a few bullet holes in the diggers," Jack Cobb pointed out.

"But what if we picked the darkest night," the scholar continued, "and all of us slipped out of the fort with our spades and hoes and lined ourselves up between here and the spring. Why, we could dig a ditch in no time!"

"Y'er right as rain, Master," Cobb answered, "It wouldn't take no time atoll fer all of us to dig that trench, but it would take even less time for them sharp-eyed savages to spot us an' snuff our candles, so to speak."

"That's why we need a diversion!" Mr. Spebbington prompted with enthusiasm.

"A dee-what?" Dirt Gurley asked.

"A diversion!" the scholar said again. "Some loud, attention-getting event that would keep the Indians focused on something other than the work we would be doing!"

"An' jus' how in the name of corn fritters do you figure on doin' that?" Dirt shot back.

"Maybe Will and his friend could help us," Katherine suggested. "They're already out there with the Indians. Maybe they could come up with a way to distract them long enough for us to dig a trench from the spring to the well."

"What do you think, Jack?" Silas Middlebrook asked.

"Well, if we don't do anything, we're gonna sit here and die of thirst. I say we call Will in an' see what he and Gray Fox can do."

Chapter Twenty-Five

THE DIVERSION

That evening Jack got Asa and Dirt to join him on top of the northwest blockhouse. Jack lifted his rifle and fired it into the air, then nodded to Asa, who fired his. A second later Dirt fired his.

"Now we wait," Jack announced to the others.

An hour later Jack heard William's voice whisper outside the gate. The bar was lifted, and one of the large doors swung slightly open, allowing the young scout to slip inside. A few minutes later William, still in his Indian disguise, stood in the school hall with his father, the scholar, Silas Middlebrook, Jack, and Dirt. Silas explained their idea for making a trench from the creek to the well.

"How can you possibly do that without the Chickasaw killing all of you?" Will asked seriously.

"We can't," the scholar answered, "without a very good diversion."

"We was hopin'," Dirt Gurley added, "that since you've been out there so much, you might could come up with a plan to keep them varmints occupied while we dig the trench."

"How much time do you need?" Will asked.

"The trench doesn't have to be very deep," Mr. Middlebrook said his thoughts out loud. "Maybe an hour."

William thought on this for a few minutes. Finally he said, "When we decide to do this and you're ready to go, Gray Fox

236

and I can get behind the Indian camp on the west side, cause a ruckus, and try to get them to chase us like they did when I first came back here."

"I don't believe an army of Chickasaw warriors is gonna chase two men," Jack Cobb said skeptically.

"Will, I'm afeered that I'm in agreement with Jack," said Dirt Gurley. "You may get a small war party after you, but not the whole grubaree of em. To get all of their attention, you'd have to hit 'em with a small army yerself."

"Well then," William answered with a smile, "Gray Fox and I will just have to be a small army. I've already got two muskets hidden out in the woods that I took from some of their lookouts. If I could carry a couple of extra rifles with me when I go back, that will give us six total. If we fire them off rapidly, making as much noise as we can, I think we can sound like small army."

"If we're serious about this plan, then I think we can do better than that," said Kate's father. "In my house I have a brace of old pistols that my father left me. They would be easy to carry and give you two more shots."

"Do you think they'll still fire?" Cobb asked.

"They should," Silas returned. "They've been taken care of, but we'll inspect them to be sure."

"When were you thinking about trying this?" Will asked, looking at the group of men. After several moments of hesitation, they all looked at the school master.

"Well, we are in desperate need of water," Mr. Spebbington began, "and based on how early the moon's been rising and setting, I'd say tomorrow night is going to be about the darkest night we'll have this month. We should attempt the plan tomorrow night or the next. If it were left up to me, I'd say the sooner the better."

"Alright, men," John Hackett announced, "unless someone has any better ideas, let's start figuring out the best way to do this."

"I honestly don't think we can count on an hour for the diversion," Will said as he considered his part of the plan. "I figure I'm going to be fortunate to keep those warriors busy for thirty minutes. Is there a way to dig the trench faster?"

At this point plans began to be made in earnest. John Hackett, Charles Spebbington, and several other men began to devise the most effective way to construct the ditch. They needed it to be dug as straight as possible from the spring to the corner of the fort where the well was located. Several of the men went up into one of the blockhouses and sighted the exact lay of the proposed trench. They decided to bring it straight from the spring to southern edge of the gate, whose opening was the only place where water could flow into the fort without being stopped by the buried ends of the palisade logs. Once the actual location was determined, workers inside began digging the portion of the trench that was to run from the edge of the gate to the mouth of the well.

William and Dirt spent part of the next day looking for extra rifles for Will to carry with him, while Jack went with Mr. Middlebrook to examine his pistols. As it turned out, the pistols were still in good enough condition to fire, which is all they needed to do.

No one could think of any reason for waiting, so they all agreed to try the plan that night. John Hackett called the villagers together, except for the few guarding the walls, and explained what was to happen. When everyone had been given their assigned position and job, and Mr. Hackett and the scholar were sure that everyone understood, they were sent back to their homes to prepare. Everyone going outside the walls put on the darkest clothing they had. All of the spades and hoes were sharpened. Several of the ladies collected balls of the lightest colored yarn that was available in the fort. It was unrolled, the end of each ball tied to the next, and the whole length of it rewound on a straight stick and given to Jack Cobb.

When the preparations were completed, the whole community gathered to pray for the desperate endeavor. The school master suggested that everyone rest and eat an early supper. The quarter moon was already high in the sky when the sun disappeared below the horizon. The scholar calculated that the moon would be set and the sky would darken sometime close to eleven o'clock, and that's when they would begin the plan.

Tension was high in Larkinboro as everyone anxiously waited. Shortly before eleven, Will Hackett, dressed and painted as a Chickasaw warrior, slipped quietly out of the gate. Even the hinges of the gates had been greased so that they would not squeak when opened. Along with his own rifle carried in his arms, William had tied pieces of rope to the barrels and stocks of two other rifles and had slung them over his left shoulder. In addition he had two loaded pistols stuck in his belt. William gave Jack Cobb and Dirt Gurley a smile and a nod before he bent low and disappeared into the darkness.

Time passed slowly for those in the fort waiting for their young scout and his Miami friend to start the diversion, but it seemed to pass even slower for William. He made his way through the first line of sentinels at the edge of the forest, but discovered that Indians were moving through the woods near the Chickasaw camp. He wound up having to backtrack and swing wide to the south in order to get to the rear of the Indian camp without being noticed.

Returning to the familiar sweet gum tree, he was soon reunited with his companion. William quickly explained the plan and handed Gray Fox a pistol and one of the extra rifles. Then the young scout led them further away from the Indian camp.

He found the familiar large, moss-covered rock in the dark woods west of the camp that he and Gray Fox had used before. He left his friend and most of the weapons there. Taking his rifle and a loaded pistol in his belt, he gave Gray Fox final instructions and set off to find the muskets he had hidden. William traveled in a general westerly direction through the forest, away from the Indian encampment. After several minutes of hard walking, he found himself in a small clearing that he followed to the south, arriving at a large beech tree. Climbing several limbs up, he found the two muskets hanging where he had placed them. In less than a minute, he had the weapons and was hurrying back through the woods toward the Indian camp.

As soon as he smelled smoke from the Chickasaw fires, he moved more cautiously. Satisfied with his position, William laid out his weapons. He loaded the two muskets, and carefully

239

collecting all of his arms, the young warrior cautiously approached the enemy camp. When he was close enough to see someone to aim at, he stopped, quietly cocked his weapons, and laid them on the ground. Satisfied that he was ready, Will stepped over to the first rifle, took deliberate aim, and squeezed off a shot. He was certain that he hit the warrior he aimed at, but he didn't wait to see. Just then he heard another rifle fire into the camp and knew Gray Fox was doing his job. Grabbing the two muskets, one in each hand, William fired them both at the camp from the hip, one after the other. More shots came from the Miami's position, so Will whipped out his pistol and, screaming his war cry, fired at the nearest warrior. Stuffing the pistol into his belt and snatching his rifle, the young scout sprinted west through the woods, screaming his war cry and making as much noise as he could. He smiled to himself as he heard Gray Fox doing the same a little to the north.

Bedlam broke out in the Chickasaw camp. Bullets began to fly through the limbs and branches where William and Gray Fox had been firing. When the enemy warriors heard their taunting war cries, their pent up rage exploded, and hundreds of blood-thirsty savages rushed through the woods after them. Turning, William quickly loaded the pistol and fired it toward the most noise. Again giving his war cry, he changed directions and headed northwest.

Everyone in the fort knew when William started his attack. They heard his gunfire and, while he was still shooting, they heard cries of pain and then the full chorus of screaming yells as the enemy army, mad with rage, rushed to destroy the unseen foe who had dared to attack their camp.

Jack Cobb and Dirt Gurley stood by the gate. They waited a few moments, then Jack slipped through the opening and crept quietly across the open land toward the spring. Dirt Gurley followed and began letting out the light colored yarn. It had been tied to a stake driven deeply into the mouth of the trench on the inside of the fort that they had already dug to the well. Hurrying toward the water source, Dirt unrolled the yarn as he went. When Jack arrived at the spring, he searched the area around it. Finding no sign of enemy lookouts, he gave the call of a whippoorwill.

Immediately two yoke of oxen came out of the gate, each pair pulling a plow carried by the plowman behind them. They were followed by an army of settlers trotting quietly out in single file, each carrying a hoe or a spade.

As soon as Dirt arrived at the spring, he pulled the yarn tight and tied it to one of the large rocks beside the pool of water. When the plowmen reached the pool, the first turned his oxen until they were straddling the yarn and facing the fort. Dropping his plow point in the ground, he prodded the oxen with his goad and began cutting a deep furrow in the ground straight toward the southernmost post of the fort's gate. When the second plowman cleared the gate, he dropped his plow point in the ground and, following the yarn, cut a trench straight toward the oncoming plowman.

The rest of the workers from the fort lined up along both sides of the plowed trenches and spread out equidistant from each other so that they reached from beside the spring all the way to the gate. Without a word and as quietly as possible, they dug furiously, excavating along the plowed cut, deepening it to two feet. As soon as one villager connected his hole to the next, he ran down the line to help someone else. When the plowmen met in the middle, the one closest to the fort lifted his plow and moved his oxen to the side, allowing the other to keep plowing to deepen the trench to the well.

As the men desperately strove to complete the trench, Kate Middlebrook, Gardenia, and several of the stronger women and girls ran from the gate carrying two buckets apiece. When they arrived at the spring, Kate filled her two buckets with water. Gardenia set her two empty buckets beside Kate and grabbed the full buckets and began to walk rapidly back to the fort.

"What are you women doin'?" Jack whispered sharply to Kate when he saw her at the spring.

"Just in case something bad happens," Katherine hissed back, "we thought it would be best to fill a few buckets!"

The scout saw the wisdom in their work, but he didn't like it. "Well, just hurry up and get back in the fort!" he returned. "Those savages could show back up any moment!"

William had heard his friend fire twice more and yell. He sounded to be about a hundred yards behind him and still a little north of where he stood. The young frontiersman reloaded his weapons and fired them once more to keep the enemy warriors coming after him. Yelling and screaming his war cry, he couldn't tell if all the Chickasaw were following him or if some might be threatening the settlers, so he decided to find out. Spotting a large, rotting log, he crawled underneath, pulled a few leaves in front of him, and waited. It wasn't long before the lead group of Indians chasing him went running by. William stayed hidden until no more warriors passed. Quietly he slipped out from his place of concealment and headed back toward the Indian camp. He hadn't gone far when he came upon another group of warriors. They were crowded around one who appeared to be a chief. When he got close enough to see, he realized there were two people standing in the center of the large war party: one was Trask, and the other was Girty.

"I know, I know," Trask growled at his companion, "but we can't leave that fort unwatched! Those people have foiled our plans twice, and I'm not going to let them do it again! You take six warriors with you to watch them. If you see anything suspicious, fire a shot to call us back. Tell the rest of this group to come with me to catch that bunch who attacked us!"

Girty spoke to his men quickly and, after picking six warriors, led them back toward the Indian camp.

Oh no! Will thought to himself, *I've got to warn the others!*

Trask led the main group to the west, chasing their unknown attackers. William hung back and hid in the darkness. As soon as everyone was gone, the young warrior crept silently to the north. When he was far enough away from Trask's and Girty's groups, he began running as quietly as he could, circling back towards the fort.

Thanks to the work of the plows, the trench was completed quickly. At that point all that was left to do was to burrow into the side of the deep pool below the spring. Two of the men with spades dug furiously to remove the dirt and rocks from the side wall of the pool.

Kate had just handed a bucket full of water to one of the girls and was turning to fill her last bucket when a shot rang out. Suddenly one of the men at the pool grabbed his chest and, with a groan, fell to the ground. At that moment Jack Cobb, standing nearby, fired his rifle into the shadows behind them. Throwing his empty rifle down, the scout grabbed the dead man's dropped spade and helped finish digging.

"RUN, LADIES! RUN!" he called as he shoveled furiously.

Suddenly there was a scream beside Kate. The girl to whom she had handed the bucket of water was struggling with a Chickasaw warrior. Katherine lifted her full bucket of water and swung it powerfully into the head of the Indian, dropping him on the ground, unconscious.

"RUN TO THE FORT, ALICE!" Kate yelled and started after her friend.

As this was happening, two more Indians charged from the forest to attack the diggers. A shot from Dirt Gurley's rifle dropped the first.

"KEEP DIGGIN'!" Dirt shouted as he ran to confront the attacking warrior. When they met, Dirt blocked the Indian's tomahawk with the barrel of his rifle and quickly swung the butt of his gun into the side of the Chickasaw's head, dropping him instantly. "WE GOT'S TO GO, FELLERS!" Dirt yelled as he watched the shadows for more enemies.

"There!" Cobb cried. "We got it!" At that moment water began to gush from the pool and surged down the trench. Just then there was another scream to their right. The men turned quickly and saw Kate Middlebrook in the grasp of two more enemy fighters. . .one of them was Girty.

"NO!" screamed Cobb as he jumped the trench, spade in hand, and ran toward the struggling girl. A shot suddenly rang out from the north, and the Chickasaw warrior dropped to the ground. Seeing his companion struck, Girty threw Kate to the ground and pulled out a pistol from his belt to face his enemy. William materialized out of the darkness from the north and charged forward, knife in hand, screaming his war cry. With a smirk Girty raised his pistol and aimed at his attacker's chest. William was only three steps away from Girty when, with a thunk, the British agent dropped to the ground. Will and Jack arrived at Girty's prostrate form at almost the same time. Standing over the unconscious villain stood Kathrine Middlebrook with a large rock in her hands.

"He wasn't nice to me!" she huffed angrily. "And. . .and. . .it made me mad!"

"Mores a'comin'!" yelled Dirt nearby as he loaded his rifle. He saw a powerful warrior charging straight for them out of the darkness. Dirt quickly shouldered his long gun and aimed at the attacker.

"KAJIKA!" the warrior called.

"HOLD IT!" Will yelled and pushed Dirt's rifle barrel up. "That's Gray Fox!"

"Well, tell him I'm sorry," Dirt cried, "but in the middle of a Injun fight, a Injun's a Injun!"

"Run for the fort, Kate!" Will urged as he grabbed her arm. "Run!"

Once Katherine was on her way, Dirt tossed Jack his rifle, and the two of them, with William and Gray Fox, faced the Indians and backed hurriedly toward the fort, loading their guns and firing as they went. When they had covered half the distance, rifles began blasting from the top of the palisade. With the covering fire, the four turned and raced for safety. As soon as they entered, the gates were shut and barred. When Will looked down, he saw the trench was full of water, and a small waterfall splashed forcefully into the well opening.

"*He, he, he,*" Dirt Gurley chuckled with exhausted relief, "I never thought we'd pull that off!"

"Then why didn't you try to stop us?" William asked with concern.

"Two reasons," Dirt shot back, still smiling. "First, we had to do somethin', an' that was the best plan on the table. Second, I figured Miss Kate would be prayin' hard enough to get us through it!"

"All you fellas on the west wall keep firing into the woods," Jack called up to the guards. "If we can keep their heads down, maybe they won't discover our trench till daylight."

"Well, certainly when the sun comes up, they will discover our work," Charles Spebbington observed.

"That they will, Scholar," Jack returned, "but our sharpshooters will be able to see them too."

"It'll be tomorrow night, when it gets too dark for us to see 'em," Dirt Gurley voiced his thoughts, "that them weasels'll slip out thar an' cork our trench."

"Probably," answered Jack, "but by that time, we'll have plenty of water in the well hole."

Chapter Twenty-Six

THE RISKS

Trask and the rest of the Chickasaw army arrived just as the last of the settlers made it into the fort. The continuous rifle fire from the top of the palisade forced the Indians back into the shelter of the trees to return fire.

After several minutes Trask heard a familiar voice crying for help somewhere in front of him. Trusting in the darkness to hide him from the American marksmen, Trask ran to the sound of the cries. He found Girty struggling to get to his feet.

"Get up, Girty!" the British major barked as bullets whined overhead. He grabbed his injured companion's arm and helped him stand. "Hurry!" Trask called again as he pulled Girty towards the woods. "We could get killed out here!"

When they made it into the shelter of the thick woods, the injured agent collapsed on the ground.

"What happened to you?" Trask demanded.

With a groan Simon Girty sat up and grabbed the back of his head. "When we got back here," he began, "we found a bunch of 'em near the pool fillin' buckets, so we attacked 'em."

"Ha!" the British major said with satisfaction. "They're running out of water!"

"Trask, that girl was out there!"

"What girl?"

"You know," Girty snarled back, "that purdy one we ate dinner with. She was standing right out there with the rest of 'em.

Running Bear and I grabbed her, but he got shot. I jerked out my pistol and turned to see who it was. That's when I got hit from behind."

"It was probably the girl," Trask shot back. "Do you know what the Chickasaw will do to us if they find out you got defeated by a..."

"Trask!" Girty barked, cutting off his accuser. "I think I saw our assassin."

"Who was it?" Trask asked eagerly.

"The one who shot Running Bear," the injured agent continued. "He came charging straight at me. It was dark, but he was close enough that I could tell that he looked like a Chickasaw...his clothing, face paint, everything."

"So that's how they've outsmarted us," Trask said his thoughts out loud. "They've put a spy among us! Can you remember anything else about him?"

"Just that he was big," Girty said, trying to jog his memory. "He was taller and had broader shoulders than most Indians."

"Hmmm, that makes me think of that big Miami we met," Trask said thoughtfully. "But it doesn't make any sense that he would be down here fighting us. It must be one of their scouts that they've dressed up like a Chickasaw."

"We've got to get that man!" Girty said firmly.

"And I think I know how to do it," the major said with an evil grin.

"How?" Girty asked.

"We'll announce to the whole tribe that there's a spy slipping in and out of the camp and get all the warriors looking for anyone they don't recognize. If they find anyone they don't know, they are to capture him and bring him to us."

An enormous feeling of relief filled the fort the next morning when they found that water still poured into the well. When the sunlight revealed the trench, several attempts were made by the Chickasaw to block the flow, but the best marksmen among the settlers were able to keep the Indians from accomplishing that goal. At the end of the day, when the sun began to set, Jack was pleased to report that the well was almost full.

"They'll likely block off our trench sometime tonight when we can't see 'em," Cobb said to some of the men standing nearby, "but it'll be too late. We've already got all the water we need."

"I figure stoppin' up the trench will actually help us out," Dirt chimed in. "That'll keep the well from over flowin'. *Hee, hee, hee*! Them Chickeesaws can be quite neighborly at times."

At twilight Jack and Dirt saw William and Gray Fox walking up to them. The young woodsman was dressed like a Chickasaw warrior, complete with war paint.

"What chu doin' wearin' your varmint suit, Will?" Dirt called out as his friend drew near. "I was hopin' you were done with all that."

"By God's grace we've been able to turn the tables on them a few times," Will answered as he stepped beside the two scouts, "and I know they're getting frustrated, but I don't think Trask is gonna let them give up yet."

"So you figure we might need to outsmart 'em one more time?" Jack asked.

"After all the braves they've lost fighting us," Will answered, "Trask knows that, if he lets them quit without taking this fort, they'll probably scalp him and his friend out of frustration."

"I see yer point," Dirt agreed. "That no good Trask is likely desperate for a victory right now."

"An' you don't think Girty is too?" Jack asked with a slight smile.

"Oh, he would be," Dirt returned confidently, "if he weren't nursin' that big, fat headache Kate done give him."

"As soon as it gets dark," Will said, "Gray Fox and I will slip out of the gate and see what they're up to. Once we know what Trask is planning, I'll come back and let you know."

"Just be careful, Will," Jack said with concern. The young scout gave his friend a smile and a nod. Jack then turned and signed the same message to Gray Fox.

A few minutes later, when darkness had completely fallen, the guards cracked open the gate, and William and the Miami slipped out.

"Watch yer top knot," Dirt Gurley called in farewell.

Will Hackett and Gray Fox knew quite well where the Chickasaw usually placed their lookouts, so staying low to the ground, they crept silently forward, making their way around the enemy sentinels. Almost an hour later they squatted in a dark thicket near the Indian camp. Using sign language, William told his friend to stay and watch their enemies while he crept to the other side so he could enter the camp from the west.

Once William was in position, he sat in the darkness for several minutes, observing the activity. Something was different, but the young scout couldn't decide what it was. There seemed to be more moving around and more conversation among the warriors than usual.

When he saw Trask and Girty come into camp, his focus shifted to the two agents. They walked around together, talking with several of the braves as they continued their private conversation, but Will was unable to figure out what was happening. Finally Trask and Girty retired to their teepee.

They'll be discussing their plans, Will thought to himself. *I've got to get to the back of their tent so I can listen in.* William slipped from his place of concealment and took the time to gather an arm-load of fire wood before he strolled casually into camp. He had only taken ten steps across the open area before a hard-faced warrior stepped in front of him. He spoke angrily and loud enough that several other Indians turned to look at them.

William didn't know what he was saying but decided to bluff, so he just shrugged his shoulders and continued to walk past the fellow. Just then the warrior grabbed Will by the arm and began crying out. As other warriors nearby started toward them, Will swung hard with his firewood, hitting his captor in the head. When the stunned Indian released his grip, William turned and dashed back the way he had come, sprinting as fast as he could.

He didn't know how they had discovered him, but by the screams behind him, he felt sure the entire camp was on his heels. Taking a quick glace back, Will could tell that the majority of his pursuers were about forty yards behind, but two of them were much closer.

The young frontiersman checked the stars and saw that he was running southwest through the woods, away from where Gray

Fox was hiding. Another quarter of a mile, and he would be at the river. If he could get far enough ahead, he could hide his rifle and dive in the water. William was a strong swimmer. He also knew that most of the Indians he had been around didn't swim. He hoped that was true of the Chickasaw as well.

The young scout sprinted through the woods as fast as he could, trying to outdistance his nearest pursuers, but when he looked back, he was surprised to find that they had actually gained on him. Just then he crashed through some brush and found himself at the water's edge. Choosing his best option, Will sprinted south along the bank. When he heard footsteps pounding close behind him, he quickly turned and, with no time to aim, raised the barrel of his rifle from the hip and pulled the trigger.

The warrior closest to William was in the act of throwing his tomahawk when Will fired. The young frontiersman saw the Chickasaw grab his chest and drop just as the thrown hatchet glanced off the top of William's head. Stunned by blow, Will dropped his rifle and staggered backward. He was shaking his head, trying to clear the stars he saw, when the second Indian slammed into him. They landed hard on the ground and rolled through the brush, with the Indian winding up on top of his dazed victim. The warrior grabbed Will's throat with his left hand to hold him down and lifted his tomahawk with his right.

Though still hurting from the blow to his head, the young scout saw and thought clearly enough to realize that death was only a split second away. Throwing up his left arm, William was able to block the descending tomahawk. At the same time he threw a hard fist into the side of the Indian's head, catching his enemy off guard and driving him to the side. As the dazed warrior tried to straighten back up, Will caught him with an even harder blow that dropped the Indian face first onto the ground beside him.

Hearing lots of noise in the woods to his right, Will saw many shadowy figures racing towards him. Rolling to his feet, the dazed youth took two shaky steps toward the river and threw himself from the bank.

He crashed more or less headfirst into the deep, dark waters as he heard rifle bullets zipping all around him. The cold water and the pain of his wound was enough to clear his head. He swam deep, trying to put as much distance between himself and the bullets as he could. He felt the river's current driving him downstream as he swam.

When he could hold his breath no longer, he broke the surface and gasped for breath. Immediately he heard the cries of Chickasaw warriors as they spotted him. A couple of rifle shots clipped the water close by as he dove again.

The strong current pushed him steadily along, so Will concentrated all of his strength on swimming toward the opposite bank. When he surfaced the second time, the cries of the Indians were further away. He took a glance up river and couldn't see any warriors in the darkness. That told him they couldn't see him either, so he quietly began stroking toward the west bank. He managed to reach some overhanging limbs near the shore and used them to pull himself out of the water.

Exhausted, he dragged himself onto land and lay in the darkness, breathing hard and shivering in the cold. He knew the wound on top of his head needed attention. He could feel the warm blood flowing down between his eyes. Grateful that the intense pain had diminished to a dull throb, William managed to force himself onto his feet. He thought for a moment in order to decide his next move. He had to get back to the fort, but there was an army of angry, determined warriors in his way. He tried to decide what the Chickasaw would expect him to do. *It would be closer and a little easier to continue south, then swing east to get back home,* he thought to himself. *If I were them, that's what I would expect me to do, so I'll go north.*

Once the decision was made, the young scout started walking west to get further away from the river. He moved quietly so as not to give away his movements to those listening on the other bank. When he felt he was far enough away from his enemies, he struck out to the north.

Will tried not to make noise as he traveled, but he was dizzy and several times lost his balance. He had been moving north for a quarter of an hour when suddenly a large figure confronted him out of the darkness. Will no longer had his rifle, so he snatched out his knife and tomahawk.

"Kajika!" the voice in the darkness called.

"Gray Fox!" Will sighed back in relief and sank to his knees.

"You are hurt!" the Miami said as he knelt beside his friend.

"I need help getting back to the fort," Will grunted as he tried to get back to his feet. "How did you find me?"

"Gray Fox watched them chase you out of the camp, so I followed. When I knew you had jumped into the river to get away, I thought that you would try to swim to the other side. When none of the Chickasaw could see me, I swam across. They thought that you would go south, so I thought you would go north. Gray Fox was right."

"You're smart, my friend," Will returned. "Let's keep going north until we are past the camp, then we'll turn east and swim the river again."

The injured scout had to endure the cold water once more as he and his friend silently swam back to the east bank. As they eased themselves out of the river, all of their senses were on the highest alert. They were now back among their enemies.

William thought the Chickasaw camp should be south and east of where the two crouched on the bank, and their adversaries were looking furiously for him. William could tell he was getting weaker from the slow but steady loss of blood from his wound. He needed to get to the fort as quickly as possible, but he was also aware that, if they made a mistake now, it would cost them their lives.

It was well past midnight as the injured youth and his loyal companion crept cautiously eastward, attentive to the slightest sound or smell that might indicate nearby enemies. After two hours of maddeningly slow progress, they were both sure that they were past the Indian encampment, so they turned south.

Eventually they found themselves at the edge of the large meadow in which the fort was built. The temptation to run for the gate was strong, but they had done this enough times to know that the Chickasaw had lookouts stationed all around. They eased their way along the edge of the woods, alert to any sound or movement. Suddenly Gray Fox froze, warning Will. He had heard the faint crack of a stick in front and to his left. Momentarily leaving his injured friend, the Miami warrior inched his way forward in complete silence until he spotted them. Will and Gray Fox had taken out so many sentinels that they were now sent out in pairs.

As weak as he was, William didn't think he was up to fighting one brave, much less two, and he signed this to his companion. Gray Fox quietly returned, and they slipped deeper into the woods to get further away from the guards. When they had distanced themselves from the lookouts, the two friends began their slow crawl to the fort.

The edge of the eastern sky was just showing the first hint of dawn when the guards at the gate heard a weak voice call to them. "Don't shoot. . .it's me. . .Will Hackett."

"Will!" one of the guards returned in a low voice. "Is that really you, boy?"

"Mr. Jeffers. . .yes. . .it's me, Will. I'm here with Gray Fox. Please, let us in. . .I need help."

Chapter Twenty-Seven

MUCH NEEDED HELP

When the guards opened the gate, they were stunned at the appearance of the blood-covered youth being aided by his Indian friend. William stumbled wearily into the fort and stood leaning against Gray Fox. "Thanks for letting us in," the injured warrior said to the lookouts. "I'm in trouble."

"Will!" Frank Jeffers gasped as he saw his wounded neighbor. "Sit down here on this barrel and rest. You look terrible!"

"I know I must look a sight," the young scout answered. "My head wound bled for a while, but I think it's mostly stopped now."

At that moment Frank turned to one of the other guards standing nearby. "Ben, run to the Hackett home and get John! Tell him his son just came in and needs help. . .and hurry!"

"Here's some water for you, Will," another of the guards said as he handed the youth a dipper.

"Thanks, Mr. Carson. I could use it." William drained the dipper and handed it back to Ned Carson, who immediately hurried to fill it again.

"What in the world happened to you, boy?" Frank Jeffers asked with concern.

"Somehow the Chickasaw spotted me when I tried to enter their camp," Will began. "I managed to get free and ran off with most of 'em chasing me. I left all but two of them behind and was eventually able to drop one as he threw his tomahawk at me. I guess it bounced off the top of my head."

"It should have split your skull in two!" Frank replied.

"Mother always said I was hard-headed," Will smiled back.

"I guess you proved her right," Frank answered good-naturedly.

"I guess I did. The long and short of it is that I jumped in the river to get away from all of them, then Gray Fox found me and helped me get back here."

Will was working on his third dipper of water when John Hackett trotted up with a look of concern. The son assured his father that he was all right, then with the Miami on one side and his father on the other, they made their way to their cabin.

Betsy Hackett almost fainted when she saw all the blood on her son's head, face, and chest. William tried to smile through the mess and assure his mother that it wasn't as bad as it looked, but when she finally got his head cleaned and could actually see the wound, she had to disagree with him.

Fortunately for William and his mother, it was not the first time Betsy Hackett had been forced to deal with similar injuries. "Mary," Betsy called to her daughter, who was standing with her brother Jay in their night shirts, staring wide-eyed at their injured older sibling, "go get my sewing basket, and be quick!"

"Yes, Mother," returned the girl as she hurried to her task.

"Does it hurt much, Will?" Jay asked with concern.

"It hurt a lot at first," William said from his chair, smiling at his scared young sibling, "but it doesn't hurt much now, although I think Mother's about to change that. . .*hee, hee.*" As he said this, the chuckling older lad ruffled the hair of his concerned younger brother.

Betsy had William move his chair next to the table. She sat a wooden chest about eighteen inches tall on top and placed a bright oil lamp with a glass chimney on the flat top of the chest. This allowed plenty of light to illuminate the wound on William's head.

Betsy shuddered when she examined the cut more closely and discovered that it went all the way to the skull. She breathed a sigh of relief when she saw that her son's head bone had not been harmed. The large gash started at the top of Will's forehead and extended back into his hair for over four inches. "Well, at least it is no longer bleeding," she said her thoughts out loud.

"That's good!" Will returned with a smile. "I wasn't looking forward to you having to stick a hot poker in there to stop it."

"Me either," Betsy smiled back at her son. "Alright, now you need to sit still while I shave the hair away from the edges. Then I'll finish cleaning it, and after that I'll sew it closed."

"Mary! Jay!" Betsy said as she looked at her two youngest children. "Thank you for your help, but I want you both to go back to bed."

Without a word Mary spun on her heels and quickly disappeared. Young Jay hesitated, and Betsy noticed. "You too, young man!" his mother said firmly. "Back to bed!"

"Aw, Mom!" Jay grumbled as he turned to leave. "I never get to have any fun!"

Just then there was a knock at the door. When John answered, he found Jack Cobb standing there. After the scout inquired about Will, he whispered something to Mr. Hackett, who nodded his answer. John walked over to Gray Fox, who was watching Betsy work on Will. He touched the Indian's arm and motioned for him to come outside where Jack was waiting.

The scout signed a greeting to the Miami and asked him if he was hurt. After Gray Fox signed back that he could use some food, Jack led him to the cabin where he and Dirt Gurley stayed. Pulling out meat, bread, and a jug of fresh water, Jack let the Miami eat all he wanted. After he finished, Jack began asking him what he had seen in the Chickasaw camp and if he had any ideas what they would try next.

It took over an hour for Betsy to shave, clean, and carefully sew up the large wound. Finally she wrapped a bandage around Will's head for protection. When she had finished, Betsy Hackett gave the bandage an appraising gaze. "If you feel up to it," she finally said, "I want you to eat a bowl of beef stew we had left from supper. I put the pot back over the fire just before I started this, so it should be nice and hot."

The grateful smile from her son informed her that he definitely felt up to it. There was actually nearly two bowls of stew left, and the tired young scout had no trouble finishing off both.

William stood shakily to his feet, wrapped his arms around his mother, and hugged her. "Thank you," he whispered in her ear. As he pulled back, he looked his step-mother in the eye as said, "I love you, and I praise God for you!"

Tears welled up in the eyes of the tough pioneer woman. Her mouth opened, but the words she wanted to say caught in the back of her throat.

"I know, Mother," her son said with a gentle smile, "you love me too." Will squeezed her shoulder as he walked past her and slowly climbed the ladder to the loft and his bed.

It was after noon the next day before William awoke. His head still hurt, but he was pleased to notice that he felt stronger and was not dizzy. As he joined his family in the big midday meal prepared by his mother, he answered all of their questions about what had happened to him.

"It sounds like they were looking for you," John Hackett surmised.

"They were," Will replied, "and that's my fault. I had charged at Girty the night you dug the trench for the water. I knew he saw me, but I figured that it was too dark for him to know who I was. I guess I was wrong."

"It is a wonder that they didn't kill you!" his mother exclaimed.

"I agree, Mother," William returned humbly. "It was only God's grace and your prayers that saved me."

"Did you get a chance to learn any of their plans before you were discovered?" his father asked.

"I was trying to get to Trask and Girty's teepee when I was spotted, so I never heard their conversation. But I did notice that a number of the Indians around the camp were all doing the same thing—tying pieces of pine rosin on the tips of arrows."

"So they're going to try the fire arrow thing again."

"That was my guess," William answered.

When the meal was finished, young Hackett walked out of his family's home and headed toward the gates.

"WILL!" called a voice behind him.

Looking back, William saw Asa running to meet him.

"Hey, Whit! I was hoping I would run into you."

"I heard you came in hurt last night," Asa said with concern as he spotted his friend's bandaged head. "Are you okay?"

"Just a little headache," William smiled back. "I'll be fine."

"I need to find Jack and Dirt. Have you seen them?"

"No," Asa replied, "but I expect they're on the wall near the gate. They both like to keep a watch on the western forest where the Indian camp is."

"That's where I was headed," Will returned.

A few moments later the two friends strode to the front gate. They spotted the scouts on top of one of the west blockhouses, scanning the tree line in the distance. Gray Fox stood with them. When Asa and Will joined them, the young scout wasted no time in telling his friends about the preparations that he saw the Indians making in their camp.

"Last evening while you were gettin' your head sewed up, your friend Gray Fox and me had ourselves a nice talk," Jack said. "He told me the same thing."

"If they're gonna use fire arrows again, then we jus' foller the same plan as before, right?" Dirt asked, looking at Cobb.

"It worked fine last time," Jack returned. "We've got plenty of water now, so soaking the roofs will be no problem. Dirt, get the men started on making more of those torches on poles to light up our field of fire."

"If we've got plenty of sap wood," Will spoke up, "why not make extra torches? If we shine more light, we could probably see a greater distance, and maybe we could keep the Indians back far enough to keep their fire arrows from even hitting any of the homes."

It was almost midnight when the Chickasaw began their attack. As soon as flickering lights were seen moving in the distant darkness, the guards on the walls lifted torches on multiple poles on all sides of the fort. Once again sharp-eyed marksmen from among the settlers were able to keep the enemy archers at too great a distance to allow their fire arrows to do much damage to the fort. As torches burned out, more were lifted in their place. The gunfire of the frustrated Chickasaw erupted from the forest, and the defenders of the fort returned it for most of the night.

As the sun broke the eastern horizon, the entire open area around the palisade was illuminated, and the marksmen had even more targets. The exasperated Indians were forced to melt back into the forest.

"You'd think them painted heatherns would get tired an' quit," Dirt Gurley said to Will, Jack, and Mr. Spebbington later the next day.

"After their persistent failures, one would think that would be the logical conclusion," Charles Spebbington agreed with his friend.

"Trask and Girty won't let them," William answered, "and so far the Chickasaw leaders seem to be going along with them. After we beat them again last night, the Indians have got to be getting to the end of their patience with those two. I've seen the looks that some of the warriors were giving the British agents, and I don't think they'll be able to muster more than one more attack out of that angry bunch."

"Well, I'm hoping Trask can't even do that," Jack said as he looked with concern at the western sky, "because if he can get them to attack tonight, we're gonna be in trouble."

"What!" the scholar sputtered. "See hear, what do you mean by that?"

Instead of answering Jack just continued to stare into the western sky.

Big storm coming, Gray Fox signed.

"I feel it," Will said.

"Yup," Dirt agreed. "Storms abrewin'. . .an' it's gonna be a big one."

"You can tell that by looking into the sky?" Mr. Spebbington asked in amazement.

"It ain't so much how the sky looks right now," Jack answered. "It's more a certain feel to the air. I think Gray Fox already knew, but Dirt and Will picked up on it when they took

259

the time to concentrate. I've heard folks smarter than me say it has something to do with the pressure of the air."

"Well, yes, that's true," the scholar spoke up. "Air pressure does change when storms are approaching, but I didn't know you fellows could actually feel it."

"There's definitely a unique feel to the air as storms come," Will said, "but if you watch the leaves on the trees, you will see some of them turn upside down when storms are brewing. The Miami tribe showed me that."

"The point is," Jack said, taking charge of the conversation again, "when that storm hits, we won't be able to use our rifles much beyond the first shot because the rain will dampen our powder."

Will began signing Jack's words to his Miami friend.

"Well, the Indians will not be able to use theirs either," the scholar added.

"That's true," Jack agreed, "so it will be mostly hand-to-hand fighting when they come. But also, if the storm hits us at night, which I'm figurin' it will, we won't be able to use our torches to see 'em comin'. That means they can creep right up to the walls before they rush us."

"If they all come at once an' on multiple sides, an' we ain't got our rifles, we won't be able to keep 'em out of here!" Dirt said with alarm.

"Even rifles won't keep them out if they get that close to us," Jack observed.

"But shotguns might," William voiced his thoughts.

"Hey, yeah!" Dirt agreed. "With all of us using shotguns, we could send six or eight times as much lead into 'em! There're several shotguns in the village, an' I saw two or three wooden boxes full of buckshot down in the storeroom."

"We'll have those without shotguns load their rifles with buckshot instead of bullets to increase our firepower!" the scholar added excitedly.

"But that ain't gonna work!" Jack said firmly. "Don't you remember? The rain's gonna keep us from using any of our firearms!"

"Unless we use our heads," the scholar said with a grin, "and come up with a way to keep our powder dry!"

"What 'chu got in mind, Perfesser?" Dirt probed.

"We're going to need wooden supports and all of the canvas from our covered wagons," Mr. Spebbington ordered as he rubbed his hands together vigorously, "and there's not much time to do this, so we will need everyone to help. Let me explain my idea."

Chapter Twenty-Eight

GOOD NEWS AND BAD NEWS

After Mr. Spebbington described his idea to the scouts and William, orders were quickly sent throughout the fort. Within a few minutes the entire settlement was a bee hive of activity. Wood for poles was scrounged from everyplace it could be found. A number of bed frames had their corner posts donated. The settlers were desperate for any long piece of wood that could be used for the scholar's plan. Even a few rafters were pulled out of roofs.

All of the canvas tops of the covered wagons were taken from storage and distributed equally around the walls. Jack, Dirt, William, and Mr. Spebbington each took a wall and supervised the construction of the frames. By the late afternoon the sky was darkening, and the wind was picking up from the approaching storm. This made stretching the loose canvas over the tops of the frames very difficult and required lots of hands, but as the sun was setting, the walkways around the tops of the walls and the blockhouses had canvas roofs over most of the areas where the guards needed to stand to defend the walls. The canvas was left long enough on the sides to serve as wind and rain breaks.

It had been dark for two hours when the heavy wind hit. It tore at the canvas awnings, but they had been lashed down tightly, and they held. After a while misty rain could be felt in the wind, but no attack came. Lightening popped and flashed in the distance, and thunder rolled as the vigilant guards strained to see any sign of their enemies.

It was past midnight when the first large drops began to fall. This soon turned into the expected heavy downpour. All during the raging storm, the defenders on the walls huddled with their weapons under their makeshift canvas pavilions.

Almost an hour after the storm became intense, gunfire began to erupt from the east side of the fort as creeping warriors were spotted near the base of the walls. At the same time both war cries and screams of the injured rose above the roar of the tempest. Blasts of lead shot roared in rapid succession from the guns of the defenders as they fired and reloaded buckshot as rapidly as possible.

The men on the other three walls scanned the darkness below their posts for signs of the enemy, but none were seen. Jack, who was standing above the gates on the west side, heard someone calling his name from the courtyard behind him.

"There's too many of them, Jack!" the voice cried. "The scholar says we need help on the east wall!"

"Run to the south wall!" the scout called back down. "Tell 'em I said to send half their men to the east wall, and hurry! I'll do the same to the north wall!"

As Jack hurried to the ladder, he called to the men standing nearby, "KEEP YER EYES OPEN!"

He quickly dropped to the ground and sprinted to the base of the palisade on the north side of the fort. "DIRT!" the scout called to his friend.

"What's goin' on?" Gurley returned.

"We need more guns on the east wall! Take half your men and get over there quick!"

"Gotcha!" Dirt answered, then turned to address the others on the wall with him. "LISTEN TO ME, ALL OF YOU!" he called loudly so everyone could hear. "STARTIN' WITH HAYWARD SIMMS DOWN THERE ON THE END, I'M TAKIN' HIM AN' EVERY OTHER MAN TO THE EAST WALL! LET'S GO NOW!" Dropping from the cat walk, Dirt led his small group of reinforcements quickly to the battle.

Jack Cobb returned to his post on top of one of the west blockhouses overlooking the gate. It was clear to everyone by the sounds of the battle that the fighting was intense on the east side of the fort. Jack looked back, trying to see what was happening through the dark storm. The constant flashes of gunfire from the defenders under their canopies gave just enough light to see.

Just then he heard one of the men beside him yell. Whipping around, Jack saw dark shapes in the pouring rain below the wall. Suddenly the cut trunks of small trees began to appear over the top of the wall.

"THEY'RE TRYIN' TO SCALE THE WALL!" Jack yelled. "LET 'EM HAVE IT!"

Gunfire exploded from the top of the palisade and from the holes in the upper floors of the blockhouses over-looking the gates. The war cries of the attackers and the screams of the wounded joined with the roar of the storm as the fight for the west wall began.

"TRY TO SHOVE THEM TREES OFF SO THEY CAIN'T CLIMB UP!" Jack ordered.

The Indians were caught off guard when the settlers were able to use their guns in the storm, but they would not be stopped again, so on they came.

While the battles raged on the west and east ends of the fort, six shadowy figures crept toward the north wall. Heedless of the heavy rain pouring down, Trask and Girty led four warriors through the stormy night until they were only a few yards from the wall. Trask had draped his British officer's coat over all six of the rifles that Girty carried to keep the powder dry as they crept through the storm. The Chickasaw braves carried the trunk of a small tree with the limbs cut so that the whole thing could be used as a ladder. The constant gunfire from the defenders provided enough light for Trask's group to spot the few remaining defenders on the north side.

Calling the four warriors near, the leader nodded to his companion, and Girty told them to begin their planned attack. The Indians dropped the ladder, and all of them took their rifles. Leaning over their weapons to keep the rain from dampening the powder, they spread out in the dark along the front of the wall and took deliberate aim at the silhouette of each guard above them.

The discharge of six weapons close to the wall on the north side was drowned out by the roar of the storm and the noise of battle on both ends of the fort. After the salvo, Trask and Girty were pleased to see the guards were no longer visible over the top of the wall. Dropping their empty rifles, Trask's party grabbed the makeshift ladder, propped it against the palisade, and one by one quickly climbed to the top.

When the last of the warriors had joined them on the cat walk, Trask had them grab the rifles of the fallen guards and sent them to attack the guards defending the gate.

Charles Spebbington had been moving back and forth along the east wall, directing the defense. At first he had been scared when he saw so many of the enemy attacking them at the same time, but once he had received reinforcements from the other two walls, the tide had shifted noticeably. It was clear to the defenders and attackers that the Indians were not going to be able to breach the walls on his end. Hearing the battle raging behind them at the gate, Mr. Spebbington grabbed Dirt Gurley.

"Dirt, my good man, we seem to have our fight under control, but I'm concerned about Jack and the others defending our front door. If you would be so kind, run back to the gate and ask if they need some of our men to help them."

"Right you are, Perfesser!" Dirt answered with a grin as he finished ramming some shot and wadding into his rifle. Quickly the scout descended to the ground and splashed his way to the gate. Just as he reached the courtyard, a movement to his right caught his eye. To his horror he saw the shadowy forms of four Indian warriors creeping along the catwalk of the north wall, preparing to attack the defenders.

"BEHIND YOU, JACK!" Dirt yelled as he raised his rifle and sent a blast of buckshot towards the sneaking Chickasaw.

Will Hackett, who was in charge of the south wall, heard Dirt's warning and spotted the attacking Indians. Calling to Gray Fox, who was with him, to watch for enemies coming from the south, the young frontiersman leaped down and, landing in the muddy courtyard, ran to help.

Jack as well as several other guards also heard Dirt's call and, whipping around, saw the three remaining Indians on the catwalk in the act of raising their rifles. "CUT 'EM DOWN!" Jack yelled as he and several of the others beside him brought their rifles up. Eight guns fired at almost the same time, sending a flood of buckshot in both directions. All three Indians went down, as well as four of the defenders on top of the blockhouse.

"JACK!" Dirt screamed as he saw his dear friend drop. Dirt quickly scaled the ladder, followed closely by William. The guard closest to the Indians had died instantly. Jack and the other two had all received multiple wounds but were still alive.

Just then the front gates shuddered under a heavy blow. William ran to the edge of the blockhouse and looked down at the gates. He saw several Indians holding a log and drawing back to ram it into the wooden gates again.

"THEY'RE TRYING TO BREAK THROUGH!" Will yelled to the rest of the defenders along the east wall. "FIRE AT THEM! FIRE. . .FIRE!"

Just then gates were struck another powerful blow and a loud crack was heard.

"Dirt," Jack said weakly as he looked into the eyes of his distraught friend, "don't mind me! Get over there an stop them warriors before they break in the gates, or we're *all* done for!"

Dirt gave a quick nod and jumped to his feet. He rapidly loaded his rifle with powder, a handful of lead pellets, and a patch. He rammed it once, dropped the rod at his feet, and fired into the mass of attackers in front of the gates below. The motivated defenders concentrated their fire at the warriors holding the ram, and the attack at the gate was stopped, although others continued to attempt to storm the walls.

At that moment a small group of men who had been fighting on the east wall came running up to help defend the gate. Charles Spebbington could tell by the gun fire that the fight for the west wall was intense, so without waiting for Dirt Gurley to report back, he had sent some of his men to help. These men quickly joined the others on the wall and in the blockhouses to make life miserable for the attacking Chickasaw.

Trask and Girty had remained crouched on the catwalk in the shadows on the north wall. They had seen their warriors cut down and the failure to ram open the gates.

"You see what happened, didn't you?" Girty whispered to his companion. "With all the men they have defending the gate, there's no way the warriors are going to break through!"

"I know, I know!" Trask hissed back. "This battle's finished!"

"And that means *we're* finished!" Girty shot back angrily. "After losing so many braves and getting nothing, they'll scalp us as soon as we get back to camp!"

"You're right," Major Trask agreed. "While they're still fighting, you and I can slip back over the wall and head to Canada right now."

"We'll head to Canada all right," Girty returned, "but I ain't leavin' empty handed. Come on!"

Quickly Simon Girty descended the ladder into the dark interior of the fort and rushed deliberately through the paths between the log houses.

"This is their house!" Girty whispered as he glanced around stealthily. "I remember it from when we were here last time. Follow me." He grabbed the handle of the wooden door and burst inside.

Rebecca Middlebrook sat by the fireplace with her two daughters, Katherine and Grace. They were praying for God's help for the outcome of the battle when the men entered.

Even sopping wet and muddy, Rebecca recognized both men as those she had hosted as guests many weeks before. "What are you doing here?" she cried. "GET OUT! GET OUT AT ONCE!"

"Shut your mouth," Girty shot back, "or we'll cut your throats!" To emphasize his threat, he jerked his knife from his belt.

"Where's all that silver you used when we were here before?" Girty demanded, glaring at Rebecca. "Get it now!"

Mrs. Middlebrook fearfully got to her feet and hurried over to a large trunk sitting against the wall. Pulling open the top, she pointed inside. "It's here," she said.

"Trask, grab a blanket off the bed, and we'll put the silver in it."

The bedding was quickly obtained and spread on the floor beside the trunk. While Girty kept his eye and his knife on the others, Trask quickly tossed all the silver into a pile in the middle of the cover. Grabbing the four corners, Trask hefted the load onto his shoulder.

"Now," Girty said with an evil grin, "you two girls is comin' with us."

"Oh no, they isn't!" yelled a small voice by the bedroom door. All the noise had awakened five-year-old Seth Middlebrook. Fearlessly the lad charged at the man threatening his sisters.

Girty was caught off guard as the determined boy threw himself at the villain's leg and sank his teeth into his thigh. "YEEOW!" Girty yelled and pulled the boy away by the collar of his night shirt. Angrily he shoved the boy towards his mother and grabbed for Gracie.

"Momma, no!" Grace exclaimed fearfully as she looked at her mother.

"NO!" screamed Rebecca and lunged for Girty.

The British agent saw the mother coming and swung his right hand that held the knife, but instead of slashing Rebecca, he hit her in the jaw with his fist. The stunned woman fell into a nearby table, knocking it over and spilling the contents of her sewing basket on the floor. The children saw their unconscious mother drop.

"MOMMA!" all of them gasped and rushed to her fallen form.

Stooping down, Girty grabbed Grace by the arm and jerked her to her feet. When she started to scream, the British agent held the knife in front of her face.

"Scream, and I'll cut your throat," he growled threateningly, "and that goes for you too," he added, looking at Katherine. "You are both coming with us, and if either of you yell or try to run off, then I kill this one." To emphasize his point, he put the blade of his knife against Grace's throat.

"Oh no, you don't!" the small boy cried and started to rush at them again.

"SETHIE, STOP!" Katherine yelled at her brother. "These men will hurt Gracie if we don't do what they say. You stay here with mother until help comes. Gracie and I will be all right." As Katherine said this, she put her hands on the floor to push herself back to her feet. Spotting a pouch full of buttons close by, she stealthily grabbed it, hiding it in the folds of her dress as she stood.

"Please," Katherine said earnestly as she faced Girty, "don't hurt her!"

"Just behave yourselves, and you will both be fine," Trask said as he shifted the bundle of silver on his shoulder. "Now let's get out of here!"

Neither girl wanted to leave their little brother nor their unconscious mother, but the knife against Grace's throat convinced them to submit to the rogues. Dragging Kate to the doorway, Trask scanned the dark shadows and, seeing no one, darted out into the rainy night, followed by Girty with Grace. Keeping to the shadows, the pair forced their captives toward the north wall.

As soon as they disappeared around the corner of the Middlebrook's house, Gardenia Leavenworth ran out of a dark shadow nearby, wringing her hands and dancing nervously in the rain as she watched the two agents drag her friends away. Hearing crying inside the house, she quickly ran through the open door and found young Seth sitting beside Mrs. Middlebrook, who was groaning on the floor.

"My girls!" Rebecca moaned. "Where are my girls?"

"'Dose men took 'em, Ma!" Seth exclaimed.

"Don't worry, Mrs. Middlebrook," Gardenia said soothingly as she knelt beside the fallen woman. "I saw where they went, and I'm going for help!

"Seth, you stay with your ma till I get back!" the girl then jumped to her feet and raced out the door screaming.

Chapter Twenty-Nine

TRACKIN' POLECATS

William, standing on the blockhouse overlooking the gate, had just taken a last shot at the retreating Indians when he felt a hand on his shoulder.

"It took some doin' this time, but praise the Almighty, we burned their britches again!" Dirt cried out.

Turning from the wall, Will and Dirt quickly checked on Jack and the other injured defenders.

"Are you hurt bad, Jack?" William asked as he leaned over his friend.

"Bad enough, I reckon," Jack grunted. "Although I had more holes in me fightin' that panther the time me an' Dirt were down on the Arkansas."

"Yeah," Dirt agreed. "You looked like a sieve that day."

Just then they heard Gardenia screaming in the darkness behind them.

"Something's wrong!" Jack said anxiously as he grabbed Dirt's arm. "Grab some men, and you an' Will go check! Some of 'em may have gotten into the fort!"

They found Gardenia standing in the dark and the rain, yelling near the open door of the Middlebrook's home.

"What's happened?" Dirt asked urgently.

"During the battle," Gardenia began, "I had to go to the privy. I was just coming back when I saw two strange men coming out of the Middlebrook's home dragging Kate and Gracie. I was

270

watching them when I heard Seth crying inside. I found Mrs. Middlebrook lying on the floor where she had been knocked down."

"WHAT!" exclaimed Silas Middlebrook as he came trotting out of the darkness to join them.

"SILAS!" Dirt barked. "YER WIFE'S BEEN HURT!"

Without waiting for any more information, Mr. Middlebrook dashed into his house to see about Rebecca, followed by William and Dirt.

"Is she hurt bad?" Dirt asked.

"She's got a large knot and a bruise under her left eye where the blackguards hit her," Silas returned, "but I think she'll be alright."

"THEY TOOK THE GIRLS, SILAS!" the distraught mother cried in agony. "THEY TOOK THE GIRLS!"

"The Injuns?" Dirt asked again.

"It was that Mr. Trask and his worthless friend!" she shot back. "They came in here, stole our silver, and took the girls!"

"I tried to stop 'em, Pa," little Seth said angrily, "but they would'a hurt Gracie!"

"Do we know where they went?" Dirt asked anxiously.

"I do!" Gardenia declared from where she stood in the doorway. "I saw them drag the girls to the north wall."

"Mr. Gurley," Rebecca said earnestly to the scout, "you must save my girls!" As she said this, her eyes suddenly rested on Will's face. "William!" she said with a pleading look. "Your mother told me you know the forest better than most Indians. You saved my girls once. I need you to do it again! PLEASE!"

Will Hackett looked compassionately into Rebecca's tear-filled eyes and smiled, "Dirt and I will do everything in our power to find them and bring them safely back."

"Will's done took the words right outta my mouth, Mother Middlebrook," Dirt agreed, throwing his arm across William's shoulder. "Me an' Will's gonna go out there, track down them girl-stealin' polecats, get the little ladies back, or die tryin'! You got Solomon Ambrose Gurley's word on that!"

"Fellows," Silas spoke up, "the battle with the Indians is over, but they're still out there. If you go now, they will kill you."

"They'll try to if they see us," William returned, "but Dirt and I are pretty good at not being seen. Right, Dirt?"

"What 'chu talkin' about?" Dirt Gurley said, puffing out his chest. "Why, I'm purt'near invisee-bule when I wants to be!"

"Gardenia," Will said turning to his friend, "can you show us where the two men took Kate and Grace?"

"Sure I can," the excited girl returned. "Follow me."

As soon as they stepped out of the house, they saw the Miami hurrying towards them. "Kajika, what has happened?" Gray Fox asked with concern.

"Trask and Girty snuck into the fort and took two of the girls," William explained in the Miami language. "Dirt Gurley and I are going after them."

"Good," his friend returned. "Gray Fox go with you."

The rain was diminishing as Gardenia led them out of the house and retraced the path she had seen the kidnappers take.

"Is the Miami comin' with us?" Dirt asked when he saw Gray Fox following.

"Yes," Will answered.

"Good," Dirt returned confidently. "He'll be a big help."

When they got to the wall, Will quickly climbed the ladder and scanned the other side.

"They used a cut tree to scale the wall while the others attacked the west and east palisades," Will called down to Dirt.

"The sun'll be comin' up in another hour," Dirt called up, "an we need to be across that open area an' in them north woods before it gets light enough for the Chickeesaws to see us. So I say let's get our packs together quick-like an' skee-daddle."

"I agree," Will returned, climbing down to join his friends and Gardenia, "but we need to use our heads. It's going to be too dark to trail them until the sun comes up, and we don't want to just be wandering around in the woods."

"What're you thinkin'?" Dirt asked questioningly.

"If you were Trask and Girty, where would you go?"

"*Hmmm*," Dirt said, considering the question. "After losing another battle with us and with so many of the Chickeesaws' braves gettin' their candles snuffed, so to speak, I suspect Trask and Girty know they'll get their hair lifted if they go back to camp."

"Right," agreed Will. "So where would they go to be safe?"

There was a long pause and finally Dirt answered. "The closest place would be Fort Dee-troit, way north of here, an' from there to Canada."

"Then that's where they'll go," Will decided. "Let's grab our packs and head north."

"Alright," Dirt returned thoughtfully, "we'll do that, but I want to check on Jack afore we leave. Oh, I almost forgot." Dirt pointed his rifle in the air and fired it. "Be sure an' reload your rifle with a ball. We won't be needin' buckshot where we're goin'."

"Until the rain stops, it will probably be best to wait to reload at all," Will returned, then explained the plan to Gray Fox.

In twenty minutes Will, Dirt, and the Miami were standing on the catwalk of the north wall, saying goodbye to their friends on guard. Slipping quietly over the palisade, they dropped lightly to the ground. The sun had not yet signaled its appearance, so the early morning darkness covered the movements of the three as they moved cautiously across the open meadow. They crept silently along, undetected, until they entered the edge of the forest. Dirt paused to listen, and when he heard no sound around them to give them alarm, he moved deeper into the woods.

Suddenly they froze. The faint snap of a twig had sounded off to their left. Without looking back at his two companions, Dirt's left hand rose and pointed into the darkness on that side. As William and Gray Fox stared at the dim shape of their friend's hand, they saw the palm turn towards them, indicating that they should stay where they were. Dirt glanced back at his companions and signed his intention. After seeing them both give an understanding nod, Dirt stood up and began walking forward, realizing that, with the rain still falling, there was little chance of him being shot.

The young frontiersman and his friend remained still, watching their friend's form fade into the darkness, when suddenly a figure burst from some brush to their left and raced for Dirt. At the same instant William and Gray Fox shot forward to protect their friend.

Dirt heard the movement and turned to face the attacking Chickasaw lookout. Just as the warrior drew near to his victim, a noise was heard from behind. The Indian turned quickly to meet this unexpected threat and was quickly dropped by the butt of Dirt's rifle.

"Let's get outta here," Dirt hissed urgently to his two friends, "afore any more of them rascals gets after us!" Turning quickly, the scout lead them deeper into the dark forest.

"You do know how to get to Fort Detroit, right?" William whispered to his companion once they were a safe distance from the Chickasaw camp.

"Oh, purdy much," Dirt returned off-handedly. "I seen it once. . .from a distance, so I knows where it is. We need to go north, then a little east for a long ways. The sun ain't up yet, and we cain't see the stars with these heavy clouds, so for now, since we know this way is north, we'll do what I'm figurin' them two worthless polecats did, and that's head due north."

The three rescuers had worked their way quietly through the woods for a quarter of an hour when they noticed a pink glow in the eastern sky. A short time later, as the growing light began to reveal more of the trees and forest floor around them, they increased their speed.

"I figure that, once Trask and Girty spotted the glow of the sun, they turned northeast," Dirt Gurley said in a low voice. He signed a basic form of this message to Gray Fox as he spoke. "Let's keep goin' north for a little longer afore we turn. We jus' might spot their trail."

"Alright," William whispered back, "but how about we let Gray Fox lead for a while? He's about the finest tracker I've ever known."

"Well then, let's put 'im to work." Dirt returned and gestured to the Miami to take the lead.

With a nod of understanding, Gray Fox guided them forward at a steady pace. The rain stopped a short time later. When it was light enough to see clearly, they halted their march.

"The clouds are breaking up," Will announced as he studied the sky.

"Good!" Dirt declared as he pulled up his powder horn. "I feel kinda neked trapsin' around out here without a loaded rifle."

As William and Gray Fox finished loading theirs, the young frontiersman said, "Now that we can see, how about we range a little as we work our way along. It may make it easier to spot their trail."

With their firearms ready for action, they resumed the chase. Gray Fox maintained their line of march while Will waved Dirt off to the left. At the same time Young Hackett ranged a stone's throw to their right. They wove back and forth as they continued north. Almost thirty minutes had passed when suddenly Dirt and the Miami were stopped by the sound of a thrush off to their right. Gazing at the source of the sound, they both spotted their young friend waving at them. Quickly the two made their way to where William stood pointing at the ground.

"Well, lookee there!" Dirt exclaimed under his breath. "That Kathrine, she's a smart one all right!"

Lying on the ground at William's feet was a light-colored, wooden button.

"There was a lot of sewing stuff lying all over the floor in their house where Mrs. Middlebrook fell," William recalled. "Kate must have been able to grab some buttons before they got kidnapped." Will made sure Gray Fox understood his reasoning.

"So along with watchin' out for their tracks," Dirt replied, "we need to keep our eyeballs pealed for more of them signs!"

Finding no more dropped items nearby, Will continued their march north. They found two more buttons as they pressed their way forward. After another quarter of an hour, the three came to a large, rotted log near the trail. On top of it were three buttons lying in a row.

"They must have rested here," Will said as he studied the ground in front of the log. "I can see the girls' foot prints where they sat together."

"Why the three buttons?" Dirt wondered out loud.

"My guess is that, as they rested, Kate heard Trask and Girty talking about changing directions. See how the buttons are lined up?"

"Yeah," Dirt agreed, "an' their all pointin' northeast."

"Let's range some to the northeast and see if we spot any more clues," William suggested, then repeated his words in Miami.

They had just begun scouting in that direction when Dirt stopped and called to his friend. "You're right as rain!" he announced. "There's another button right here! She dropped the next one quick to make sure we found the turn. That girl's somethin'!"

"Well, come on!" Will called over his shoulder as he broke into a long distance trot, following the new trail.

They traveled as fast as they dared while still scanning the area in front and around them for more signs. In another thirty minutes Will stopped again. Something in the brush to their right caught his eye. Retrieving it, he showed it to Dirt and Gray Fox.

"That there's a piece of cloth," the scout announced. "It's been torn off somethin'."

"Kate's got a dress that color," Will observed. He began studying the ground near where the piece of cloth was found. Finally he walked back to his friends.

"It looks like the girls rested here again," Will said. "Kate's trying to slow them down."

"She's doin' her part," Dirt responded proudly. "Now let's do ours!" The scout signed to the Miami to lead them on.

Once again they began their determined march, constantly on the alert for signs. Both William and Dirt were pleased with the pace that Gray Fox set. The Miami's eyes missed nothing, constantly scanning the forest floor as they hurried along. The two scouts felt sure that they had to be gaining on the kidnappers. Eventually they called a halt beside a large outcropping of moss-covered rocks. Here they paused to take a drink from the canteen Will carried in his pack.

The rescuers had only been on the trail ten minutes more when a grunt a short distance away stopped them in their tracks. Not thirty yards in front of them was a large black bear clawing at the bark of a dead tree trunk. Running around beneath her feet were three cubs.

"NO, NO, NO!" Dirt hissed urgently as he grabbed Will and Gray Fox by their shoulders and pushed them back the way they had come. "Momma bears is bad medicine!"

"This is gonna make us lose time!" William whispered anxiously

"It cain't be helped!" Dirt returned. "If we shoot that thing, we'll let the two weasels we're chasin' know that we're after 'em, an' they'll either change directions or, more likely, ambush us. An' besides that, if we only wound that monster instead of killin' it, we'll be in a whole heap of trouble! So come on, an' let's start backin' away from this dee-saster."

They had only retreated ten steps when suddenly Dirt's foot landed on a dead branch, causing a loud snap. Instantly the four bears turned and look straight at them.

"Run!" Dirt whispered, then he turned and sprinted back the way they had come, with William and Gray Fox right on his heels. With an angry roar the mother bear galloped after them, her three cubs playfully bouncing in her wake.

"IS SHE COMIN'?" Dirt shouted over his shoulder.

"WHAT DO YOU THINK?" Will shouted back. "CAN YOU GO ANY FASTER?"

"I DON'T NEED TO AS LONG AS I'M AHEAD OF YOU. . .*HEE, HEE, HEE!*"

They continued running until they came to the outcropping of rocks.

"QUICK! FOLLER ME!" Dirt yelled as he ran past the formation and darted around it to the south. At least for the moment, they were out of sight of the furious bear. When she reached the end of the rocks, she stopped to try to locate the strange creatures, who she saw as a threat to her cubs. By the time she looked behind the rocks and spotted the three humans racing away, they were so far ahead that, instead of chasing them, she pawed the ground and gave them a roar of good riddance.

Chapter Thirty

THE CRY FOR HELP

"**H**o. . .*huff, huff.* . .Hold up!" Dirt puffed as he slid to a stop. Grabbing a small tree nearby to support himself, he heaved to catch his breath. "It looks. . .*huff, huff.* . .like we finally. . .*huff, huff.* . .lost that bear."

"Are you okay?" Will asked his winded companion as he handed him the canteen of water.

"Oh, I'm jus' peachy!" the scout said sarcastically after taking a long drink. "I run fer my life a couple a times a day, don't chu know."

"Well, when you get your wind back, let me know, and we'll circle back and try to find their trail again."

"I'll be alright," Dirt returned as he straightened up and handed the water back to his friend. "Go ahead on. I'll be right behind you. . .jus' take 'er easy at first."

Will stole a secretive look at Gray Fox as Dirt finished. The Miami nodded his understanding. Replacing the canteen in his pack, Will scanned the sky through the tree tops to get his direction, then walked to the northeast, followed by Dirt. Gray Fox came last to keep an eye on the still panting older scout. They had run downhill to escape the bear, so now that were moving uphill again, William traveled slowly to let Dirt get his breath. They had only been walking for a few minutes when Will suddenly stopped.

"What's wrong now?" Dirt called out.

"You remember those rocks we rounded to get away from that bear?" Will asked.

"Sure. What of it?"

"Well, just look up ahead of us," Will said as he pointed in the distance. "From this downhill side of those rocks, we're now facing a sizable ridge to climb."

"Whoo-wee!" Dirt exclaimed as he studied the series of ledges in front of them. "That there's a serious bluff! It must be thirty to thirty-five feet tall."

"Look there," Will said, pointing to the east. "The ridge gets taller the further east we go."

"We cain't go back, or that bear'll have us for lunch!" Dirt snapped in frustration. "Great granny's garters! We've got ourselves in a fine mess, Will! You know we're gonna have to climb that rascal!"

"Yep," Will answered matter-of-factly, "and it's gonna put us even further behind."

With an exasperated sigh Dirt Gurley dropped his head and shook it slowly in disappointment.

"Are you ready?" Will asked.

"Aw, skunks!" Dirt huffed, staring at the rocks in front of them. "I should've left this to you young bucks. I'm getting too old fer all this foolishness. Alright, lead on."

William walked along the base of the bluff until he came to a spot that seemed to offer the most hand and foot holds.

"I don't know, Will," Dirt said as he studied the rocks above them. "This is gonna be a tough climb with us holdin' our rifles."

"We could use our powder horn straps to loop around the guns and slide the straps over our heads and shoulders," William thought out loud.

"That might work," Dirt answered, "but I'm afeared the weight of the gun will break the strap."

"Hey, wait a minute!" the young frontiersman said excitedly as he dug into his pack. "Yeah, I thought so. The strap on the canteen is thicker. It should hold. So we'll loop the canteen strap around your gun for you to carry, and I'll loop the straps of both powder horns around my rifle. With the weight of my gun distributed between both of them, they should hold."

It took several minutes to attach the makeshift slings, but just then Dirt noticed Gray Fox standing nearby holding his rifle.

"What a meathead I am!" Dirt exclaimed. "We plum fergot about poor ol' Gray Fox. We ain't got no more straps fer his rifle. What's *he* gonna do?"

"Dirt is concerned with how you are going to get your rifle to the top of the bluff," Will explained to the Maimi.

With a snort Gray Fox laid down his rifle and whipped out his knife. Finding a small sapling, he cut it off at the base and quickly shaved off all of the side branches. He ran the stick that was left through the trigger guard of his rifle and shoved it into the back of his belt. Walking over to the bluff, he began to climb.

"Well, I'll be a cross-eyed gopher!" Dirt said in amazement. "I reckon I didn't need to cut the straps off our canteen."

"Yeah," Will added, "he's pretty smart!"

"Next time," Dirt declared as he walked over to the bluff, "we'll ask him first."

They followed the Miami, climbing with their rifles hanging from their backs. They spread out to avoid hitting each other with the bits of stone and dirt that might be knocked loose.

With starting, stopping, and moving around to find the best grips on the ledges, it took nearly half an hour for them all to reach the top. When the three tired rescuers finally did drag themselves over the edge, they lay for several minutes with their arms quivering from the exertion.

The first thing Will did after he sat up was to pull three pieces of jerked deer meat from his pack and hand one to each of his companions. When they felt the strength returning to their arms and legs, they shared the canteen again and took up their fire arms.

With their equipment back in its place, the three were ready to resume their march. They took a moment to study the land around them, then they all turned and looked at each other at the same time.

"I know what yer gonna ask," Dirt spoke first, "an' the answer is, 'I ain't got no idear.'"

"So do you know where the trail we were following is?" Will asked the Miami. Gray Fox only shrugged.

"Well, since none of us knows where to look," William reasoned, "we're going to need to backtrack along this bluff until we find where we were before the bear got after us."

"That's all fine an' dandy," Dirt returned, "jus' as long as you don't run us back into momma bear."

"Right," William agreed. "We're going to have to be cautious."

The trip along the top of the ridge was much slower than they wanted it to be, but fear of confronting the fearsome beast again demanded it. The sun was getting lower in the west when Dirt called in a low voice: "See that dead tree jus' up ahead?"

"The one to the right?" Will asked.

"Yeah, that one. It looks like the place mamma bear was scratchin' when we first come up on her an' the cubs."

As they drew closer, they spotted the deep claw marks in the rotted trunk.

"Yep," Dirt said again, "that's it, all right."

"Okay, good," William agreed. "Now we just head northeast from here, and we should be going in the right direction."

"Well, let's get movin'," Dirt growled, "afore that grumpy she-bear comes back."

Gray Fox led as they once again pursued the kidnappers. The Miami constantly kept his eyes searching the ground for more of Kate's buttons, but he saw none. They kept moving until it began to get dark.

"I hate it, Dirt," Will announced to his friends, "but we're going to have to stop."

"I know," Dirt agreed. "With this heavy cloud cover, we cain't see the stars, an' we won't be able to keep a proper direction if we kept marchin'. But the good news is that they'll have to stop too."

William reached into his pack and pulled out three more pieces of jerky and handed them out.

"We'll hole up here for the night," Dirt added as he received the offered meat, "an' start after 'em at first light."

"I hope they didn't change directions on us again," Will said as he sat down with his back to the trunk of a sweet gum tree and chewed his supper. "You know, I haven't seen any more buttons since we climbed the ledge. It'll take more time, but if we're going to find their trail, we'll have to wait until it gets light enough to see, then start ranging again to try to find some sign of them."

"Will," Dirt said, suddenly very serious, "have you prayed about this? What we decide to do next could mean life or death for these two girls, an' I don't want to make that decision without His help. You know what I mean?"

William was thoughtful for a moment before he answered. "Yeah, I know exactly what you mean. I was so worried about getting Kate and her sister back that I forgot to ask the Lord Jesus for His help."

"Well," the older scout returned, "we got several hours on our hands to do it. Since our All Knowin', All Mighty Father in Heaven knows where they are AN' how to catch 'em, let's ask Him how to do it. You go first, then I'll pray a spell too. . .jus' fer good measure."

William explained to Gray Fox what his friend had said and what they were going to do.

"Good," the Miami answered. "You and Dirt pray to Gitchie Manitou. Gray Fox pray too."

Laying down his rifle and crawling onto his knees, William began to cry out to his Heavenly Father in the name of his King, Jesus Christ. The lad voiced his anger at the injustice of what these men had done. He cried out for safety and protection for the two sisters, for God's grace and power, and that the girls might be rescued and returned safely to their family. Finally the young frontiersman petitioned the Almighty for His wisdom and direction so that he, Dirt, and Gray Fox might find them in time. His prayer was so intense that, when he finally finished, there was sweat trickling down his face. Eventually he said, "Amen."

Dirt cleared his throat and began his prayer: "Hello there, Yer Majesty, Sir," the crude scout said. "I'm sure You remember me, Sir. . .Yer ol' friend Solomon. That fine Son of Yers, King Jesus, said we could talk to you whenever we need to, so here we are. It's awful good of You, Sir, to take the time to listen to us like this! It really does mean the world to us to know that we can come to You an' ask fer Yer help. An' to be abso-tively factical about it, Sir, we've got a whoppin' need fer it right now.

"Them two scallywags, Trask and Girty, has done injured Mother Middlebrook, and on top of all their wicked shenanigans, has kidnapped her two daughters right outta their own home! It's fallen to the three of us to try to get 'em back, but Lord, we're in a fix! This rescue ain't been goin' so well fer us, an' I suspect that the enemy has been up to more of his foul doin's to help these two reperbates do his evil work.

"Now, Lord, we know that you're bigger, stronger, an' smarter than Satan, an' you've already whupped him at the cross. But Lord, me an' Will an' our Injun friend here, need you to whup him again.

"We've done tried our best to catch 'em, but we jus' keep getting' further an' further behind. You see, Your Immenseness, it's like this: You know where they are right now an' where they're agoin', but we don't. So, You see, Lord, we're desperate fer some of Yer wisdom. Fer the sake of them two sweet girls, we're askin' you to tell us what to do to catch 'em.

"Well, Sir, I reckon that's it, except that we thank you fer listenin' to us an' fer what yer gonna do. . .uh, Amen."

Dirt was suddenly surprised when he heard solemn words coming from the Miami warrior. He was standing a short distance away with both arms raised to heaven.

William smiled as he listened to his friend's sincere prayer. "Oh Great Spirit, who is Gray Fox that he would dare speak to You? But You know my good friend, Kajika. I know You hear him and have shown great favor to him. It is my friend Kajika who has told me about Your Son. Kajika says that if we pray in His name, You will hear us. So in the name of Great Chief Jesus, I ask You to show us where these bad men who have taken the two girls are. Let us catch them and save the maidens, Great Spirit. Only You can help us. I am Gray Fox."

The three friends sat in the darkness in silence for several long moments after they finished praying. Finally William spoke. "Well. . .did the Lord say anything to you?" he questioned Dirt and then asked the Miami the same thing.

"*Hmmm,*" Dirt began, "you know, I didn't hear no actual words, but I did get a idear."

"What is it?"

"I know they're travelin' slower with the girls," Dirt began, "but think about it, Will. With all the bad luck we've been havin', we're so far behind 'em that, even if we find their trail in the morning, we will have lost so much more time that there's no way we'll catch 'em."

"I can see that," the youth return. "So what do you want to do?"

"Well," Dirt answered, "if'n I was them two gutless slime balls, I'd wanna get to Fort Dee-troit jus' as fast as I could. So I figure, since they think they escaped the Chickeesaws, they'd head straight fer safety. Do you agree with that?"

"Yeah, that makes sense."

"Alright then," the older scout returned, "let's save as much time as we can an' lite outta here as soon as the Good Lord shows us where east is an' make a straight line fer Dee-troit. There's a big river a good day's march ahead of us, an' them rascals is gonna have to figure out how to cross it whilest draggin' two girls with 'em."

William thought about this suggestion for a few minutes before he voiced his opinion: "I can see a lot of problems with that plan," the young scout explained his thoughts. "We could easily miss them, you know?"

"You're right as rain," Dirt agreed. "They may not go straight, an' we might never find 'em, but. . ."

"But," Will interrupted, "you're right. If we wait till it's light enough to find signs of their trail, we'll be too far behind to do the girls any good."

"Plus," Dirt added, "we could search all day an' not find their trail."

Once again William nodded his agreement.

"Lest we make another mistake," Dirt said, "how about explainin' it to yer smart Miami friend and see if he can think of a better plan."

After several minutes of conversing with Gray Fox, Will turned back to Dirt. "He agrees that your plan is the best."

"Alrightee then," Dirt announced decisively, rubbing his hands together vigorously, "I doubt it's gonna happen, but if the sky clears an' we can see the stars well enough to get our direction, we'll leave tonight. If not, then as soon as we spot the first hint of dawn in the eastern sky, we high-tail it to the northeast."

Chapter Thirty-One

DESPERATE MEASURES

"**L**et's get movin'!" Girty announced loudly to the rest of their party.

Katherine had slept on a patch of damp leaves, holding her younger sister in her arms. Both of them jerked awake at the agent's gruff call.

"UP, YOU TWO!" snapped Trask as he slung his powder horn around his neck.

The two tired girls groaned as they sat up.

"I'm so hungry!" Grace complained.

"We need some food!" Kate demanded.

"EITHER STAND UP ON YOUR FEET," Girty yelled in Katherine's face, "OR I'M GONNA YANK YOU UP BY YOUR HAIR!"

Both girls struggled wearily to their feet, groaning again at the soreness in their overly taxed leg muscles.

Girty pulled a stick of Indian pemmican from the leather pouch on his hip and shoved this at the older girl. "Share that!" he ordered. "Now follow me. . .AND KEEP UP!"

Katherine looked with disdain at their nasty-looking breakfast. She tried to blow and brush some of the dust and bits of leaves off the leathery food. Finally she stuck one end into her mouth and, with difficulty, bit off a large piece, handing the rest of it to her famished sister.

As soon as she had realized that Trask and Girty were taking them, Katherine had clung to the desperate hope that someone would come to their rescue. That's why she had grabbed the pouch of buttons. In an effort to do her part, she had tried to slow down their progress in order to give anyone who might be chasing them a chance to catch up. Katherine was confident that her friends and family would want to save them, but with the Indians attacking the fort, they might not be able to. If she let herself think about it, she understood that realistically their rescue was not very likely, but she was not ready to give up hope.

She had tried moving slowly and struggling in the brush they passed through, but then Girty had dragged Grace up next to him and threatened to hurt her sister if Katherine didn't keep up. The older captive then came up with another plan. She had pretended to trip a couple of times, then be slow about getting up. But the last time she had done this, Trask had hit her hard across the back with a large stick that was lying nearby. That had happened the afternoon before, and the painful whelp was still prompting her to avoid trying that trick again.

She had run out of buttons yesterday before sunset and had resorted to dropping bits of cloth torn from the edge of her dress. When she felt she was being watched too closely to do that, the older girl had started occasionally dragging her foot to attempt to leave some kind of recognizable mark for pursuers to follow.

As this second day of their horrible ordeal began, Katherine cried out to God for her sister and herself. He was a God of hope, she told herself, and she would cling to that.

After an hour of hard marching through the woods, Girty suddenly stopped and urgently forced everyone further into the brush to their right. Facing the two girls, he put his finger to his lips, then drew his index finger across his throat to show what would happen to them if they didn't do what he wanted. Holding perfectly still, the four of them watched and waited anxiously from their hiding place.

At one point as they hid, Grace had let out an involuntary sigh, which instantly produced another murderous look from Girty. The two girls were both curious and fearful of whom or what they were hiding from. It was only a few more moments before they got the answer.

As the sisters looked past the two British agents crouching in front of them, they spotted first one, then two more Indians creeping through the woods where they had been. As they watched the warriors moving stealthily along, the brave in the lead stopped suddenly, held up his hand, and began sniffing the air.

"They know we're here," whispered Girty as he put his mouth close to Trask's ear. "I'm gonna show myself. Stay hidden."

"Hatito!" Girty called as he stood and held up the palm of his right hand. All three Indians whipped around to face the agent. "Howisiwapani," Girty said again with a smile. "Niwisi Girty."

"Ho, Gir-tee!" one of the warriors returned and held up his hand in friendship.

"They're Shawnee," the agent whispered to Trask. "I met with their tribe before, so I'm going to go talk to them. If I call you, come out smiling. . .but keep your knife handy."

Girty stepped out of the brush and walked over to the warriors. He had an animated conversation with the three for several minutes. They began pointing to the brush where Trask and the girls were.

"They know there are more people with me," Girty called out. "Trask, come out with the girls and act friendly!"

The three Shawnee looked surprised when they saw Grace and Kate. There was even more animated discussion after that.

"They're from a larger hunting party that's not far from here," Girty translated for Trask. "They are really interested in the girls. Show them the silver, and we'll try to distract them."

"I'm not giving them our silver!" Trask growled.

"I didn't say *give* it to 'em," Girty snapped impatiently. "I said *show* it to 'em!"

Trask dropped the sheet, and Girty unwrapped it quickly and lifted out pieces of the silver service. The warriors looked at it curiously for a moment, then tossed it down and turned back to the girls. Girty tried to explain the worth of the silver, but they didn't listen. Even Trask could tell that the attitudes of the Indians were changing from friendly to something more ominous.

The three Shawnee focused all their attention on the two terrified prisoners. The braves began smiling and elbowing each other as they reached out and touched the girls' arms and shoulders. They seemed to be especially fascinated with Grace's golden hair. The fearful sisters drew close to each other. Katherine threw both arms around Grace and hugged her protectively.

With a look of grim realization, Simon Girty turned to Trask. "They're gonna kill us and take those girls," he whispered.

"So we kill them first," Trask returned coldly.

"Right," Girty answered, "but there's three of them, so we have to put them off their guard. I'm going to tell them that friendship with the great Shawnee is more important than two squaws, so I'm going to give the girls to them as a present. That will take their thoughts off us and onto the girls."

"That's when we'll take them," Trask said emotionlessly.

"Right," Girty agreed, "but we have to use our knives! If a rifle goes off. . .theirs or ours. . .we're gonna have that whole hunting party on us, and we won't be able to explain our way out of that mess! Now be ready!"

Girty called to the three to get their attention. As he gave them his little speech, the smiles came back on the Indians' faces, and the braves turned to take possession of their *gifts*. When the fearful sisters saw the leering savages eagerly reaching for them, they began backing away.

"NO! NO!" Katherine cried, hugging Grace tighter. "LEAVE US ALONE!"

"NO. . .PLEASE, NO!" Grace sobbed as she buried her face in her older sister's shoulder.

The three Shawnee rushed forward as one and grabbed the girls at almost the same time. Just then the Indian in the middle heard his two companions give grunts of pain and saw them collapse on the ground. Turning to see what had happened, the unfortunate warrior saw the same two knives that had dropped his friends deal him the same fate.

When Grace saw it happen, she started to scream in horror. Girty anticipated the girl's reaction and whipped his knife up to point at her. Katherine saw the agent's move and quickly slapped her hand over her sister's mouth. Girty cut his eyes to Katherine and gave a nod of approval. "Smart," he said to the older girl.

"Listen to me, both of you!" Trask said in a low voice. "These three were part of a larger hunting party, and the rest of them are somewhere nearby. The only hope that any of us have of getting out of here alive is if we slip through these woods as quietly and as quickly as possible. Do you both understand?" He stared hard at Katherine, who nodded her head. He then looked at Grace who, with Kate's hand still over her mouth, nodded her head as well.

"Enough talk!" Girty snapped. "Let's get going!"

Girty grabbed the younger sister by the arm and forced her to walk beside him as they hurried through the woods. Katherine followed, pushed along by Trask, who had picked up the silver. As they traveled, Girty kept an eye on the position of the sun to make sure they headed in the correct direction.

They kept going at a quick pace until they arrived at a small creek flowing almost north and south. At the edge of the stream, Girty paused and glanced back the way they had come. Making a decision, the agent stepped into the water, dragging Grace with him, and waded south with the flow.

"When the rest of the Shawnee hunting party find their friends, they'll be after us," he called back to Trask. "I think we need to hide our tracks. Follow me, and don't touch the banks on either side."

As Katherine thought of a band of Shawnee chasing after them, she decided that now was not the time to leave more signs.

Girty led them steadily along the creek, constantly searching the eastern bank. They followed the course of the stream for almost half an hour when Girty stopped again. "Okay, here's where we get out," he finally announced.

He turned Grace to look him in the eye and spoke sternly to her. "Listen to me, little girl. If you don't want the Shawnee to get you, you had better do exactly what I tell you."

With her eyes wide in terror, the girl nodded her understanding and agreement.

"I'm gonna lift you up so you can grab this limb over the creek. I want you to hang onto it and use your arms to work your way along it until you get to those rocks over there. Once you get there, sit until the rest of us join you. If you try to run off, we still have your sister, and we'll kill her."

Once again Grace nodded her understanding.

"Hold my rifle, Trask," Girty said to his companion. With both of his hands free, he lifted the girl up until she gripped the limb.

"Alright," Girty said when Grace hung from the limb, "use your arms and climb along that branch until you can drop down on those rocks just over there."

"I. . .I don't know if I can," Grace gasped as she began shuffling her hands along the limb.

"Well, you'd better do it if you want to live!" Trask barked.

She moved her arms stiffly as she slowly but steadily shifted closer to the outcropping of smooth rocks. She got halfway there and stopped to get her breath.

"Don't stop!" Girty called out.

"Keep going!" the other agent yelled.

Once again Grace began shuffling her arms forward, continuing her difficult journey. When she was close to the rocks, she stopped again and tried to reach out with the toe of her foot, but she was still too far away.

"My arms are tired. . .can't go any farther!" she groaned.

"DON'T YOU STOP!" Trask shot back.

"If you drop in that dirt below you and leave tracks," Girty barked, "you and your sister are scalped. . .and that's a fact!"

"MY HANDS ARE SLIPPING!" the girl cried in panic.

"You can do this, Gracie!" Kate called to her sister encouragingly. "You're strong! It's only a little farther, and you can DO this!"

At her sister's urging, Grace gritted her teeth and repositioned her sore hands on the limb. Once again she began shuffling her arms forward, inching closer and closer to the coveted slab of stone. Finally, with a painful groan, her hands slipped from the branch, and she dropped, landing hard on the shelf of limestone below her.

As Grace lay exhausted and crying, Girty turned to Trask: "I'm going next. Once I'm across, send the other girl." Without waiting for an answer, the British agent leaped up and grabbed the limb. After watching her sister struggle so hard, Katherine was surprised at how quickly Girty swung across. "Now toss me both rifles," he called back to his friend.

Trask sent the first weapon flying across. Girty caught it easily and laid it down by his feet. "Now yours," he called again. Once more a rifle went sailing through the air, and as before, the agent on the rocks was able to grab it. "Good! Now send the girl!"

With his hands free, Trask helped Katherine as she jumped for the limb. When she tightly gripped the branch, she began to work her way across. Girty gave a nod of approval at Katherine's strength as he saw her moving smoothly and quickly over to join them. When she reached the slab, Kate dropped down and wrapped her arms around her still crying sister.

A few moments later Trask dropped lightly onto the rock to join them. Handing his partner back his rifle, Girty turned and led them along the shelf of granite and into the woods towards the northeast.

Chapter Thirty-Two

GOTCHA

Since making their decision to race to the river where they expected the kidnappers to eventually be, the three rescuers covered lots of ground in a hurry. No longer searching for signs to follow, they pushed themselves at a long-distance run to the northeast in an effort to make up the time they had lost.

It was late morning when William slid to a sudden stop. Holding up his hand for quiet, he listened carefully to the sounds of the woods. He had caught just a faint noise as he ran and wasn't sure of its source, but it wasn't natural. Hearing only one distant note, the confident, young frontiersman knew it was man-made.

Dirt Gurley also concentrated as he tuned his ears to the distant sounds of the forest.

"You hear that?" Will asked after a moment.

"Yeah, I hear it," Dirt returned. "It's a ways off. Can you make it out?"

The Miami said something to William.

"He says it's a death chant," the young scout translated. "He's right. I've heard them before."

"In this neck of the woods," Dirt reasoned, "it's most likely Shawnee."

"Do you think the Shawnee caught up with them and grabbed the girls?" William asked with concern.

"Well, I ain't gonna lie to ya," Dirt returned. "There's a ver' real possibility that they might have 'em, but let's use our headbones fer a second. If the Shawnee don't have the girls, and we diddle around here tryin' to figure that out, we'll lose any chance of getting' 'em back. I'm fer skirtin' around them Injuns an' to keep makin' tracks fer the river, in case them worthless polecats made it through. If we get there and we cain't find no sign of 'em, then we backtrack, find the Shawnees, an' see if they've got the girls."

William thought on this for a moment and nodded his agreement. He turned to his Miami friend and explained what Dirt had proposed. The scout was surprised at the animated discussion that passed between the two friends.

"He ain't said that many words since I've knowd 'im," Dirt said to William when the talk ended.

"He changed the plan," the young frontiersman returned. "He says we're to head to the river as fast as we can, and he will go scout the Shawnee. If the girls are there, he will come get us."

"Alright, let's get movin'!" Dirt said urgently.

Without hesitating any longer, William struck out to the southeast in an effort to give the Shawnee ahead of them a wide berth while Gray Fox headed straight for the Indians.

Once William judged that they were well past the enemy warriors, he turned back toward the northeast. Focusing on catching up to the kidnappers, they pushed themselves hard in their race through the forest.

It was midday when they cautiously emerged from the woods and found themselves on the shore of a wide, slow-moving river. They quickly scanned up and down the bank but saw no sign of any others.

"Okay," Dirt spoke up, "here's where it gets kinda tricky. First, we don't know if they even made it here or not, an' second-wise, if they are here, we don't know if we're above 'em or below 'em."

"Alright," Will returned, "you go down river, and I'll go up. We'll look for them or for signs of their crossing. If by sunset we find nothing, we'll meet back here."

"An' if you do find 'em," Dirt added, "come get me if you got time, an' if you don't, then do yer best."

"Right," agreed the youth. Quickly turning, he trotted along the bank to the north, carefully scanning the ground along the shore.

Dirt turned to the south and discovered that he could only see about three hundred yards ahead before the river made a sharp bend to the right and disappeared. He hurried on, being careful to search the ground for footprints as he passed.

When he reached the bend, he followed it, looking and listening carefully as he went. He noticed boulders in front of him, blocking his way and extending out into the water. When he reached the rocks, since they weren't very high, Dirt decided to climb over them rather than take the long way around. As his head cleared the top of the rocks, the scout froze. Standing a short distance away was Trask and the two girls.

Gotcha, you black-hearted varmints! Dirt thought to himself. Continuing to watch from the top of the boulders, the scout saw Simon Girty drag a canoe down to the river from where it had been hidden in the woods.

As Dirt looked for the easiest way to climb down from his hiding place and slip up closer to the group, a rock broke loose under his hand and clattered down the face of the boulders.

"HOLD IT RIGHT THERE!" a voice shouted. Dirt cringed as he looked up and saw Girty looking straight at him. The villainous agent had one of his hands around Grace's throat, and the other one held a knife in front of her. "THIS GIRL DIES IF YOU DON'T DO EXACTLY WHAT I SAY!"

"DON'T HURT HER!" Dirt called back, standing and lifting his arms in the air. "YOU GOT ME!"

"THE FIRST THING YOU'RE GONNA DO," Girty yelled back, "IS TOSS THAT RIFLE DOWN HERE ON THE GROUND SO I CAN SEE IT!"

"THAT MIGHT BREAK MY GUN IF I DROP IT THAT FAR!" Dirt yelled back, stalling for an extra moment. As he said this, Dirt pointed to the ground below with his left arm, but with his right he carefully cocked his rifle.

"WELL, WOULDN'T THAT JUST BE TOO BAD!" Girty yelled back sarcastically. "NOW TOSS IT, OR I CUT THIS GIRL!" Dirt and Jack had both filed the trigger mechanisms on their rifles down so that the slightest touch would set them off. That way when they pulled the trigger, it did not upset their aim. Knowing this, Dirt tossed his rifle down but made sure that when it hit the ground, the barrel would be pointed away from everyone. Just as he expected, the impact of the rifle with the ground jarred the trigger, and the gun went off.

"I TOL' YOU IT WAS TOO FAR TO DROP IT!" Dirt yelled back.

"YOU BONEHEAD!" Girty cried in anger. "WHY DID YOU COCK IT? NOW YOU'RE GONNA HAVE EVERY SHAWNEE IN THE TERRITORY AFTER US! GET DOWN HERE NOW!"

William had been making steady progress to the north along the bank of the river, but so far had seen and heard nothing. He stopped for a moment to study the shore ahead. Suddenly he heard a rifle shot some distance behind him. Immediately the young frontiersman turned and raced in the direction of the noise. After several minutes of hard running, William reached the bend in the river. He cautiously scanned the shoreline as he followed the curve of the shore. When he looked ahead and could see no one between himself and the rocks in the distance, he sprinted furiously to the base of the boulders. He was about to climb them when he heard a conversation on the other side.

He recognized Dirt's nasally voice and knew that he had to be talking to the kidnappers. Taking deep breaths to calm his pounding heart, the young woodsman began to follow the edge of the rocks away from the river and into the woods, where they were swallowed by a low, wooded slope a short ways in.

When William entered the forest and made his way to the other side of the rocks, it was evident why the Miami Indians called him Kajika, or Walks Without Sound. When he was within thirty yards of the party on the shore, he halted. Grass and shrubs hid him from the view of the others.

Girty had the canoe in the river. The agent himself was seated in the back with its bow resting on the shore. Will saw Grace carefully using both hands as she walked along the rocking canoe to a place just in front of Girty. Katherine stood on the shore, ready to climb in after her sister was seated. Trask too was still on the shore, but with his rifle trained on Dirt, who was several yards closer to the woods.

As William watched Grace struggle in the rocking boat, he carefully assessed the situation. The British agents had to know that Dirt, to have caught up with them so soon, was a scout of no little ability. They also had to know that, if they let him live, he would keep coming after them until he had rescued the girls. The logical conclusion came to the young frontiersman in an instant. *They're going to kill Dirt!* Will realized. *They have to kill him to stop him!*

With this clear understanding of what was about to happen, William laid his cheek along the stock of his rifle and drew careful aim at Trask.

When Grace was finally seated in the bottom of the canoe at Girty's feet, the agent called to Trask. "Alright, finish that scum. Then you and the girl climb in, and we'll push off."

"Right," called Trask as he readjusted his rifle on his shoulder.

Realizing that he was about to be shot, Dirt's eyes got big, and he began backing away as he cried, "NOW, DON'T BE SO HASTY..."

Suddenly the crack of a rifle sounded from the woods behind Dirt, and with a grunt Trask was knocked backwards and fell lifeless into the river.

At that instant both Kate and Grace cried out in terror as Girty snatched up his rifle from the floor of the canoe, aimed it at Dirt, and fired.

Dirt had anticipated what would happen and tried to jump to his right, but grunted in pain as the bullet arrived. Girty immediately began using the stock of his now empty rifle as an oar and backed the canoe away from the shore as quickly as possible.

Just then William came sprinting out of the woods and dropped beside his injured friend. "Dirt!" he called urgently.

". . .the ball creased me across my back," he grunted through clenched teeth. "I'll be okay. Jus' save that girl!"

Without hesitating, William sprang to his feet, ran over, and snatched up the still-loaded rifle that Trask had dropped. When Girty saw the weapon now aimed at him, he grabbed the crying Grace and held her like a shield in front of him.

"LET GO OF THAT GIRL, YOU COWARD!" Will yelled.

"WHY?" Girty called back, "SO YOU CAN SHOOT ME? NO WAY! YOU PUT DOWN THAT RIFLE, OR I'LL KILL THIS GIRL!"

"THAT'S NOT GOING TO HAPPEN," Will answered, "AND YOU'RE NOT GOING TO HURT HER EITHER, OR I WILL PUT THIS BALL BETWEEN YOUR EYES!

"YOU TRIED YOUR BEST TO GET AWAY, AND MY FRIEND AND I FOUND YOU EASILY. I PROMISE YOU THAT WE WILL NOT GIVE UP UNTIL WE GET YOU. I WILL GIVE YOU ONE CHANCE TO SAVE YOUR LIFE. IF YOU ROW BACK OVER HERE AND GIVE GRACE TO US, I GIVE YOU MY WORD THAT I WILL NOT SHOOT YOU!"

Girty thought about those last words for several long moments. Finally he made his decision. "ALRIGHT," he yelled, "SHE'S YOURS. . .BUT YOU HAVE TO COME GET HER!"

As he said this, he gave a powerful shove and threw the terrified girl over the side into the deep river.

"GRACIE!" Katherine screamed when she saw her sister thrashing in the water.

As Girty began making powerful strokes toward the opposite shore, Will dropped the rifle and dove for the girl.

The young frontiersman plowed through the water with all of his strength. The weight of her wet dress pulled at Grace, but the terrified girl managed to keep her head above the surface long enough for William to reach her. Grabbing the crying girl around the waist, the scout kicked and swam for the shore.

"Calm down, Grace," the scout said gently. "You're alright now. I need you to help me kick to the bank. Remember...we've done this before."

The soothing words did a lot to settle the panicking girl's nerves, and she was able to use her legs and the arm that wasn't around Will's neck to aid their journey to safety. When they arrived at the shore, Katherine helped Grace up the bank. Dirt stumbled over to join them just as William crawled out of the water.

The two sisters cried and hugged as Dirt stepped up and extended his hand to shake Will's. "A fine piece a'work!" Dirt exclaimed as he welcomed his friend. "Yessiree-bob, a fine piece a'work! I couldn't a' did it better my-self!"

"What about you?" William asked with concern. "I need to see to that wound of yours!"

"Yeah, I'd be much obliged," Dirt grunted back. "If we could come up with some kind of bandage for it, I think that would help."

Will sat Dirt on one of the rocks beside the river and helped him pull off his shirt. The injured scout grimaced as the youth used handfuls of water to clean the wound.

"How bad is it?" Dirt asked after Will studied the injury.

"Well, the ball cut about a three inch long grove below your left shoulder blade. It's not deep and didn't do a lot of damage, but it's still bleeding, and it's going to hurt for a while."

"Can you figure out a way to wrap me up so's I don't lose much more blood?" Dirt questioned.

"I didn't bring any bandage material," Will returned.

"We can take care of that," Katherine responded eagerly. "If we can borrow your knife, Grace and I can cut the bottom three or four inches off our dresses for you to use."

"Now ain't that somethin'!" Dirt Gurley said with a grin. "Leave it to she-males to come up with brilliant idears!"

Using the wide strips of fabric, William wrapped a snug bandage around the injured man's chest and back. Putting his shirt back on was a painful ordeal, but eventually Dirt was ready to travel.

"Thank you both so much for saving us!" Grace said with feeling.

"Yes," Kate added, "thank you! Since they took us, we have been praying to God to deliver us, and He sent you!"

"We should thank Him!" Grace said sincerely.

"Yes, we should!" agreed Dirt. "All of you bow yer heads, an' I'll do the honors."

Dirt pulled off his hat, and all four of them bowed their heads. "Almighty God, Yer Honor, Sir. . ." Dirt began. But he didn't get any further.

Loud calls came from the woods a short distance away. "KAJIKA! KAJIKA!"

Looking over, they saw Gray Fox waving fiercely for them to come to him. "Now what's he blabberin' about?" Dirt asked with a confused look on his face.

Just then angry yells, war cries, and several guns erupted in the distance, causing the four friends to look to their left. They saw a large party of Shawnee warriors burst out of the forest three hundred yards to the south and charge along the bank straight towards them.

"HELP US, LORD! AMEN!" Dirt called out his brief prayer. "NOW LET'S GET OUTTA HERE!" he cried as he and Will each grabbed a girl and ran into the western woods to join Gray Fox.

Chapter Thirty-Three

THE SACRIFICE

William, tightly gripping Grace's arm, ran quickly into the thick forest to the west. The ground slopped upward from the river, and rocky limestone outcroppings were thickly scattered through the woods.

"You know them sneaky rascals probably sent flankers angling up through the woods to cut us off!" Dirt Gurley called from behind as he ran with Katherine. The Miami followed as their rear guard.

"Yes, I do!" Will called back over his shoulder. "That's why, when we get over this hill, we're turning north." The young frontiersman wanted desperately to move faster, but with the girls as tired and as hungry as they were and with Dirt's injury, he knew they were traveling as fast as they were able.

When William got all of them over the top of the low, rocky hill, he halted briefly. "Is everyone okay?" he asked, looking at each one of them. He saw that both girls were red-faced and breathing hard.

"We're doing our best!" Katherine huffed back with an attempt at a smile. Grace, panting hard, just nodded her head.

"I think I'm slowin' you down," Dirt said honestly. Will studied his face and could tell that his injury had weakened him.

The young scout considered each of them. Looking realistically at the task ahead, Will quickly made his decision. "Step exactly where I step," he ordered, leading them rapidly due north using rocks and ledges as stepping stones to hide their tracks. As they traveled hurriedly, working their way along the western face of the rocky, forested hill, William scanned the terrain around them for a way to implement his plan. Suddenly he saw what they needed to their right—a dark shadow close to the ground below an exposed shelf of limestone.

"This way, quickly!" Will called back as he hurried to the ledge.

"Listen, Will," Dirt called from behind. "These girls' lives is at stake. You need to leave me behind an' get 'em to the fort!"

"I'm leaving all of you behind," William called back. "Over here—as fast as you can!" their young leader said as he rushed to the ledge he had seen. Throwing himself onto his stomach, Will stuck his head into the dark opening under the shelf to explore it.

"Alright, this will work!" he announced. "Dirt's right. We're not going to be able to out-run them, so here's the plan: there's just enough room for the three of you to hide under this ledge. Be quiet while Gray Fox and I get the Indians to chase us to the north."

After saying this, William quickly explained his idea to the Miami, who nodded his agreement.

"Give me plenty of time, Dirt," Will said earnestly to his injured friend. "Hole up in there nice and quiet for at least half an hour before you crawl out and head to the fort."

"Are you sure about this?" Dirt asked with concern.

"Absolutely! Now get moving!"

"Alrightee then," Dirt agreed. "I know you both know how to take care of yerselves, but. . .take care of yerselves!"

"Quickly!" William snapped. "We've got no more time to spare. All of you get under that ledge. . .and be quiet!"

When Grace dropped to her knees and looked into the ominous dark opening, she hesitated.

"Just go ahead on!" Dirt said urgently to the fearful girl. "I'd carry you across the threshold, but I'm kinda in-kee-pacitated right now with this here hole in my back."

Katherine saw her reluctance and knelt beside her. "Let me go first, Gracie," Kate said with a smile. "Just follow me."

When the younger girl saw her brave sister crawl into the dark opening, she gave a shudder and followed her. Dirt slid in last with his rifle.

Standing back, William had them push further into the crevice until they were completely concealed by the darkness. As the young scout and his Miami friend hurriedly threw limbs and brush around the opening to hide it, he gave Dirt some parting instructions. "Give us plenty of time to get the Shawnee to chase us a good ways to the north before you crawl out."

"That won't be no problem," Dirt's voice called back out of the darkness. "We'll just curl up in here nice an' snug-like an' take ourselves a little ol' nap."

William quickly turned and, with Gray Fox on his heels, ran back in the direction of the enemy warriors, trying to get as far away from his hidden friends as possible. Dirt said a silent prayer for Will and Gray Fox as he saw them leave.

"Ughh!" Dirt heard Grace's voice whisper in disgust. "There're bugs under here!"

"Jus' remember, little missy," Dirt hissed back, "them bugs is yer friends. . .the Injuns ain't!"

Will and the Miami raced to intercept the pursuing Shawnee. The young frontiersman suspected that the Indians had split into two groups. The first would be the ones that had run after them along the river bank and would have followed them where they darted into the woods. The second group would be their best runners, who would have split off into the forest to try to intercept the fugitives.

Will knew that, in order to protect Dirt and the girls, he and Gray Fox had to find both groups and make sure they all chased them north. The young frontiersman had just topped a rocky rise when a movement in the distance caught his eye, and he slid to a sudden stop behind a tree. He spotted eight Shawnee warriors creeping carefully through the woods, looking for tracks. The leader of the group stood up and pointed north toward the direction Will and his friends had taken. *They're good,* William said to himself.

Just as the warriors began moving towards him, Will took careful aim and squeezed his trigger. Almost immediately Gray Fox's rifle barked as well. Looking under the powder smoke, Will saw the Shawnee leader and a brave beside him drop. The rest of the warriors dove out of sight, and the two comrades quickly reloaded their weapons.

William didn't want the Shawnee to trap them, so he and Gray Fox kept moving. As they ran they sent several rifle balls in the direction of the approaching enemies to force the Indians' heads down. Will knew there were more braves in the party than the ones he could see, and he was getting desperate to discover where they were.

From behind a tree where an Indian had hidden came a loud cry. A few seconds later an answering cry echoed from the woods to the south and west.

"So that's where the rest of them are," the young pioneer said to the Miami. "Alright then, let's get everybody together."

After several more shots were fired his way, William made a sudden dash to his right, followed quickly by Gray Fox. When the Shawnee warriors in front saw their prey heading west to get away, more screaming was heard, and hidden warriors popped up to fire at them. The two friends dashed from tree to tree, relentlessly making their way toward the sound of that cry further away. As they ran, Shawnee rifle balls zipped close by or tore bark off nearby trees.

As near as Will could tell, he was running toward the southwest. The Indians they had been fighting jumped from their places of concealment and ran west, trying to catch them. The young frontiersman topped a low hill and looked ahead. He saw the other group of Indians heading straight for him. Their leader saw Will at the same moment and gave his war cry, snapping his rifle to his shoulder. Before he could fire, he was dropped by Gray Fox's rifle.

"Okay," Will called to the Miami, "we've got them all together. Now let's lead them north away from our friends!"

Before he turned to run, the young scout gave a loud Indian victory cry to taunt his enemies. Gray Fox lifted his enthusiastic yell as well. It apparently worked, because as they turned to run north, both groups screamed their rage and furiously gave chase.

To keep from getting too far ahead of his pursuers, William slowed his pace a little. He was actually feeling proud of himself for finding all of the Indians and getting them to chase them. Just then rifle balls began to zip past and tear through branches and leaves very close to their heads. It was at that moment that he had the thought that slowing his pace may not have been the best idea.

"You run like turtle!" Gray Fox called from behind. "RUN!"

Increasing his speed to an all-out sprint, Will led the small army of blood-thirsty warriors in a desperate race through the woods and away from Dirt and the girls.

Jumping logs, dodging thick brush patches, and ducking under low branches, William and the Miami continued their mad dash through the thick woods for almost an hour while the shrieking savages kept close behind them.

The young scout slid to a halt at the edge of a dry creek bed. Taking a quick glance left and right, he decided his best option was straight across. Leaping down the steep bank, he took three strides across the bed and clambered up the other side, not bothering to hide his tracks, with Gray Fox close behind. William sped on for another thirty yards and stopped again beside a hickory tree. He could hear his pursuers as they approached the creek bed.

"Let's slow them down," he called to his friend who hid nearby. The young scout reached into the ammunition pouch that hung at his side and snatched out a ball and a patch. He stuck them in his mouth, after which he raised his rifle and watched for a target.

When the first of the Indians reached the creek, the leaders immediately spotted William's tracks and yelled to those that followed. A rifle suddenly fired, and one of the warriors clutched his chest and fell to the ground. The others dropped or leaped behind tree trunks and shot at the gun smoke thirty yards ahead of them. Another rifle went off a little to their right, and they blasted away at this new threat.

As soon as he had fired his gun, Will snatched up his powder horn and poured a small amount in the pan, snapping the frizzen shut. An instant later he poured black powder down the muzzle, re-plugged his horn, and let it fall to his side. He pulled the ball and patch out of his mouth and shoved them, patch first, into the muzzle. One hard tamp with his ramrod, and he was ready to fire again.

Gunfire still erupted from many places on the other side of the creek, but William was not able to get a clear shot at any of his enemies. Knowing that they were already sending flankers in both directions along the creek to cross and cut the two of them off, the clever scout signed his intentions to Gray Fox, and they retreated quietly into the thick woods behind them.

When they were sure that the trees and thick brush blocked the Shawnee's view, they began sprinting again. They hadn't run quite a hundred yards before hearing the familiar war cries behind them. Not bothering to look back, the young scout led his friend in a rapid race northward. Despite having to dodge around tree trunks and leap over logs, the two friends maintained their fast pace through the woods.

Bursting through a barrier of leafy limbs, William suddenly found himself at the edge of the river again. He had come on it so unexpectedly that he had to grab a nearby bush to stop himself from falling into the water. He thought they had been running parallel to the river, but obviously its course turned west here. His mind raced for a plan. His first idea was to jump in and swim to the other side.

"Shawnee too close!" he heard Gray Fox warn from behind. "If we try to swim now, their rifles will not miss us! If we go right, we go back to the river. Go left!"

William immediately saw the wisdom of his friend's words. It was their only option. The Miami quickly dashed to their left, leading the way along the river bank to the west.

The loud cries of their enemies seemed closer as they ran. When a few rifle shots zipped past them, it was clear that the Shawnee were gaining. William berated himself for not making his decision at the river faster.

The young frontiersman found himself breathing harder and felt his chest tightening, making him realize that the ground was sloping upward. He pushed himself to keep up his pace as he ascended the gradual climb. The fugitive also noticed that there were more rocky outcroppings in the woods before them. After several grueling minutes of heavy exertion, William felt his lungs burning and had a cramp in his side. His body was begging for rest, but he knew they were in a race for their lives, so on they ran.

When they reached a more level place on top of the wooded hill, Gray Fox stopped so they could catch their breath and look back for their enemies. Will spotted them running up the slope towards them. There were three in the lead, but the rest were further back.

Suddenly an alarm went off in his head. He studied the group of Indians running towards him. As he mentally counted them, the lead warrior pointed at William and aimed his rifle at him. Will squatted to make a smaller target as the ball flew over his head.

"There's only eight of them!" the young scout said his anxious thought out loud. "WHERE ARE THE REST?"

Just then the loud crack of a rifle sounded behind him, and a split second later he felt a hammer blow against the back of his right shoulder, knocking him to the ground.

"KAJIKA!" Gray Fox yelled and leaped to his friend's aid.

In his pain William heard the yells of the Shawnee warriors as they raced through the woods behind them and realized that they had been outsmarted. The Indians had known about the bend in the river and had sent part of their group to the west to cut them off.

Painfully William pushed himself to his knees. Making a rapid survey of their situation, they saw more enemies than they could handle racing for them in front and behind. William snapped off a quick shot, dropping the closest enemy, and exclaimed, "HELP ME UP!"

Gray Fox lifted his injured friend painfully to his feet. The young scout dropped his empty rifle and yelled, "WE'VE GOT TO GET TO THE RIVER!"

In five strides they were looking at it, but there was no bank. They were on a bluff over a hundred feet directly above the dark green water.

"Kajika, we are dead men!" the Miami said as he stared at the terrifying drop.

"Not yet we're not!" Will shot back as rifle balls whizzed past them. "JUMP. . .AND PRAY!"

The desperate youth leaped away from the edge and dropped.

Gray Fox hesitated for only a moment as he watched his friend falling away. Suddenly a bullet tore through his right sleeve and sliced his arm. Sufficiently motivated, he too threw himself off the ledge.

Down, down, down they fell. When Gray Fox saw Will hit the surface, he was still a long way above the water. The Miami slammed feet first into the river with tremendous force. Water blasted up his nose and burned his sinuses. Suddenly he felt his feet hit the rocky bottom, and he pushed himself back to the surface. Looking around, Gray Fox spotted Will thrashing with one arm towards the base of the bluff. Bullets began to hit the water around him, and he too swam for the rocks.

Once the Miami arrived beside his friend, it was clear that the Shawnee warriors on top of the bluff could not see them.

"I see you lived," William said with a smile.

"No thanks to you," Gray Fox shot back.

"What?" the young frontiersman returned. "You didn't think that was fun?"

"Not fun!"

"Oh, come on, Gray Fox!" Will responded. "That was just like flying!"

"You fly like you run. . .like a turtle! Bullet in your shoulder makes you talk like a crazy man. We need to get you to the fort."

"You're right," Will agreed, "but let's stay here under the bluff a bit longer until the Shawnee leave. Then we'll let the current take us down the river. We should wind up close to where we met Trask and Girty."

"Then we travel southwest to the fort," stated Gray Fox. "Kajika will give out before we get there."

"I'm strong," Will protested. "I won't give out."

"You shot," the Miami returned confidently. "You will give out."

"Oh, yeah?" William retorted. "Well, just watch me!"
Gray Fox just rolled his eyes and snorted.

Chapter Thirty-Four

TOO CLOSE FOR COMFORT

"**M**r. Gurley," hissed a nervous voice from the darkness, "do you think it's safe to crawl out yet?"

The earnest query was met with silence.

After a few moments Katherine tried again. "Mr. Gurley?"

Still no answer.

"Mr. Gurley!"

Again, no response.

"Gracie, is he alright?"

Grace quietly crawled forward until she was right beside the scout. She placed her hand on his shoulder and shook it saying, "Mr. Gurley!"

Suddenly there was a gasp and a snort as Dirt attempted to rise up and smacked his head hard on the rock ledge above. "OH, MY HEADBONE!" he groaned as he grabbed the back of his skull. "GREAT HONKIN' GEESE, LITTLE MISSY, YOU ABOUT SCARED ME SPITLESS!"

"I'm so sorry, Mr. Gurley!" Grace returned with feeling. "I didn't realize you were sleeping!"

"Oh. . .uh. . .well, I weren't actually sleepin'," Dirt responded, still rubbing his head. "I was meder-tatin' on our sitcheeation."

"Meder-tatin'?" Grace questioned.

"Well, shore!" Dirt answered confidently. "Didn't you girls realize? We've done found ourselves in what's known in the scoutin' world as *dire straits*. That means that we don't need to be

310

amakin' no snap dee-cisions. Nosiree-bob! We need to put on our thinkin' caps an' do us some meder-tatin."

"Well, Mr. Gurley," Grace persisted, "in all your *meder-tatin'*, do you think it's safe enough yet for us to crawl out of this bug-infested mud hole?"

"To be factical," Dirt answered, "I ain't heard no sounds of enemies fer quite some time. Meanin' that it looks to me like young Will and Gray Fox has done led them wild men far off to the north. So, yes, ladies, I do believe it's safe enough for us to ee-merge from our hidy hole."

"Well, could both of you start ee-merging," Kate said with some irritation, "because I desperately need to get out of here!"

The process of crawling from under the low ledge was slow and required a lot of painful grunts and groans from the injured scout. Once he had extricated himself, Dirt stood holding his sore head as he watched Grace and her sister claw their way into the sunlight.

"Oh, my goodness!" Grace exclaimed when she viewed the effect the crawl had on their dresses. "Kate, just look at us! I have never been so filthy in all my life!"

"I don't think our dresses will ever be clean enough to wear again," Katherine agreed with a smile.

"It's a small price to pay fer yer lives," Dirt said wisely.

Katherine saw the scout still held his head. "Are you going to be alright?" she asked with concern.

"I'll be fine," Dirt returned. "It don't hurt near as bad as it did. As a matter of fact, I'm kinda glad I did it. When I first smacked my headbone on that rock, Bertha's bunions, that hurt. In fact, it hurt so bad that I didn't notice the pain from my back wound. Now that my head pain's calmin' down, I'm startin' to feel my back again. I've dee-cided that if my back wound starts givin' me too much trouble, I'll jus' hit my head again. *Hee, hee, hee!*"

Both girls giggled at his comment.

"So how do we get back home?" Grace asked.

"We needs to head southwest," Dirt answered as he looked for the position of the sun through the thick canopy overhead, "an' it looks to be that dii-rection." The scout pointed off to his right, then began walking that way. "Jus' foller me, ladies."

Dirt was cautious and alert as he led them through the thick woods. He trusted William to have led the Indian war party that they knew about away, but there had been so much activity in this part of Kentucky in the last few weeks that he was not about to let his guard down now.

They had only been hiking about an hour when Grace spoke up. "Mr. Gurley, can we rest?"

Dirt turned to face the two sisters and saw the weary look in their eyes. "We really ain't traveled very far," he returned. "Are you sure you can't keep goin' fer a while longer?"

"I'm sorry, Mr. Gurley," Katherine answered for her sister, "but we've had almost nothing to eat since we left the fort, and we're both getting weak."

"Well, o' course you are!" Dirt blurted out. "What a meathead I am! I never thought about you girls needin' some food. Both of you sit down on that log, an' I'll see what I got."

The scout dug into the leather pouch at his hip and finally came out with three thick pieces of jerked deer meat. "Sorry, ladies, but that's all I got. You can each have a piece and a half."

"But you need something to eat also," Katherine said, trying to hand one of the pieces back.

"Oh, I'm alright," Dirt said with a smile. "If'n I get real hungry, I'll jus' chew on some green brier roots or find some shelf mushrooms to eat.

"I'd really like to go shoot us a deer an' broil some big, fat steaks, but I cain't shoot my rifle or start a fire without havin' every blood-thirsty cut-throat in the territory down on our heads. For now we'll jus' have to make do."

When their meal was finished and the girls thought they could keep going, Dirt located the sun, found his direction, and continued their journey. Occasionally he would move ahead of the slower moving sisters to scout for enemies, but would then quickly return to make sure they didn't get lost.

Late in the afternoon the girls were once again traveling alone when suddenly Dirt came rushing back to them with a grave expression on his face.

"Mr. Gurley, what's wrong?" Kate asked with concern.

"*Sssshhhh!*" the scout hissed as he anxiously looked all around them. "We got big trouble! Quick. . .over there! Get in that low spot!" Dirt pointed to a slight depression in the leaf-strewn forest floor.

"What's going on, Mr. Gurley?" Grace asked as she and her sister hurried to comply with the scout's directions.

"There's a whole passel of Injuns headed right for us!" Dirt answered. "We cain't out run 'em, so's we gots to hide! You ladies lay down in that little depression, an' I'll cover you with leaves an' branches."

The scared sisters immediately obeyed, lying face down on the ground, and the scout quickly covered them. "Now you two listen to me," Dirt whispered to them as he finished. "Yer lives depend on you doin' exactly as I say. Take small, shallow breaths, an' don't move a muscle. I'm gonna be off to the north a ways watchin', an' if they get close to findin' you, I'll cause a ruckus an get 'em to chase me instead. If somethin' was to happen to me, you girls stay here all night, and in the morning when you see the sun comin' up in the east, you head southwest...Got it?"

"Yes," whispered Katherine. "Please be careful, Mr. Girley!"

"Why *careful* is my middle name," Dirt returned with a smile.

"I thought it was Ambrose," whispered a voice out of the leaves that covered Grace.

Keeping low to the ground and using trees and thick brush for cover, the scout moved quickly but quietly to the north. He took a position behind the trunk of a large oak that allowed him to clearly see where the girls were hidden. Almost immediately the Indians came trotting into view. Dirt studied their clothing, paint, and ornaments.

Chickeesaws! he said to himself as he watched them approach. Dirt kept most of his body behind the tree, but he made sure to keep one eye always on the war party.

They traveled single file, heading northeast. It was clear to the scout that this was no hunting party. These Indians were painted for war. Dirt counted fifteen as they came near.

With his back wound and having eaten little food for the last two days, Dirt knew that, if he had to reveal himself to save the girls, he could never out run them. He might drop two or three of them, but they would definitely get him. *If'n it comes to that,* Dirt prayed to himself, *please, Lord, have mercy on them two girls and let me die quick!*

As Dirt observed the approaching enemies, he gasped when he saw the leader take a slight detour around some brush. *Great smokin' pole cats!* The scout thought to himself. *Them cut-throats is headed right fer 'em!*

Quickly he offered a desperate prayer. *Have mercy on us, Lord, an' PLEASE keep them girls still!*

As the leader of the Chickasaw trotted by, he missed stepping on the girls by no more than three feet. One by one the rest went charging by the place where the sisters were hidden.

Dirt, from his vantage point, gave a deep sigh of relief as he saw the grim-faced savages streaming past. He would have been in much more of a panic if he had known that, since just before the Indians arrived, Grace had been fighting hard to stifle a sneeze.

From where she was buried under a pile of leaves, the dust and mold were wreaking havoc with her nose. Fortunately for her, she had lain down with her hands near her face. She pinched her nose tightly in an effort to prevent the sneeze, but it wasn't working. Even as the feet of the Chickasaw warriors were landing beside her, she could feel the sneeze building, and she knew that, when it came, there would be no way to stop it.

She thought that if she gripped her nose and her mouth tightly, she might be able to muffle it, but it was coming regardless. She prayed that the Indians would pass and be far enough away that whatever sound she made would not attract their attention, but warriors kept running by. It seemed to her that there must be a hundred of them.

Panic gripped her as she felt the sneeze was on its way, and still the Indians ran past. Her body wanted her to take in a big lungful of air to help the unwanted eruption. The thought suddenly came to her that, if she didn't take in the air, there would be nothing to form the sneeze. Exhaling what air she had, Grace then gripped her nose and mouth firmly and waited for the inevitable.

She had been right. When the sneeze came, there was no air to produce the usual blast, and it resulted in nothing more than a sudden jerk of her shoulders. Unfortunately this caused a crunch sound in the dried leaves covering her. It happened just as the last Indian was running by them and. . .he heard it.

Sliding to a stop, the warrior looked around curiously for the unnatural sound. When Dirt saw the Indian stop, his heart jumped into his throat. Sliding his rifle around the trunk of the tree, he cocked it and took careful aim at the warrior, offering another fervent prayer as he did so.

The Chickasaw turned and took a step to his right to see the area around him more clearly. As he did so, Kate saw his moccasined foot land right beside her head. She held her breath and joined Dirt in his intense petition to God.

The suspicious warrior stood for several long moments, studying everything his eye viewed and listening intently. He began looking keenly at the scattered leaves next to his feet as Kate's pounding heart threatened to burst through her chest.

"Nashooba Losa!" a voice called from behind the warrior. He turned his head toward the speaker and saw another Chickasaw. "Nanta iskatihmi?"

Instead of answering, the first warrior lifted his hand toward the second and glanced suspiciously around him once more.

The second Chickasaw looked back over his shoulder and saw the last of their party disappearing in the woods to the northeast. Turning back to his companion, the impatient warrior spoke again. "Nashooba Losa, minti. . .MINTI!"

Reluctantly the first warrior turned to face his friend. As he did so, the heel of his foot bumped Katherine in the head, but he didn't notice.

Dirt Gurley finally breathed his sigh of relief as he saw the two Chickasaw braves race northeast after their comrades.

"Thank you, Lord! Thank you!" all three of them prayed sincerely.

Dirt waited several long minutes before he made his way back to the girls. "It's okay," he whispered. "It's me!"

"I have never been so scared in all my life!" Grace confessed as she sat up.

"Are you sure?" her sister asked with a knowing look.

Thinking back over all that had happened to them in the last two days, Grace nodded uncertainly in agreement. "Well," the younger girl spoke again, "let me just say that I was really scared!"

"Mr. Gurley," Kate said sincerely, "my legs are shaking so badly that I don't think there's any way I can walk further this evening."

"After all that, I'm in full agreement with you, Miss Kate," Dirt Gurley returned. "The day's nigh on to done anyway. Let's all jus' park our carcasses right here, get some rest, an' try it again tomorrow. Surely it cain't get no worse."

"DON'T SAY THAT!" exclaimed both girls at the same time.

Chapter Thirty-Five

AFTERMATH

At dawn just over two days later, the Larkinboro sentinels standing watch on the north wall spotted a movement at the edge of the woods. Sounding an alarm to call out all the reserve guards, the little fort quickly prepared itself for an attack.

Jack Cobb, limping on his left leg and with his left arm in a sling, made his way with difficulty to the top of the north wall. "What do you see, Jeffers?" the scout asked anxiously.

"Right there," the man named Jeffers answered as he pointed to the edge of the distant forest. "You see 'em? There's more than one, an' they're movin' slowly straight towards us. As good a shot as Macklin is, I think he could hit them from here."

"Now just hold yer horses," Cobb shot back. "Some of our people are still out there! We cain't be shootin' at everything we see. We'll stay alert, but no shootin' until we know for sure who it is. Pass the word down to every man on the wall! Also send word to the men on the other walls to be alert for a sneak attack!"

Every eye on the north catwalk focused on the approaching figures, but they were still too far away to identify. "I can't tell if it's two or three people, Jack," Eldridge Smith said as he stood near the scout. "They're bunched together for some reason."

"Whoever they are," Jack answered, "they're still comin', an' they don't seem to be afraid of us or the Chickasaw."

Ten minutes later Mr. Smith spoke again. "There's three of them, and it looks like the one on the right is female."

"So's the one in the middle," Jeffers added. "You can tell she's wearin' a dress."

Just then the one on the left raised his hand and waved to the guards on the wall.

"WHO ARE YOU?" Jeffers yelled at the approaching trio.

As they listened carefully, they heard a faint voice in the distance call back, "Get off yer fat hams, ya lazy varments, an' get out here an help us!"

"IT'S DIRT AN' THE GIRLS!" Jack announced excitedly. "QUICK, SEVERAL OF YOU MEN GO HELP THEM!"

"It was pretty foolish of you to walk across the open field like that in broad daylight," one of the men said. A large crowd watched as one of the ladies, Clara Leavenworth, changed the bandage on Dirt's back wound. The injured scout sat on a barrel near the home of Abner Davis because it was nearest the gate. Mrs. Davis stood beside him with a pan of warm muffins.

"It weren't foolish atoll," Dirt shot back as he shoved another corn muffin in his mouth. "All the Chickeesaws is gone."

"But how did you know that?" another man asked skeptically.

"Cuz' I spent most of last night an' before dawn scoutin' where their camp had been an' the woods around it," he answered as crumbs fell out of his mouth, "They ain't there. I reckon they finally had enough after we licked 'em in that last fight.

"Me an' the girls had to hide from a war party of 'em headed northeast."

"Northeast?" another man asked. "Their land is northwest of here. Why would they go northeast?"

"My guess is that they wanted Trask's hair for this mess he got 'em into by attackin' us," Dirt shot back. "But when they find him, they're gonna be too late. Will took care of him jus' before that red-coated rascal could send a rifle slug betwixt *my* eyeballs. Which reminds me, has Will an' the Miami made it back?"

"We thought they were with you," John Hackett said with a look of concern.

Seeing the worried look in Will's father's eyes, Dirt swallowed his muffin and retold the whole story of the girls' rescue and of how Will and Gray Fox saved them by leading off the Shawnee.

"That was three days ago," Dirt said as he finished. "We got slowed down when Miss Kate slipped and fell down a rocky embankment, twisting her ankle. From then on me an' Miss Grace had to help her with her walkin'. It slackened our pace a good bit, so I figured Will might be back here waiting on us."

"We need to send out a scouting party to find him!" John Hackett announced.

"I understand your concern, John," Jack spoke up, "but the last time anybody saw him, he was almost three days march northeast of here and headed north real fast. There's no tellin' where he is now."

"Oh, yes, there is!" called a voice from the top of the northwest blockhouse. It was an excited Asa Whitlock. "He and his Miami friend are coming in now, but I think Will's hurt! Gray Fox is carrying him!"

In response to this report, more men charged from the fort to help. William was unconscious when he was carried in and taken straight to the Hackett home.

"Dirt," Jack called to his friend, who was trying to put his shirt back on. "I've only got one good arm to sign with. Ask Gray Fox what happened."

Dirt Gurley laid aside his shirt and began signing to the Maimi. As Gray Fox responded with his and Will's story, Jack interpreted for those standing around.

"Gray Fox says that he kept trying to help Will on their walk home, but young Mr. Hackett wouldn't let him. He kept telling the Miami that he was strong enough to get back here on his own."

"That sounds like him," Dirt spoke up.

"Gray Fox says that Will's strength gave out about a mile back, and he had to carry him the rest of the way.

"Dirt," Jack said, turning to his friend, who was still trying to put his shirt back on, "tell Gray Fox how grateful we all are for what he did to bring Will back to us."

With a sigh Dirt laid his shirt back down and signed the message to the Miami. The injured man then walked over and picked up two more corn muffins off the tray. One of these he handed to Gray Fox, and the other he handed to Jack.

"Why give me a muffin?" Jack asked with a confused look on his face.

"Cuz I've been tryin' to get my shirt back on for ten minutes, an' you need to do somethin' with yer mouth besides talk to me 'til I do it!"

Two days later, when Will's mother felt that he was strong enough to receive visitors, the first ones to see him were Kate and Grace's parents. Silas had tears in his eyes as he expressed his deepest thanks to William for what he had done to save their girls. Rebecca Middlebrook was so emotional that she couldn't speak. All she could do was lean down and give the young scout a long, heartfelt hug.

A week later William Hackett was strong enough to walk out of his family's home and get some fresh air. Everyone he met expressed their gratitude for what he had done to save the fort and the two Middlebrook girls. It happened so much that Will started to feel embarrassed. He found Jack and Dirt standing on top of one of the blockhouses beside the gate and was about as relieved to see them as they were to see him.

After visiting and catching up with what had been happening over the past week, Will changed the subject. "Have either of you seen Gray Fox? I haven't seen him since we got back, and now I can't find him anywhere."

"He's been stayin' with us at night," Jack volunteered, "but I don't know where he goes during the day."

"You know, that's right," Dirt agreed thoughtfully. "I ain't seen him fer days, but he always shows back up at the cabin at night."

"Then I guess he's got to be here somewhere," William reasoned. "I'll keep looking for him."

Will was making his second circuit of the fort's interior when he happened to see Asa coming out of the school house.

"Hey, Will!" the youth called cheerfully. "I'm really glad to see up and about."

"I'm still feeling weak and sore," William responded, "but I was going crazy lying in bed.

"Asa, I've been looking for my Miami friend, Gray Fox, but I can't find him anywhere. Have you seen him?"

Oh sure," Asa answered offhandedly. "He's in the school house with Mr. Spebbington."

"What's he doing in there?"

"Taking classes," Asa chuckled. "Come on. I'll show you."

With a confused look William followed him into the log building. He saw Gray Fox and the scholar sitting together in the front of the room. As soon as the Miami saw Will, he jumped up excitedly. "Kajika! Uh. . .uh. . .how are. . .uh. . .you. . .to-day?" he said in English, smiling broadly.

"You are learning our tongue!" Will exclaimed in the Miami language.

"Yes," Gray Fox answered excitedly in Miami. "The happy fat man is teaching me. He is good! I like him. I had the scout Dirt Gurley ask the happy fat man if he could teach me to read the Gitchi Manitou's book you told me about. He is teaching me to speak and to read."

"I haven't the foggiest idea of what you two are gibbering about," Mr. Spebbington said, inserting himself into the conversation, "but Mr. Fox here, your Miami friend is an excellent student!"

"What did he say?" Gray Fox asked Will excitedly in the Miami tongue. "Did the happy fat man say Gray Fox was *ex-helent student*? What does *ex-helent* mean, Kajika? It means Gray Fox is very good student, right, Kajika?"

"It means you're a good student," William returned.

"NO!" Gray Fox snapped back. "It means Gray Fox *very* good student! Better than you!"

"Well, I don't know about that," Will teased.

"Gray Fox know about that!" the Miami shot back. "Let's ask happy fat man. Will he say Kajika was *ex-helent* student?"

William struggled to come up with an answer to that question. "Well. . ."

"*HA!* Gray Fox didn't think so," the Indian returned confidently.

"I thought you were headed back home soon," William said, trying to change the subject.

"Gray Fox not ready to go home," the Miami answered cheerfully. "I have good friends here. Dirt Gurley and Jack Cobb let me stay with them. Gray Fox has a warm cabin, a soft bed, and plenty of good food. I also have to stay so the happy fat man can teach me to read the Manitou's book."

"Well, you're welcome to stay if you want to," William added, "but if you wanted to learn stuff, you could have just asked me. I would have been happy to teach you."

Gray Fox snorted at this. "Kajika probably teaches like he runs and flies. . .like a turtle."

"So what did he say, William?" Mr. Spebbington asked eagerly.

"He said he wants you to teach him the history of the Prussian empire," Will answered as he smiled at Gray Fox and turned to walk out the door.

THE END

Appendix A
Chapter Questions and Lessons

In writing this story I not only wanted to create a fun and entertaining story for my family to read together, but I wanted to teach some important character and spiritual lessons to my children as well. I have always told my children stories, especially the ones that I heard from my father, and there were occasionally some spiritual lessons stuck in them. I was impressed by the fact that those were the lessons that my children always remembered.

It struck me that one of the reasons Jesus used stories so much in His teaching was because they made the lessons so easy to remember. I researched and learned that when teaching is placed within a gripping or engaging story, not only does the information reach the mind of the reader, but also the teaching is connected to the reader's emotions. Said another way, when the emotions are engaged, the lesson is remembered and the heart is taught, and that is where real life change occurs. Please understand, I do not believe that a teaching technique causes heart or life change. Only the Spirit of God at work in our hearts can do that. But when we follow Jesus's example of how to teach and combine it with fervent prayer, I believe that we are giving our children and students the best opportunity for the Holy Spirit to reach their hearts.

If it is your goal to use stories to reach the hearts of others, then I believe the most effective way to use these books is for parents to read them to their children or for teachers to read them to their classes. When a chapter finished, take time to talk about the spiritual and character lessons learned, giving the listeners an opportunity to verbalize their discoveries. As a help, we have assembled in this appendix a collection of discussion questions and important lessons found in each chapter. Use any or all of these questions as a place to start, but be sensitive to the direction of the discussion and add your own questions to accommodate what God is doing in the hearts of your listeners. Remember God's part in this whole process and always pray (if not audibly, at least to yourself) each time before reading, asking the Lord to use the story to teach His lessons to your listeners' hearts.

In His Service,

Alan W. Harris

Chapter 1

Describe the character qualities it will take for these pioneers to be successful in creating a new home in the Kentucky wilderness.

What important character qualities did Jack Cobb use when the accident happened to the Middlebrooks' wagon?

How would you describe young William's problems?

How does God want us to handle our fears? (*Psalm 56: 3-4*)

What are the consequences of not dealing with our fears in God's way?

Character Qualities to Identify:

Jack Cobb showed **alertness** when he saw that William was in a position to help the girls.

Alertness: *being highly perceptive and aware of difficulties, problems, or dangers around you, enabling you to make quick and accurate decisions and to act rapidly.*

This is in contrast to mental dullness, daydreaming, and inattentiveness: *being so absorbed in your own thoughts that you are unaware of what is happening around you.*

How did Jesus show alertness?

Chapter 2

What advice would you give to William about his feelings of being worthless?

Why does William feel this way?

Whenever we have thoughts of being worthless or no good, where do those thoughts come from?

What does God say about our worth and value? (*John 3: 16; Ephesians 1: 3-14*)

What good character qualities did William show in his conversation with Kate and her fears?

Character Qualities to Identify:

Jack Cobb showed **patience** with his young friend, Will Hackett, as he answered Will's questions and taught the boy about the natural world around them.

Patience: *accepting delay, trouble, or suffering without getting angry or upset, in order to express kindness to another.*

This is in contrast to resistance, being short tempered, or irritable: *becoming angry and inflexible with anyone or anything that gets in the way of accomplishing your will and desires.*

How did Jesus show patience?

_____

Chapter 3

What character qualities and abilities was William going to need to be a good hunter?

On the hunt, why was it important and wise for Dirt to mention which way the wind was blowing?

Why did Jack pick the log farthest away from the spring as the spot from which Will was to shoot? Why are difficult challenges more valuable to personal growth?

How was William helped by going on this hunting trip?

How did Asa show himself to be a true friend to William?

What did Asa's friendship mean to William?

Character Qualities to Identify:

Asa showed **compassion** to William as he struggled with guilt and fear.

Compassion: *showing sympathy and concern for the difficulties and hardships of others.*

This is in contrast with **indifference**: *the lack of interest, concern or sympathy for the needs or problems of others.*

How did Jesus show compassion?

Chapter 4

What good character qualities did Will and Asa show in pursuing the runaway cow?

How did they show poor judgment in pursuing the cow?

What character qualities are most important for someone to survive being lost in the woods for a long period of time?

When a person realizes that they are in a difficult situation, why is praying to God about it the best first step? (*James 5: 16-18; Ephesians 6: 18-20*)

William thought that exploring the wilderness and making new discoveries was the best life he could live. Asa thought Will's idea was selfish and irresponsible. Who do you agree with and why?

Character Qualities to Identify:

Because William was so upset when the boys first discovered they were lost, Asa tried to **encourage** his friend by getting him to smile and laugh.

Encourage: *to give support, confidence or hope to someone in need.*

This is in contrast to dishearten, sadden, or to trouble: *to obstruct by opposition, to express clear disapproval.*

How did Jesus encourage others?

Chapter 5

What were some of the ways that the boys showed creativity in solving their problems?

What evidence do you see in this chapter that God is drawing William's heart to Him?

After the boys decided to trust God and pray for wisdom, how did they put their faith into practice?

After they decided to follow the creek to get back home, what character qualities did they show by taking several days to prepare for the trip, rather than leaving as soon as they made the decision?

The forest fire was the results of what poor character shown by the boys?

Character Qualities to Identify:

Although Dirt Gurley wouldn't pronounce it correctly, the boys showed **ingenuity** by using what they had to make the rabbit traps.

Ingenuity: *being clever and creative enough to think of new ways to accomplish something.*

This is in contrast with **ineptness**: *showing incompetence, failure, or weakness in the face of a challenge.*

How did Jesus show ingenuity?

_____

Chapter 6

How much are you worth to God?

Pick a person from the New Testament or someone you know and describe how Jesus made something beautiful out of their broken life.

If grace is God's power to accomplish in us what we are powerless to do ourselves, then what does it look like when we are trusting in God's power to work in our lives?

William said that he wanted to make Jesus king of his life. What does that mean?

Why was it important that William forgive his birth father? (*Mathew 6: 14 - 15*)

How was William able to do that?

The boys barely got up the tree before the wolves arrived. What character qualities could they have used to have avoided such a close call with danger?

Character Qualities to Identify:

Over and over again Asa showed himself to be a **faithful** friend to William.

Faithful: *someone who is loyal, constant and steadfast.*

This is in contrast to being **false, treacherous** or **traitorous**: *a person who will likely betray the trust of another.*

How was Jesus faithful to God and to us?

_____

Chapter 7

If you had been with Asa and Will on this adventure, how would you have felt when you suddenly came upon Jack and Dirt and knew you had made it home?

Do you think the boys should have been punished for getting themselves lost?

When William told his father how much he loved the wilderness, what did that tell Mr. Hackett about his son, and how did that influence how Mr. Hackett intended to raise him from then on?

How did following Jesus affect the problems and hardships of William's life?

Why is it important to get a good education?

What character qualities does it take to study and learn?

Character Qualities to Identify:

Dirt Gurley showed **prudence** when he decided to get the injured Asa the help he needed before they butchered the dead buffalo.

Prudence: *Showing wisdom and good judgement in making practical decisions in life.*

This in contrast to **carelessness** and **inattention**: *failure to give sufficient attention to what's happening around you in order to avoid harmful results.*

How did Jesus show prudence?

_____

Chapter 8

Schoolwork was obviously very difficult for William, but what could he have done to benefit more from his time in class?

Different people have different learning styles or ways that are most effective for them to learn. Auditory learners remember best by hearing a lesson; visual learners remember best by seeing the words and examples, and tactile learners remember best by interacting physically with the new material. What learning style helps you learn the best?

What did it mean when Mr. Spebbington said William was loyal and true?

What character qualities did William show as he crept up to the Indians?

When Jack Cobb heard that Indians were in the area, what good qualities did he show by increasing the defenses of the fort?

Character Qualities to Identify:

William showed **attentiveness** when he recognized that the sound of the birds was missing in the direction where he eventually found the Indians.

Attentiveness: *being observant and paying close attention to what is happening around you and responding appropriately.*

This is in contrast to being **negligent** or **unaware**: *failing to take the proper care or make the appropriate response.*

How did Jesus show attentiveness?

_____

Chapter 9

What did Jack mean when he said, "The man that's never caught is the man who never sticks his head in the trap"?

What can you learn about God by looking at His creation?

On the march to the salt lick, Mr. Spebbington and Asa were eager to ride the horses and rest. At first William refused to ride but later he changed his mind. Why did he change his mind, and what does that tell you about Will?

What are some important uses for salt?

How did Jesus use salt to teach? (*Matthew 5: 13*)

Character Qualities to Identify:

Mr. Spebbington and Asa showed **persistence** in trying to put the bones of giant creatures together.

Persistence: *firmness of purpose, to continue in a course of action in spite of difficulties.*

This is in contrast to **laziness** or **idleness**: *contented to remain in a state of inactivity.*

How did Jesus show persistence?

Chapter 10

What are some of the character qualities that made Jack Cobb a good scout?

What were some of the qualities that Jack appreciated the most in William?

William had learned to face his fears rather than run from them or try to avoid them. Why is this good to do?

Where did William expect to find the courage to face his enemies?

After discovering the Shawnee war party, what was it that caused Jack to conclude that the Lord was with them?

How did Asa show foolishness during the fight?

Character Qualities to Identify:

When Jack and Dirt realized that the Shawnee war party was going to catch up with them, they showed **decisiveness** when they stopped the retreat and prepared effective defenses to meet the attack.

Decisiveness: *the ability to evaluate a situation and make decisions quickly and effectively.*

This is in contrast to **uncertainty** and **vacillation**: *the inability to decide between different opinions or actions.*

How was Jesus decisive?

———————————————————————

Chapter 11

When the first battle was over and they were waiting for the Indians to attack again, what did Jack have the men do that showed wisdom and good leadership?

In this chapter, how did God use this terrible storm to do good?

What good character qualities did Will and Asa show both in the fight with the Shawnee and in their escape through the storm?

William had found God to be faithful in getting them back home safely. What are some of the ways God had shown His faithfulness?

How has God shown His faithfulness to you and your family?

Character Qualities to Identify:

Everyone in the salt gathering party had to show **endurance** in order to get back home safely.

Endurance: *persisting faithfully through a difficult situation without giving way.*

This is in contrast to **apathy** and **slackness**: *having an uncaring attitude or lack of interest.*

How did Jesus show endurance?

Chapter 12

How did the men show wisdom and forethought in their plans to protect the fort?

What character qualities did Jack Cobb see in William that told him Will was born to be a great woodsman?

What character qualities did Mr. Spebbington see in Asa?

Why do you think Asa was not jealous of the skills and knowledge of the woods that William had?

When a person goes into a cave and sees the beautiful and amazing rock formations inside, what does that reveal about God?

What poor character did William show that almost got them lost?

Character Qualities to Identify:

Mr. Spebbington showed **resourcefulness** when he came up with a way for the settlers to make their own gunpowder.

Resourcefulness: *using your God-given creativity to come up with clever ways to overcome obstacles and problems.*

This is in contrast to being **dull** and **incapable**: *unable or unwilling to do what is necessary to reach a goal.*

How did Jesus show resourcefulness?

Chapter 13

What are some of the character qualities the pioneers needed to farm land that had never been farmed before?

If the land was so fertile and productive, why did the settlers still need to rely on God?

What is the difference between education and experience, and why are they both important?

In order to be able to draw reliable maps, what important attributes did the explorers need?

Character Qualities to Identify:

Mr., Spebbington made himself **available** to cook the squirrels for the rest of the party.

Available: *setting my own schedule or desires aside in order to serve others and meet their needs.*

This is in contrast to being **self-serving**: *being more interested in your desires and wants than in helping those around you.*

How did Jesus show that he was available to others?

_____

Chapter 14

If you were with them on this trip, would you be scared or excited and why?

What good character qualities did the explorers show in dealing with the coming storm?

If Asa and Mr. Spebbington were going to use the information in their journals to draw accurate maps of the land they explored, what attributes would they need to use in writing in their journals?

It was hard for William to learn his lessons in the classroom. Why was it so much easier for him to learn the lessons of the woods?

What should William have done when he heard the strange noise in the woods? Why didn't he do that?

In spite of his mistake, what good character qualities did William show in dealing with the Indians?

Character Qualities to Identify:

William showed **rashness** when he went to scout the strange sound he heard while the others slept.

Rashness: *acting too hastily, without considering the consequences of your actions.*

This is in contrast with **prudence** and **caution**: *taking the time to think through a situation and to choose a wise course of action.*

When others were rash, how did Jesus show prudence?

_____

Chapter 15

As a prisoner of the Indians, what good character qualities would help William the most during this ordeal?

How did William determine what God's will was for him in his captivity?

Can you think of someone in the Bible who was separated from his family and made a slave? How did he handle his captivity?

How can a trial like that make your faith grow stronger?

When William prayed to God to let him find food for all of them in the snow, what did William want the Indians to realize?

How did trusting Jesus as his Lord and King enable William to live his life without fearing death?

Character Qualities to Identify:

When the Indians tried to praise and honor William for saving their lives, he showed **humility** by turning the praise back to God.

Humility: *understanding and expressing that God and others are the ones who made our achievements possible.*

This is in contrast with **pride** and **arrogance**: *taking deep pleasure in and selfishly promoting one's own achievements.*

How did Jesus show humility?

_____

Chapter 16

Do you think Jack should have felt guilty for William being lost to the Indians?

How should Jack have handled his feelings?

If you were a member of the Hackett family, how would God want you to respond to this kind of loss?

Is Simon Girty's attention to Katherine acceptable behavior? Why?

If Girty had been a gentleman, how would his behavior have been different?

Character Qualities to Identify:

Dirt Gurley tried to be **astute** when he took the time to examine and question the two strangers at the gate.

Astute: *showing cleverness and mental sharpness, enabling the person to observe and understand situations clearly and make wise decisions.*

This is in contrast with **inability** and **ineptness**: *the lack of competence, judgment, or good sense.*

How did Jesus show that He was astute?

_____

Chapter 17

What seems to be William's attitude toward the Miami Indians he is being forced to live with?

How is God using William in the tribe?

What attitude does God want us to have when we are forced into difficult trials and hardships?

What good character qualities did William show in the battle?

When William was made a member of the Miami tribe, how would you describe his attitude as he received the honor?

Character Qualities to Identify:

Chief Black Cloud showed **virtue** when he risked his life to confront the Shawnee and try to avert war.

Virtue: *righteous and honorable behavior that shows high moral standards.*

This is in contrast to **dishonor, evil** and **meanness**: *unkind, spiteful and unfair behavior. To disregard what is right and honorable.*

How did Jesus show virtue?

Chapter 18

What character qualities did William show when he urged Black Cloud to make better preparations for the coming winter?

How did William honor God in all that he did for the tribe?

How would you describe the character of Trask and Girty?

Describe the attitudes that William had when he made the decision to try to outrun the Chickasaw and warn Larkinboro of the attack?

What Godly attributes helped William make this decision?

Character Qualities to Identify:

William showed **wisdom** when he encouraged the chiefs to let him go find out Trask's plans.

Wisdom: *the quality of having good sense and good judgement.*

This is in contrast to **ignorance** and **stupidity**: *behavior that shows foolishness and a lack of good sense.*

How did Jesus show wisdom?

_____

Chapter 19

William thought that God might be using him like He used Esther to save her people. How did God use Esther?

How did William use good judgment during his run to warn his friends?

After his rest, William determined enemies were near. What character qualities and attributes did he use to protect himself?

What good qualities did Gray Fox show by following and joining William?

What are important attributes to have if you are to be a good friend to someone?

Character qualities to Identify:

Gray Fox demonstrated **loyalty** by following William, even though it meant risking his life.

Loyalty: *faithful allegiance, a strong feeling of support.*

This is in contrast to **faithlessness** and **treachery**: *betrayal of trust, deceptive, deceitful.*

How did Jesus show loyalty?

_____

Chapter 20

How did Gray Fox show himself to be a good friend to William?

Who are some Bible characters who showed themselves to be good friends?

Judas was supposed to be a friend to Jesus, but he was not. Describe his character.

How did Jesus show Himself to be a good friend to us?

Character Qualities to Identify:

Gray Fox's loyalty to William showed that he was a friend with **dependability.**

Dependability: *being willing to make unexpected sacrifices to meet the needs of those being served.*

This is in contrast to **inconsistency**: *unpredictable, someone who cannot be counted on.*

How did Jesus show dependability?

Chapter 21

How did Jack show wisdom as he prepared the fort to defend against the Indian attack?

Describe the poor character you see demonstrated in Braxton Wyatt.

Describe what is happening between William's mother and Gray Fox?

What difference did it make that William's mother and Gray Fox were from different cultures and different "races"?

What good character qualities are you seeing in Gray Fox?

How does God want us to respond when people don't like us and say things about us that are not true?

When we are afraid, how does God want us to respond?

Character Qualities to Identify:

Asa and Kate believed William's report about the coming Indian attack because they knew that Will possessed **trustworthiness**.

Trustworthiness: *possessing the quality of being able to be relied on to be faithful, honest, and truthful.*

This is in contrast to being **false**, **deceitful** or **dishonest**: *a corrupted character that is unlikely to tell the truth.*

How did Jesus show trustworthiness?

Chapter 22

Even though faced with overwhelming odds, what good character qualities did the pioneers defending the walls of the fort show?

How would you describe Braxton Wyatt's behavior?

While Asa probably should not have hit the mouthy Braxton, what good character did Asa show as he defended William?

What are some of the promises God has made to us that show us He is always ready to help His children when they call on Him? (*Matthew 6: 31-33; Matthew 7: 7-11; Matthew 11: 28-30*)

Character Qualities to Identify:

All of the settlers in the fort exercised **discretion** by staying out of sight of the Indian shooters in the tree.

Discretion: *avoiding words, actions or attitudes that bring harmful results.*

This is in contrast to **inattention** or **carelessness**: *failure to give sufficient attention in order to avoid harm.*

How did Jesus show discretion?

_____

Chapter 23

What character qualities would it require for Will and Gray Fox to be successful in scouting out the Chickasaw camp?

If you're in a situation like these settlers and you need wisdom, where does the Bible say it comes from? (*James 1: 5*)

In this story, what would likely have happened if the people of Larkinboro had not used wisdom and creativity in coming up with a plan to defend themselves?

Explain why prayer is so important in dangerous, scary, or even uncertain situations?

Character Qualities to Identify:

When they only had a short time to prepare for the Indians' fire arrow attack, William had to use **creativity** to come up with a plan.

Creativity: *using your God given imagination to come up with a unique idea.*

This is in contrast to **mental dullness** and **inability**: *lack of power, ability, or motivation to accomplish a goal.*

How did Jesus show creativity?

Chapter 24

Since oxen were critical for the settlers to farm and haul loads, why was it wise to kill some of them?

If meekness is giving up your personal rights and expectations to meet the needs of others, how was William showing meekness?

In the story, how did God answer Kate's prayer for water?

In coming up with a plan for solving the problem of getting more water, what part did God play and what part did the people play?

Can we count on God to answer our prayers today? Explain your answer.

Give some examples of how God answers prayers today.

Character Qualities to Identify:

William and Gray Fox showed great **boldness** by hiding among the Shawnee and fighting them secretly.

Boldness: *confidently willing to take risks to meet the needs of those I am serving.*

This is in contrast to being **timid** or **cautious**: *lacking in courage or self-confidence.*

How did Jesus show boldness?

_____

Chapter 25

Over and over again the pioneers had to be creative to come up with solutions to the problems they faced. What are some things that would encourage you to be more creative?

What things today stifle or suppress creativity?

When faced with problems or difficult choices like the pioneers, it is easy to get discouraged and give up, but what attitudes should we use to face our challenges?

How did the settlers show wisdom, cleverness, and forethought as they prepared for and implemented their plan to get water?

What good character qualities did Kate Middlebrook show as the plan was implemented?

Character Qualities to Identify:

The women and girls showed **initiative** by collecting buckets of water as the trench was being dug.

Initiative: *the ability to determine what needs to be done and acting to accomplish it without being asked.*

This is in contrast to **apathy** and **indifference**: *lack of interest or concern.*

How did Jesus show initiative?

Chapter 26

What character qualities would motivate you to keep going or keep working even if you were hurting or tired?

Can you think of some examples of people who accomplished hard tasks even though they were injured or exhausted?

What good character did Gray Fox show in coming after and helping William?

Why is it important to be a good friend to those God puts in our lives?

Character Qualities to Identify:

William showed **diligence** as he struggled to get back to the fort after his injury.

Diligence: *carefully and persistently pursuing a goal.*

This is in contrast to **weakness** and **lethargy**: *giving in to difficult or challenging obstacles rather than doing your best.*

How did Jesus show diligence?

Chapter 27

What character qualities and attributes did Will's mother show in taking care of his wound?

Character Qualities to Identify:

Betsy Hackett used **gentleness** to clean and treat William's painful head wound.

Gentleness: *being especially kind and caring in meeting the needs of others.*

This is in contrast to being **callous, cruel,** and **harsh**: *willfully causing pain or suffering to others and being unconcerned about it.*

How did Jesus show gentleness?

_____

Chapter 28

What good character qualities does Mr. Spebbington show in this chapter?

How would you describe the characters of Girty and Trask?

What motivated five-year-old Seth to attack a grown man who was armed with a knife?

Describe how Katherine showed maturity and leadership in dealing with Trask and Girty?

Character Qualities to Identify:

Both the Indians and the settlers defending the fort fought with fierce **determination**.

Determination: *unwavering in purpose regardless of the opposition.*

This is in contrast to **hesitation** and **indecision**: *uncertainty, questioning a goal or plan.*

How did Jesus show determination?

_____

Chapter 29

William and Dirt Gurley took on the responsibility of rescuing the Middlebrook girls. Describe what it means to accept responsibility for something.

How would you describe Gray Fox's character for joining the rescue party?

How did Will and Dirt show wisdom as they pursued the kidnapers through the woods in the dark?

Describe how Katherine showed cleverness, creativity, and resourcefulness as a captive.

Character Qualities to Identify:

Dirt Gurley showed **discernment** as he reasoned where the kidnapers would be heading.

Discernment: *the God given ability to consider all the evidence and circumstances and to draw accurate conclusions.*

This is in contrast to **ignorance** and **stupidity**: *dullness of mind.*

_____

Chapter 30

How did Will, Dirt, and Gray Fox show creativity and resourcefulness in getting their rifles up the steep bluff?

Who's idea was the wisest and why?

What is Dirt's view of the value of prayer?

Both Dirt and Gray Fox worded their prayers very differently. How do you **think** God viewed their prayers?

After they finished praying, how did William show his faith that God had heard their prayers?

Character Qualities to Identify:

Dirt showed **reverence** to God when he suggested that they pray about their problem.

Reverence: *having a deep respect for God and how He is working in the people and circumstances around me.*

This is in contrast to showing **disregard** and **disdain**: *the feeling that someone or something is unworthy of respect or consideration.*

How did Jesus show reverence to His Father in Heaven?

Chapter 31

What do you think Katherine mean when she thought that God was a God of hope?

How could you find the courage to deal with a terrifying situation like Kate and Grace had to endure?

What character qualities did Grace need when she was about to give up crawling across the limb to the rocks?

The Bible says in Romans 8: 28 that *"all things work together for good for those who love God and are called according to His purpose."* How could God be working good in this terrible ordeal?

Character Qualities to Identify:

Kate was **encouraging** to her sister when Grace didn't think she would climb any farther.

Encouraging: *the ability to give someone else support or confidence in a difficult situation.*

This is in contrast to **discouragement**: *to dishearten or dampen the spirit of someone.*

How did Jesus encourage others?

Chapter 32

What are you learning about Gray Fox's character in this chapter?

After Dirt was caught, how did he show cleverness in getting a message to William?

What are some of the character qualities Dirt used in warning William?

Describe the good character qualities William used to figure out what Trask and Girty were going to do with Dirt?

When Jesus told his disciple that they were to be *"wise as a serpent and as harmless as a dove,"* what did that mean?

The girls had prayed to God to rescue them. How had God answered those prayers?

Character Qualities to Identify:

The girls had **gratefulness** to God and to Will and Dirt for rescuing them.

Gratefulness: *an attitude of thankful appreciation for what God and others have done for you.*

This is in contrast to **ungratefulness** and **thanklessness**: *an annoying attitude of showing no appreciation or gratitude for what others have done for you.*

How did Jesus show gratefulness?

Chapter 33

What do we learn about Dirt Gurley when he ask Will to leave him behind to save the girls?

Why were these men risking their lives to save these girls?

What character qualities did William and Gray Fox show in drawing their enemies after them and away from their hiding friends?

When you are faced with a dangerous situation, where does courage like this come from?

Character Qualities to Identify:

William and Gray Fox showed **responsibility** by leading the Indians away from their friends.

Responsibility: *recognizing your duty and using all your ability to accomplishing it regardless of the cost.*

This is in contrast to **immaturity** and **unreliableness**: *the inability to trust someone due to their lack of maturity and good character.*

How did Jesus show responsibility?

———————————————

Chapter 34

When they were hiding from the Chickasaw, what did Dirt do several times that showed that he was trusting in God?

Is fear a sin?

Courage is not the absence of fear. It's doing what needs to be done in spite of your fear. Can you think of a time when you did something in spite of your fear?

Why is it important to face your fears rather than run away from them?

Character Qualities to Identify:

Dirt Gurley showed **deference** to Katherine and Grace when they asked to rest and eat.

Deference: *showing respect and esteem for others and their needs instead of pursuing my desires.*

This is in contrast to **rudeness** and **disregard**: *to ignore others and make light of their desires.*

How did Jesus show deference?

Chapter 35

When the guards on the wall first spotted someone walking toward the fort, how did Jack Cobb show wisdom as he gave orders to the men?

What good character do you see in Gray Fox when he brought Will in?

What reason did Gray Fox give for wanting to learn English?

What are the advantages of having a good education?

Character Qualities to Identify:

Jack and Dirt showed **hospitality** to Gray Fox by letting him stay with them and sharing their food with him.

Hospitality: *cheerfully sharing what you have with those who God brings into your life.*

This is in contrast to **unfriendliness,** and **aloofness**: *the attitude of being distant, remote or withdrawn around others.*

How did Jesus show hospitality?

About the Author

Alan Harris is a practicing veterinarian living near Columbia, South Carolina, where he and Valerie, his wife of over forty years, make their home. They have six children whom they homeschooled for twenty-seven years, a growing host of beautiful grandchildren, whom they adore. . .and a pug.

Alan was motivated to write when he desired to share an exciting story, not just to entertain his children, but to also teach them important character and spiritual lessons. It became clear that the tale needed to be very suspenseful, and the characters had to be engaging and fun, in order to keep his children interested. The results were *The Tales of Larkin* series, which has five books. You can find out more about them as well as how to use them to teach at **StoriesChangeHearts.com**.

In searching for other subjects about which to write, Alan discovered a book in the public domain by Joseph Altsheller called <u>The Young Trailer</u>. He liked the time period, setting, and some of the concepts in the story, but it lacked a spiritual message. Basing his work on the things he liked, Alan crafted a new story, changing the plot and many of the characters, as well as giving it a biblical world view. And as in all of Harris's stories, he included plenty of adventure, lots of laugh-out loud humor, and abundant opportunities to learn character and spiritual lessons.

It is Alan's prayer that his new series, *The Flintlock Sagas*, and this first book in that series, <u>The Young Frontiersman</u>, will not only entertain his readers but also help them grow in godly character and draw them closer to God the Father and His Son, King Jesus.

Keep up with Alan Harris, his future works in *The Flintlock Sagas*, and his first series, *The Tales of Larkin* at **www.StoriesChangeHearts.com**.

If you wish to contact Alan you can e-mail him at **StoriesChangeHearts@gmail.com**.